THE
BLACK
SWAN
MYSTERY

TETSUYA AYUKAWA (1919–2002) was born in the Sugamo district of Tokyo. The son of a surveyor for the South Manchurian Railway Co., he spent much of his youth in the Japanese puppet state of Manchukuo, returning to war-ravaged Japan only in 1944. He began writing detective mysteries, and introduced the recurring character Inspector Onitsura, for which Ayukawa later became renowned. Celebrated as one of Japan's finest writers of impossible crimes and alibi-deconstruction mysteries, he won the Mystery Writers of Japan Award for *The Black Swan* in 1960 and in 2001 was awarded the inaugural Honkaku Mystery Award for his contribution to the genre. Many of his works have been adapted for radio and screen.

BRYAN KARETNYK is a translator of Japanese and Russian literature. His recent translations for Pushkin Press include Seishi Yokomizo's *The Village of Eight Graves* and *The Little Sparrow Murders*, Futaro Yamada's *The Meiji Guillotine Murders* and Ryunosuke Akutagawa's *Murder in the Age of Enlightenment*.

THE BLACK SWAN MYSTERY

TETSUYA AYUKAWA

TRANSLATED FROM THE JAPANESE
BY BRYAN KARETNYK

PUSHKIN VERTIGO

Pushkin Press
Somerset House, Strand
London WC2R 1LA

KUROI HAKUCHO © Tetsuya Ayukawa 2013
English translation rights arranged with KOBUNSHA CO. LTD.
through Japan UNI Agency, Inc., Tokyo

English translation © Bryan Karetnyk 2024

The Black Swan Mystery was first published as Kuroi
Hakucho by Kodansha in Tokyo, 1960

First published by Pushkin Press in 2024

3 5 7 9 8 6 4 2

ISBN 13: 978-1-80533-523-8

Designed and typeset by Tetragon, London
Printed and bound in the United Kingdom by Clays Ltd, Elcograf S.p.A.

www.pushkinpress.com

Contents

ONE

A Bad Day

1.

Atsuko and Fumie were strolling down an elegant, tree-lined avenue full of shops and boutiques, taking in all the window displays as they made their way towards Shimbashi. It was almost noon, and the late-spring sunlight set off the bright colours of their outfits—one Japanese, the other Western. Since mid-May, the duster coats that had been so popular had vanished entirely, and now, everywhere one looked in the Ginza, women were wearing early-summer dresses. Here, Atsuko's lace blouse, which might have seemed a little racy in other parts of Tokyo, complemented her surroundings and showed off all the more eye-catchingly her chic, sporty style.

Before long, the two women stopped in front of a jeweller's window and peered in at the display.

"What a lovely tiepin!"

On the little glass shelf where Fumie was pointing, there was a golden tiepin in the shape of a sabre. Atsuko took the remark as more of a comment than an invitation for her to share her opinion. Maybe it just slipped out as Fumie pictured the accessory on her beloved husband's chest. About ten days ago, he had gone to England to attend a textile convention in Lancashire, and, on the return journey, he'd be stopping off to inspect textile mills in various countries, so wasn't expected to land back at Haneda Airport until sometime in September.

"It's nice, isn't it? It would really suit somebody slim and with a tan."

As she said this, Atsuko in fact had no idea whether this slender, curving pin, which made her think of the body of a damselfly, would look better on a man with fair or dark skin: instead, she had merely described Fumie's husband.

"You've such a good eye, Atsuko... Say, how about some lunch? My treat."

As though having seen her friend's empty stomach with X-ray vision, Fumie laughed giddily, and, as she did, a dimple appeared on her left cheek, while her lips parted to reveal a beautiful set of white teeth.

She glanced at her watch.

"Perfect timing! It's almost noon. There's an Italian restaurant just over there, around that corner."

No sooner had the words passed Fumie's lips than she took Atsuko by the arm and set off again down the avenue. Atsuko was a little envious of her companion's decisiveness and her assertive nature, which seemed to manifest itself in even the most trivial of things, like this. And yet, this was only because she had no idea of the true purpose behind Fumie's invitation to go with her to the Ginza that day. If she had known, Atsuko might have felt very differently indeed.

There was a Japanese curry restaurant on the third corner they came to, and, sure enough, next door to it was an Italian restaurant. Under a garish peach-and-green-striped awning there hung a signboard bearing the name: Posillipo. It was Atsuko's first time there, but Fumie headed straight upstairs, with the air of a regular, and sat down next to a potted Chinese windmill palm. In contrast to the downstairs section, it was much quieter here, and the table that Fumie had chosen was in a spot far removed from

8

the few other customers who were up there. In hindsight Atsuko realized that Fumie must have chosen it deliberately so that their conversation would not be overheard.

Remarkably enough for a restaurant in this upmarket part of town, there was no music playing in Posillipo, and the only accompaniment to the meal was the tinkling of the fountains in two tiled ponds that stood in the middle of the floor. After walking in the early-summer sun, the sound of water was refreshing to hear, just like wiping away perspiration with a cool towel and applying a dash of eau de cologne. And although Fumie had chosen the restaurant partly on account of the delicious food and the cool sensation imparted by these fountains, what she really needed was a quiet place where she could talk freely.

"I've never had Italian food before," Atsuko said, after casting a brief glance at a plump Italian-looking couple seated on the other side of the room.

"They do all kinds of things here," Fumie said, handing her a menu, which was, incomprehensibly, written entirely in Italian.

"Oh, they've got something called macaroni Caruso! I think I'll try that."

Atsuko had seen this dish in a magazine somewhere and knew that it had been named after the immortal singer Enrico Caruso. But that was the sum of her Italian knowledge.

"I had that the first time I came here, too."

Wearing a dazzling smile, Fumie summoned the waiter, who, with his white uniform, jet-black hair and tanned skin, looked every bit the Mediterranean type.

As they ate, the conversation turned to the earrings, necklaces and rings set with artificial gems that they had just been admiring in the shop windows. Some women do, of course, like to talk about jewellery, even if the price tag is beyond their reach, but, in the case of these two, they were in the fortunate position of being able to get their hands on anything their heart desired. In fact, it may well have been this topic of conversation that made the food in Posillipo taste even better than Atsuko expected, compensating so well for a lack of seasoning.

When a rich Neapolitan coffee was served after their meal, Fumie pressed the napkin to her rounded lips and flashed a meaningful smile at her companion.

"Now I don't mean to pry, but are you seeing anybody at the moment?"

The suddenness of the question caught Atsuko off guard. Trying not to give anything away, she stirred her coffee impassively.

"No," she replied. "Why do you ask?"

"Well, it's just that there's a little matter I'd like to discuss with you…"

"Oh?"

Without her even having to ask the question, Atsuko knew Fumie was trying to broach the subject of a marriage proposal.

"The thing is," said Fumie, lowering her voice, "I know somebody who's interested in marrying you…"

The most distinctive feature of Fumie's face was her big eyes. Not only were they large, but they were deep and limpid. Atsuko was no poet, so she didn't see, reflected in those eyes, a cold lake found deep in the mountains, but when she peered into their fathomless pupils, searching for a response, she had the uncanny feeling of gazing into Fumie's soul, which made her unaccountably nervous. Although she tried not to let it show, she could feel her face blushing redder and redder.

"I'm sorry, I didn't mean to take you by surprise."

"That's all right," Atsuko replied off-handedly. She hadn't the least interest in the identity of this possible suitor, but if she were to say nothing, there was a risk that Fumie might suspect something. "Who might he be, this 'somebody'?"

"Mr Haibara! Surely you know him? The director's private secretary."

Atsuko immediately pictured the man's broad shoulders and stocky build. The name had come as a surprise to her, but, after the initial shock had passed, and the more she thought about it, it really wasn't so peculiar that Haibara should want to marry her. They'd crossed paths several times—at the company's garden party, at her dancing display, and so on—and, on each occasion, they had chatted to each other.

"Don't you think you'd make the perfect couple? He's kind, considerate… I'd have thought that any woman would consider herself lucky to marry a man like that."

Fumie spoke with such enthusiasm, as though she were recommending her own flesh and blood.

In Atsuko's eyes, however, Haibara did not seem quite so considerate. It was true that whenever they met, he was always pleasant and attentive, but she was sure that it was all an act, and that she could see through his motives for sidling up to her. After all, her father was the managing director of the same company. If Haibara were to marry the man's daughter, his path to the top would certainly look much shorter. Surely, a man as shrewd as he could not have failed to recognize this. But Atsuko was no soft touch, nor was she foolish enough to let herself be made a stepping stone for an ambitious man.

Yet there was no way for Fumie to know what was going on in Atsuko's mind, as she silently sipped her coffee.

"He's awfully good at what he does, and the director loves him! He doesn't really have any relatives to look after, and, as you know, he's the reliable sort. There aren't any rumours flying around about his love life, either. It's hard work, you know, when they've got too

11

many relatives; all that running around you'd have to do… You'd be worn out!"

Apparently believing this prospect of marriage to be truly a wonderful thing, Fumie kept trying to convince Atsuko. She was the wife of one of the company's senior executive directors and, still childless in her early thirties, seemed to have channelled this loneliness into the love lives of others. Three or four times already, she'd taken it upon herself to play matchmaker, resulting in the marriages of several young people within the company. On this occasion, since the proposal concerned a friend from her university days, it was perhaps only natural that she was being more solicitous than usual.

Her good intentions were well known to Atsuko. She'd heard from her father that Haibara was already in the running for one of the top positions at the company, and he'd intimated how impressed he was with this "self-starter" of a man. Even her mother seemed to have a soft spot for him after everything that Atsuko's father had said.

"I had thought about broaching it with your father, but then I decided it would be better to talk to you directly. There's no need to make any decisions now, though. Talk it over with your parents and think about it. There's no rush. After all, nothing can be done until the strike's over."

Fumie's voice trailed off into what sounded like a sigh. They both of them had reasons enough to sigh. The trade union at the Towa Textiles Company was at loggerheads with the owners; a month ago, they'd published a four-point list of demands and called a strike. Since then, the situation had only worsened, with little sign of a breakthrough.

"I know," said Fumie cheerily, trying brush off her black mood. "How would you like to go and see the roadshow release in Hibiya? If we leave now, we'll make it just in time. I've been wanting to see that thriller for so long."

12

With those words, she grabbed her crocodile handbag and got up.

2.

After leaving Fumie, Atsuko took the subway to Shibuya. Since it wasn't quite rush hour yet, the trains and stations were not too crowded. She'd just got off at Shibuya Station and was about to cross over to the Inokashira line, when suddenly a man stopped her.

At first, she assumed that he'd mistaken her for somebody else. She'd never seen this man before in her life. He had a pale, slender face and, at first glance, seemed a gentle sort. But his eyes were small and unblinking.

"It's Atsuko, isn't it? Atsuko Suma?"

Hearing her own name spoken, she realized that the man had not mistaken her. The impertinence in his voice and the brazen look in his eyes made her wonder whether he wasn't some sort of low-ranking police officer. Only, she couldn't recall having been approached by one like this before.

"I won't take up much of your time," he said. "But if you wouldn't mind coming with me for just a minute…"

"Whatever for?"

"Come and find out for yourself."

"No, I don't believe I will. If there's something you want, you can tell me right here."

"Not here," the man said, quickly scanning his surroundings. For a police officer, he looked rather suspicious.

"Who on earth are you? If you don't tell me this instant, I'll cry for help," she said, her voice already getting louder.

If the crowds of people crossing between the Inokashira and Tamagawa lines were like a river, the two of them stood there like two stones right in the middle of the flow. If Atsuko needed help, all she had to do was shout, and the station staff and policemen, not to mention the people around her, would come running—so, she didn't feel in the least bit frightened.

"Don't be absurd," he said in a low voice. Though he practically whispered, they had a startling menace about them. It struck Atsuko that this was the kind of threatening voice one imagined hearing in gangster novels and the like. "You'll find that my patience has its limits…"

"What are you talking about?"

"Don't play innocent with me, lady. I've got your number, all right. Or are you actually trying to humiliate your old man?"

"What are you talking about?"

"Still playing dumb? You don't want your future husband to be lumbered with the reputation of a traitor, do you?"

As he uttered the words, his tone was frightening. The pompous phrase "the reputation of a traitor" even sounded like a line that had been lifted straight from a badly translated novel, but Atsuko had already lost the presence of mind needed to notice this. It was clear from the man's bold, self-possessed smirk that there was no getting out of this.

"Well? Are you coming? I'm not going to eat you, you know… Speaking of which, to put you at your ease, why don't we go to a café. Choose one you like, why don't you? As I say, I won't take up much of your time."

The man's voice had regained its former quiet, even tone. There was even a hint of cultivation in his words, so unlike those of street gangs.

"No," she said resolutely. "If you want to talk, we can do it here."

"I think not. Now, I'm a busy man myself. If it were something that could be discussed here, why would I go to the trouble of suggesting a coffee with you? We can go somewhere near the station."

"…"

"Come on, stop stalling. If you don't want to see your father's and your future husband's faces with mud on them, then get a move on."

Without waiting for a reply, he walked off, leading the way. Though hesitant, Atsuko took the bait and followed him. As the man seemed to know full well, Atsuko had a secret. But she wouldn't be rushed and first wanted to find out just how much the man really knew. At the same time, she was also somewhat reassured by his belated cultivated tone.

The two of them passed through the ticket barrier and exited in front of the station. Red-and-blue neon lights were beginning to light the busy streets. The famous statue of Hachiko, that most loyal of dogs, fixed Atsuko in his bronze canine gaze.

"Choose someplace quiet. An eatery, the upstairs floor of a soba joint maybe… We wouldn't want to be overheard now, would we?"

"But I don't like that kind of place!"

"Now, now… I don't mind where we go, myself. But it's you who'll pay the price."

The man looked at Atsuko and laughed.

As they walked side by side, Atsuko noticed that he was a little on the short side. You couldn't say that he was either thin or fat, but his body, although not appearing especially sturdy, emanated a kind of lethal energy. He had an innately cunning air about him, like a man who has cheated death any number of times during adventures on the battlefield, or who has taken part in shoot-outs with fellow villains. All this put Atsuko on edge.

"That one'll do," she said.

Having crossed the road without giving him time to respond, she paused in front of a café and hurried inside. She was trying to get back at him for the confidence he had shown earlier; it was also an attempt to show that she would not simply crumble when threatened. She looked around the room and sat down in a booth in an empty corner.

"I'm afraid I haven't much of a sweet tooth," he said brazenly as he stirred his coffee, before gulping it down and devouring a choux bun in only two bites. "A drink over some cold tofu would've been much more to my liking."

Atsuko made no attempt to hide her revulsion and contempt for his unpleasant jokes and the disgusting manner in which he ate.

"What did you want to say to me?"

It would have been more appropriate to use baser language with a man like this, so it riled her that her surroundings wouldn't allow it. The man wiped his mouth with a soiled handkerchief and, with deliberately slow movements, took out a cigarette and lit it.

"Let's go over things from the very start, shall we? It'll be simpler that way. Your old man is the director of Towa Textiles, the workforce of which is currently on strike. The vice-chairman of the trade union is a man called Narumi. He's the kind and energetic sort, so I can see the allure he has for women. I suppose it's only natural that you're so keen on him." Catching Atsuko with his eye, he smiled ironically. "Quite the little rebel, aren't you? Playing the industrialist's good little girl on the one hand, and sneaking off with the young union boss on the other. In terms of status, they're worlds apart."

He was just getting into his stride, and he glared at Atsuko.

"Now, if I were to inform the union that the vice-chairman, who is supposed to rank among its most loyal of members, was secretly meeting the daughter of an enemy executive, what do you suppose they'd do? Narumi would be dubbed a traitor and kicked out of the union. And then, of course, there's you! Your old man would hardly take the news sitting down, now, would he? He'd be made a laughing stock."

"Yes, yes, I know all that, obviously. Will you get to the point? You're not the only one who's got places to be."

"Well, then, let's get down to brass tacks... I want one million yen."

The number didn't hit Atsuko immediately. The man's tone was so casual that he could have been asking for change for cigarettes.

"What are you looking so vacant for?" he said. "For a rich little girl like you, it can't be all that much."

She said nothing.

"Why don't you take it out of your own savings? You can ask your old man to make up the rest. After all, fathers do dote on their daughters. I'm sure he'd give it to you."

"Enough. There's no way I can get my hands on that sort of money."

"If you didn't have the money, I wouldn't be making these demands. I know perfectly well how much money your father has, because it's my business to know."

"Still, you'll never get it."

"Very well," he said ominously, rising to his feet. "Just remember: your father will be made to stand down from the company because of a few pennies, while your lover will become a social outcast. You do understand this, don't you?"

"Wait!" Atsuko called feebly.

It was true that she and Narumi were in love. Because of the circumstances, they'd chosen to keep their relationship a secret. While the word "tryst" has a lewd and vulgar nuance to it, which Atsuko loathed, there was probably no more fitting word

17

to describe the way they would meet furtively, lest they be found out. She would grin and bear it as she awaited patiently the day when they could marry in the open. So: when and where had this man seen them?

He sat down again and smirked, as though having seen right through her act. The expression on his pale face was dull and inert; the only signs of emotion were the menace in his voice and the gleam in his eyes, which were cut like those of a Mongolian.

"Shall I tell you the time and place of your most recent tryst with Narumi? I have it all written down in my diary."

"How do you know this?"

She couldn't fathom why he'd been surveilling her.

"Because I've been following him."

"Why?"

"So that he'd listen to me. So that he'd do as I say."

"What do you want with him?"

"That's none of your concern. Suffice it to say, I wanted something from him. But it was clear that he'd refuse me. So, what's a man to do? The best thing was to find out a secret of his and then confront him with it."

"And that's why you've been following me?"

"Precisely. Everyone has secrets. And you can't go giving up after only three or four days. It takes perseverance. I ended up following Narumi around for more than a week, ten days even! That's when I found out about his little trysts with you. I never dreamt of finding out something as good as this."

His expression remained unchanged, but a note of pride appeared in his voice.

"So, I thought to myself. My reason for wanting to find out Narumi's secret was, as I've just told you, so that he'd do something for me. But then, there's always more than one way to skin

18

a cat, isn't there? It occurred to me that I could put this story to far better use. Because, you see, now I've found the goose that lays the golden egg. And if you don't care for the goose analogy, then let's call you a swan or a peahen. Either way, you're going to make me a lot of money."

"Spare me the fairy tales. Stories like that are for children to enjoy, not for blackmailers to appropriate."

"Are they now?"

"If you must use a bird analogy, you might as well just call me a sitting duck."

The man's eyes flickered and the corners of his mouth twitched. He must have found this amusing.

"You could be a mandarin duck for all the difference it makes to me. The question is whether you're going to give me the 1,000,000 or not. If you sold off that car you've just bought, that would get you seven or eight hundred thousand right there."

Taken aback by this, Atsuko peered into the man's eyes. He knowledge of her seemed to know no bounds. Only in March she had bought a new sports car.

"It's very cowardly, you know, to take advantage of a lady's weak spot like this."

"I'll do anything so long as there's money in it. Cowardice and conscience are not words in my vocabulary, you see."

He snorted and smiled at her with contempt.

"But I'm telling you, it's impossible."

"I certainly hope not. Women are miserly by nature. The woman in her tenement house is every bit as miserly as the lady in the mansion. You may wear pretty clothes and have a pretty face, but I'm willing to bet you've got a lot saved up."

"That isn't what I mean," she replied. "I understand that you mean to blackmail me for a million yen, but what kind of guarantee

19

do I have? Forgive my saying so, but you aren't very good at this. What I'm saying is that it's impossible to trust a man like you. Paying you the money would be one thing, but I've no desire to be blackmailed again with the same material afterwards. Unless you can give me some guarantee, I simply can't help you."

The man was silent.

"Think it over," she said. "Then we can talk about it."

"Quite the operator, aren't you?"

"I'll even pay for your choux bun."

Taking the chit, she stood up and went over to the till. She had wanted to say something rude but didn't care to demean herself. Still, she was upset. Stubbornly, she refused to look back while the cashier returned her change. She could feel distinctly on her back the eyes of her blackmailer as he sat there, taken off guard and temporarily defeated, a dumbstruck look on his face.

Finally aboard the Inokashira Line train and having regained her composure more or less, Atsuko had time to reflect on the events of the day. Not only had she been cornered about a marriage proposal from a man she didn't much like, but a perfect stranger had tried to blackmail her for a vast sum of money, too. It had been a bad day, she thought.

TWO

The Private Secretary

1.

Haibara watched on in a daze as the typist's fingers with their lobster-pink nails worked nimbly to extract the letter from its envelope. There was no doubt about it: he was utterly exhausted.

"That's the last of this morning's post, Mr Haibara."

"Give it here, will you?"

He took the letter and began to read it, but his expression quickly changed. Clearly, something was wrong.

"Another petition?" she asked.

"No, it's a letter trying to blackmail us. They're persistent, this lot."

"It's downright harassment!"

"I suppose so, yes. I'm certainly not taking it seriously though."

When he had finished reading the letter, Haibara folded it neatly and replaced it inside the envelope. On his desk were about thirty letters divided into three piles. One of these was for private correspondence addressed personally to the company director. These were not to be opened. It was his job, however, to open all those that were official or whose senders were unknown.

To support the strike at the Towa Textiles Company, which had begun in mid-April, the wives of union members sent in letters complaining repeatedly about their living conditions. These complaints were all alike and often exaggerated the actual situation, claiming, for instance, that they couldn't buy rice because their husband's wages had been cut or that they hadn't enough money for baby formula—all of which, however, had only made the executives laugh at their pathetic efforts.

As the union's prospects had gradually begun to worsen, however, the content of these petitions had become more and more harassing, to the point whereby some of them had become out-and-out specimens of intimidation or blackmail. Such letters were to be reviewed by the company director.

"That makes three of them today, doesn't it?"

"They're panicking," Haibara said. "More than that, they're getting desperate. It's because the union is patently losing."

While the typist gathered up the letters, Haibara turned and looked out of the window. In the sky over Nihonbashi, there was an advertising balloon floating languidly in the air, bearing the words: SPRING CLEAR-OUT: EVERYTHING MUST GO. Bathed in the early-summer sunlight, the translucent sphere looked like a jellyfish swimming in a great cobalt-blue sky.

"Spring clear-out…" he murmured softly, surprised once again by how quickly the days were passing.

Since the factory workers had gone on strike, Haibara had spent many days between board meetings and the negotiating table, enveloped in a tense and acrimonious atmosphere. There were even times when he'd worked throughout the night or had to sleep on the office sofa. The results of the collective bargaining round held at the end of May had shown conclusively that the unions were losing ground. Of their four demands, the company had agreed to accept two of them and settle the dispute on a fifty-fifty basis. On the surface, it looked like there was no clear winner, but since the two most important items had been rejected, the executives were in effect winning the battle. Now, at last, Haibara had found a moment to take in his surroundings and was astonished to see that it was already early summer, a fact that brought him to reflect upon the fifty days of bitter conflict that had just passed.

"I've lost weight," he said to himself, as he touched his arm through his sleeve.

Haibara had always been a little on the heavy side, but even if it was difficult to see, he had lost around two stone. He extracted a cigarette from his briefcase and lit it. He'd had a light breakfast of only toast and was ravenous. As he inhaled the smoke, he began feeling mildly dizzy. Unlike the cigarettes he would have to calm his nerves at the negotiating table, this one he could truly enjoy.

"They're all ready, Mr Haibara."

Coming to his senses, he saw that he was being presented with three neatly organized bundles. He left the bundle of petitions on the desk and stepped out of the room, taking with him the letters personally addressed to the director as well as those that were trying to blackmail them.

The director's office was situated two doors down. Gosuke Nishinohata was standing by the window, puffing on a Vegueros and looking down at the miniature-seeming cars crowding the road. Carried on the warm summer's breeze, the powerful aroma of the cigar caressed the tip of Haibara's nose. He had tried a cigar himself once—a Legitima—but he simply couldn't get used to the phenomenal strength of it. Nishinohata's was a prized cigar, given him by the director of an American textiles company who had come to visit the factory last winter, and so Haibara could tell that the director must have been in a very relaxed frame of mind in order to light it.

"Letters, is it?"

"Yes, sir. As usual, there are three of a threatening nature."

"Very well. Leave them over there, will you? It's risible that they think they can blackmail me into accepting their demands. I'm not one to be cowed by that sort of thing."

Whenever the director spoke, his big belly would roll like a wave. Besides being overweight, he was short, which made his belly seem to stick out even more. His employees said he looked like the folk hero Kintaro because of his short neck and red face. His hair, which he wore close-cropped, was still jet black, while his eyebrows were bushy and his lips full. You could tell from the very first glance that he was an energetic man.

"I'm heading out after lunch. Could you arrange the car for me?"

"Of course. Only, you do have an appointment with the director of Maruta Trading at half past one…"

"I've had to postpone it until this evening. I rang to inform them myself," Gosuke Nishinohata said matter-of-factly.

"And where are you going, sir?"

"Nihonbashi. I'm going to see about a painting in a department store there. I'll be back in a couple of hours."

"Very well, sir. I'll have them bring the car around. Only…"

"What is it, Haibara?"

"Might it not be better to keep a low profile for the moment?"

The private secretary glanced at the letters lying on the table.

"They're a scare tactic," said Nishinohata, sitting down. "A man in my position would never leave the house if he worried about letters like those."

"True, but there are some violent men in the union. And with things the way things are, there's no telling what they might do out of spite."

"I'm well aware."

Sitting back in his chair, twirling the long moustache that was his pride and joy, he looked up at his private secretary who was still standing there and said slowly and deliberately:

"Don't worry, Haibara. I value my life. I've nothing to fear in broad daylight."

"I can accompany you if you'd like?"

"Thank you, but there's really no need. You stay here and man the fort. I'll go alone."

Was it just Haibara's imagination, or had there been a hint of irritation in the director's words?

2.

After seeing off Gosuke Nishinohata, Haibara ordered some eel from a nearby restaurant and treated himself to a leisurely luncheon. Most of his colleagues had gone off to the Ginza, so the office was deserted. Taking advantage of this lull, he pulled out of his bag an economics magazine that he had just bought and opened it, red pencil at the ready. A swot in his schooldays, Haibara had changed little in the years since.

The man didn't much fancy spending his life working for a company where success meant, at best, retiring after rising up to the head of a department. His aspirations lay a little higher than that. But to achieve them required constant application, and from what he could see, what robbed people of their diligence was entertainment and the opposite sex. This is why he hadn't the faintest idea how to play *go* or chess. Nor had he ever been to the cinema or the theatre. After all, if a man finds purpose in striving towards his future goals, such an austere life won't seem so dull or monotonous.

It was the same when it came to women. Deeming them to have nothing but a negative influence on men, he had never been in a relationship, and now, at the age of thirty-eight, he was still a bachelor. After all, he would think, isn't the most intelligent woman still just a woman? Heedless of Haibara's views, some women, with a certain gleam in their eye, would make overtures to him, but no matter how beautiful she might be, she would always be flatly refused. Of course, being a man in his prime, Haibara had his needs and was known, on occasion, to frequent tea houses. Yet he never thought of geisha as objects of his affection.

The first time Takeshi Haibara set eyes on Atsuko was when the company held a garden party for its shareholders the previous autumn. It was then, seeing Atsuko dressed in her long-sleeved kimono, watching her graceful movements as she performed the tea ceremony in the open air, brilliant sunshine raining down all around, that the fires of love were lit in this shameless careerist's heart. His theory that women were an impediment to career progression did not apply to Atsuko, since marrying her would mean becoming the managing director's son-in-law, thus securing his future at the company. From that day forth, he would often find himself getting carried away, daydreaming about what it would be like to have her as his wife.

This alone, however, would not have been enough to stir Haibara's heart. Ever since that first meeting, a curious connection had developed between them. They had bumped into each other a further three times, riding in the same lift at a department store, at a dismal *kouta* party hosted for the executives of the company and at Atsuko's dance display. There can be few things more depressing than seeing an executive put on the trappings of a connoisseur and hearing him croon a *kouta* song at the top of his lungs, but what had made the pain bearable for Haibara was Atsuko's presence there. It had been a chilly day at the end of January, and Atsuko was wearing a kimono with a light silver design of peonies on a dark-red background. Her crêpe *haori* with its delicately crinkled pattern seemed a little plain, but it had suited Atsuko's tidy demeanour very well. At the dancing display, she had danced *The Heron Maiden*. For this, Haibara had bought a ticket and gone to see it. On each occasion, the fire in his chest seemed to burn stronger and stronger, until at last his heart itself was set aflame.

This being Haibara's first encounter with desire, he didn't know how to assuage his infatuation with her. And while his days were spent dealing with the workers' strike, when he would lie down at the end of the day, his only thoughts were for Atsuko. Ordinarily a man of great competence, when he was distracted by something it was all the more apparent. And so, it was in the taxi on the way back from Haneda Airport, where he had seen off the deputy director and the senior executive director as they left for Lancashire, that he was grilled by the latter's wife, Fumie Hishinuma, who in the end succeeded in extracting a declaration of love from him.

"You are rather naïve, aren't you?" she'd said. "But just leave it to me. I'll let her know how you feel."

Thereafter, he would repeat Fumie's words back to himself several times a day, eagerly awaiting the good news.

He opened the magazine and began to read an article, but not a single line of it went in. Atsuko's face appeared from behind the printed text. With her short stature and wide-set eyes, she didn't correspond to the conventional image of a great beauty, but she had a certain freshness about her, and her features were intelligent. In the end, Haibara abandoned the article and, closing the magazine, gave himself over entirely to daydreaming about Atsuko. The office was still quiet.

But why had he not heard anything yet? As he counted on his fingers, he thought it all seemed to be taking far too long. His heart suddenly seemed to darken. And he had good reason to be concerned. It all had to do with the secret the company director was keeping.

Perhaps "secret" was too strong a word, though. After all, it was something that anybody in Haibara's position would have done. And yet, what may seem insignificant to some could be perceived as all too significant by others. Maybe this was the case with Atsuko.

Atsuko was a wholesome young woman. If the director were to tell her, or if she were to get wind of it somehow, it was obvious that whatever feelings she might have had for Haibara would instantly turn to loathing and contempt. And that is what he feared.

Simply waiting for the director to blurt it out was out of the question. But what could Haibara do to stop him talking? What could he do to shut him up?

"… Kill him?" he mumbled, still half-dazed.

The words returned Haibara to his senses with a jolt. It was an horrific thought, although it had never occurred to him before, not even in his wildest dreams.

But sure enough, having put those thoughts out of his mind, he found himself only a few minutes later picturing once again the murder of Nishinohata. Besides, he was in favour with the deputy director, Haruhiko Ryu; his position wouldn't be affected by the director's death.

"No, it would never work," he thought to himself, sitting up and brushing off this ridiculous fantasy. "Better think about something else. Anything else."

Just then, he received a telephone call, informing him that Hanpei Chita was at the reception desk, asking to see him.

"Send him away," Haibara snapped. "I know what he'll be after."

Mr Chita, who was disagreeable at the best of times, wouldn't be happy.

THREE

By the Tracks

1.

It was close to four o'clock on the morning of 2 June. Dawn was breaking, but countless stars could still be seen in the early-summer sky. Up ahead, the blinking red-and-green wing lights of an aeroplane seemed to skim the treetops of a pitch-black forest, but the roar of its engine could not be heard at this distance.

In his faded blue overalls, the strap of his cap tight around his chin, a driver was sitting on his hard seat, his right hand gripping a lever, his eyes fixed on the two parallel rails illuminated by the headlights in front of him. The fireman beside him opened the firebox door with a clatter and shovelled in some coal. The violent vibrations of the engine had taken their toll on the driver's stomach, and all the colour had drained from his face. Every time the fire door was opened, however, the burning red light would be cast on his cheeks, and for a moment his complexion would improve so much that he was almost unrecognizable. Driving a steam engine was much harder than driving an electric locomotive. And yet the reward for it was scant at best.

As the driver watched the fireman's movements out of the corner of one eye, his other was fixed firmly on the track ahead. There was a reason that he felt a little more nervous that night than usual. Just after passing Shimojujo Station at around 11.10 p.m., the No. 783 Aomori-bound freight train had collided with a

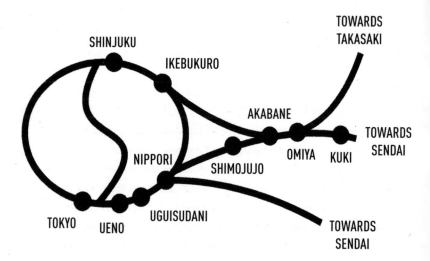

truck that had crashed straight through a crossing barrier about 400 yards down the track. It was clear that the owner of the vehicle had been at fault, but he had died instantly, and the train driver, who had been taken to hospital with steam burns on the entire right side of his body, had to be questioned by the police in his bed, his face contorted with pain.

The truck had been dragged for around a hundred yards after the train sped into it, not only destroying the front of the locomotive, but also damaging the upbound freight and passenger lines and suspending all traffic on the Tohoku mainline for several hours.

The downbound freight line was the first to be restored, at around 2 a.m., after which the off-duty driver, Ubajima, had been woken and told to go to work. The locomotive had been replaced, but the thought of his poor injured colleague, who had been pulling dozens of freight wagons, instilled in him a feeling of dread that naturally set him on edge. What troubled Ubajima most, however, was his colleague's predicament; drivers involved in collisions, even those that were unavoidable, would normally have a black mark placed on their service record. In a worst-case scenario, they could even be sacked. And when a driver steps off a locomotive, he's like a fish out of water; he can't even provide for his family. Such a fate could befall any one of them, at any time.

Ubajima may have felt despondent, but he was wide awake. He used every trick in the book to calm, cajole and coax the roaring engine that rattled his body. His face was black with soot and smoke, even though he'd been gripping the lever for a mere hour, and only his eyes glittered.

As they approached Kuki Station, he gave a loud blast of the whistle. The reason being that, about half a mile from the station, there was an unmanned railway crossing situated on a big curve in the track. As soon as they reached the curve, however, the driver leant out of the cabin and cried out in a strangled voice.

"What's the matter?" the fireman asked.

"I saw something strange out there. It looked like a body."

Before his colleague could say anything more, the driver pulled on the brake. Since the train had already begun to slow down, it only took a hundred yards for it to come to a complete halt. The locomotive was belching out steam, apparently unhappy at having to stop.

"It looked like a jumper."

The fireman nodded. He had been paying attention to the oncoming track, too, but hadn't spotted anything like this. Having been on the job for only a year, he was impressed with his colleague's vigilance. Article 15 of the service regulations stated that, in cases like this, the accident must be investigated and reported.

For all his apparent composure, the driver's mind was racing. He had never had an accident before. Still, the cool night air helped to calm his nerves.

"I'll go and check," the fireman said, stepping down onto the embankment.

With a torch in one hand, he made his way back along the tracks. The round light danced as he ran, illuminating the boxcars and open wagons one by one, before disappearing behind them. The train was stopped on a bend, so there was no clear line of sight. At the very end of the long line of freight cars, a pale neck craned out of the window in the guard's van.

"What's happened?"

"I think there's been a jumper."

"A man or a woman?"

"I don't know," said the fireman, out of breath. "It was Ubajima who spotted the body."

The guard's head vanished, and, while the light of the fireman's torch continued the search, there was a crunch of gravel as he jumped down onto the ballast.

"I'll go with you," he said, seeming to intuit the fireman's apprehension.

The guard took the lead.

It didn't take long before they found the body. Two trouser-clad legs were sticking out of a ditch by the track on the inside of the curve. The right foot was wearing a black shoe, but the left one had only a sock on. The fireman, who'd imagined a corpse cruelly mangled under the wheels of the train, heaved a sigh of relief when the ditch was lit up. All the body's limbs were intact.

"He's only been hit. Let's pull him out."

If the man was still breathing, he'd require treatment. The two of them clambered down, took one end of the body each and finally managed to carry him up onto the embankment. The man was short but heavy, and so, even with two of them, it required every ounce of their strength. By the time they laid him down, they were both sweating.

When the fireman shone the torch on him, he saw that the man had his eyes closed, as though he were blinded by the light. He wore the ash-grey upturned moustache of an old army general and had a pale, bloodless face. The guard placed his ear to the man's chest, but as he glanced back at the fireman, he was struck by the electric light shining right in his eye and looked away.

"Hey! Watch it, will you!"

"Sorry. Is he alive?"

"He's dead. Such an impressive moustache, too… What a waste."

"Isn't it," the fireman said, nodding in the dark. It was common knowledge that those who killed themselves on the railway tended to be poor, patients suffering a nervous breakdown, or else lovers who had decided on a double suicide. There was something decidedly odd about the death of this waxen-faced, energetic-looking man.

"Shall I call it in?" the fireman said, pointing his torch at the top of a nearby telephone pole.

"Kuki Station is just up the tracks. It'd be quicker to run and tell them in person."

Making a snap decision, they left the body where it lay and returned to the train. Before long, there came a short blast of the whistle, rending the night air, and the No. 783 shuddered violently into motion.

2.

By now it was light all around. The stretcher with the body on it had been placed on the grass beside the tracks, ready to be carried off at any moment. The dewdrops covering it glinted beautifully in the morning sun.

The station attendant and the police officer who rushed to the scene had thought at first that the incident was a simple case of suicide. They supposed that the man had been hit by the oncoming train and fallen into the ditch. But when they examined the body, they found something unexpected.

The left breast of the brown jacket worn by the man was soaked in blood, and when the body was rolled over onto its front, they found a single hole right between his shoulder blades. On closer inspection, the area around it was charred black. Irrespective of whether this was a case of suicide or murder, it was clear that the train had not caused the death. The station attendant had then rushed back and, using a railway telephone, called the duty officer up the line at Omiya Station. Upon receiving their report, he in turn had immediately contacted the police station in Omiya.

As the officers arrived and continued their investigation, it became clear that the amount of blood loss was extremely small. Normally, the blood should have been spilt over a wider area, but there was hardly any at the scene. An examination of the wound revealed that the gun had been fired at point-blank range. Given the location, it was thought definitely not to have been self-inflicted. And yet, no murder weapon had been found in the vicinity of the crime scene. The officer in charge concluded on the basis of the available evidence that the man had not been killed by a passing train, but that he had been shot dead by an assailant who had then dumped the body at the scene. Not only was there no murder weapon, but there was a shoe missing as well—all of which pointed to the corpse having been moved.

The victim appeared to be in his mid-fifties. His immaculate grey moustache and fine figure suggested that he enjoyed a comfortable lifestyle. His clothes were cut from a superior summer wool and bore the name of a leading tailor. Only when they looked inside his business-card holder, however, was his identity established conclusively.

Neither Gosuke Nishinohata nor the Towa Textiles Company were exactly what you would call eminent, but, in spite of this, their names were familiar even to the station attendant, because the demands made by the striking workers and the fact that the company director had dug his heels in had drawn public criticism. The photographs of Nishinohata, which had appeared in all the daily newspapers and weekly magazines, had left an indelible impression on those who saw them precisely because of his distinctive moustache.

Upon receiving the report, officers from the police headquarters in Urawa and the district public prosecutor's office immediately travelled to the area. After everything had been checked over thoroughly, the Nishinohata household in the Yoga neighbourhood of Tamagawa was informed of the incident by the metropolitan police. It had just gone eight o'clock on the morning of 2 June.

3.

Philosophers deny the existence of chance. Even if something appears to be accidental at first, it is only perceived as such because the cause has yet to be investigated fully. When the painter, Yoshihara, found a strange stain on the roof of a train, not only the people around him, but even the local newspaper described it as an accidental discovery. On closer examination, however, the reason would become apparent.

That morning, Yoshihara had dozed off right in the middle of painting—the result of a lack of sleep the previous night. The reason for him going to bed so late was that he had been so excited to see his girlfriend and lost track of time, and his reason for being so excited about their rendezvous was that she was kind and beautiful and loved him with all her heart.

Yoshihara and his colleagues had been tasked with painting the footbridge at Shiroishi Station, and, before they'd set to work, the duty assistant had told them to take special care to avoid accidents. If any of the men were to lose their footing and fall inadvertently onto the tracks, they would likely lose their lives in the event of an oncoming train. As a painter, Yoshihara was used to working at great heights, and the more he became accustomed to it, the more he began to relax up there.

Broadly speaking, the only colours used to paint stations are grey, black and yellow. The buildings and structures, moreover, are large and have vast surface areas, which means that the work tends to be quite monotonous. Thus, even if you start the work feeling alert, there's no way that you'll be able to keep it up.

Yoshihara had just begun to nod off when he suddenly opened his eyes, his brush having fallen out of his hand and landed with a bang on the roof of the stationary train that had just stopped right below him.

Damn it! he thought, contorting himself in a panic, his hand clutching the rope as he looked down. What drew his eye, however, wasn't so much the brush that he'd dropped, but the dark-red marks covering around a fifth of the carriage roof next to where it lay. These marks appeared to be dry, but, perhaps as a result of the wind when they were still wet and the train was in motion, they had formed backwards-facing little tails that looked like exclamation marks. "Those look like drops of blood," Yoshihara thought to himself. "There must have been an accident…"

Suddenly the train bell rang. Several passengers went tearing past him, dashing down the stairs and hopping aboard, using the nearest steps. The stationmaster, holding a pocket watch in his white-cotton-gloved hand, was counting down the seconds. Yoshihara glanced helplessly at the brush lying on the carriage roof. It was only a short stop, so there had been no time to go down and fetch it. He knew he would get a good scolding from his supervisor later; it had been a bad start to the day. But just what were those marks?

It wasn't until a break with his co-workers that he thought about the marks on the carriage roof again. The station attendant, whom he knew vaguely, had come over and told them that a body had been discovered by the tracks near Kuki Station.

"I've just had a call from Tokyo," he said. "Let me know if you spot a train with blood on the roof."

"With blood on it? Why?" one of the men asked.

"They think the body must have fallen from the roof of a passenger train, so there ought to blood on one of the carriages."

"What should we do if we find it?"

"I'm not really sure, but apparently the police are searching for it."

Yoshihara was annoyed with himself for having dropped his brush; uncharacteristically taciturn, he just sat there, puffing away on a cigarette. But as he listened to the conversation, he recalled the train from earlier.

"That must have been what I saw!" he exclaimed. "It was one that pulled out around nine-twenty. There'd been an accident, so it came in twenty minutes behind schedule."

He paused, trying to recall what the loudspeaker on the platform had said.

"That's right!" he said. "I think the announcer said it was the second- and third-class stopping service bound for Aomori."

"That would make it the No. 117, the 8.59 service." The station assistant began to stand up, but he stopped halfway. "And you're sure it was blood?"

"How should I know whether it was blood? All I saw was a dirty great mark on the carriage roof. It looked like the mess left after butchering a rabbit…"

4.

Early that same morning, a young man was leisurely walking his dog along the road that ran parallel to the railway tracks connecting Ueno and Uguisudani Stations. Although he was recovering from a chest ailment, he had never yet missed a morning walk.

UENO – SENDAI (TOHOKU MAINLINE) (DOWN TRAINS)

Station	537 Oyama	539 Ujiie	515 Utsunomiya	115 Utsunomiya-Kiryu	541 Oyama	543 Aomori	411 Akita	401 Sendai	133 Aomori	413 Aomori	117 Aomori	3111 Kuroiso	3113 Kuroiso	45 Aomori (Freight)
Ueno dep.	18 00	18 25	18 50	19 25	19 50	20 10	20 35	21 30	21 50	22 30	23 40	9 30	13 15	22 12
Oku "	18 08	18 34	18 58	19 33	↓	20 17	20 42	↓	21 58	22 38	23 48	↓	↓	↓
Akabane "	18 16	18 43	19 07	19 42	20 06	20 25	20 50	21 42	22 06	22 47	23 56	9 43	13 30	22 28
Omiya "	18 38	19 06	19 29	20 06	20 28	20 46	21 12	22 04	22 30	23 09	0 19	10 06	13 50	23 00
Hasuda "	18 48	19 16	19 38	20 16	↓	20 56	21 21	↓ [a]	22 40	23 19	0 29	10 17	↓	↓
Shiraoka "	18 55	19 23	19 44	20 22	↓	21 02	21 28	↓	22 46	23 25	0 35	10 25	↓	↓
Kuki "	19 02	19 30	19 51	20 30	20 48	21 10	21 35	↓	22 54	23 35	0 43	10 33	↓	23 22
Kurihashi "	19 12	19 40	20 01	20 40	20 57	21 20	21 45	↓	23 03	23 45	0 53	10 43	↓	↓
Koga "	19 23	19 51	20 10	20 51	21 07	21 30	21 56	↓	23 14	23 58	1 03	10 54	↓	↓
Mamada "	19 33	20 00	20 20	21 01	↓	21 40	22 05	↓	23 24	0 06	1 13	11 05	↓	↓
Oyama arr.	19 42	20 09	20 28	21 10	21 23	21 49	22 14	22 48	23 33	0 15	1 22	11 15	14 34	23 53
Oyama dep.	...	20 12	20 30	21 14	21 34	[b]	22 16	22 50	23 35	0 20	1 28	11 16	14 34	0 04
Koganei "	...	20 21	20 38	21 23	21 43		22 25	↓	23 45	0 29	↓	11 41	↓	↓
Ishibashi "	...	20 30	20 47	21 33	21 52		22 34	↓	23 55	0 39	↓	11 51	↓	↓
Suzumenomiya "	...	20 39	20 55	21 42	22 01		22 43	↓	0 04	0 48	↓	12 01	↓	↓
Utsunomiya arr.	...	20 48	21 04	21 52	22 11		22 53	23 17	0 14	0 58	1 59	12 11	15 02	0 35
Utsunomiya dep.	...	20 55	[c]	22 05			23 00	23 24	0 28	1 05	2 12	12 18	15 08	0 45
Okamoto "	...	21 04		22 14			↓	↓	↓	1 15	2 24	12 37	↓	↓
Hoshakuji "	...	21 11		22 21			↓	↓	↓	1 23	↓	12 44	↓	↓
Ujiie "	...	21 19		22 30			23 21	↓	↓	1 32	2 41	12 52	↓	↓
Kamasusaka "	...			22 42			↓	↓	↓	1 39	↓	12 59	↓	↓
Kataoka "	...			22 47			23 36	↓	↓	1 45	↓	13 05	↓	↓
Yaita "	...			22 55			↓	↓	1 04	1 54	3 01	13 21	↓	1 25
Nozaki "	...			23 03			↓	↓	1 19	2 03	3 15	13 30	16 00	↓
Nishi-Nasuno arr.	...			23 11			23 57	0 07	1 26	2 11	3 22	13 37	16 08	1 39
Nishi-Nasuno dep.	...			23 13			0 19	0 09	1 29	2 14	3 24	13 40	16 14	1 43
Higashi-Nasuno "	...			23 22			↓	↓	↓	2 24	3 37	13 49	16 24	↓
Kuroiso "	...			23 30			0 38	↓	1 47	2 33	3 46	13 57	16 32	↓
Takaku "	...			↓			0 52	↓	↓	↓	↓			↓
Kurodahara "	...			23 42			↓	↓	↓	2 48	4 03	[e]	[f]	2 21
Toyohara "	...			↓			↓	↓	↓	2 55	4 10			↓
Shirasaka "	...			↓			↓	↓	↓	3 16	4 22			2 37
Shirakawa arr.	...			0 04			1 20	0 51	2 19	3 24	4 30			2 46
Shirakawa dep.	...			0 11			1 34	0 57	2 26	3 32	4 36			3 10
Kutano "	...			↓			↓	↓	2 32	3 38	4 43			↓
Izumizaki "	...			↓			1 57	↓	2 43	3 46	4 50			↓
Yabuki "	...			↓			↓	↓	2 51	3 54	4 59			↓
Kagamiishi "	...			↓			↓	↓	2 58	4 02	5 07			3 39
Sukagawa "	...			0 41			2 22	↓	3 06	4 11	5 16			3 52
Asakanagamori "	...			↓			↓	↓	3 15	4 20	5 24			↓
Koriyama arr.	...			0 54			2 36	1 38	3 22	4 27	5 32			4 06
Koriyama dep.	...			1 03			2 44	1 47	3 32	4 35	5 52			4 20
Hiwada "	...			↓			↓	↓	3 40	4 43	6 01			↓
Gohyakugawa "	...			↓			↓	↓	3 47	4 50	6 10			↓
Motomiya "	...			1 20			3 04	↓	3 54	4 57	6 18			4 42
Sugita "	...			1 34			↓	↓	4 03	5 08	6 30			↓
Nihonmatsu "	...			1 42			3 17	↓	4 11	5 16	6 39			5 02
Adachi "	...			1 48			↓	↓	4 17	5 22	6 46			↓
Matsukawa "	...			↓			↓	↓	4 25	5 31	6 57			5 17
Kanayagawa "	...			↓			3 37	↓	4 31	5 37	7 06			↓
Fukushima arr.	...			2 20			3 48	2 36	4 42	5 51	7 22			5 34
Fukushima dep.	...			2 47			4 00	2 45	4 52	6 02	7 42			5 50
Seno-Ue "	...			↓			[h]	↓	5 00	[h]	7 51			↓
Date "	...			↓				↓	5 06		7 58			6 05
Koori "	...			↓				↓	5 14		8 07			6 14
Fujita "	...			↓				↓	5 20		8 13			6 22
Kaida "	...			↓				↓	5 32		8 27			↓
Kosugo "	...			↓				↓	5 38		8 34			6 50
Shiroishi "	...			3 33				↓	5 58		8 58			7 11
Kita-Shirakawa "	...			↓				↓	6 08		9 11			↓
Ogawara "	...			3 49				↓	6 17		9 18			7 32
Funaoka "	...			3 55				↓	6 24		9 28			7 40
Tsukinoki "	...			4 01				↓	6 31		9 35			↓
Iwanuma "	...			4 10				↓	6 41		9 44			8 01
Masuda "	...			4 20				↓	6 50		9 54			↓
Rikuzen-Nakada "	...			4 25				↓	6 58		9 59			8 19
Nagamachi "	...			4 32				↓	7 02		10 05			↓
Sendai arr.	...			4 40					7 11		10 13			8 28
TERMINUS	...			...		17 30	18 40	9 12	...	21 04	22 21	...	...	18 52

Notes:
[a] 401: Special Express
[b] 543: Does not run Saturdays
[c] 515: Diesel locomotive
[d] 539: (Shinbashi dep. 18 06 / Tokyo dep. 18 15)
[e] 3111: (Runs every weekend until 11.11)
[f] 3113: (Runs every Saturday until 10.11 and also on 2.11)
[g] 117: Front part continues to Aizu-Wakamatsu (205), arr. 7 38
[h] 411 / 413: To Aomori (via Ou Mainline)

Amid the polluted air of the crowded Shitamachi, he had felt as though his lungs, which had just begun to get better, were once again being filled with soot. Hence his need to take a refreshing stroll through Ueno Park that morning, breathing in the abundant fresh air and cleaning out his lungs. Ordinarily, his route would take him past the Science Museum and around the University of the Arts, and, by the time he returned home, his mother would have breakfast all laid out on the table for him.

Around three hundred yards past Ueno Station, the road divided: the path to the left led up a gentle slope before going down again to remerge with the original road. The young man was walking up this hill at a slow enough pace not to get out of breath. Every winter, the young people from the neighbourhood liked to gather there and go skiing down it. When he'd been healthy, the young man had enjoyed skiing a lot himself, but after this recent illness, he would never be able to take part in such energetic sports again. Whenever he climbed this hill, he would think about this, forgetting the joy of his recovery, and he would feel angry and remorseful that he had ever contracted that damned disease.

If you stood at the top the hill and looked to your left, you would see an overpass leading across the railway tracks to the park on the other side. Known as Ryodaishi Bridge, it was an imposing concrete structure with a carriageway in the middle and a footpath on either side. The young man crossed it almost daily.

The dog, which was waiting ahead of him, knew the routine. As his master began to cross the bridge as usual, it dashed over to the edge of the footpath and began to sniff around excitedly.

"Pesu! Pesu!" the man tried calling it.

But the dog didn't come back. It just kept barking, rubbing the tip of its nose on the ground. There was something strange about its bark, as though the animal were pleading for something.

"Pesu! What is it, boy?"

As the young man drew nearer, the dog, sensing his approach, started barking even more. There was a large smear on the black surface of the footpath. He couldn't tell what it was, but, judging from the strange barking of the dog, which had a keen sense of smell, it wasn't anything as mundane as motor oil.

Since the path was damp with dew from the previous night, the stain had not yet dried entirely. The young man wanted to test it, so he looked around for a handy stick to prod it with; as he did so, his eyes came to rest on the railing in front of him, and what he saw stopped him dead in his tracks. The railing of the overpass was also made of concrete, but, in contrast to the blackened footpath, it was a paler shade of grey—and on it, the shock of blood stood out much more clearly.

Before, the young man would have trembled at the sight of this. He had an instinctive aversion to and fear of blood. But ever since his chest ailment, frequent haemorrhages in his lungs had sadly accustomed him to seeing the red liquid. And so now, unfazed by the sight of it, he carefully examined the stains on the railing.

Placing his hands on it and leaning over, he saw that there were also dark-red stains on the other side of the concrete. With a little imagination, he could picture somebody being injured on the footpath, climbing over the railing and falling onto the tracks below. Embellishing the scene still further, he was horrified to see in his mind's eye the struggle that had taken place on the dark overpass.

Running directly under the section of the bridge with the bloodstain was the downbound Tohoku mainline. Surely, the victim would have been cut in two under the wheels of a train. The young man peered down at the track nervously, but there was no grue-some sight to be seen. "Maybe the train was able to brake sharply and stop in time," he thought. "It would've just left Ueno Station, so it wouldn't have gathered much speed. Stopping would've been easy." At any rate, his morning walk had been thoroughly ruined by the discovery of this ominous bloodstain.

The young man gave his dog a nudge and carried on his usual route. Before long, he came across a policeman on patrol, just in front of the Science Museum.

"I'm sorry to bother you, Constable, but was there some accident on Ryodaishi Bridge earlier?"

The police officer turned and, fiddling with his baton, looked at the man quizzically.

"On Ryodaishi Bridge? No, not that I'm aware of… Why do you ask?"

Finding himself under scrutiny, the young man seemed flustered. He panicked, realizing that the question had sprung from his own imagination.

"Well, you see," he said, blushing, "I thought I saw some blood on it, so I wondered whether somebody hadn't been injured…"

The policeman was around the same age as the young man. He was shorter than him but had broad shoulders and was of a sturdy build, as though he'd come from some farming village. He had a sunburnt, ruddy-looking face, in the middle of which were two beady eyes. As he listened to the youth's story, those eyes suddenly lit up.

"A bloodstain, you say?"

"I believe so, yes. Though it could be the blood of an animal, of course."

The young man cringed. He didn't want the policeman to laugh at him if it turned out that he was wrong, and now he regretted letting his curiosity get the better of him.

"Never mind about that. Where exactly on the bridge was this?"

In his capacity as a police officer, he was not all that interested in what the man had said. After all, once he had inspected the scene and filed a report with his superiors, he would be discharged of responsibility. Yet there was no way that the young man could have known this, and, since he couldn't talk his way out of it now, he stood shoulder to shoulder with him, and together they made their way back the way the dogwalker had come. His dog wagged its tail in excitement.

They'd just turned the corner at the Science Museum and taken a couple of steps towards the overpass when a voice called out from behind them. About two hundred yards away, at the main gate of the National Museum, was a man who looked like a security guard, waving to them.

"We should go over there. It looks as though something's happened."

The ailing youth hurried as best he could, following the policeman's lead.

"I'm sorry," said the man as they approached, "but it's getting in the way. You couldn't have it moved, could you?"

The security guard was indicating a parked car beside them. He must have been around fifty, and although he looked quite scrawny, his eyes were sharp. There were deep wrinkles running from the sides of his nose down to his mouth, and he had a sour look on his face.

"I'm sure the owner will be back any minute," the policeman said matter-of-factly.

The car door had been left slightly ajar, lending the impression that the driver had just stepped out on an errand. Yet, on closer inspection, the grey body of the car was covered in night dew and the engine was cold to the touch. It was clear that the car had been abandoned for several hours. Having been left directly in front of the main gate, it was getting in the way of visitors now that the museum was open.

"How long has it been here?"

"Well, it wasn't here last night," the guard replied brusquely. Though he said nothing more, he looked as though he had no time for such silly questions and just wanted the obstruction to be removed as quickly as possible.

The vehicle was a Kaiser. As cars went, it was mid-range, but new. The black characters against the white background of the number plate revealed that it was registered for private use.

"Couldn't you drive it?" The guard had adopted a prickly tone.

Ignoring him, the policeman peered into the vehicle. There was a black fedora lying beside the accelerator.

"What's this?" the young man said, venturing to pick the hat up.

You could tell, just by looking at it, that it was a top-quality item. It was a brand-new Borsalino and it smelled faintly of hair oil.

The policeman's face suddenly took on a troubled expression. He looked much more serious now than when he'd heard about the bloodstain on the bridge. He rummaged around in the pocket of the door and extracted the driver's licence. As he unfolded it, his beady eyes alighted on the name written there, before looking off into space, as if trying to recall the person.

"Why does the name Nishinohata ring a bell? Gosuke Nishinohata…"

"Isn't Gosuke Nishinohata the director of Towa Textiles?" the dogwalker ventured. "The company that's on strike at the moment?"

"Ah, yes, I remember now. The Towa Textiles Company. But then…"

The policeman stopped mid-sentence and pulled a wry face as the suspicion dawned on him. He was thinking the same as the youth.

44

"But then why has the director of the company left his car here?" the security guard asked.

"Why, indeed... At any rate, don't touch the car until you hear from me later, old man."

"Oh, for heaven's sake! If you don't hurry up and move it, then—"

But before the guard could finish what he was saying, the policeman tapped the young convalescent on the arm and, in a tone of enthusiasm that was a far cry from his earlier reaction, said:

"Come on, as quick as you can. I need to see those bloodstains on the bridge."

FOUR

A Suspicious Errand

1.

It was about eleven o'clock by the time it was established that the bloodstains on Ryodaishi Bridge belonged to Gosuke Nishinohata. It was impossible to determine whether the director had been killed and his body thrown over the railing or whether he had jumped of his own volition in order to escape his assailants; what was easy to imagine, however, was that his body had landed on a train that had been passing directly beneath the overpass and been carried all the way to Kuki in Saitama Prefecture.

An incident room was set up on the first floor of Ueno police station just after noon, a little over eight hours after the body was discovered. To say that the investigation did not get off to a smooth start would be an understatement. The original intention had been to set up an incident room at the local police station in Omiya, with the aim of conducting a joint investigation together with the Saitama prefectural police, but after the unexpected discovery of the crime scene on Ryodaishi Bridge, it was formally moved.

The forensics were carried out by a team of investigators that included detectives from both the metropolitan police and the local force. The two officers who paid a visit to the head office of Towa Textiles in the west Ginza were Detective Inspector Sudo, a veteran of the force with over twenty-five years' experience, and Constable Seki, who had been appointed to the post only last year.

This combination of experience and inexperience was standard procedure, so that the new recruits could learn the ropes from their superiors. Or at least that was the theory.

"Reporting for duty, sir," the constable said, bowing his head.

"Oh," was all the inspector could muster as he slumped back in his chair.

This response, which would have appeared arrogant to anyone else, didn't offend Seki in the least, for the inspector's ruddy face and downward slanting eyes gave him a kindly air. He also wore a little moustache, which looked as though it had been painted on with tip of a brush. This in turn lent him the louche appearance of many a man like him from the down-at-heel streets of Tokyo's Shitamachi.

It had taken about fifteen minutes for the investigation team to split itself into nine pairs. After that, the eighteen men received a briefing from the police chief, before being sent on their various ways. Some headed off to conduct interviews, while others were dispatched to look for evidence at the crime scenes. Sudo and Seki entered the subway at Ueno and headed for the Ginza. After all, it's only in film and television that detectives flag down taxis; the reality was that they seldom went anywhere by car—not because they couldn't, but because the budget was so tight.

After exiting at Ginza 4-chome and emerging from the crowd onto Sukiya Bridge, the pair turned left at the crossing. Having only a few years ago been the setting for a popular radio drama that brought tears to eyes of so many housewives across Japan, the famous bridge was now about to be demolished.

"Nothing lasts for ever, does it?" Seki said, unable to help himself. But the noise of a passing tram drowned him out.

"What lasts for ever?" Sudo shouted back, causing a passing office girl to look at them both strangely.

The Towa Textiles Company was situated right beside a car park. As the two entered the building, they were greeted by the receptionist. Ordinarily, she would have flashed her sweet, well-rehearsed smile, but today, having received the news of the company director's untimely demise, she had none of her usual cheer.

They took the lift to the sixth floor. The cold marble floor stretched the entire length of the corridor. Normally, it would have been abuzz with activity, workers racing busily back and forth with documents.

Taking a seat on the sofa beside the lift, as instructed, they waited, and presently a heavy-set man of around forty approached them. He was dressed like a typical Ginza salaryman but had a rather dowdy air about him. He introduced himself as Haibara, the director's private secretary, and invited the two men into his office.

"Care for a cigarette?" Haibara offered amiably. He spoke standard Japanese, albeit with a pronounced Tohoku accent.

"Thank you, I have my own," Sudo said flatly, taking out a cigarette case, the gilt of which was peeling. "Don't mind me."

He lit the cigarette he'd extracted from it and took a long drag before requesting, with a polished tone, the secretary's cooperation with their investigation into the murder of Nishinohata.

"Do you know of anybody who might have wanted Mr Nishinohata dead?"

"As it so happens, I can think of not one, but three."

Haibara spoke very clearly. He appeared to have been waiting for this question.

"And who are these people?"

"Yoshio Koigakubo and Shusaku Narumi, for starters. They are, respectively, the chairman and vice-chairman of our trade union. As you may know, our company is embroiled in a labour dispute that's been going on for the last month and a half. We had another round of negotiations the day before yesterday. Of the four demands made by the union, we accepted two of them and were on the verge of reaching a compromise."

"I see…"

"The fact that the company has agreed to half of their demands makes it look as though we're level-pegging, but the reality is that it's a defeat for the union."

The secretary looked alternately at the detectives, as if trying to satisfy himself that both were listening.

"As you've probably already read in the newspapers, the union's demands are fourfold: an increase in wages, the introduction of severance pay, and the other two, to use their terms, concern 'questions of their fundamental human rights'."

This gist of all this was indeed already known to the police detectives. Among the more peculiar of their demands, however, was a call to abolish the censorship of private correspondence. According to reports in the press, women living in the company dormitory had their letters screened by an administrator, who would open every item of post received from outside and go through it with a fine-tooth comb. Clearly, this practice was against the law, and not only had Nishinohata received criticism for ordering that these outdated inspections be carried out, but so had the employees, who, in their ignorance, had acquiesced to it until now.

"At the final round of talks two days ago, the company agreed to only two of the demands made by the union: abolishing the censorship of private correspondence and acknowledging their so-called freedom of religious expression. The union leaders took the deal back to the shop floor and held a meeting, during which they listened to everyone's opinion and discussed whether or not to accept it. But you see, gentlemen, the two items for which they'd really been holding out hope—wages and severance pay—had been rejected out of hand. Effectively, the strike had achieved nothing. Great cry and little wool, as the old saying goes."

"But they did win those two concessions, did they not?"

"Well, I wouldn't quite put it like that."

The secretary quickly rebutted the detective inspector's statement. He was quite eloquent, although he spoke with a slow tongue.

"To believe that the company was actually opening private letters is preposterous. It's a totally baseless fabrication. It was nothing more than a plot to court public sympathy; a sob story invented to make the director out to be an ogre and to cast the factory girls as heroines. Addressing a grievance that never even existed is hardly a win."

This was news to the two detectives. They were impressed by how much the secretary knew about the goings-on behind the scenes.

"Even on the matter of religious freedom, the company has been much misrepresented. Everybody is in search of some kind of spiritual comfort. The company director, with the love a parent has for a child, merely tried to guide them towards the religion he believed in, so that they might share in the joys of a happy and secure life. Only, the workers didn't much like this. They'd rather play pachinko than worship the gods. You see, originally it was an act of goodwill on the director's part, but when he heard about their complaints, he felt it was wrong to press the matter, so he agreed to the union's demand. After all, what difference did it make to the company? On the other hand, the union would be able to claim a victory that in real terms had no substance to it whatsoever."

"I see."

"During these latest negotiations, the director gave the union an ultimatum. He told them that since the company had agreed to two of their demands, they must now withdraw the other two; otherwise, there would be a lockout. Ordinarily, this might have been done earlier, but the fact that it wasn't is surely evidence of the director's patience and restraint, irrespective of any fatherly feelings he may have had."

"Yes, I see."

"It's an important point, actually. It was the director himself who ultimately took such a hard line on the lockout. He was intransigent. If the dispute had been settled liked that, it would have meant a total defeat for the union, and Koigakubo's and Narumi's reputations would have lain in tatters."

Getting carried away with himself, the secretary seemed oblivious to the contradiction in his depiction of the director, who was supposed to have been a caring, fatherly kind of employer one minute, and a hard-line martinet the next.

"Koigakubo and Narumi may be in control of the union, but this is their first strike since being elected to office, so this will be seen as a touchstone to test their skills. To make matters more difficult, they labelled the old leadership company lackeys before ousting them, so now, whenever anything goes wrong for them, they're subject to scorn and ridicule from that faction. Recently, there have even been rumours that the former leaders are plotting to form a second union. It isn't beyond the realms of possibility that Koigakubo and Narumi would be tempted to bump off the director."

"So, are the other executives sympathetic to the strike?"

"I certainly wouldn't say that, no," the secretary said sharply, frowning. "You might say that they aren't as hard-line as the director, though. Were it not for him, they might have reached a more favourable solution. In the grand scheme of things, they'd have been able to keep the union members happy, and, on a smaller scale, it would've spared the other executives the ridicule of their rivals. I'm sure this cannot have escaped the notice of the union chairman and his deputy. It's for these reasons that we believe Koigakubo and Narumi may have had something to do with all this. Narumi, especially, is forever saying incendiary things like, 'Let's bury the director!'"

When he had finished, the secretary lit his third cigarette. He was fair-skinned, but his face was flushed, probably because of all the talking.

2.

Resting his cigarette in the ashtray, Haibara moistened his throat with a sip of tea and carried on talking.

"As I touched on earlier, our director was a believer in a new sect of Shintoism, known as 'the Shaman'. It's one of these new religions that have been springing up all over the place ever since the war. There's no time to go into its doctrines or anything else about it right now, but it's a big religious group with a growing number of followers, so I'm sure you've heard the name, at least."

The secretary waited for the two detectives to nod before carrying on.

"As you'll know, it's not uncommon for big companies to have a certain sway over the personal lives of their employees, and so, wanting his workers to be happy, our director urged them all to join the fold. If we accept the union's demands, however, its members will leave. And that will be a big problem for the Shaman."

"How many members does the union have?"

"Let me see now. The factory in Tokyo alone has around six and a half thousand workers. It's located in Adachi Ward, so if all its members left, it would leave the Shaman shrine in north Tokyo empty. The prospect of this came as a great shock to the high priests, and even the founder himself dispatched letters and messengers to the director several times, entreating him not to accept the union's demands. Nevertheless, as the situation became less and less favourable—that is, as the director was on the point of accepting the union's demand for freedom of religious expression—the Shaman began to adopt a more uncompromising attitude. Eventually, we received a notice stating that a mass defection would be regarded as an act of betrayal by the company director against the sect's founder."

"Meaning what, exactly?"

"Meaning that traitors would be dealt with accordingly, and that, if that was a frightening prospect, then the union's demands shouldn't be accepted."

"So, he was being blackmailed... As new religions go, the Shaman is a powerful organization. Why were they so worried by the potential loss of only six and a half thousand members?"

"We also have factories in Nagaoka and Osaka. If all their employees were to leave, it would be a heavy blow to the sect. Not only that, but there's also a serious risk that other discontented elements who've been critical of the sect's doctrines but unable to do anything about it, would follow suit. If this were to cause a chain reaction and other groups were to leave, too, all in quick succession, the sect would be devastated."

"Yes, I can see that."

Detective Inspector Sudo nodded, as though finally convinced.

Rumour held that the founder of the sect was a Japanese repatriate from Oroqen in northern Manchuria, where he'd had the opportunity to observe folk shamanism. According to one university professor, who was a well-known social critic, the doctrine of the Shaman was exceedingly shallow, clothing primitive shamanism in a modern veil. And, since shamanism and sorcery were linked inextricably, the founder had joined forces with a travelling conjurer he had found in the countryside to show his devotees all manner of mysterious phenomena. This was how the cult had captured the public's interest to begin with. In the three short years since it was granted status as a religious corporation, it had acquired as many as 1,250,000 members and now had branches in every prefecture. There was seemingly no end to the number of people who flocked to its main shrine in the Ryudocho neighbourhood of Tokyo's Azabu. A bus stop had been built outside the shrine for this very reason, and the Metropolitan Transport Authority had allocated four state-of-the-art trains for a branch line that served it. Such was the prosperity of the Shaman.

"So, are you saying that Mr Nishinohata could have been killed by the Shaman?"

"Yes, by a certain somebody within the organization."

"Do you mean a somebody in particular?"

"A man by the name of Hanpei Chita."

At the very mention of this name, a look of tension appeared on Sudo's face. The secretary seemed to sense this.

"Do you know him?"

"No, but I'm familiar with the name. Only, why do you suspect *him*?"

"Why, because he's capable of anything—even of killing a man."

Haibara paused, as though weighing what to say next. Meanwhile, Seki gulped down his tea.

"… The lower shrines of the Shaman are organized into small circles known as *rinban*. It's different for men of stature like our director, but they make the average man repent of his past in one of these circles when he enters the organization. I believe Christians do something similar, so it's hardly surprising that the Shaman make them do such things. One after another, the senior members of the circle confess their past transgressions, and so, encouraged by this, the newcomers try to unburden themselves by revealing their true faults. But you see, the headquarters make recordings of these confessions and, if ever a person should become disillusioned and want to leave the organization, they'll use the material to blackmail them. So, it's a mechanism wherein believers whose weaknesses have been exploited can never leave. Hanpei Chita is the shadowy man in charge of these tapes, and it's his job to threaten and dissuade anybody who wants to leave the group. In Soviet terms, his position is like that of the chief of the secret police."

"Quite an unscrupulous little set-up, isn't it?"

"I should say it's more than just unscrupulous. It seems this Chita fellow used to work in the intelligence services, and it's because of these skills and expertise that he was employed by the founder. Only, if the director were to have given into the union's demand, Chita wouldn't have time to go around threatening each and every one of the 6,500 members just in Tokyo who would try to leave the organization. Moreover, since most of them didn't join the Shaman in good faith, the confessions they made to their respective *rinban* were often quite lacklustre. Under pressure, they'd invent half-baked stories, saying they got drunk and knocked over a post-box, that sort of thing. So even if they were presented with the recordings, I doubt they'd take much notice. From the Shaman's point of view, at least as far as the union members are concerned, their trump card has turned out to be a joker."

"So, you're saying Chita had no choice but to deal with Nishinohata personally?"

"Exactly. He came to the office several times. Each time I saw him, he made crude and threatening insinuations. The last time he showed his face here was yesterday afternoon."

"And what exactly did he say?"

"He said that their patience was running out and that if the company didn't do as he said, there would be grave consequences."

"And you told Mr Nishinohata?"

"Of course. He was out at the time, but I told him the moment he got back."

"What did he say?"

"He laughed at me," Haibara said in his heavy northern accent. "He said that he was taking precautions just in case, and that he could never run a business if he concerned himself with threats from 'those idiots'. He had a tendency to push back even more forcefully when he was pushed; it wasn't just Chita but rather the whole organization that he was furious with."

3.

The three of them lapsed into silence as they drank their tea. All you could hear was the sound of sipping and the noise from the street coming through the wide-open window. Since they were on the sixth floor, however, the noise was somewhat muffled, like a musical instrument with the dampener applied.

"It's so quiet up here," Detective Inspector Sudo said, setting down his teacup.

"Business has ground to a halt. Only an hour ago there were dozens of reporters here. We couldn't fit them all into the reception area, never mind this room, so we had no choice but to talk to them up on the roof."

"Did you mention Chita or Koigakubo?"

Sudo looked flustered. It was unconscionable that anybody should have blithely mentioned the suspects' names.

"No, of course not," Haibara replied in a clipped tone. "I believe I know what constitutes an official police secret."

The question appeared to have offended him. Blood rushed to his ordinarily pale face.

"On another note," Sudo asked, ignoring the expression on the secretary's face, "now that Mr Nishinohata is dead, who will succeed him in the company?"

"Nothing official will be decided until the board meeting, of course, but it seems evident enough that our deputy director, Haruhiko Ryu, will be promoted. But, Inspector, you mustn't think that Mr Ryu would have killed the director just to get ahead."

A wry smile appeared on the secretary's plump face, as if he had read the detective inspector's thoughts.

"Oh, and why not?"

"Because he's in Lancashire in England at the moment, attending a textile convention with his wife."

"I see. I certainly didn't mean to cast doubt on the deputy director. But it is my job to ask these things. On yet another note, how much of an estate does Mr Nishinohata leave?"

Haibara's eyes suddenly seemed to light up. He blinked several times, perhaps to hide his reaction, and averted his gaze.

"I really couldn't say. I'll fetch Mr Nukariya, Mr Nishinohata's lawyer, directly. You should address that question to him. Well, if there's nothing else, gentlemen?"

"One last thing... Do you happen to know where Mr Nishinohata went after he left the office yesterday?"

"I'm afraid not. When I heard about his death this morning, I telephoned half a dozen places to try and piece together his movements, but without any luck."

"Who was the last person to see him?"

"His driver. If you'll kindly wait here, I'll call for him."

As Haibara stood up to leave, his assistant came in, bringing tea and shortcake on a tray which she carried with her beautifully manicured hands. She had probably come to work unaware of the director's demise, but, in hindsight, her shiny nails and flashy clothes looked somewhat inappropriate.

"Mr Nukariya will be here in just a moment," she said politely. "If you wouldn't mind waiting a little?"

Seki was keen to ask what had caused the detective inspector's reaction upon hearing Chita's name mentioned earlier, but, stayed by the idea that somebody somewhere might be listening, he kept quiet and drank his tea.

Just as he was finishing his cup, a slender man of around sixty entered. His hair, eyebrows and even his lips were pure white, against which his berry-brown face seemed almost black. On first appearances, he gave the strong impression of being a difficult person with a short temper.

"If you don't mind, we'd like to ask you a few questions regarding the content of Mr Nishinohata's estate," Sudo said rather tentatively, apparently having formulated the same impression of the man as Seki.

"Mr Nishinohata has liquid assets of 30,000,000 yen and real estate valued at 50,000,000. Most of the liquid assets are in the form of shares and securities, while the real estate includes his residence at Tamagawa, as well as land and forests in Ito and Karuizawa, and in his home town of Nagaoka."

Constable Seki had no idea whether 80,000,000 was a large

or small amount for a businessman, so he said nothing and simply noted down the colossal figure in his notebook.

"And who stands to inherit all this?"

"Everything goes to his wife. He was lucky in business but not blessed when it came to children. Was there anything else?"

Ever the typical lawyer, valuing his own time, Nukariya shot to his feet the moment the conversation was over.

4.

Haibara entered again, this time accompanied by a man with a hunchback and an ashen complexion. At the age of thirty-five, Jiro Iba was supposed to be a man in his prime, but his clothes were plain and his movements so lacking in vigour that he looked a good ten years older. When they resumed their seats, Haibara was the first to speak.

"I think it would be best if I gave you a run-down of the director's movements last night. At the end of the business day, he met with the director of Maruta Trading in our reception room. Ordinarily, such meetings would have been conducted somewhere more convivial, but Mr Maruta is a little stuffy and abhors the atmosphere of tea houses, restaurants and the like. With no alternative, Mr Nishinohata skipped dinner, having only a sandwich instead, and held the business meeting here in the office. I won't go into the details of the meeting, but I saw Mr Maruta out just before eleven. The director himself left just after that, at around eleven o'clock."

"Where did you and Mr Nishinohata part ways?"

"Right in front of the office. The director got into Mr Iba's car and went home, while I called for a car to pick me up. The last person to see him was Mr Iba here."

The driver moistened his lips, realizing that it was now his turn.

"We left the office and drove towards Shimbashi. That's where Mr Nishinohata told me to stop the car. He said that he'd drive the rest of the way himself and told me to take the subway home. So, I got out of the car as he asked me to do…"

"Just a moment," Haibara cut in. "For clarity's sake, I should point out that dropping Mr Iba off halfway isn't exactly a rarity."

"Why is that?"

"It's like this, you see. Because of all these threats from the labour union and Mr Chita's bizarre attempts at blackmail, the executives at the company have been jittery. They were worried these people might find the director at home and kill him as he slept. He had nerves of steel, so he wasn't bothered, but the others prevailed on him to change where he slept regularly."

"Ah…"

"So, after dropping off Iba here, he'd drive himself to a hotel or a *ryokan* he knew well. In such cases, only his wife would be informed where he was staying. Nobody else, not even I, his private secretary, would know. He had to be consistent in everything he did, you see."

His tone suggested that he was a little disgruntled that Nishinohata hadn't trusted him.

"And he was able to drive himself?"

"Yes, I believe he'd been a very able driver ever since he was young. He was proud of the fact that he'd worked his way through university moonlighting as a truck driver."

The story went that Gosuke Nishinohata's family had fallen into ruin when he was a child and that they had practically fled under cover of darkness, leaving Nagaoka and moving to Miyazaki Prefecture on the island of Kyushu. There, he completed his first six years of schooling, before continuing his studies while working as a manual labourer. A local elder took note of his diligence and hard work and paid his school fees, allowing him eventually to finish high school and go to university. It was rumoured that his wife was the daughter of this benefactor, and that the reason he'd put up with her selfishness and criticisms of him without threatening to divorce her was because he felt obligated by the kindness he had received from the old man. When the lawyer described Nishinohata as not having been blessed with children, what he was really referring to was the director's wife. At any rate, Mrs Nishinohata not only was selfish, but also had a reputation for being plain, spendthrift and severely prone to hysteria.

"You were saying about the hotels and *ryokan* he frequented…"

"Yes, there were half a dozen of them. He seems to have gone to whichever one took his fancy. There was no rhyme or reason to it. These are the places I telephoned this morning, trying to find out where he'd been."

Sudo nodded to Haibara, before turning his attention to the dismal face of the driver.

"Did you notice anything unusual last night, Mr Iba?"

"No, not really. Mr Nishinohata seemed the same as always."

"I don't necessarily mean Mr Nishinohata himself. It could be anything at all that was different. Please, try to think."

The driver paused. Finally, something occurred to him just as he was about to place his cigarette to his lips, making him stop halfway.

"I can't be sure, but I did think at one point that a car seemed to be following the boss."

"Tell us more."

"It was when I stopped the car in Shimbashi. Mr Nishinohata had got into the driver's seat and, just as he was about to set off, there was another car that started its engine and seemed to follow him."

"What kind of car was it?"

"A grey Plymouth."

"Did you see the number plate?"

The driver averted his eyes awkwardly.

"No, that's the thing. It only occurred to me after I heard about the accident. I didn't think much of it at the time."

"What model was it?"

"A '52 or a '53, I think."

"A '52 or a '53… And which in direction did Mr Nishinohata drive off?"

"Well, he was heading towards the intersection at Tamuracho, but as for where he went after that…"

Trailing off, he scratched his head. Once again, Haibara butted in; even if his intention wasn't to save the embarrassed driver, that was certainly the effect of it.

"Constable, there was something else I noticed that was a little odd about the director's movements yesterday."

"Please, go ahead."

"Well, I'm not sure whether it has anything to do with the case or not, but it happened yesterday afternoon. The meeting with Mr Maruta from Yokohama was originally scheduled to take place in our reception room here at one-thirty in the afternoon, not in the evening. But for some reason Mr Nishinohata decided to postpone it and went to a department store in Nihonbashi. He said he was going to see an exhibition of paintings from Mexico."

Both Sudo and Seki were aware that such an exhibition was indeed being held there.

"The director must have been very keen on art."

"If he were, there'd be nothing strange about it, but the fact is that he wasn't interested in art in the slightest. I remember once hearing that, because he had to work so hard from a young age, he hadn't time to cultivate much of an appreciation for the arts."

"But isn't it possible that he'd had a change of outlook?"

Once again, Haibara's face reddened.

"Mr Nishinohata was a very busy man. His schedule of meetings and dinners was fixed a month in advance. Mr Maruta is the same in that regard; if they missed yesterday's appointment, neither of them would have a free day for the foreseeable future. That's why Mr Maruta was asked if he'd go to all the trouble of meeting in the evening. My point is rather whether it was strictly necessary for Mr Nishinohata to go and see those paintings, what with all the inconvenience it caused."

"It is curious, isn't it?" said Sudo, who was momentarily distracted by the driver awkwardly clearing his throat. "Then you believe the story about the paintings to have been some kind of ploy?"

"Well, I did wonder..."

"Mr Iba," the detective inspector said, suddenly turning to the driver with a friendly smile. "Did you take Mr Nishinohata to the department store?"

"Well, sir... I don't really know how to answer that."

The driver looked at him like a frightened animal.

"What? Why? Did you drive him there or not?"

"The thing is, sir, the boss gave me a thousand yen to keep it a secret..."

"The circumstances couldn't be more different now! Your employer has been killed, hasn't he? You have to tell us whatever secrets you know so that we can find out who killed him."

Fear once again clouded the driver's eyes. Seki thought he looked like a rabbit in the headlights.

"You see, Officer, we took turns driving around the Ginza, after which I spent an hour gambling in a nearby pachinko parlour."

"On the instructions of the director?"

"Yes, sir."

"And you've no idea where he went?"

"No. I thought it would be improper to spy on him, so as soon as the car moved off, I ducked into a side alley. But I am certain that the car sped off towards Shimbashi…"

"And can you recall what exactly Mr Nishinohata said to you at the time?"

"I think so… At first, I just thought we were going to Nihonbashi. But when we reached the crossroads at Owaricho, he asked me to stop the car, just like he did in Shimbashi. 'Go and find a pachinko parlour to play in for an hour,' he said, handing me a thousand yen. 'Here's some money for the balls.' He'd given me the money a couple of times before on the way home from work, but this was the first time he'd done it in the middle of the day, so I was surprised. I asked him whether he was going to the department store, but he just said, 'No, I'll go there tomorrow. I have some urgent business to attend to.' That was when he took out another 1,000 yen note and said to me, 'Only, don't tell anyone, mind. We're going to pretend that we went to see the exhibition of Mexican paintings…' And with that, he headed off round the corner towards Nihonbashi."

The two detectives were not the only ones who were interested in the driver's tale. Haibara, too, appeared to be hearing this for the first time, and he listened to the entire story almost without blinking, his eyes fixed on the man's profile.

"At around what time did Mr Nishinohata return?"

"After about an hour. He tapped me on the shoulder from behind while I was playing. This time I sat behind the wheel and took us back to the office."

Mr Iba looked happy to have got everything off his chest.

"At what time did you leave the office?"

"Around half past noon, maybe a little later."

"And he left you at Owaricho when?"

"Hmm… It must've been around ten to one."

Hence, if he took the car on his own for an hour or so, he would have got back to the pachinko parlour at 1.50 p.m. and returned to the office at 2 p.m. Having noted this down, Sudo nudged Seki and stood up.

"Thank you, Mr Iba," Haibara said, while the driver sat there in silence, wearing a look of relief.

5.

After leaving the head office of Towa Textiles, the two detectives took the subway towards Asakusa, retracing the journey they had just taken. There were no empty seats to sit on, so they stood directly under the spinning electric fan.

"Who exactly is this Hanpei Chita, sir?"

Seki was finally able to ask the question that had been gnawing at him all this time. The inspector answered almost in a whisper, just loud enough to be heard over the rattling of the train. It was a strange way of speaking.

"The name of that travelling magician taken on by the Shaman to trick its followers was Keiichi Owase. As the numbers of adherents increased, however, relations between Owase and the founder of the cult became strained. It's the usual story. Or at least it was, until Owase's body was found floating in Tokyo Bay in the spring of last year."

"I remember now. It was a ferry bound for Kisarazu that discovered the body, wasn't it?"

"Yes, that's right. Chita came to our attention in the course of the investigation, but some of the followers gave witness statements saying that he had been at the Shaman headquarters at the time of the incident, so we were never able to pin anything on him."

"Did you believe their statements?"

"No, in a word. But these so-called witnesses are all fanatics, so they were unfazed by the prospect of being charged with perjury."

Every time the train would pull into a station, they would stop talking and wait for the noise to resume before returning to their conversation.

"Then there were the killings of two Shamanists in the summer and autumn of last year: one in Meguro, the other in Nerima. The only thing they had in common, besides being believers, was that they both wanted to leave the cult. One was a wealthy man who'd given a lot of money to the organization—which is to say they'd used him as a milch cow—while the other one was the head of a local branch. These weren't your average followers, so it would've been a bit of a blow to the Shaman if they'd left. They probably tried various things to coerce or intimidate them into not leaving, but when that failed, they must have resorted to more extreme measures. In effect, they made examples of them."

"It's outrageous."

"Incident rooms were set up at the two local police stations. I even went to Nerima myself. Both investigations concluded that Chita was the likely culprit, but unfortunately there wasn't enough evidence to prove it, and the investigations hit a brick wall."

"It's a slippery organization, isn't it?"

"Well, Chita did work for the intelligence services, after all. He's adept at sniffing out other people's secrets and turning the screws. He's also got a knack for going to ground. If it *was* Chita who did

Nishinohata in, proving it won't be easy. We'll have to show him what's what this time."

Sudo laughed as though what he'd said were a joke. Yet Seki couldn't help but notice the curious glint in his eyes.

When they returned to police headquarters, they found the crowd of reporters that had been there earlier had gone, and the chief constable was sitting alone in his office with the door wide open.

"Some reports came in while you were out," he said as he poured out two cups of chilled barley tea. "We've identified the train that carried the victim's body. It was the 23.40 from Ueno to Aomori, a second- and third-class stopping service. The university lab has taken a look at the bloodstain and confirmed that it's a match for Nishinohata."

"Which university lab, sir?"

"Sendai. The bloodstain was spotted on a carriage roof at a station up there called Shiroishi."

"Shiroishi... Where have I heard that name before?"

"It's in Miyagi Prefecture. It's a small, flat town in the country-side. Although, I was surprised recently to see that a row of chic modern apartments has been built up in the hills behind the station," the chief constable said, recalling a business trip made there last spring.

"Then we know precisely at what time the murder was committed."

"I should think so, yes. It's safe to assume that the attack took place just before the train passed, which would put the time of the murder at eleven-forty. They're saying that with a wound like his, he would likely have died instantly, but even if not, he would have survived another five minutes at most. Besides, the impact of falling onto the carriage roof would have done a fair bit of damage, too."

"What did the coroner's office say about the results of the autopsy?"

"They estimated the time of death to be around midnight."

The detective inspector slurped his barley tea. Not only was it cold, but it was also sweet. By nature, he was no drinker, so, after a day's walking outside, this was much better than beer to quench his thirst.

"Another thing is that Hayashida's team has managed to locate the missing shoe. I'm sure it'll be the matching pair for the one found on the body, but just to be sure we've sent for Nishinohata's maid to confirm it."

"Where was it found?"

"Between Uguisudani and Nippori. Some maintenance guys working on the Tohoku line found it and are keeping it for us," the chief constable said, replenishing his empty cup with some more of the brown liquid. "So, how did you two get on?"

FIVE

Testing the Waters

1.

The director of Towa Textiles had once, during the umpteenth round of negotiations, courted controversy by comparing the trade union to the tuberculosis bacterium residing in his own body. Two or three of the weekly magazines were quick to pick up on this and used the material to lampoon Nishinohata in their publications. One of the best cartoons was drawn by a mid-career satirist and depicted the director as having, for fear of the disease, overdosed on antibiotics, which had in turn led to hearing loss, allowing him to listen to the union's complaints with a calm and impassive face. Never had the phrase "falling on deaf ears" rung truer.

Had that same cartoonist seen the union headquarters, which was located on the site of the company factory in Adachi, he would surely have drawn it as a hovel. No other company building was as unloved and abused as this one: it was cramped and dirty, with poor ventilation and no natural light. The walls were crumbling in parts and water-stained. Once, some of the plasterwork on the ceiling had come crashing down, hitting a typist, who was working directly below it, right on the head. Naturally, the company paid out neither for compensation nor for the cost of repairs.

Ever since they'd called the strike, the agit-material pasted to the walls served a dual purpose. Motivational posters bearing the slogans "We will achieve our aims!", "Let's take on the fight for basic human rights!" and even the old wartime motto "Never surrender!" may have been decorative, but they also covered the flaking plaster and watermarks on the walls. The strike had certainly helped cheer up this dismal room.

News of the director's death had spread like wildfire throughout the factory and caused a sensation among all the employees. The union members were both surprised and dismayed, as the death of the director was like the anticlimactic fall from a horse of an enemy general in the midst of a decisive battle. The whole day was spent discussing the death and its implications for the strike.

Although it was already past clocking-out time, five or six top members of the union were gathered in the head office, feverishly discussing the events. Since both Koigakubo and Narumi had just returned from a trip, this was the first time that the other leaders had been able to discuss the situation with the chairman and vice-chairman.

"It's a sorry state of affairs, of course, but I'm glad he's dead."

"It's a godsend. With the stubborn old man gone, the rest of the executives will be more reasonable. I'm optimistic about the negotiations."

Not a single voice there lamented the death of the director. Instead, everybody was all smiles, suggesting that it would be advantageous to the union. Compared to yesterday, when the union members had been in the doldrums, now they spoke cheerfully, as though they were different people entirely. They were full of fighting spirit, and once again there was a glimmer of hope in their eyes.

"What did that lot down in Osaka have to say about it all?" one of them asked.

"They said that this is the best thing the old guy's ever done for us," Koigakubo joked with his distinct Osaka drawl.

"Did they now?"

All of a sudden, one of the men interrupted before Koigakubo could reply.

"By the way, I had a call from some police detective earlier."

The room suddenly fell silent.

"He was asking whether you and Narumi were here. When I told the bastard you were coming back on the *Tsubame* train, he said he'd pay us a visit here this evening."

"Oh? They're a suspicious lot, aren't they? But I suppose it's only natural. After all, who had more cause to bump the old man off than we did?"

Koigakubo's tone was matter-of-fact. He was short and a little stocky, just like Gosuke Nishinohata, but he had a cheerful, easy-going face, perhaps because the situation had developed so favourably, or perhaps because he was an eternal optimist.

Narumi, by contrast, was slender in both face and body and had pale skin. His limpid eyes and straight nose hinted at an intelligent personality. As a fighter for the union, Narumi may have seemed a little unpromising, but, when paired with Koigakubo's nerves of steel and easy, modern manner, each was able to compensate for the other's shortcomings, and, between them, they made a formidable duo.

"If we're clear on what we were doing when the director was killed, the detective won't be able to lay a finger on us. Apropos of which…"

Narumi paused mid-sentence. From the corner of his eye, he saw the security guard approaching with two men. Both visitors were wearing open-necked shirts and panama hats and looked like door-to-door insurance salesmen. A salesman, of course, would have come carrying a case, but these men limited themselves to a fan.

"Speak of the devil," one of the men said.

2.

For a few moments there was a loud clattering of shoes on the wooden floor as the union members left the room, but eventually things quietened down again. The four men sat around the rectangular table, all facing one another. Narumi placed the scattered teacups to one side and mopped up the spilt tea with his handkerchief.

"I suppose you'll have heard about Mr Nishinohata's death?" Sudo asked.

The two union men nodded silently.

"Where were you at the time?"

"What do you mean by 'at the time'?"

"Why, at the time when Mr Nishinohata was killed, of course," the detective inspector replied unhurriedly. As he cracked his fan open, his manner was relaxed, as though they were having a cosy chat.

"You must be kidding! How should I know when the director was killed?"

There was a provocative, confrontational quality to the way Narumi spoke. Koigakubo grinned broadly, showing his contempt for this underhand trick.

"Oh, don't look at me like that, gentlemen. It simply slipped my mind," Sudo said, narrowing his eyes and grinning back at Koigakubo. "The director was killed at eleven-forty yesterday evening."

"My, my, that's awfully precise, Inspector," Koigakubo said teasingly. "So precise, in fact, you don't even bother to say, 'killed at *around* eleven-forty'."

"As I say, at eleven-forty."

Narumi glanced at Koigakubo. He stood up and went over to fetch a small suitcase that was standing in the corner of the room. Pushing aside his change of underwear and toiletry bag, he extracted a timetable.

"Allow me to explain," Koigakubo said, returning his gaze to the two detectives.

His round, optimistic-looking face exuded confidence, although Seki thought that he was a little too cocksure.

"During the last round of negotiations, we were given what might be termed an ultimatum by the director."

The two detectives had already learnt this piece of information from Haibara, but Sudo wore a blank expression, as though he were hearing it for the first time. He wanted to hear with his own ears where they would lie and what kind of lies they would tell.

"It was a real blow to the union. After all, they haven't paid us for two months. And what's more, since we're talking about employees who're poorly paid and have no savings, their wives, who're trying to make ends meet at home, have begun kicking up a fuss. So, it's little wonder that some of the members have bowed to pressure from their other halves and decided to go over to the other camp, hoping for a better time of it. At any rate, we—and by 'we', I mean Mr Narumi here and myself—had to canvass opinions at the factories in Nagaoka and Osaka and decide on the best course of action. So, on the morning of the thirty-first, we took the Joetsu line from Ueno to Nagaoka, where we spent the night and the following morning in discussions. I don't think you need to know what the conclusions of those discussions were—they're a union secret, so we can't discuss them with you in any case. All you need to know is that we left Nagaoka by train that afternoon for Osaka," said Koigakubo.

"I see."

"It's on the Hokuriku mainline, and there was only one express train heading to Osaka—the *Sea of Japan*—so I had the union buy the tickets and then we boarded it. It left Nagaoka at…"

"At 16.08. It's right there."

Narumi held the timetable open, while Koigakubo pointed to the *Sea of Japan* column with the tip of his pencil.

"So, if the company director was killed at eleven-forty, the *Sea of Japan* would have just pulled in at Kanazu."

Narumi turned the page to show more times for the Hokuriku line. He scanned down the list of numbers with his finger, and, sure enough, the *Sea of Japan* departed Kanazu at 23.41. If it was true that they had been on this train, that would have placed them in Fukui Prefecture, far away from Tokyo, when the incident occurred. Sudo had little choice but to go through the standard questions.

"Is there anybody who can corroborate that you were both on this train at the time in question?"

"Yes, the conductor," the chairman was quick to reply, as though he'd been rehearsing it for some time. "Naturally, we set out in third class. But the guys at the Nagaoka factory felt sorry for us and worried we'd be too exhausted if we took the third-class overnight train, so they donated money for two third-class sleeper tickets to Osaka. Of course, the station counter was sold out and there were no sleeper tickets available. So, I asked the conductor after we boarded the train. I'd almost totally given up hope, when a trio who were supposed to join the train at Toyama failed to show up and three spaces became available. The conductor came to inform us, and we moved into the sleeping car. That was around ten minutes after we left Toyama, so, let's say, nine o'clock, give or take."

According to the timetable, the *Sea of Japan* left Toyama Station at 20.35, so the conductor could well have come to find them at nine. Needless to say, there was no way that somebody who was in Toyama Prefecture at nine o'clock could have shown up in Tokyo only two hours and forty minutes later to commit a murder.

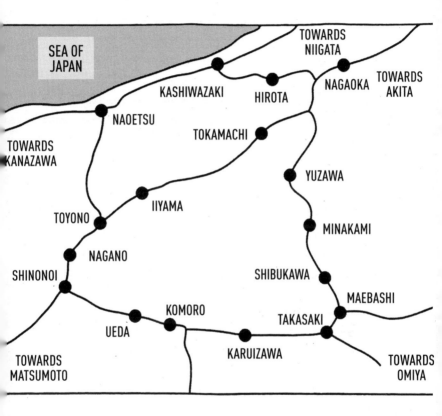

NAGAOKA – NAGANO – TAKASAKI (SHIN'ETSU MAINLINE) (UP TRAINS)

Station	Ueno 316	Kami-Suwa 336	Takada 340	Osaka 522	Nihongi 342	Komoro 348	Arai 918	Osaka 524	Osaka 502	Ueno 328	Takada 920	Naoetsu 338	Ueno 612	Arai 922
Niigata dep.	9 00	...	...	11 19	...	...	...	13 25	↙		...	14 54	...	...
Niitsu "	9 38	...	...	11 52	...	...	...	14 05	15 08	Aomori dep. 5 35	...	15 38	...	...
Higashi-Sanjo "	10 22	...	...	12 40	...	...	...	14 49	15 36		...	16 26	...	...
Nagaoka "	11 06	...	...	13 45	⌐	...	⌐	15 38	16 08		...	17 20	...	...
Miyauchi "	11 12	...	...	13 51	2nd & 3rd cl.	...	2nd & 3rd cl.	15 45	↓		...	17 28	...	...
Raikoji "	11 21	...	...	14 00		...		15 55	↓		...	17 38	...	...
Echigo-Iwatsuka "	11 26	...	...	14 05		...	...	16 01	↓		...	17 44	...	...
Tsukayama "	11 39	...	...	14 13		...	...	16 09	Sea of Japan Special Express		...	17 52	...	...
Nagatori "	11 47	...	...	14 30		...	...	16 18	↓		...	18 01	...	...
Echigo-Hirota "	11 52	...	...	14 36		...	...	16 24	↓		...	18 07	...	...
Kitajo "	11 58	...	...	14 41		...	...	16 47	↓		...	18 13	...	...
Yasuda "	12 07	...	...	14 46		...	...	16 53	↓		...	18 19	...	...
Kashiwazaki arr.	12 14	...	...	14 54		...	...	17 01	16 48		...	18 26	...	...
Kashiwazaki dep.	12 16	...	...	14 59		...	...	17 08	16 55		...	18 36	...	...
Kujiranami "	12 23	...	...	15 05		...	...	17 16	↓		...	18 45	...	...
Omigawa "	12 28	...	...	15 11		...	...	17 24	↓		...	18 51	...	...
Kasashima "	12 33	...	...	15 16		...	...	17 29	↓		...	18 57	...	...
Hassaki "	12 39	...	...	15 23		...	...	17 35	↓		...	19 03	...	...
Kakizaki "	12 47	...	...	15 33		...	...	17 43	↓		...	19 12	...	...
Jogehama "	12 53	...	...	15 39		...	...	17 50	↓		...	19 18	...	...
Katamachi "	12 58	...	...	15 45		...	Diesel locomotive	17 55	↓	Diesel locomotive	...	19 25	Maibara dep. 8 15	Diesel locomotive
Saigata "	13 04	...	...	15 51		...		18 02	↓		...	19 31		
Kuroi "	13 10	...	...	15 58		16 36		18 09	↓	2nd & 3rd cl.	...	19 38		
Naoetsu arr.	13 15	...	...	16 02		16 41		18 14	17 38		...	19 43	19 08	
Naoetsu dep.	13 32	14 38	15 15	16 24	16 06	16 46	17 43	18 36	17 57	18 22	19 31	...	19 48	20 30
Kasugayama "	13 38	14 46	15 29	Osaka arr. 8 30	16 12	16 53	17 49	Osaka arr. 7 50	Osaka arr. 5 51	18 28	19 39	...	19 54	20 35
Takada "	13 44	14 52	15 37		16 20	17 00	17 55			18 35	19 44	...	20 01	20 45
Wakinoda "	13 40	14 59			16 27	17 06	18 02			18 41		...	20 08	20 53
Kita-Arai "	↓	↓	...	...	↓	↓	18 08	...	...	↓	...	...	↓	20 58
Arai "	13 59	15 13	...	...	16 37	17 18	18 14	...	...	18 50	...	...	20 19	21 04
Nihongi "	14 14	15 28	...	...	16 51	17 36	...	...	...	19 05	...	...	20 38	...
Sekiyama "	14 31	15 45	...	...		17 52	...	...	...	19 22	...	...	20 55	...
Taguchi "	14 54	16 09	...	...		18 15	...	...	...	19 45	...	...	21 18	...
Kashiwabara "	15 13	16 32	...	...		18 35	...	...	...	20 03	...	...	21 36	...
Furuma "	15 19	16 39	...	...	Karuizawa	18 41	...	...	...	20 10	...	...	21 42	...
Mure "	15 31	16 48	...	...		18 47	...	...	...	20 19	...	...	21 51	...
Toyono "	15 48	17 00	...	...		19 05	...	...	...	20 31	...	...	22 03	...
Yoshida "	15 57	17 10	...	...		19 15	...	...	...	20 40	...	...	22 12	...
Nagano arr.	16 03	17 16	...	...	346	19 20	...	...	...	20 46	...	...	22 18	...
Nagano dep.	16 15	17 25	...	...	17 35	19 30	...	...	...	21 00	...	...	22 30	...
Kawanakajima "	16 23	17 33	...	...	17 44	19 38	...	...	...	21 08	...	...	22 38	...
Shinonoi arr.	16 28	17 38	...	...	17 50	19 44	...	...	...	21 13	...	...	22 43	...
Shinonoi dep.	16 30	17 39	...	...	17 52	19 48	...	...	...	21 15	...	...	22 44	...
Yashiro "	16 38	Kami-Suwa arr. 21 30	...	...	18 01	19 56	...	...	...	21 24	...	...	22 52	...
Togura "	16 48		...	...	18 12	20 04	...	...	...	21 33	...	...	23 00	...
Sakaki "	16 59		...	...	18 21	20 12	...	...	...	21 42	...	...	23 12	...
Nishi-Ueda "	17 08		...	...	18 31	20 21	...	...	...	21 51	...	...	23 21	...
Ueda arr.	17 14	...	...	...	18 39	20 27	...	...	...	21 58	...	...	23 27	...
Ueda dep.	17 19	...	...	...	18 44	20 32	...	...	...	22 03	...	...	23 30	...
Oya "	17 28	...	...	...	18 55	20 41	...	...	...	22 13	...	...	23 38	...
Tanaka "	17 34	...	...	...	19 04	20 47	...	...	...	22 20	...	...	23 44	...
Shigeno "	17 43	...	...	...	19 16	20 55	...	...	...	22 27	...	...	23 52	...
Komoro arr.	17 56	...	...	...	19 28	21 07	...	...	...	22 39	...	...	0 05	...
Komoro dep.	17 59	...	...	...	19 32	...	...	...	...	22 45	...	...	0 08	...
Hirahara "	18 07	...	...	...	19 39	...	...	...	...	22 50	...	...	↓	...
Miyota "	18 24	...	...	...	19 54	...	...	...	...	23 07	...	...	↓	...
Shinano-Oiwake "	18 42	...	...	...	20 09	...	...	...	...	23 22	...	...	↓	...
Naka-Karuizawa "	18 48	...	...	...	20 15	...	...	...	...	23 29	...	...	↓	...
Karuizawa arr.	18 54	...	...	...	20 21	...	...	...	...	23 35	...	...	0 53	...
Karuizawa dep.	19 02	...	...	...	...	...	...	...	...	23 42	...	...	1 02	...
Kumanotaira "	19 21	...	...	...	...	...	...	...	...	0 01	...	...	1 26	...
Yokokawa "	19 53	...	...	...	...	...	...	...	...	0 46	...	...	1 57	...
Matsuida "	20 02	...	...	...	...	...	...	...	...	0 55	...	...	↓	...
Isobe "	20 13	...	...	...	...	...	...	...	...	1 11	...	...	2 17	...
Annaka "	20 21	...	...	...	...	...	...	...	...	1 21	...	...	↓	...
Gunma-Yawata "	20 27	...	...	...	...	...	...	...	...	↓	...	...	↓	...
Kita-Takasaki "	20 33	...	...	...	...	...	...	...	...	↓	...	...	↓	...
Takasaki "	20 37	...	...	...	...	...	...	...	...	1 38	...	...	2 37	...
UENO	23 03	...	...	...	...	...	...	...	...	4 25	...	...	5 00	...

"If you need to confirm our alibi with the conductor, I'd rather you did it as soon as possible. If his memory were to become a little hazy after a few days, we'd be in trouble."

"It isn't just you who'd be in trouble," the detective inspector retorted ironically. "We'd also find ourselves in a pickle."

"Do you happen to remember the name of the conductor?" asked Sudo.

"I haven't the faintest idea. It never occurred to me that I'd need to rely on him. How about you, Narumi?"

"No idea, I'm afraid."

"Well, if you don't remember, you don't remember. Do you by any chance remember the number of your berth?"

"I didn't pay much attention to that either, I'm sorry to say. But then who does? You can't expect people to note down the carriage numbers of each and every train they ride on."

"Actually, I do remember," Narumi said, cutting in.

This man, playing the role of the wife, had left Koigakubo to do all the talking while he observed the two detectives silently from the sidelines.

"What were the numbers?"

"Yours was 107, and mine was 207."

"Lower and middle bunk, if I remember rightly."

"That's right, yes. And I don't much relish being looked at with suspicion either, Detective Inspector, so I hope you'll do as you say and investigate the matter in a timely fashion."

"I quite understand," Sudo said resolutely, as though to cut the conversation short. For his part, he wasn't best pleased at having an outsider try to dictate his line of investigation. "So, the *Sea of Japan* must have arrived in Osaka this morning. You hotfooted it back to Tokyo awfully quickly, didn't you?"

"Yes, we headed over to the dormitory first thing and had

breakfast. We were just about to begin our first meeting when news of the director's death came in. The guys in Osaka were amazed to hear he'd been killed, weren't they? The thing is, though, his death changes the situation entirely, so there was no point holding the meeting. That's why we came back."

"What was your opinion of the late director?"

Just like that, Sudo changed the subject. The chairman, who had been able to answer the questions easily up to this point, hesitated for the first time because of this rapid change of tack and the vague, ambiguous question, which seemed to conceal a trap.

"If I were to tell you that we thought he was worthy of respect, would that satisfy you?" It was Narumi who, with a smile on his face, answered the question in Koigakubo's stead. "I thought not. Because you'd see right through the lie straight away. Since I've little choice but to tell the truth, I despised the man. But it wasn't just me, you understand. Everybody did."

"And why was that?"

"He was devious, an egotist, had absolutely no morals whatso-ever, was a terrible womanizer, and, to top it off, he was a paranoiac. How can you respect a man like that?"

"Perhaps that's what it takes to rise up in the world of capi-talism," Sudo suggested casually, laughing. "In what way was he 'devious'?"

"Well, just take the business with the Shaman. Some would have it said that the director made us workers join the cult en masse for our spiritual edification. But that just isn't true."

Perhaps because the conversation had turned into an attack on the director, the vice-chairman's tone became combative, and with it his eyes began to glitter.

"So, what's the truth, then?"

"The director had his heart set on standing for the Conservative Party in the next general election. But even he, for all his vanity, knew that he didn't stand a chance of winning the seat on his own. You see, the sitting member of parliament is a local big-shot, so it was obvious to everybody that he'd never win against him. So, what was a man to do? That's when he hit upon the bright idea of lumping all his employees together into one congregation. After all, there were so many of them that the Shaman was hardly going to turn their noses up at it. And in exchange, he was to receive all the votes of the Shaman followers in his constituency and win a landslide victory in the election. It was a good deal for the Shaman, too, so the negotiations between the director and the founder came off very easily."

Director Nishinohata, however, had accepted the demand for freedom of religious expression in the recent strike and was about to allow a mass withdrawal of employees. The detectives simply couldn't fathom what had caused this sudden volte-face.

"It was because of a change in his constituency affairs. The two biggest names have both died in the past year. All that's left are the small fry. And not only that: he was then able to receive the official seal of approval from the party in place of the deceased representatives. That being so, he'd nothing left to fear. He was sure now to win the election and no longer needed the backing of the Shaman to do it. It can't have been very gratifying for the director to bow down to the shady founder of a bogus religion, or to pay the enormous donation required of him every year."

"Was your experience of Shamanism really all that bad?"

"It was a right pain. For a start, there were those morning and evening prayers they made us do. It wasn't just about bowing your head; on sunny days, they made us go out into the public square and chant sutras none of us understood. Once that was over, they'd beat drums and have us form a circle, doing some out-of-season O-Bon dance. The chanting and dancing took half an hour, but it wasn't only in the mornings. They'd make us dance in the evenings, too, even when we were completely exhausted after work. And to make matters worse, they didn't even pay us for this hour of service. So, in effect, we were coming to work thirty minutes early, leaving thirty minutes late, and if anybody dared complain about this, they'd be summarily dismissed. That is the truth of it."

Thus were they faced with a clutch of inconsistencies between Narumi's version of events and what Haibara had told them. Neither Sudo nor Seki had any idea whom to believe.

"And when you say that Mr Nishinohata was an egotist, what do you mean, specifically?"

"I say it because he only ever thought of profit. That our union is demanding wage increases isn't some regular, yearly event as it is for other big groups that go on strike. We're doing it to survive. We don't have the luxury of saving money, and if we're forced to retire due to the retirement cap one day, we won't be able to put food on the table the very next. All we want is to live a decent life without this constant worry. I don't think that's unreasonable. The company has plenty of money, so there's no reason why they can't accept our demands. But the director didn't see things that way. I would've thought that a boss who'd experienced poverty as a child would have been a little more willing to listen to us."

"And what about his womanizing?"

"He was an old lecher… We know this because we have a secret organization that collects information on the company's side of things. Most of the girls in the typist pool have found themselves at one time or another the object of the director's affections. Not that they're as pure as the driven snow themselves, of course. I suspect you'll have met Haibara already. Didn't it strike you as odd that someone with Nishinohata's proclivities would employ a man as his private secretary?"

"I can't say that it did. This is the first time I've heard these allegations of womanizing."

"It was a means of placating his wife. He meant to show her implicitly that, while every other company director may have some pretty young thing for his secretary, not him, oh, no—he knew where his priorities lay. Ah, yes…" Narumi looked as though he had just remembered something. "There's a story doing the rounds that the director was supposedly sleeping in various *ryokan* all over the place as a precaution in case somebody wanted to do him in while he slept. Perhaps you've heard it. Well, we aren't the forty-seven *ronin*, and there's no chance that we'd be idiotic enough to bump him off in the night. He must have been perfectly aware of this himself. The real reason that he was running around, pretending to be Yoshinaka Kira, was so that he could get up to no good under the guise of preventing attacks from radical elements in the union. That way, even his lady wife would have no cause for complaint, and he could entertain himself with geisha in peace."

"I see."

"That's the sort of guy our company director was, Inspector. That's why I say he was a conniving and contemptible man."

"I do seem to be forming a picture of him, yes," Sudo said, glancing at Seki, who was taking notes. "What, incidentally, is your opinion of Mr Haibara?"

"The union takes a dim view of him. Just as the company does of me. In the balance, I suppose we're about even." This time it was Koigakubo who had replied, laughing heartily. The two of them were like doubles players in tennis, each taking turns to return the ball batted at them by their opponent. "He has a reputation for being a callous and calculating man, does Mr Haibara. The proof of it is that he hasn't any friends. Even if he were to cultivate a friendship, he'd discard it as soon as it was no longer of any use to him. Yes, he's a cold-hearted and ruthless piece of work. And anyway, he's the boss's flunkey, his faithful mouthpiece, so you can hardly expect us to sing his praises."

He opened his mouth again and beamed. His laugh was carefree, perhaps because he placed such absolute faith in their alibi.

"Is it true that private correspondence is subject to censorship here? Or rather, what exactly is it that happens to the letters?"

"It's done to suppress any complaints about low pay," Narumi replied, once again taking over. "Many of our women workers come from rural areas, so they're housed in the factory dormitories. If they were to divulge the low wages to their parents, or if they were to receive a letter from their parents advising them to move to better-paid places of employment, these modern-day slaves would likely run away. That's what the company fears, so they check all private correspondence, lest these complaints reach the outside world, or the girls take to their heels."

"I understand that you've been calling for the director to be 'buried'? Why, there's even a poster here that—"

"That's a matter of interpretation."

The vice-chairman didn't look in the least panicked.

"I didn't mean that they should kill him, just that we should bury him *as director*. What I really wanted was for him to step back as director and be appointed the company's president, leaving the way for a more capable man who understands the union—our deputy director who is currently abroad, for instance—to be promoted."

Despite his fragile appearance, Narumi was apparently quite a tactician, and an eloquent speaker to boot. He had to be, otherwise he would never have been chosen as a union representative.

By the time the interview was over, Seki's hand holding the pencil was slick with sweat.

The summer solstice was three weeks away and the days were long, but it was so late that when the two police detectives stepped out through the factory gates, the ramshackle streets so typical of Adachi Ward were about to fade into darkness.

"Do you think it's true that they were on that train?" asked Seki.

"I don't know, but they both seemed pretty sure of themselves."

"Doesn't it seem strange that they travelled together like that? There's something fishy about it if you ask me."

"Maybe they needed two heads, given the stakes were so high. Had they been successful here in Tokyo, they could've gone out to Nagaoka and Osaka in triumph. But instead, they had to go and make their excuses."

"That's true enough."

Having said this, Seki was not so convinced by the inspector's straightforward thinking. He couldn't help suspecting that there might have been some contrived link between Koigakubo and Narumi's trip and the fact that the director had been killed while they were away.

"I may well have to send you to see whether their story checks out, Seki," the detective inspector said after they'd walked a short distance.

"By asking the conductor, you mean?"

"Yes. We have to be clear on this. Just be sure to take photos of them with you. If we have any decent ones on file, take those; if not, we'll have to have them taken."

Taking photos that weren't a good likeness would only confuse matters. Seki had already got into trouble with something similar while working on a previous case, which made him very unpopular with the chief constable.

The two of them walked on in silence. Inside, they were both going over all that they'd just heard. When the smell of cooking reached them from the noodle shop down the street, they both suddenly realized how hungry they were and turned to look at each other.

"Let's grab something to eat," Sudo said. "Just a minute… Before we do, I should probably make a call to the Shaman."

Skulking along the dusky streets, Sudo looked for a telephone box.

3.

The headquarters of the Shaman was located in a side street, about a hundred yards off the main thoroughfare in Azabu's Ryudocho. The two detectives stepped off the bus at a stop called "Shaman Headquarters". Their surprise was obvious when almost ninety per cent of the passengers on the packed vehicle alighted there, too, leaving the bus to drive off practically empty. Though he'd heard about the shrine there already, Seki in particular hadn't expected it to be quite so popular.

Every time a new busload of believers arrived, they would pass the others already waiting at the stop and place their right palm to their chest, mumbling something as they went.

"Do you hear what it is they're chanting?" Sudo said.

"I can't make it out."

"They're saying *iyasaka-iyasaka*… 'Fortune and prosperity'."

"Not a very efficient way to say hello, is it?"

Seki laughed. He could well imagine them scurrying around like ants on the scorching summer ground, bumping into one another, their antennae waving about. Around the corner from the headquarters stood a man dressed in a white *hakama*, with a white *hachimaki* tied about his head, directing traffic; in his hand, he carried a lantern bearing a hexagonal crest with a plum blossom in the middle of it. Guided by the movement of the red lantern, the footsteps of the faithful flowed and stopped in an orderly fashion.

"That's quite some crest."

"He's better than our guys in the traffic department."

As the two commented on their surroundings, the flow of believers continued apace. They were of various ages and wore all manner of clothing. Some looked like beautiful office girls, while others were dressed in the plain apparel of housewives. There were young men who had all the lively spirit of fishmongers, and old men wearing scholars' caps.

The two detectives pressed on, jostled by the surging crowd.

"Last year, when the founder of the sect was hospitalized with a stomach ulcer, the faithful lined the street all the way to the headquarters, holding oil lamps in their left hands and praying for his full recovery."

"They're a bunch of fanatics, aren't they?"

"Apparently they charged them for the oil, the use of rush mats, and even for the space they took up in the street. Very enterprising, wouldn't you say?"

"I'm speechless… But if this founder is truly possessed of divine powers, shouldn't he be able to cure a stomach ulcer without being hospitalized?"

"You'd think so, wouldn't you? By rights, he ought to have forgone the anaesthesia, too, but apparently he screamed in pain the moment the scalpel was inserted."

"You don't say," Seki said flatly.

As they entered through the gate, they saw, tucked away at the back of several thousand square feet of gravel, a magnificent shrine, which was said to have been inspired by a picture postcard of the Todaiji temple at Nara. Bonfires in the four corners of the garden brightly lit the drapery bearing the same hexagonal crest and the gravel, which had been swept clean. Sudo and Seki picked their way through the crowd to the far side of the grounds. To the side of the shrine, a long corridor with a gently arched roof stretched out, leading to the tea-arbour-like building where the founder lived.

"What is the founder's background?"

"When he came back from what used to be northern Manchuria, he opened a tofu shop in the countryside over in Chiba Prefecture. Apparently, waking up early and grinding soybeans with a millstone can help purify your spirit. The story goes that it was then that he hit upon the idea of founding a new religion."

As they drew nearer to the man himself, they automatically began to speak in hushed tones. On both sides of the front door, bathed in the light of electric lamps, hydrangeas were in bloom. Even the plants were growing untrammelled, as though borrowing the founder's authority.

Hearing Sudo's voice, a middle-aged woman dressed in a kimono came to the door, but, doubtless because he'd called in advance, she showed them directly to a formal room used for receiving guests.

This modestly sized room, in which a red carpet was spread over the tatami mats and a lounge suite placed on top of it, had an uncanny feel to it, in stark contrast to the classical cypress construction of the building. Both Sudo and Seki felt uneasy as they looked about the room inquisitively.

After five minutes or so, they could hear the rustle of clothes, and a shrine maiden, who looked the very image of a dancing girl from a Heian-period novel, appeared. She led the dazed pair down a long corridor with an air of almost provocative aloofness, as though knowing full well that her costume would take the visitors' breath away. They were shown into an even bigger tatami room that looked over a garden. In the middle stood an eight-foot-long table, which was dwarfed by the size of the room.

"A room fit for the Buddha himself, don't you think?" Seki said.

"Well, Shamanism draws its roots from Shinto, so I'd venture we're more likely to see the goddess Amaterasu manifest herself."

As Sudo spoke, he looked around the room. Where the alcove would normally have been, there was an altar covered with offerings of sacred sake, paper and sakaki branches, among which stood an idol depicting an animal with a pointed mouth—possibly a fox or a racoon. Hanging in the centre of the wall was a scroll on which several characters were boldly inscribed in black ink, but, perhaps because of a certain manneredness in the calligraphy, Sudo couldn't make out a single one of them. The detective inspector, who had been staring at them in puzzlement, eventually gave up and turned his attention to the garden. Illuminated by fluorescent lamps, the garden was as bright as though it were daylight.

Two maples and one old plum. One maple was of a small-leaved variety, and even though it was early June, the leaves had already turned red. To Seki, even the speed of this change seemed to be very much in the spirit of the day. There was a fine garden stone beside the plum tree, and a row of large-leaved chrysanthemums thriving under a rough-woven bamboo fence. There was a refined simplicity to the garden. The great Sen no Rikyu might have been moved perform a tea ceremony there, or Matsuo Basho to compose a line of poetry.

As Seki took out a cigarette to light it, he heard the shuffling of footsteps approach from the corridor. The sliding screen glided open to reveal the founder dressed in a sombre *haori* and a pair of *hakama*; as he entered, he nodded solemnly to the shrine maiden who was prostrating herself on the floor beside him. He was an unimpressive-looking man of around sixty with a very ordinary face. Ignoring the presence of the visitors, he bowed before the altar and began intoning something with a peculiar melody. For all they knew, he could have been reciting a poem, singing a beggar's sad, mournful lament or perhaps even a pilgrim's song. The words he was uttering were incomprehensible, but perhaps that was the point of it, though it might have been the sort of thing that brought comfort to his followers.

The founder's worship became more and more fervent. Several times he waved the offertory paper in the air, and on each occasion clapped his hands. Fearing to set the sacred paper alight, Seki waited for the performance to end before lighting his cigarette.

The founder's exaggerated gestures revealed a kind of showmanship, done for the benefit of an audience; his profound desire to be seen as a spiritual figure came off as both absurd and repugnant.

"I have been expecting you ever since your telephone call, gentlemen," he said rather stiffly, when they were at last sitting across the table from one another. "How may I be of assistance to you?"

It might have been Seki's imagination, but he thought the founder's words betrayed a certain eagerness to bring the interview with the detectives to a close as quickly as possible.

"I assume, sir, you are aware of the murder of one of your followers? Mr Gosuke Nishinohata?"

"I am indeed aware. I do not read the papers or listen to the radio, but the shrine maiden informed me of it. A most regrettable affair."

"We understand that Mr Nishinohata wasn't exactly popular around here ever since he betrayed the organization…"

Whether it was his strategy for dealing with the wily old man, Sudo was adopting an ever-breezier tone.

"Not at all. It is up to every individual whether they choose to believe in our religion or not. Just as there are many whom Buddhism cannot save, so too are there those who cannot understand our teachings. That is something that cannot be helped, nor is it something with which we should interfere."

"That may be so for a man as tolerant and broad-minded as you, but I believe there are also those who are not quite so enlightened; those who would be, shall we say, not too happy about the mass desertion Mr Nishinohata was about to allow. Mr Chita, for example…"

The founder did not reply, but instead turned his gaze towards the garden. His eyes flashed violently, and his nostrils twitched. Though his face may have been ordinary, there was something unexpectedly chiselled and impressive about his profile. Seki had no interest in or knowledge of physiognomy or phrenology, but he couldn't take his eyes off him, admiring this different aspect of a man who had founded a new religious sect.

"I cannot believe that Chita would have done such a thing."

"I don't wish to believe it either," Sudo retorted without missing a beat. "But we do know that he threatened Mr Nishinohata on more than one occasion, telling him he wouldn't get away with it in the most forceful of terms."

The founder turned, leant over the table and said in a hushed tone:

"The fact is, Inspector, I wondered myself whether this might have been Chita's doing."

"Meaning?"

Once again, the founder lowered his voice.

"Chita has been of great service to us ever since the founding of our sect. But, perhaps owing to an overabundance of zeal, he occasionally resorted to violence. Whenever word of this reached my ears, I would always try to admonish him, but, perhaps because of his wild, wily nature, he would not listen to me and, I gather, just carried on in his reckless deeds. I was indignant when I heard about these recent encounters with Mr Nishinohata, and I instructed him repeatedly not to act so rashly."

That Chita's actions threatened to damage the Shaman's reputation seemed to be the only thing that caused the founder concern.

Sudo enquired about Chita's movements on the previous day.

"He got up at ten o'clock and took a late breakfast, after which I believe he went out. He seldom discloses his itinerary."

"And you haven't seen him since then?"

"He telephoned once."

"What was he wearing when he left?"

"I asked the maid before you got here. She said he had on a black polo shirt and grey trousers, a grey flat cap and a pair of black shoes. He took the office car."

"What kind of car is it?"

"I'm no expert when it comes to cars, but I believe it's an American make. Blymouth or Plymouth, or something like that."

"And the colour?"

"Grey."

Bingo. It had to be the car that Mr Iba had spotted in Shimbashi.

"Do you have any idea where he's gone?"

"I'd imagine you'll find him in one of our branch offices. There are twenty-five across Tokyo, and five more in the greater metropolitan area."

"If you'd be so good as to let all the heads of branch know we're looking for him, would you contact us when he shows up?"

"I'm afraid that won't be possible," the founder said, looking fearful. "I'd prefer not to get too involved. And I would request that you mention our discussion here this evening to no one. Anybody who crosses that man takes his own life in his hands."

It seemed that even divine power offered no protection against the redoubtable Mr Chita. Rather than have the police intervene directly in these religious circles, it would have been far more effective to have the founder contact them, and it would also have avoided causing a stir; no matter how Sudo tried to persuade him, though, he just wouldn't budge. The founder's fear of Chita may have seemed comical at first, but it also spoke to the fact that Chita was a dangerous man.

Sudo and Seki subsequently had Chita's room searched and discovered that he had left with only the clothes on his back and a bank book for an account holding a little over 3,000,000 yen. It seemed likely that he had planned to kill the director and then go into hiding.

The detectives left the main shrine, having borrowed some photographs of Chita. The bonfires in the garden were burning even brighter than before, bathing the crowds of the faithful in a fierce crimson light. Behind them, the drums, resounding with mockery, suddenly began to beat, chasing the men out.

"The neighbours won't much like all that racket. I hear that guests stopped visiting the upmarket *ryokan* next door, and it eventually went out of business."

Seki could only hear snatches of what the detective inspector was saying.

SIX

The Safety Deposit Box

1.

To rest for an hour after breakfast without any interruption whatsoever had been Mr Nukariya's habit for the last thirty years. Even if the telephone rang or visitors came to see him, he wouldn't lift a finger. Being the busy, overworked lawyer that he was, he didn't have the time to play golf, and so, although it was a very passive mode of relaxation, a complete rest after his meal was surely of immense benefit to him. As proof of this, almost never in all those thirty years had Nukariya fallen ill. The only time he had seen a doctor was when his pet dog bit him on the hand. So, on the morning of the third, it was Mrs Nukariya who answered the phone, as usual.

"That was Mr Haibara," she said, standing at the dining-room door.

The telephone was in the sitting room.

"What did he want?"

"He said he'd had a call from the Showa Bank."

"And?"

"He said he didn't quite know what to do, so he wanted to ask your opinion."

Lawyers being peevish by nature, Nukariya frowned. Noticing this, his wife looked a little sheepish and wary.

"Come on, out with it! Surely that wasn't all he said!" Irritated,

Nukariya closed his *manga* book and plopped it down on his lap. "Start from the beginning."

"Yes, dear. Well, on the afternoon of the day of the accident, Mr Nishinohata went out without telling anyone where he was going. They say he even left his driver at a pachinko parlour."

"Right…"

"The investigators are very keen to know where he went during that time. It was in this morning's papers."

"Right…"

"Well, apparently he stopped off on the way at the Showa Bank in Kyobashi."

"What?"

"According to Mr Haibara, he used one of the bank's safety deposit boxes and went to fetch something from it."

"Whatever for?"

The furrows on his brow had disappeared. The lawyer, who had been annoyed at first, now seemed to be interested. He sat up in his chair and, straightening himself, adopted a serious expression.

"What did he say then?"

"The manager in charge of the vault informed the lead investigator of this. He was told that officers would be paying the bank a visit as soon as possible."

"To open the safe?"

"Yes. That's why Mr Haibara wonders whether it wouldn't be better if you were present for it."

"Right, I'll go there at once. Kindly let him know," he said in a harsh tone.

When the lawyer, having changed his clothes, arrived at the Towa Textiles office in the west Ginza, Haibara greeted him with sleepy eyes.

"Good morning. Thank you for last night."

By "last night", Haibara was referring to the fact that Nukariya had attended the wake for the director. The lawyer had stayed for an hour or so before heading home, but, judging by Haibara's red eyes, the secretary must have worked throughout the night.

"The service is at one o'clock, isn't it?"

"Yes. Mrs Nishinohata has decided she wants it to be as lavish an affair as possible."

"And he's to be buried in his home town?"

"Yes, the director had his ancestral grave restored at great expense, and he's to be buried there."

"Just like that…" the lawyer lamented, with a shake of his white head.

In the course of a single night, Mr Nishinohata, the stubborn, pugnacious backbone of Towa Textiles, would be reduced to a handful of ashes. Status and wealth were powerless in the face of death.

"Do you have any idea who could have done this, Mr Nukariya?" the private secretary suddenly asked.

"I don't know…"

"I think it was *them*."

Haibara's narrow eyes suddenly seemed to glitter.

"And who exactly do you mean by 'them'?" asked the lawyer.

"Why, the union leaders, of course. And if not them, then Hanpei Chita. It's so obvious I thought they'd have arrested the lot of them yesterday. The police are really dragging their heels, aren't they?"

Haibara was convinced from the outset that it was one of them. He seemed sure of it. Yet the lawyer, frankly, did not share his indignation. Not because he opposed the secretary's notion that it could have been either the union or Chita, but because he was aware of yet another motive.

"Did you know that the director used the safe at the bank?" he asked, ignoring Haibara's display of emotion.

Haibara was momentarily taken aback.

"I did, yes. Only, I didn't think he'd be going there."

"When he went there in the past, did he always go alone?"

"No, he always had the driver take him."

"So why all the secrecy this time?"

"I really don't know…"

The secretary was at a loss.

"Maybe we'll understand when we get there…"

Before the lawyer could finish, the telephone rang. Haibara immediately placed the receiver to his ear and looked at Nukariya.

"Some police officers have arrived. Very well, we'll be right down," Haibara said calmly, seeming to have forgotten his earlier outburst.

The lawyer, however, could see all too well behind the mask his joy that the director's secrets were at last beginning to come out.

2.

In a reception room on the first floor of the Showa Bank, in addition to the manager in charge of the vault, were the two detectives, Sudo and Seki, who had met only the previous day. Sudo was dressed smartly in a business suit, while Seki wore an open-necked shirt with a white linen jacket. Their white canvas summer shoes were dirty and grey, which gave some idea of how much running around the pair had done in the last twenty-four hours.

"Apart from ours, there are only a handful of banks that keep safety deposit boxes," the manager said, launching straight into an explanation once the usual pleasantries were over. "Ever since the Shimoyama incident, we've become quite famous, and we have so many applicants that we've had to give priority to those who already hold an account with us."

"How big are they, these safety deposit boxes?" asked Sudo.

"They're divided into seven categories, from A to G. A-type boxes are small and used for storing documents, whereas the G-type are big enough to fit two or three people inside. Well, shall we, gentlemen, seeing as you're all here?"

No sooner had the manager stepped out of the room than he returned with a young employee.

"This is Mr Koine. He's one of the clerks responsible for our safety deposit boxes. There are two of them, but it was Mr Koine here who attended Mr Nishinohata when he paid us a visit the day before yesterday."

Thin and pale-faced, the young man, whose hair was slick with pomade, greeted them tactfully.

"Do you recall seeing Mr Nishinohata?" Sudo asked without delay.

"Yes, sir. It was only the other day, so I remember it well."

"Was there anything unusual about his visit?"

"Not that I recall."

"At what time did he arrive?"

"It would have been… a little after one. I'd just finished lunch and returned to my desk. It would have been about forty minutes later that he came back the second time."

"The second time? You mean to say that Mr Nishinohata was here twice that day?"

The young bank clerk, who didn't know what was going on, was taken aback by the suddenly much louder voice of the lead detective and looked at him in astonishment. Sudo was not alone in his astonishment, however; the lawyer, the private secretary and Seki were also surprised by this revelation.

After Gosuke Nishinohata left the office, he'd driven himself
to the bank and then completed some business at an unknown
location, before returning to the office, once again via the safety
deposit box. Their immediate thought was that Nishinohata must
have taken something from the safe and put it back there after
the meeting. The contents of the safe would no doubt reveal what
this "something" was.

"How long did he spend in the vault?"

"Mr Nishinohata? Hmm, let me see... Three, maybe four minutes at most. That's how long it usually takes to fetch anything
from one of the safe boxes."

"Thank you. Shall we take a look then, gentlemen?"

Having finished his questions, Sudo stood up.

The four men followed the young clerk and the vault manager
down to the ground floor and then down the stairs to the basement. Seeing the polished marble steps glistening in the fluorescent light, the lawyer suddenly had the impression that he was
descending into an ossuary.

At the foot of the stairs there was a steel door. Koine inserted
a key and pushed it open.

"There are four of these doors," the vault manager explained,
turning to the group as the second door was being opened, "each
requiring a different key, of course."

To open all four, they had to pass through three antechambers.
At last, the heavy fourth door was opened to reveal a vast room
several thousand square feet in size, full of safety deposit boxes.
The black steel boxes stacked on neat rows of shelves maintained
a discreet silence and really did resemble an ossuary.

"It's like Fort Knox with all those doors."

"We take additional precautions, in fact, sir. There was no need
with Mr Nishinohata, since we know him well, but with ordinary

97

clients we ask for their name, address and age and check every-thing against our own records. Only after they go through these checks can they be shown into the vault. And, of course, they need their *inkan*—that is to say, their personal seal—as well."

The manager and the clerk guided the four men, walking swiftly and assuredly between the dozens of rows of shelves.

"Here it is. Mr Nishinohata's box is a C-type. It's a medium-sized box and, as with the A-type, is used for storing documents. Would you do the honours, Mr Koine?"

There were two keyholes in the box. At the manager's bidding, Koine inserted a key and gave it a single turn.

"This means that the box is now half open," the manager explained. "As with all safety deposit boxes, two keys are required to open it: one for the client and one for the bank. As soon as Mr Koine had unlocked it, he would have left and waited outside the door to the vault. Mr Nishinohata would then have been free to take out his own key, insert it into the other hole and finally open the box. In this case, however, the responsibility falls to us."

The vault manager then took out the master key, which was used only in such instances, unlocked the box and stepped aside.

"Please, gentlemen."

"Mr Nukariya, would you be so kind as to open it?" Sudo asked hesitantly.

The deceased's legal adviser was, he reasoned, the most suitable person to open the box containing his secrets, even if it was for the purpose of investigating the case. He also calculated that, by making this kind of concession now, he would be able to pry into other things later on.

Nukariya pulled towards himself the black steel container, which clattered slightly as he did. He opened the lid and took out several kraft-paper envelopes that had been tied together with a faded green ribbon. There were nine envelopes in total, each of which appeared to contain a document of some kind. Ten eyes gazed intently at Nukariya's hand as he examined their contents.

Seven of the envelopes contained share certificates of prominent companies, all of which were considered to be leading shares. The eighth envelope contained shares in a Nagaoka-based company.

"What is it, this Hikari Industries?"

"It's a paint-manufacturer."

"Why would he own shares in such an insignificant regional concern?"

"He's from those parts, so it's possible he was made to buy them," the secretary replied, looking wholly disinterested.

The final envelope contained deeds pertaining to land and property along with three photographs. The deeds were all contracts that had been exchanged upon the sale and transfer of various mountain forests and villas, so there seemed to be nothing out of the ordinary about them. Sudo then turned his attention to the three photographs. One of them had been torn in half, so it would have been more correct to say that there were two and a half photographs. Two were of children, both girls. The inscriptions on the back—"Hisako Wakatake (aged 2)" and "Hisako Wakatake (aged 5)"—indicated that they were both of the same child. Both appeared to be amateur photographs: the contrast between the sky and the clouds was blurred because the photographer had not used the correct filter. On a path through a forest stood a crude, handcrafted pram made of offcuts of timber, inside which sat two-year-old Hisako, shouting something with her little open mouth. Judging from the baby's clothes, it looked as though it had been taken sometime in the summer. In the other, the five-year-old Hisako stood in the garden with a friendly smile on her suntanned, healthy-looking face. The straw-thatched roof of the house behind her and the fruiting persimmon tree in the background made clear that this was a snapshot taken in some rural village in the autumn.

In contrast to the other two, the subject of the third photograph was a young-looking woman. She was facing the camera and looked a little unkempt in her flashy kimono and sandals. The buildings in the background and the car parked behind her suggested that it had been taken in an urban area. Yet everything from the waist up was missing, making it impossible to judge her looks from the part of the photograph that remained.

"Well? Does it mean anything to you?" the lawyer asked Sudo.

"This photo? I don't know."

"Mr Haibara?"

"I don't know, either."

Judging by the curiosity with which Haibara had been peering at the photographs, however, one might have wondered whether that "I don't know" wasn't a lie. And yet, it was no easy task to guess what Mr Nishinohata might have taken from among the photographs and all these deeds and share certificates.

"If that will be all, gentlemen, I'll lock the box back up now," the manager said.

The lawyer placed the kraft-paper envelopes back into the box, and Sudo followed suit with the photographs. There was no point in looking at them for ever.

"Should the need arise in the course of the investigation, you will let me see them again, won't you?"

"Of course. If you'll kindly go through the correct channels, we can make them available to you anytime."

"Whether or when the need will arise, I can't say, but until the case is solved, I'd like you to leave the contents of the box undisturbed, if possible. I doubt it will be long before the matter is laid to rest."

"That shouldn't be a problem. If the widow should decide to liquidate the estate and dispose of the stock certificates, I'll be sure to let you know in advance."

The lawyer also gave his word, which was a relief to Sudo. He feared that, if he didn't keep Mr Nukariya sweet, the curmudgeonly old man could hinder the investigation.

Having thanked the manager in charge of the vault and the clerk, the four men left the bank. After the artificial light of the basement, their eyes were unaccustomed to the fierce early-summer sun, and so, dazzled and squinting, they each of them placed a hand to their forehead. Having bid farewell to the two detectives, Haibara opened the car door.

"Can I drop you off, Mr Nukariya?"

"No, thank you. I have somewhere else to be, so I'll take the subway."

After the car drove off with the secretary inside, the old lawyer turned to the detectives.

"Inspector," he said in a serious tone. "I didn't like to mention this earlier while Mr Haibara was around, but I think I know who the girl in those two photos is…"

3.

The three of them went to a nearby café and ordered some cold drinks.

"The Wakatake girl has eyes very similar to Mr Nishinohata's, don't you think?" said Mr Nukariya. "I thought so the moment I set eyes on her."

Wiping his hands with the damp towel that had been given him, the detective inspector laughed, creases forming under his eyes.

"Could she be the director's illegitimate child, do you suppose?"

"You have a keen eye, Inspector."

"The jawline, the shape of her eyes, those eyebrows—they were all identical. If you tell us whose child she is, you may rest assured that we'll keep it in the strictest confidence."

It goes without saying that, as a lawyer, Nukariya was unable to divulge his clients' secrets. But since Nishinohata's death, the situation had changed entirely. Still, lest there be a stain on his professional conscience, he could not have told the inspector straight out.

Nukariya nodded silently now as he took out a cigarette case slowly and offered it to his two companions. Seki took a cigarette and lit it.

"Last autumn, out of the blue, Mr Nishinohata asked for some confidential advice. He told me he wanted to have the child officially recognized as his own and asked if I would begin the proceedings. Up to that point, I'd been under the impression that Mr Nishinohata had no children, so this came as something of a surprise to me. According to what he told me, the child was born to a maid called Tazuko Wakatake, who used to work at his house in Yoga. Seemingly, his wife had no knowledge of it, because he put Tazuko on leave before the pregnancy started to show. He gave the girl some money, which of course was meant as severance pay, and thought that he had washed his hands of her completely. Only…"

"Only…?"

The lawyer had paused to sip his cream soda, but Sudo, impatient for the continuation, urged him on.

"Only, he'd heard a rumour on the wind that Tazuko had died. He hadn't cared much while the child's mother was alive, but now that she was dead, he couldn't help feeling sorry for the orphan. He took a gift with him and went out with the intention of just peeping over the fence, but when he saw her, he found that she not only had some features of her late mother, but also resembled him. He fell in love with her immediately. Until then, you see, he'd never considered himself a parent. He'd never known what it is to be a father."

"Where was this?"

"In the countryside, in Tochigi Prefecture. Fortunately, he knew the blood type of the late Tazuko, so it wasn't hard to prove that the girl was his own. That's when he called on me and asked me to make the arrangements."

"Excuse me! Miss!" Sudo called to the waitress. "Would you mind turning the music down a little? Thank you. Now, Mr Nukariya, if that child were officially recognized, wouldn't she stand to benefit in the event of Mr Nishinohata's death?"

The strains of jazz music suddenly abated. Sudo frowned.

"That is correct, Inspector. Even without a will, a certain amount of money would have gone to the girl."

"How did his wife take this?"

Sudo asked the obvious question. The lawyer slowly looked from Sudo to Seki, who was busy taking notes.

"Not well. A few days later, Mr Nishinohata came to me and asked me to delay the finalizing of the paperwork."

"Why?"

"I wasn't made aware of the reasons, but I suspect his wife must have kicked up a fuss when she found out about it. I say this because she later sent a proxy to me, asking all sorts of questions about the possibility of a legal case against her husband for her reduced share of the estate."

"Her 'reduced share'?"

"Put plainly, he'd decided that when the time came to divide his estate, two fifths should go to his widow, with the other three fifths going to the Wakatake girl. In which case, his widow would have been within her rights to challenge the will with a view to equal distribution."

"Then, if the wife was envisaging a situation such as the one you're describing, and was seeking information on her rights, would it be fair to assume there had been a certain cooling of their affections for each other?"

"That isn't for me to say, Inspector," Nukariya replied firmly.

The fact that he had not denied it out of hand, however, could be interpreted as tacit confirmation. Sudo could easily imagine Mr Nishinohata's sharp-eyed wife stumbling across a photo of Tazuko that the director had left lying around and tearing it up in a blind rage.

"Did you ever meet the mother?"

Sudo was interested in the woman who had given birth to the girl, and not only in a professional sense. It seemed a pity that the photograph had been torn in half, for he imagined Tazuko to be a beautiful woman.

"Yes. It must have been about six years ago now. She served me tea when I visited the Nishinohata residence in Tamagawa. She had very Japanese features, as I recall. If I were being kind, I'd say she had a pretty, oval face, but, truth be told, she was on the plain side and her jaw was rather masculine. She wasn't my type, that's for sure."

This was a rather harsh criticism on Mr Nukariya's part. However, next to the lawyer's wilful, selfish wife, who was so emaciated that she looked like a dried-up vegetable, Tazuko must in fact have seemed quite beautiful.

"So, what ended up happening with the acknowledgement of the child?"

"She was never acknowledged. The strike got in the way, and he died before he could resolve it."

"So, Hisako hasn't received a penny of the inheritance?"

"It is not inconceivable that Mr Nishinohata could have entrusted the matter to a lawyer other than myself, but I find it doubtful that he would have involved anybody else, as it would have meant disclosing the secret needlessly to another person. Just to be sure, though, why don't you send for a copy of Miss Wakatake's family register?"

"We'll do that," Sudo said.

In his heart of hearts, though, he thought it would be far simpler to look into the widow's movements in order to ascertain whether or not she had killed her husband.

He was a little nervous to have discovered a suspect with a new motive.

4.

Sudo and Seki got off the Tamagawa tram at Yoga. The director's residence was in the fourth district, on the northern edge of the town. The two detectives mopped the sweat off their brows as they trudged along the parched street, musing that this, of course, would not have been a problem for Gosuke Nishinohata, who drove a luxury car everywhere he went.

When at last they reached the residence, Seki spotted the nameplate on the gate.

"It certainly looks big, doesn't it?" he said, gazing up at the high wall.

"That's capitalists for you."

Having said this, Sudo suddenly came over all queer. He had

meant to say that it was because Nishinohata was the director of a company, but the word "capitalists" just slipped out. Apparently, after his talk with Koigakubo and Narumi the previous evening, he had inadvertently picked up some of their vocabulary.

Nishinohata's body had been returned to the residence the previous night. According to Haibara, the funeral was to take place later that afternoon, at the Hongwanji temple. The three cars parked in front of the gate hinted at a lack of calm inside.

"Do you suppose that's the maid over there?"

Further down the wall, a young woman had just stepped out of a side door and into the street.

"Let's see what she's got to say. Leave it to me."

No sooner had Sudo said the words than he went striding off towards her. The young woman had her back to the two men and began to hurry off in the opposite direction. She was dressed as though she was going shopping in the local area.

"Excuse me, miss?" Sudo called out as he caught up with her. "Do you happen to work in this house?"

Startled, the woman stopped in her tracks and regarded the two plain-clothes detectives with suspicion.

"Who's asking?" she retorted.

There was a note of reproach in her voice, and she had an air of arrogance about her, so typical of maids in these large mansions, as though she had every right to wear the mantle of her employer's fortune.

The detectives introduced themselves.

"Oh, I thought you might be journalists," she said.

Her look of suspicion vanished and was replaced by one of alarm.

"I believe," said Sudo, "that the lady of the house dropped her purse the night before last when she was out. Is that right? A member of the public picked it up and called out to her, but it seems that she didn't hear and drove off in a taxi she'd flagged down. The good citizen had no choice but to hand it in at the local police box…"

The maid turned to look searchingly at Seki before returning her attention to Sudo. There was a curious trace of scepticism mixed with disdain in her eyes.

"There must be some mistake."

"Oh?"

"The mistress was at home that evening."

"The member of the public picked up the bag, though, and handed it in to us."

"But…"

She looked back and forth between the two of them, then her lip curled. The movement made her cheek twitch, which in turn made it seem as though she were sneering at the detectives.

"The mistress has bad legs," she said in a calm yet ironic tone, as though having seen through Sudo's little falsehood. "There's no way she could have gone out. She hasn't been able to walk these last couple of years."

"Really? Which doctor is she seeing?"

"Dr Wakao… Now, if you'll excuse me," she said brusquely, before walking off.

She'd made quite a forceful impression—and not in a good way. Still, her shapely legs, which peeped out from under her gingham skirt, were beautiful, despite her personality.

"Damn it!" After the woman disappeared around the corner, Sudo laughed. "She caught me red-handed."

"Women are perceptive, aren't they? But is it true that she can't walk?"

"We'll have to go and ask that doctor. What did she say his name was? Wakao?"

"I'll ask at the tobacconist's," Seki said, recalling having passed one a little earlier. He had just run out of cigarettes.

A few moments later he returned.

"He's a little up that way. I was told he's a reputable doctor."

They chose to walk on the shaded side of the street. It wasn't so bad when they'd been at the bank, but now, as it approached noon, the temperature was rising, and it was as hot as midsummer. The two of them alternated between using their fans and their handkerchiefs.

"I've never been to Joetsu before," Seki said. "I hope it's cooler than in Tokyo."

"That'd be nice, wouldn't it? I don't know it very well myself."

"I've never made it past Takasaki."

Seki's thoughts were racing ahead of him to that unknown land by the Sea of Japan. He was to depart on the last train for Naoetsu that night.

The purpose of his trip was to meet the conductor mentioned by Koigakubo and Narumi. After enquiring with the rail company, Seki had learnt that, after his shift had ended, the conductor in question had spent the night in Osaka and was to travel back on the Aomori-bound service departing that very day. Seki therefore planned to meet the train at Naoetsu and check the union men's alibis with the conductor.

As they walked along, talking about the journey, they found themselves in front of the Wakao Clinic. It was a large private surgery with an imposing porte cochère. Outside, there was a white painted signboard gleaming in the midday summer sun, lending the place a clean, hospital-like appearance. The words on it indicated that three doctors shared responsibility for internal medicine, surgery, paediatrics and otolaryngology. A pram had been left by the entrance, and the two detectives could hear, coming from the consultation room at the back, the noise of a baby screaming as though it were on fire.

When Sudo explained the situation at the reception desk, the nurse, who seemed to know the patient well, told them that she was attended by the director, escorted them into the waiting room and immediately disappeared through the door on the other side. Four or five patients, each holding a film magazine in their hands, were leafing through the pages without much interest.

Once the doctor was free, the detectives were shown into the consulting room. They were met by an elderly man sitting behind a desk, glancing over some clinical records. He closed the file and looked at the visitors, his close-cropped white moustache lending him an air of refinement. Sudo introduced himself once again and, without going into details of the case, asked whether it would be possible for Mrs Nishinohata to walk.

"Impossible," the doctor said categorically. "She has chronic sciatica. It's caused by... by a certain pathology. If it's caught in the early stages, that's one thing, but for her there's no cure. At the moment, all we can offer is palliative techniques to alleviate the pain."

All this curious skirting around the issue made Sudo think that the real cause of Mrs Nishinohata's disability might in fact be syphilis. It was known, after all, to cause sciatica in the later stages. And, what with Mr Nishinohata's well-known philandering, it was conceivable that she could have contracted the disease from her husband. If this were so, Sudo could well imagine the fury of a wife who not only had to deal with such chronic nerve pain, but, as if that weren't enough, was being threatened with a much-reduced inheritance to boot. And yet, at the same time, the fact that she suffered from chronic sciatica had to dispel any suspicions Sudo had about her.

Having thanked the doctor, the two detectives left the clinic. The pram outside was gone.

SEVEN
Death on the Move

1.

"ALIBI CONFIRMED"

It was midday on the 4th when the telegram arrived from Constable Seki. It had been sent from the telegraph office at Kashiwazaki and showed that he had successfully managed to board the *Sea of Japan*, confirm Koigakubo and Narumi's alibi, get off at the next stop and immediately dispatch the message.

There had been three leads. Yesterday, at Dr Wakao's clinic, one of them had gone cold, and today, in Kashiwazaki, a second one had done the same. That left only one: Hanpei Chita. Once again, everybody's energy was poured into tracing his whereabouts. The Plymouth car that Chita had taken from the Shaman headquarters was found in the early hours of the morning, abandoned on Rokugo Bridge. If he'd crossed the bridge, he would already be in Kanagawa, so the metropolitan police formally requested the assistance of the local prefectural force. His whereabouts, however, remained unknown.

It was a little after six o'clock that evening when the call came in. The division chief laid down the receiver, looked around the room and beckoned the inspector over.

"I hate to trouble you, Sudo, but you need to go down to Yurakucho."

"What's the problem?"

"There's a guy on the phone who's got a tip for us. It seems important."

"Do you know what it's about?"

"He says he's too busy to talk on the phone. He's apparently got a break at six-thirty, so he's asked us to send someone over."

Sudo had no idea what was going on. What could this man possibly have to tell them?

"Whereabouts in Yurakucho?"

"Radio Nippon. He's a voice actor, of all things." The division chief laughed. "His name is Toshio Murase."

"What, him?"

The name of this man was known even to the detective inspector. He didn't play in anything as serious as literary works, but he was good in comedies and enjoyed an unrivalled reputation for playing drunkards. Although Sudo rarely had the time to sit down and listen to the radio, he would split his sides laughing whenever he heard Murase, his favourite voice actor.

"Take a taxi," said the division chief, thrusting a 500-yen note into his hand.

On the main street, Sudo flagged down a car.

Among the public broadcasters, Radio Nippon was a first-rate company. It owned an eight-storey building in Yurakucho. The first-floor stage was leased to the Tokyo outfit of a local commercial broadcaster, while the second floor and above were used by the station itself.

Sudo took the lift to the sixth floor, and, when he mentioned Murase's name to the charmless young woman on the reception desk, she seemed to have been informed in advance and sent a girl to show him in.

Coming out of the lobby, the corridor twisted and turned in a labyrinthine fashion, and, were it not for his guide, Sudo would never have found his way. He went up and down flights of stairs twice over, losing all sense of direction in the process. And not only that, but he could no longer tell which floor he was on.

He arrived in a large hall consisting of a stage with audience seats in front of it: it appeared to be a public recording studio. Stagehands were scurrying about, taking the instruments that had been used in the previous set backstage. The floor of the auditorium was littered with scraps of paper and empty bento boxes.

"He's over there," said the girl, pointing to a corner of the hall, before leaving.

Sudo looked over in the direction indicated. Behind a folding screen, a group of seven or eight men and women were holding a read-through, each one with a script in their hand.

"I think the gangsters need to sound a little more ruthless."

The one clutching a stopwatch in one hand and giving notes seemed to be the producer. As Sudo sat in the auditorium, waiting for a break in the rehearsal, he looked at the men, trying to work out which one was Toshio Murase.

"Could I have a cue here?"

A pretty actress was pointing out a part of the script to the producer. Even for a voice actress, her voice was particularly beautiful.

"Yes, I'll give you one. Right then, Mr Murase."

The producer had called out the voice actor's name. Sudo looked up and spotted the actor being addressed.

"Could you give these lines a little more sadness. We want the audience to be roaring with laughter, but *you* shouldn't be laughing. Rather, you should be so sad that you almost want to cry."

"Got it," replied the low, nasal voice that was familiar from the radio.

Most of Murase's body was hidden by the folding screen, and the only parts of him that could be glimpsed were his protruding forehead and belly. This voice actor, whom Sudo had never pictured as he listened to him on the radio, appeared to be rather fat in real life.

The producer's attention to detail was extraordinary. He explained everything in a generous, animated manner, using a combination of words, gestures and body language to ensure that they grasped his intention. The plot appeared to be one involving gangsters. Murase was playing the role of a drunkard, his speciality, to leaven this crime drama, full of thrills and suspense with moments of laughter and pathos. It was clear to see the work Murase was putting in by the way he kept mopping his brow with a handkerchief, despite the air conditioning in the auditorium.

The producer carried on giving notes for another five minutes or so before finally taking a break. The voice actors dispersed to their seats and began reading over their scripts. A man and woman who until just now had been lovers were back to being strangers, sitting in chairs far apart from each other.

"I'm sorry to have kept you waiting. I'm afraid we're in the middle of a rehearsal," Murase said as he approached Sudo. He was a stout and jolly-looking man, just like the characters he played on the radio. He was so hot that he'd taken off his dress shirt and now had on only a T-shirt. He looked more like a clerk in a pawnbroker's than a voice actor. The only thing out of place was the beret he wore.

"What is it you wanted to tell us?"

"The thing is, I saw Mr Nishinohata on the night of the incident. I thought I should inform you."

So far, nothing was known about Gosuke Nishinohata's movements or what he had been doing between the time when he left his driver in Shimbashi and when he was killed on Ryodaishi

Bridge. The actor's story could well fill in some of these blanks. Sudo leant forward expectantly.

"I'd assumed the investigating team would have known his movements already, so I didn't see the need to report it. But when I saw the evening papers, I realized that they were still in the dark. That's why I rang up like that out of the blue."

"Right, when you say you 'saw' Mr Nishinohata, you mean...?"

"Before all that, I'd like to ask something," he said gravely. "When exactly was he killed?"

It was a strange question.

"At eleven-forty p.m. on the first."

"And you're absolutely sure about that?"

"There may be a certain latitude, a couple of minutes maybe, but definitely not later than eleven-forty."

"I see. The thing is—cutting to the chase—I happened to see Mr Nishinohata at ten minutes to midnight."

In a flash, Sudo found that he wasn't taking in anything else that his vis-à-vis was saying. Instead, he was just staring blankly at the man's face. It took him a few moments to realize that a man who'd been shot at 11.40 couldn't have been alive ten minutes later.

"Could you have been mistaken?" he eventually asked.

"I suppose it isn't a rarity to come across a person who might bear a passing resemblance, but this man had that same splendid grey moustache... I'd have recognized it anywhere. After he left, I immediately turned to the friend I was with and said, 'Wasn't that Gosuke Nishinohata?' He was, after all, being raked over the coals in all the weekly newspapers, wasn't he?"

"I see. And where was this?"

Sudo had no choice but to ask the question. Though the voice actor was insistent, he had to have been mistaken. Not only had Sudo got to look around the rarely seen broadcasting studio, but he'd also met a voice actor whom he'd previously known only through the wireless; in the balance, it hadn't been a fool's errand, but still, to go all the way to Yurakucho at the drop of a hat just to hear this story of mistaken identity had been an absolute waste of his time from a professional point of view.

"It was by the east exit of Ikebukuro Station. We'd finished recording early that day, so my friend and I had gone for a drink. We were feeling peckish as we were walking back, so we went to grab a bite to eat in a Chinese restaurant called the Orchid. Nishinohata came in while we were eating there."

"Had you ever met Mr Nishinohata prior to this?"

"No. As I say, I'd only seen pictures of him in the press. But really, there's no mistaking a man with such a distinctive moustache."

Murase seemed to be thoroughly convinced that the man he'd seen was Gosuke Nishinohata, and now he was getting a little irritated by Sudo's scepticism.

"We were sitting facing the entrance, so we spotted him right away. He ordered eight-treasure noodles, ate, then left. He was done in about ten, maybe fifteen minutes."

When he heard the name of the dish, Detective Inspector Sudo was startled. The autopsy report had revealed that Gosuke Nishinohata had indeed eaten a dish of noodles right before he died.

"Was he there with anyone?"

"He was alone."

"What was he wearing?"

The voice actor looked away for a moment and stared at the soundproof wall, as though trying to recall a line he'd forgotten.

"He was wearing a grey Western-style suit. I'm afraid I couldn't say what kind of material. Oh, and he was also wearing a fedora. A black one."

The colour of both the clothes and the hat were spot on. Could the man at the restaurant really have been Nishinohata?

"And you're certain that this was at eleven-fifty?"

"Yes. That night there was a broadcast of the Polish bass Doda Conrad singing some songs by Chopin. It was scheduled to go out at midnight, and I remember thinking that if I drove home, I'd be just in time to catch it. The recording hasn't yet been released here in Japan, and the record is sold out abroad, so it was a rare opportunity to listen to the performance."

Sudo had little interest in music, so he failed to grasp even half of what the voice actor was saying, but he understood why the time had remained in Murase's memory so exactly.

"Was it eleven-fifty when this man resembling Mr Nishinohata entered the restaurant, or eleven-fifty when he left?"

"When he left. So, he must have arrived around fifteen minutes before that."

"And were you going by your watch or the clock in the restaurant?"

"My watch."

"And there's no chance it was running fast?" Sudo pressed.

"None," said the actor, shaking his head. "It's never failed me yet."

He seemed certain, and indeed it did look like a high-quality watch.

"Thank you, Mr Murase. You've been most helpful."

Having offered these hackneyed words of thanks, Sudo stepped out into the corridor. The truth was that he had not been helpful at all. Murase must have been mistaken. After all, even though moustaches were no longer in fashion, there must have been hundreds if not thousands of old men in Tokyo who still wore them in a style similar to Nishinohata's. To insist that it had been

Gosuke Nishinohata solely on the basis of the moustache was scarcely any different from seeing a withered pampas grass and convincing yourself that you'd seen a ghost. And if, for argument's sake, it really had been Nishinohata, then surely Murase's watch had been running fast.

Thus ran Detective Inspector Sudo's thoughts as he walked down the red-carpeted corridor. Little did he imagine that in the next few days both of these theories would be refuted.

2.

The *Moonlight* express was heading westward towards Osaka along the Tokaido mainline. It had been three hours since the train left Tokyo, and most of the passengers were already asleep. In the third-class sleeping car, all the passengers were supposed to be in bed with their curtains drawn. However, the attendant, Sonobe, couldn't go to sleep just yet, because he still had duties to attend to. A passenger was due to join the train at Hamamatsu, and he had to be shown to his berth. He was annoyed, not being able to sleep just because of one person. It wouldn't be so bad if it turned out to be a stunningly beautiful woman, but if it would be a tragedy if it was some wrinkled old codger.

A balmy summer's breeze was blowing in through the half-open window in the attendant's office. As the wind caressed him and he gave himself over to the monotonous rhythm of the train, it was a wonder that he didn't doze off, so hypnotic was the repetition.

The lights of a station shot past the window like an arrow. He looked at the clock. It was a little before two. It had probably been Kanaya or Kikugawa. Another forty minutes and they would arrive at Hamamatsu. Then, after they departed, he'd be able to sleep peacefully without being disturbed by anyone. Forty more minutes of patience, forty more minutes of…

Suddenly, he opened his eyes and looked up. Through the haze of drowsiness, he thought he'd heard somebody knock at his door. He was unsteady on his legs as he stood up. When he peered into the corridor, he saw a man standing there in a *yukata*, a look of exasperation on his face.

"I can't sleep because of the person in the bunk below me. Can you do something about it?"

Only a well-seasoned traveller would change into a *yukata* on a sleeper. And only that kind of traveller was wont to complain about such trivia.

"Is he snoring?"

"I'd sooner describe it as groaning."

"Maybe the passenger's feeling unwell."

"He may well be, but the noise is disturbing me."

The man showed no sympathy for his fellow passenger's plight. He seemed to be concerned only with his own sleep being interrupted.

Sonobe put on his cap and followed him.

The man led him to a berth in the middle of the carriage and pointed to the bottom bunk. Sure enough, there was a noise coming from behind the curtain. Only, instead of groaning, it sounded more like somebody muttering in a delirium. Every now and then, it would suddenly break off, only to continue a few moments later. It sounded as though he was talking, but the words were so indistinct that it was impossible to catch the meaning of anything he said.

"Excuse me, sir?" the attendant called to him through the curtain. He kept his voice low, trying not to disturb the other

118

passengers. The man in the bunk appeared not to hear him and carried on muttering.

Sonobe placed his hand on the curtain, knelt down and peeped in. The slanting light from the ceiling revealed a man in his sixties asleep on the bed. Both the pillow and the blanket had been pushed aside, and a large amount of drool was running down one cheek. It was a curious sight.

"Excuse me? Hello?"

Sonobe tried to rouse the man by shaking him, but to no avail. Half of his face seemed to twitch drowsily, but then he immediately began to mutter once again. The attendant recalled that the man had boarded the train at Tokyo. He had with him a single suitcase, which was both new and small, so he did not strike Sonobe as a regular traveller. He seemed to like a drink, and when Sonobe had looked in on him at Yokohama, he'd seen him with a half-empty bottle of whisky, his red face shining. He must be travelling to Osaka, the final stop on the journey.

The attendant turned around. The man from the middle bunk was still standing there. He had both hands in his pockets and a cigarette in his mouth; he looked down on the ailing man with indifference, blinking from the smoke. The young passenger in the bunk opposite appeared to have woken up and was peering out through a chink in the curtain.

"Oh, dear, I expect he'll have to be taken off the train?" the youth said, pretending to talk to himself and, in so doing, hinting at his own desire.

Even without that suggestion, Sonobe knew that the man would have to be taken off the train. Not to get rid of a nuisance, as the man seemed to suggest, but rather so that he could receive medical attention. The attendant looked at his watch. It was another fifteen minutes before they reached Hamamatsu. There was a big hospital there… He had to contact the train guard right away and have him dispatch a message cylinder. Sonobe hastened to his feet.

The message warning that a passenger had been taken ill and would need to be carried off at Hamamatsu was thrown out as the train passed Tenryugawa Station.

Everything seemed to go as planned. As they pulled into Hamamatsu Station, a doctor and a nurse, as well as a member of the station staff with a stretcher, were waiting for them. Seeing their silhouettes on the dark platform, Sonobe heaved a sigh of relief, happy that the passenger would be helped.

When the train came to a full stop, the station attendant got on and, under the doctor's direction, transferred the patient to the stretcher before carrying him off, treading as softly as possible so as not to disturb the other passengers. Sonobe gathered up the man's belongings, which were scattered about the bunk—among them, his hip flask filled with whisky, his jacket and his flat hunting cap—and handed them to the nurse.

The entire operation was accomplished within the five minutes for which the *Moonlight* was scheduled to stop at Hamamatsu. As it pulled out of the station, Sonobe looked back at the retreating platform and prayed that the man would make a full recovery.

"Attendant! Where is this bunk?"

Hearing the voice behind him, Sonobe turned around and saw the passenger who had just boarded proffering a sleeper ticket.

"It's just down here, if you please," he replied politely, leading the way.

The passenger was not the beautiful young woman he had hoped for, but, just as he'd feared, a short, cantankerous old man. His disappointment was tempered, however, for he was now wide awake.

3.

The patient who had been dropped off on the platform at Hamamatsu Station was taken immediately to a deserted waiting room in the small hours of the morning and laid down gently on a sofa, still wearing his black shoes. By now, he had stopped babbling and had fallen helpless into a comatose state.

The doctor gave him an injection of camphor as a precaution. His pulse was irregular and would occasionally flutter. His body temperature had also dropped to almost thirty degrees. When they rushed to check his blood pressure, they found that it, too, was dangerously low.

"Nurse, fetch me some solution of vitamins and glucose."

The doctor lifted the man's malnourished arm and gave him another injection. He observed him for five minutes, but there was no change in his condition whatsoever.

When the doctor shook his head as if to say, "It's useless," the nurse nodded in tacit agreement. The patient's breathing was gradually become shallow and irregular, with longer intervals between breaths. Even the station staff could see that he was nearing the end. It was not long after that that the patient's lips began to show signs of cyanosis.

Outside, a freight train blew its whistle as it slowly passed. Just as the roar of the train died away, the traveller on the sofa breathed his last.

The doctor took his pulse, listened to his heartbeat, checked his pupils and then pronounced him dead. The nurse covered the man's face with gauze.

"What was it? A heart attack?"

"No. Despite appearances, the man seems to have been a drug addict. My guess is that he'd taken some harmful substance, but we won't know for sure until we conduct the autopsy. Would you notify the police that there's been a suspicious death?"

In an attempt to identify him, the dead man's clothes were examined by the police officers who rushed to the scene, but when they did so, they discovered something strange: all the name tags had been removed.

The wallet in his pocket was made of pigskin and contained twenty brand-new 1,000-yen notes that had been folded neatly in two, but no business cards or anything else of the kind.

"Curious… It's almost as though he didn't care what became of him."

Grumbling all the while, the policeman carried on rifling through the jacket pockets of the deceased, but all he found was a tissue, a handkerchief and a third-class ticket. He then checked over the trousers once more, but found even less. All he discovered in the back pocket was a strangely crumpled clump of grey wool.

Finally, he gave up on the pockets and began to search the man's suitcase. But there he found only a change of clothes and some toiletries—no name or address, and certainly nothing to suggest an identity. It was inconceivable that this man would have chosen the sleeping car of a train as a spot to commit suicide, so it was natural to assume that somebody else must have slipped him something. It also seemed likely that that same somebody had removed the name tags from his clothing and the business cards from his wallet in order to conceal his identity.

"I'm sorry, Officer, but… isn't that a false moustache?"

This unexpected question was asked by the young station attendant, who was standing beside the policeman. That spring, he had dressed up as an army general for a flower-viewing party and had worn false whiskers himself, hence why he recognized it. And sure enough, it did indeed look like a false moustache. It was misshapen slightly, crammed as it had been into the dead man's pocket, but originally it must have been a fine piece.

Meanwhile, the policeman was still rummaging around in the inside pockets of the suitcase. He found a scrap of paper, which he took out and examined carefully. It looked like a clipping from a newspaper or a magazine, and, when he turned it over, he saw the dense text printed on it.

"What's that?" the attendant asked.

"It's a photograph... Hey, look! It's that guy who was killed in Tokyo. Gosuke Nishinohata."

"Oh, the one from the what's-it textile company?"

"The very same."

"That's odd, isn't it? Why would he have a clipping of his photograph?"

"Wait. Hand me that false moustache, will you?"

The policeman reshaped the crooked hairs, removed the gauze covering the dead man's face and placed it gently under his nose. He then adjusted the moustache twice, using the photograph as a guide, before stepping aside and looking at the cadaver intently, as though admiring a work of art.

"What do you think? Doesn't he remind you of someone?"

"He does! He really does," the doctor exclaimed excitedly. "Why, he's the spitting image."

The rest of the group just stared at the corpse in amazement.

4.

It was the following evening, back at the incident room at the police station in Ueno, and more than fifteen hours had passed since the mysterious passenger breathed his last in Hamamatsu.

"Good work, Sudo. Let's start with your report," the division chief said, setting the ball rolling.

Sitting on either side of him were the station chief, the duty officer and two constables, all flanked by staff from headquarters. For the past week, each of them without exception had continued to ignore the voice actor Murase's first-hand account, writing it off as some kind of optical illusion. Yet when reports came in that a double had been found poisoned in Hamamatsu, they were not a little panicked. Several of that evening's newspapers had even poked fun at the division chief for having been so blasé during the press conference. That's why they had been waiting all day for the return of Detective Inspector Sudo, who had gone to Hamamatsu to investigate.

"A Professor Mori from the University of Shizuoka came and performed the autopsy at the police station in Hamamatsu," Sudo began, reading from his notebook. "The results showed significant damage to the internal organs, especially the stomach and small intestine. A sample was taken to the university for testing, and it turns out that it was arsenic poisoning."

"And that's what caused the death?"

"Yes, sir."

"How did it enter his body?"

"We believe he drank it. An analysis of the leftover whisky revealed trace amounts of arsenious acid. Based on the quantity of it dissolved in the whisky and on the volume of whisky we believe the deceased consumed, the amount of arsenic absorbed into his body is estimated to be 0.5 grams. This far exceeds the lethal dose for most people."

Sudo opened his bag, took out the dead man's grey clothes, which he'd brought back with him, and pushed them towards the division chief.

"As you can see, all the name tags are missing, and there's nothing to establish the identity of the deceased."

"I see. They've been removed with great care. What kind of fabric is this?"

An older detective who specialized in clothing stood up and touched them.

"It's tropical worsted."

"Nishinohata wore poral, didn't he?"

"Yes, sir. Indian silk poral."

"And this suit is an off-the-shelf number?"

"It certainly looks that way. Judging by the shallow stitching, I'd say they were made in Osaka."

"Thank you."

"Shall we find out where they came from, sir?" asked the lead investigator, cutting in.

"Yes, do that. Please, carry on, Sudo. Were there any identifying marks on the body?"

"He appears to have been a manual labourer. His fingers are exceptionally gnarled. We estimate him to be around sixty years of age, and there's evidence that he's recently had some dentistry work done. Judging by the fact that he has a bridge without a gold crown, we're working on the assumption that he probably had health insurance."

"I see. There's no way a labourer could afford clothes like this. The killer must have either given them to him or else given him the money to buy them. If it's the latter, that won't be much use to us, but if it's the former, we might just be able to connect him to Chita if we find out where they're from."

"We'll get on it first thing tomorrow."

"Do that. Remember, this Chita guy used to work in intelligence. He's good," the division chief said, addressing everyone as he looked around the room. "You all remember that Nishinohata's last meal was a plate of noodles, right?"

"Yes, sir. It was in the autopsy report."

"So, Chita was counting on us finding this out."

"Yes, sir."

"Let's try to put ourselves in Chita's shoes and imagine what he was planning."

The division chief took out a cigarette, placed it in his mouth and, after trying several times with a lighter that was nearly out of fluid, finally managed to light it. He was a man possessed of a forceful nature, but his thick black eyebrows and his thick-framed, thick-lensed spectacles gave the viewer a clear indication of his character.

"The first thing Chita had to do was to get Nishinohata to eat the Chinese noodles without giving away his intent. With a bit of skill, this wouldn't have been too difficult. After that, he must have taken him to Ueno Park, and, just as he was about to kill him, the double did what he'd been ordered to do. That is to say, he walked into a Chinese restaurant in Ikebukuro, wearing the false moustache he'd prepared earlier. He then ate the same kind of food that the victim had been fed while he flaunted the distinctive moustache. Since Nishinohata had been making quite a splash in the press, Chita could be certain that he'd be noticed. He'd factored this into his plan as well. The double then removed the moustache the moment he left the restaurant, so that he wouldn't draw any more attention. That way, he'd just blend into the crowd. After all, as photos of the body show, this mystery victim has a pretty ordinary face."

"That's right, Chief!" the duty officer agreed. "The voice actor, Toshio Murase, claimed to have seen Nishinohata, but it would be more accurate to say that all he saw was a man dressed in a grey summer suit who had Nishinohata's moustache."

"It goes without saying that Chita's aim in all this was to create an alibi for himself by staging this scene to make it look as though the murder took place later than it really did. Having committed the murder at eleven-forty, his plan was to leave the scene of the crime immediately and then show up at a suitable location ten minutes later. Meanwhile, the false Nishinohata would waltz out of the Orchid, so that nobody could possibly suspect Chita of being the culprit. It was the perfect alibi."

"But then why would he go on the run rather than insist on his alibi?" the station chief asked, turning his sweaty face towards the division chief.

"Why, because of the unexpected blunder, of course. Quite by chance, the body fell on top of the moving train at eleven-forty, thus revealing the actual time of the murder. Because of this, the alibi confected at the Orchid, making it look as though the murder took place more than ten minutes later, isn't worth a penny."

"Ah, yes, I see," the station chief said, blushing slightly. He had long heard rumours that this man was quite the theorist, but now he had irrefutable proof of it.

"In short, we need to establish the identity of the man who died in Hamamatsu. Naturally, we need to look into his records, but it might be quicker if we enlist the help of dentists in Tokyo. If he's a labourer and, what's more, one who's been receiving treatment on his insurance, that should narrow the field significantly."

With that, the division chief drew the discussion to a close. The investigative meeting was over for another day.

5.

The death of the man in Hamamatsu was reported in considerable detail by the morning papers. The reports also included a reproduction of the man's likeness, which had been made in great haste. As they waited for some response, the police were like patient Jiang Ziya, his eyes fixed steadfastly on his fishing hook, but in their hearts they were not so optimistic. After all, it had been ten days since the incident, and they still had no idea where Chita was. This in turn placed a burden on them, with the result that even more was expected of Jiang's fishing hook.

It was a little after 3.00 p.m. when the call came through from the police station in Asakusa. A dentist in the area had notified them that he recalled a man with similar features. An officer was dispatched to check it out. The person in question proved to be a man named Genkichi Obata, who had been staying at a sort of *ryokan* in San'ya 5-chome and had left on the evening of the eighth, claiming that he was going away on a trip. He was fifty-four years of age, which was a good match for the murder victim. Sudo and Seki therefore decided to take a tram immediately and pay the *ryokan* a visit.

San'ya 5-chome was situated to the north of the Namidabashi stop on the metropolitan tramway. The backstreets of this entire district were known as "the San'ya hostels", owing to the many cheap lodgings, which, as places where the illicit trade in methamphetamine and barbiturates went on, had been the subject of many outraged articles.

After they alighted from the tram, they found themselves standing on the pavement, looking at a painted map directly in front of them.

"Ah, here it is," Sudo said, pointing to the street they needed. "So, we should go this way."

Seki nodded. If they headed towards the Sumida River and turned right down the second side street they came to, then five blocks down they would find the *ryokan* were looking for—the Tachibana-ya.

"We should get a move on. It looks as though it might rain," Sudo said.

The dreariness of the day reminded them that the rainy season would soon be upon them, and, even though it was only four o'clock, the whole place was bathed in the slate-grey of dusk. The two detectives quickened their steps. Neither had on a jacket, let alone a raincoat.

Advertisements for cheap lodgings and flyers offering part-time jobs were plastered all over crumbling concrete walls and utility poles, which, when coupled with the overcast sky, added to the down-at-heel atmosphere so characteristic of San'ya. As the map had indicated, there was a cobbler's shop on the corner. The way he was scraping by, repairing old shoes, seemed almost like a symbol of the poverty of this run-down area.

The term "hostel" covers a multitude of sins. Some of the places here had big dining rooms and large tiled bathrooms and could have been called second-rate *ryokan* rather than hostels, while others had only half a dozen three-mat rooms and sooner resembled cramped dosshouses.

No matter how one looked at it, the Tachibana-ya was at the lower end of these establishments. The roof on the upper floor was so damaged that you could see the warped corrugated iron from the street below. The entire building looked quite old. The blackened panelling had turned green with moss, and some of the panels had fallen off, exposing the rough walls.

"Hello? Is anybody there?" Seki called out, opening the lattice-work door. He was about to step inside, but the concrete floor was so strewn with muddy sandals, *geta* and work-*tabi* that there was nowhere to stand. The two men waited outside. The reply came soon enough, and a young woman dressed in a simple blue dress appeared, drying her hands on her apron.

"Is this… about Mr Obata?" she said, realizing that the two men were police officers.

"Yes, miss. We'd like to find out everything we can about him. Could we start with his age?"

"Of course. He told me he was fifty-four, but whether that's true or not, I couldn't say. Mind you, there's no use pretending to be young at that age. It's not as though he had a girl in tow."

Conveniently, this young woman seemed to be the talkative type. She was in her early thirties, and, with her slender face and widow's peak, she was a great beauty, although the simple dress she had on didn't suit her at all; were she to put on a nice little *yukata* instead, she would have looked very elegant indeed.

"Did he have a job of any sort?"

"He used to go to the job seekers' office in Minowa every morning, though I think he mainly worked as a street sweeper. I once spotted him at the foot of Ohashi Bridge when I was taking some *o-hagi* rice balls to my aunt's in Senju. I was on the tram, so I couldn't say hello. Oh, hang on, that's right—it wasn't *o-hagi*, it was *sekihan*. It was during the festival for the local guardian deity, so it must have been *sekihan*."

"And before that?"

"Come again?"

"What did he do before that?"

"Oh, I do beg your pardon. He said he used to be a gardener. Apparently, he was quite good at it, but he lost all his family in the war and went a bit off the rails. I don't mean he did anything really wrong, but he did start drinking. In the end, his clients all let him go, and so he had to find work as a day labourer. But he's only been here since January. Before that, he was staying at the Narikoma-ya."

Covering her mouth with one hand, she divulged, in an even more gossipy tone, that the Narikoma-ya was a hostel in a neighbouring district and that Genkichi Obata had quarrelled with the owner there and been thrown out.

"Was he the quarrelsome type, would you say?"

"No, I'd sooner chalk it up to the owner. She's a real piece of work, she is, and she's forever causing trouble with everyone. Mr Obata was a good sort."

"And what about the company he kept?"

"Hmm… He rarely had visitors. In fact, he hardly went out."

"Did he receive any letters?"

"Not really. He did once receive a reminder from the local tax authority though…"

"When did you last see him?"

"On the eighth. He took the day off and spent the afternoon sleeping on the futon. He didn't look unwell, and I was surprised to see him not at work. Then, a little after three, he got up and took a bath. I wondered why he was acting so strangely and finally asked him why he was drawing a bath in the middle of the afternoon. With a big grin, he told me that he was going away on a trip and that he'd be gone for five days. That wasn't the only thing that was queer, though. Lately he'd been a bit hard up, but he'd paid the rent he had owing for the last two months as well as what was owing for this month all at once. I was so stunned that I asked him where all this money had come from. But he just smiled and said, 'My luck's finally changed!'"

All this, she rhymed off breathlessly.

"Did he mention where he got the money or where he was going on his trip?"

Sudo couldn't help staring at the woman's lips.

"Not a thing," she said. "I'd the impression that he was keeping me deliberately in the dark."

"I see," the detective inspector muttered. For a few moments, he stared at a spot on the wall, trying to gather his thoughts.

Of course, the money Obata used to pay for the room must have been some of his reward for playing the double. It was unclear how he had come to know Hanpei Chita, of course, but it was easy enough to imagine that he had been sweet-talked into a trip to Osaka, slipped a bottle of poisoned whisky as a farewell gift, and he had hurried out of Tokyo, unaware that he was speeding towards his death.

"You know, sir, I read in the papers that Mr Obata was killed in Hamamatsu…"

"That's correct."

"That's in Niigata, isn't it?"

"Er, no, it's in Shizuoka Prefecture."

"Ah, Kyushu…"

Her geography was hopeless. Still, she seemed oblivious to the wry smile that had appeared on Seki's face.

"They're saying he drank poisoned whisky on the train. What a terrible way to go. The man was no saint, but he didn't deserve that. If you catch the murderer, he will be executed, won't he? These days, murderers seem to be getting away with just two or three years inside. It's scandalous, that is!"

The thought appeared to enrage the woman.

"Where was he heading, anyway?" she asked.

"He had a ticket to Osaka."

"To Osaka…"

"Not the one in Hokkaido, the one beside Kyoto."

"Oh, I know the one you mean all right, but Genkichi was a real Tokyoite. He was proud of the fact he'd never set foot outside the city. I think Saitama Prefecture was the furthest he'd ever gone."

"Is that so?... Incidentally, was Mr Obata a member of the Shaman sect?"

Sudo wondered whether Chita might have known Obata because he was a believer. However, the woman merely shook her head and mimed beating a drum.

"I was once a member myself."

"I see. Well, seeing as we're here, would you mind showing us Mr Obata's room?"

"Of course not. Please, this way," the owner said, indicating the stairs.

Genkichi Obata's "room" was three tatami-mat size at the far end of the first floor. Some faded paper from a department store had been pasted onto the sliding door of the built-in wardrobe. The space was spartan, with only a futon and a wicker basket, so the search clearly wouldn't take long.

"What have we here?" said Seki, holding between his fingers a sweat-stained army cap that he'd found in a corner of the wardrobe. "*Ke-ta-ba-ko*? 'Shoebox'? What do you suppose it means?"

On the side of the khaki-coloured cap, in white cotton thread that had yellowed over time, the four katakana characters were embroidered horizontally.

"Try reading it from right to left..."

Realizing his mistake, Seki blushed. It was a name: Kobatake.

It took less than ten minutes for them to see everything they needed to see, but they uncovered nothing.

"Well, thank you, miss," Sudo said as they were leaving. "We're sorry to have put you out like this."

"I hope you catch whoever did this soon. And when you do catch him, I hope he swings for it."

The owner slipped on her sandals and saw the detectives out the door.

"Oh, it looks as though it might rain," she said, looking up at the sky anxiously. "I've just hung the laundry out to dry. I wonder whether it'll be all right."

The pair then walked back the way they came, towards the tram stop in Namidabashi. Grey dust seemed to float in the dimly lit road. It looked as though raindrops would start falling at any moment, but still the rain stayed off. Hopefully they'd make it back without getting soaked.

The trundling of the trams mixed with the distant rumble of thunder.

"I wonder where that bastard Chita's hiding himself…"

Just as Seki was about to kick a stone on the pavement as hard as he could, he decided against it.

"It won't be long now," the detective inspector said. "We'll find out where he is soon enough. I can feel it."

And he was right.

EIGHT

A City in the North

1.

Nagaoka, with a population of some 130,000, was the second largest city in Niigata Prefecture. Bounded by mountains to the east and the Shinano River to the west, the city stretched out from north to south. Home to the Makino clan, it had once flourished, and, like most castle cities set amid the remote countryside, it had a quiet air of tranquillity.

On the evening of 10 June, in Nagaoka's Asahimachi, about 800 yards south of the station, a guest checked into a small *ryokan* called the Okesa. He was a pale-looking, rather short man of around forty, and when he arrived, the first impression he made was an altogether dark one. That isn't to say that he seemed despondent or gloomy, but rather that there was something suspicious about him, something to suggest an element of criminality. He had light-brown eyes, and the mere sight of them flashing in the corner of his narrow eyes created an uncanny aura around him.

The Okesa was a third-rate inn with only five rooms. The guest was put in a comparatively superior one of six *tatami*-mat at the back of the first floor. The view from the room—with a tax office, a temple and a hospital scattered on the other side of the Kaki River—was not what one would call spectacular, but when the east window was opened, the magnificent red flowers of a balsam plant in the garden behind the inn could be seen in full bloom.

And, if ever the mood so took him, the guest could always indulge his curiosity and catch a glimpse of the lives of common people in this northern city. The guest did not appear to care for this pastime, however.

"How was your journey, sir? It's a pleasure to welcome you to Nagaoka. We haven't had much rain this year, you know…"

The proprietor of the inn was kneeling in the corridor, bowing repeatedly across the threshold.

Trying to judge from the owner's ambiguous expression whether it was a good thing or a bad thing that there hadn't been much rain, the guest simply laughed inscrutably. As he sat there drinking tea, he was already in his underwear, his hairy legs in full view.

"Forgive me for getting straight to the point, sir, but it's just the small matter of the hotel register…"

The guest took the blunt pencil that was nestled between the pages of the ledger, glanced askance at the neighbouring columns and began to fill in all the necessary information.

Mikawacho 1-7, Kanda, Chiyoda Ward, Tokyo
Kazuhiko Mabuchi (39), writer

"That's wonderful, sir. Thank you," said the owner, bowing and scraping as he glanced down at this bewildering profession. Recently, his rivals in the local area had been renovating their *ryokan*, and he'd noticed a marked decline in his own custom. Because of this, he now had to focus on the quality of service and make a good impression on his guests. "Oh, you live in Kanda? Such a bustling, dynamic area."

The proprietor had been to Tokyo during the war and was now recalling his time there.

"Oh, yes, it's as bustling as ever."

"Which part of it is Mikawacho, if I might be so bold as to ask, sir?"

"It's where that fictional Detective Inspector Hanshichi lived."

"Ah, yes, of course. I thought the name sounded familiar."

The owner once again looked at the man's profession. It crossed his mind that he, too, might be a writer of historical detective novels. When he took another good look at him, he thought there was something about the guest's eyes to suggest that he really was a writer of fiction.

What the proprietor didn't know, however, was that the place name Mikawacho had long since vanished. Even among the residents of Kanda, there were very few who could tell you where Mikawacho had once been. Still, it was understandable that he didn't appreciate the guest's humour or, by the same token, realize who he really was.

"I've taken the liberty of running a bath, sir, but perhaps you'd like to eat first?"

"Is it occupied?"

"No, sir, there's nobody in it at the moment."

"Good, I'll take a bath first, then. And I'll have a cold beer with my meal."

The proprietor withdrew, while Mabuchi was shown to the bath by a maid.

He liked the Okesa and had decided that he would ensconce himself at the inn for a few days. In addition to leaving handsome tips, he went out to see things during the day, so, although his menacing eyes became a topic of conversation among the maids, he was considered a welcome guest by the proprietor.

Nagaoka was only a small city, but there were the ruins of the old castle in Zao Park to see, not to mention Mount Yukyu and various other touristic spots, so a sightseer could well spend a leisurely three or four days there. Every morning, the guest would ask the owner about places of scenic beauty and historical interest before setting out in his short-sleeved shirt.

"How was your day, sir?" the owner would enquire whenever the man returned, but not only would he never divulge where he'd visited and what his impressions had been, he would offer no words at all, merely chuckling in the back of his throat. In all truth, he was not a very likeable man. Setting aside the fact that he was a guest and an older gentleman, he was not the kind of person whose company one would ordinarily want to keep. Though the proprietor thought this deep down, he smiled politely, bowing to the guest every time.

On 14 June, the fifth day of his stay at the Okesa inn, the man, contrary to his habit, did not go out, but instead spent the morning in his six-mat room, lying on the floor with a cushion folded in two beneath his head, reading a weekly magazine. He appeared to have exhausted all there was to see in Nagaoka. Then, around noon, he sent out for two plates of rice curry from a nearby Western restaurant and, after eating, changed out of his *yukata* into a shirt and trousers. The radio had just begun to play popular songs, so it must have been around 12.30 by the time he went out.

"He's an odd one, isn't he?" the owner's wife commented as she watched him go.

"Yes?"

"Well, he always pays on time, but… I don't know, there's just something I don't like about him. He says he's a writer, but I'm not so sure. Isn't that the sort of stunt a politician might try? Maybe he isn't who he says he is."

"For the love of god, woman! Don't go saying things like that about paying customers! He's a writer of historical fiction. That

look in his eye is from thinking about samurai from dawn till dusk.
I'm sure of it."

"Hmm, I wonder…"

"Of course he is. Just look at the face of *rakugo* storytellers. They
spend so long talking about that fool Yotaro that they all end up
looking like him."

"If you say so, dear."

"And what about those policemen we see always after robbers?
They all wind up looking like criminals, don't they?"

Though he tried to rebuke his wife with the best examples he
could think of, he knew in his gut that he agreed with her. Still,
he was convinced that the surest way to assert the dignity of his
station as both husband and proprietor was by opposing his wife,
no matter what the topic.

2.

Gosuke Nishinohata was a native of Nagaoka. Though his parents had fallen on hard times and fled to Kyushu, the temple of
his ancestors was in this city, and, while his father had died in
Miyazaki, this was where he was buried. Now the director too was
to be laid to rest there.

The Nagaoka factory was located in Zaomachi, on the northern edge of the city, and since not only the factory workers but
also many members of the Nishinohata family lived in Nagaoka,
a large number of people were expected to attend the ceremony.
Naturally, executives from Tokyo would come with their wives, as
would the chairman and vice-chairman of the union, which had
called a temporary truce, as well as the factory manager and union
representatives from Osaka. The factory in Nagaoka had taken

care of all the arrangements at the temple and the dormitories, but they couldn't be relied on to do everything on their own, so Nishinohata's private secretary had hurried there from Tokyo and given them instructions on various matters.

On the evening of 12 June, three days before the burial ceremony, Haibara had arrived in Nagaoka unaccompanied. He immediately set about meeting the factory manager and the director's relatives and inspecting the rooms that had been reserved for the family at the hotel in the Sakanoue-machi neighbourhood, while the following day he made arrangements with a taxi company, contacted the undertaker's and the temple, telling them to get more sakaki branches, shikimi branches and joss sticks, and generally spent his time running around, either with people from the factory or on his own. Back at the hotel, since many of the guests were elderly, they would prefer rooms overlooking the quiet garden at the back of the building rather than those facing onto the busy street—details to which only seasoned travellers pay attention.

Haibara's efforts over the course of those few days were praised by the staff, who thought his attentiveness just the sort of thing one would expect of a man who worked at head office. What hadn't occurred to them, however, was that this display of industry was also calculated to advance his career prospects.

At 6.30 p.m. on the 14th, the eve of the funeral, the top management of the Tokyo head office and the Nagaoka factory were to meet in the hotel's dining room to discuss the details of the ceremony. Haibara had seen to everything, even down to the meal they would be served, and he met the executives who had arrived on the 17.13 express at the station, which was only a few hundred yards from the hotel.

When the older men arrived at the hotel, they thanked him for his efforts.

"Well, you've done us proud, Haibara," one of them said. "It's a decent room."

"Are you sure it won't rain?" his wife added.

"They said on the radio that it should be sunny," Haibara replied.

"That's a relief. It would be a disaster if it rained."

The company executive's wife was worried, of course, about the rain staining her precious mourning clothes.

The representatives of the factory in Osaka came on the Hokuriku line. Some of those from head office were yet to arrive, and three or four of the reserved rooms still lay empty, but even so, it was rare to see so many of the top executives and their wives gathered in the same place at once. Despite the sombre purpose of the trip, there was a sense of occasion among the ladies and their daughters, as though they were on some kind of group excursion.

Pretending not to look, Haibara stole a few glances at Atsuko. Wearing a light-brown blouse with a white suit jacket over it, not only did Atsuko compare well with the other women there, but she even stood out among them. *One of these days, I'll be able to hold her in my arms.* The very thought made Haibara tremble with excitement. He interpreted Atsuko's behaviour—all throughout, she acted nonchalantly and avoided his gaze—as the shyness of a young woman who had led a sheltered life.

It was a little before nine o'clock by the time that he took the bus back to his lodgings and lay down on the bed, without bothering to remove his trousers, feeling a sense of relief that the hour-long dinner had gone off without a hitch. He still had the ordeal that was tomorrow's funeral to prepare for; even after it was over, he would have a few matters left to tie up, but, for the moment, all the important things had been seen to. As he stared up at the ceiling with his hands behind his head, his mind found its way back to Atsuko. Their eyes had met fleetingly at the dinner table; he had nodded in recognition, while she had bowed her head slightly. Her image was seared onto his retinas and refused to disappear. Yet, as any photographer would do, he retouched the picture, until Atsuko's darkish eyes gradually acquired a warmer, more passionate tone, and at last she now smiled at Haibara with an air of coquettishness.

His heart was so stirred by sweet fantasies that in the end he couldn't sleep. In an attempt to calm himself, he put on his jacket and headed down to the hotel lounge. The room was about a thousand square feet and was located on one side of a corridor that connected the main building to an annexe. It was furnished with a Zenith record player, a television and a bookcase filled with the latest publications. If nobody was around, he'd listen to the radio, and if people were there, he'd leaf through the magazines.

He found a guest sitting on the sofa next to the window, reading under the glow of a fluorescent light stand. Two shapely, attractive legs stretched out tantalizingly below the hem of her skirt. As he looked at the woman's face, his heart began to beat madly. With feverish eyes, he scanned the room, checking to make sure there were no other guests there before making a beeline for the sofa. The sound of his footsteps was muffled by the carpet, so Atsuko didn't appear to notice his approach. Amid the silence, only the sound of a page being turned could be heard.

"Well, hello," Haibara ventured in a half whisper.

"Oh!"

Atsuko turned around in surprise and smiled when she saw that it was Haibara. Her rouged lips parted to reveal a set of pearly-white teeth. The private secretary was at liberty to interpret this sociable smile in whichever way he pleased.

"Are you reading?"

He asked to see the book. She nodded slightly, continuing to hold the book in her hand. With the French doors in the background, her petite stature, newly coiffed hair and slender face combined to make her look every bit as lovely as a Chinese doll.

This is the woman I'll marry! Haibara gulped. Forgetting himself, he plumped his corpulent body down on the sofa and gazed into Atsuko's eyes. Perhaps it was the effects of the alcohol.

"I believe you might have heard about me?"

"About you?"

"Yes, that I... that I'm in love with you. The senior executive director's wife told you, didn't she?"

"Why, yes, she said something, but..."

Her words trailed off, leaving the impression that she'd wanted to say, "... but what of it?" Yet the infatuated Haibara didn't have the presence of mind to notice anything like this.

"Miss Atsuko!" he called out excitedly, shifting closer to her. Haibara had lost all sense of shame and propriety. Before he knew it, he had flung off his everyday mask of composure.

Atsuko recoiled in disgust.

"Miss Atsuko!"

The private secretary's pitch rose once more as he inched still closer to her. Without a word, she again edged away.

"Miss Atsu—"

Midway through her name, his face turned to desolation as at last he noticed the stiff expression on her face. Just as he'd feared for some time, she must have heard about the incident. That's why she was trying to avoid him. Yes, of course. He ought to confess the truth and clear up any misunderstanding. His dazed mind had run away with him, run amok, and was coming to its own conclusions now.

"Miss Atsuko! You probably heard from the director about my visit to that tea house. But nothing happened, I assure you. I just went to collect something I'd forgotten at a banquet the previous evening and got chatting to some geisha. You have to believe me! It's the truth. When the director found out about it, he assumed the worst and thought I was some kind of philanderer. It's unfair of him to tell you such a baseless rumour. No, I'm not trying to make excuses for myself. I really did just go to pick up something I'd forgotten there. I swear it! Oh, Miss Atsuko… I… I… I'd never…"

He kept talking and talking, leaving no opportunity for Atsuko to get a word in. Instead, she just watched Haibara's crazed eyes in shock.

"I had the utmost respect for the director. But it was cruel of him to slander me with such a false accusation as this and spoil things between us. I was afraid he might talk. I'd have done anything, anything at all to make sure he didn't—"

Her soft red lips were so intensely alluring. It must have been the alcohol that finally gave him the courage.

"Ah! Mr Haibara, no! You mustn't!"

Twisting and turning, Atsuko struggled in Haibara's arms. His pale, bloated face drew nearer, breathing heavily. Her eyes flashed with anger and indignation, while her lips twitched with disdain for the man. But that didn't seem to put him off. All he was interested in was tasting the sweet fruit. As he pinned Atsuko down on the sofa, his lukewarm breath caressed her cheek.

The very next instant, he jumped up, looked around himself in a fluster and rushed out through the French doors. Before she could comprehend what had happened, Atsuko stood up, smoothed her dress and picked up the book, which had fallen on the floor. Just then, Fumie came in. Atsuko was startled to see her.

"Oh, you're alone? I thought I heard a noise, so I assumed you were with somebody."

Fumie smiled her usual broad smile. She didn't appear to notice that her friend's hair was dishevelled. Atsuko, however, felt she had to do something to restore an atmosphere of normality in the room. This was not to protect Haibara, but to have been on the point of having a kiss snatched from her by the private secretary was hardly the most dignified situation.

"It's already gone ten," she said. "I wonder what the weather will be like tomorrow."

Atsuko hastily turned on the radio, pretended to listen to it and averted her eyes. Her heart was still pounding. She knew that if she spoke, her voice would tremble, and Fumie would suspect something.

The national news bulletin had just ended, and they were about to turn to local news. The chimes rang and the announcer's voice changed. The Niigata broadcasting station reported on a fire and the arrest of a thief, but Fumie seemed to have little interest in the goings-on of this unfamiliar city.

"The announcer's voice always sounds the same, no matter where you are, doesn't it?" Atsuko said, sitting down on the sofa. "NHK can't help it, of course, but I do think it'd be more interesting if commercial broadcasters didn't use standard Japanese. It'd be better to use local accents. In Aomori, for instance, they…"

Atsuko was about to say something but suddenly stopped short. The voice issuing from the radio was reporting the discovery of a murder in Nagaoka.

"… an analysis of fingerprints has revealed the victim to be one Hanpei Chita, thirty-seven years of age. Chita was wanted for questioning by the Tokyo metropolitan police in connection with the murder of Towa Textiles director Gosuke Nishinohata. After

145

slipping the police net, however, he is believed to have fled the capital and been hiding at a *ryokan* called the Okesa in Nagaoka's Asahimachi since the tenth of this month…"

The two women looked at each other in stunned silence. They listened for more details, but the announcer had already moved on to the next item.

"Chita was the one who was threatening the director. Remember, that guy from the Shaman?"

"Yes… yes, you're right."

Atsuko's thoughts drifted back to the stranger who'd accosted her at Shibuya Station. She'd never seen him again after that.

3.

It was said that, when the funeral was held on the 15th, every florist in the city ran out of sakaki and shikimi branches. Jugwanji, Nishinohata's family temple, was a famous Buddhist site of the Shingon sect and was situated just beneath a water tower on the western outskirts of the city, with the Shinano River flowing behind it. Usually, there was hardly a soul to be seen in its shaded gardens populated by old trees, but that day the ordinarily peaceful sanctuary had all the bustle of a marketplace. And though the partitions had been removed in the great hall, those mourners who still couldn't fit inside had to sit in temporary marquees that had been erected in the gardens.

Before the photo of Gosuke Nishinohata that was adorning the altar, several monks were kneeling, reciting sutras and banging fish-shaped temple blocks. The sutras must have been a blessing, but for those who didn't understand their meaning, the monotony of the voices intoning them only added to the overwhelming heat.

Atsuko, who was sitting beside her parents, kept trying to cool herself with her little fan.

Just as the funeral at Jugwanji was getting under way, Detective Inspector Sudo and Detective Constable Seki were being shown the crime scene in Kurojo by an officer from the police station in Nagaoka. The two detectives had rushed all the way there from Tokyo, and Sudo, dressed in his panama and white shirt, looked bewildered—or, rather, not only bewildered, but a touch dismayed and panicked too. The sun was high over their heads, and the inspector nodded as he listened to the briefing, mopping up the sweat that kept streaming down his brow, with a used cotton handkerchief.

Nagaoka is an industrial city, but once you set foot into the suburbs, there are rice paddies and fields all around. Kurojo, the site of the murder, was located north of the industrial district of Zaomachi, and, although it was incorporated into the city on the map, it was still a desolate place with many fields, because the area had started to be developed only recently. There, in a small forest of broadleaves, the assassin Hanpei Chita had been found dead, stabbed multiple times in the chest. When on the previous evening the incident room in Tokyo received the unexpected report from Nagaoka, they were so stunned that for a few moments nobody knew what to say.

The local police station was located on Ote Street, right in front of Nagaoka station. By the time officers had jumped into a car and arrived on the scene the afternoon before, Chita's body was almost cold. However, the blood that had spurted from the wound and stained the blades of the green grass had not yet dried, and here and there it still glistened in the evening sunlight that poured in through the gaps between trees.

The victim's hat was found about six feet away, lying upside down under a chinquapin tree. A search of the victim's wallet revealed four 1,000-yen notes and some small change, as well as a receipt for the Okesa, so a local detective was immediately dispatched to the inn. That the register bore the name of a town that no longer existed made it apparent that the victim was no honest man. The reply received from Tokyo several hours later confirmed that this was indeed Hanpei Chita.

Initially, the incident room in Tokyo had wondered how Chita, who was ordinarily so cautious and alert, could have been killed with such ease. However, the mystery was soon solved when analysis of the contents of his stomach revealed traces of barbiturates. It was assumed that he must have been given a dose of the drug secretly by the perpetrator and stabbed while in his drowsy state.

After inspecting the site, Sudo, Seki and the local officer left the forest and sat down on a nearby grassy knoll. Directly in front of them was the road leading to a village called Fukujima. There was hardly another person to be seen, and the only sound they could hear was the chirping of cicadas.

"What's that factory over there?" Sudo asked, pointing to a tall grey smokestack rising in the distance.

"That's Osaka Manufacturing's Nagaoka plant. And just to the left of it is Hokuetsu Electric."

Smoke was rising straight up from one of Hokuetsu Electric's two smokestacks. There was no wind that day.

Suddenly, there was the blast of a whistle. A train bound for Niigata had just left Nagaoka North Station and was moving slowly from left to right across their field of vision. The cream-coloured flowers of the evening primrose on the railway embankment were swaying in the breeze.

"Why do you suppose Chita was killed here in Nagaoka, Inspector? In a place he didn't have any connection to?"

Having been watching the passing train get smaller and smaller, Seki now turned his ruddy face enquiringly to his colleague.

"If you ask me, he probably came here to hide. But it's also possible that he came here on the killer's instruction," Sudo answered ruminatively. "Remember what Nishinohata's driver said about Chita's car following him at Shimbashi?"

Seki remembered all right. Sudo pinched his little moustache and began to twirl it as he carried on speaking.

"Here's what I think. As we know, Chita was going after the director, trying to deliver a crushing blow from the Shaman. But what if there was somebody else who had it in for the director as well?"

"Who, sir?"

"I don't know yet, but what if in following the director that evening, Chita happened to witness that other person murdering him. What do you suppose his course of action would have been then?"

"He'd try to blackmail the perpetrator, naturally."

"Precisely. After all, he had form with this, didn't he? He was bound to try it. In the end, whoever did this must have agreed to his demands and told him that he'd pay his travel and lodging and give him the money in Nagaoka."

"That must be it," the local officer chipped in. "The owner of the Okesa said that Chita had been splashing his cash around. Apparently, he'd been living it up, going out, eating expensive food, the works!"

"I agree, Inspector," Seki said. "But in that case, who was the person pulling Genkichi Obata's strings?"

While Chita had been suspected of Nishinohata's murder, it was thought that he had been the one who used Genkichi Obata and, consequently, that he had disposed of him for fear that he might reveal his secret. In other words, by having the decoy Nishinohata appear in a different location after the time of the murder, it was assumed that he had tried to create a false alibi by making out the timing to have been later than it really was. With the unexpected coincidence of the body falling on top of the train, it was thought that all Chita's efforts to create a false alibi had been in vain; hence why he'd had no choice but to go to ground. If, however, it turned out that Chita had been a mere spectator in all this, then who could have made Obata don the false moustache and put in an appearance at the Orchid?

"Who indeed…" Sudo seemed to have forgotten all about Obata. He was now twirling his moustache furiously. "When it comes down to it, everything we thought we knew about Genkichi Obata as an imposter until now must be true of this new perpetrator."

"I don't follow, sir."

"I mean that if it wasn't Chita who killed the director after staging the scene at the Orchid, then it must have been whoever did this. The fact that the corpse fell on top of the train, and also that the blackmailer Chita had witnessed the crime, must have rendered the actual murderer's false alibi using Obata completely useless."

It stood to reason that Sudo could be right. Seki was silent for a moment, but then he looked up again. A question had presented itself to him.

"But we can't say with any certainty that it was the murderer who was taking advantage of Obata, can we? If Chita had intended to kill Nishinohata, wouldn't he have needed an alibi for himself, too?"

"Hmm…" Furrowing his tanned brow, the detective inspector twirled his moustache once again and lapsed into silence. "Here's a thought. If it was Chita who was using Obata as a decoy and set

150

the whole thing up in order to kill the director, then, judging by the time that Obata left the Orchid, Chita must have planned to kill him at around 11.30."

"What makes you say that, sir?" Seki asked reflexively.

Sudo was still thinking things through. He spoke deliberately, following his own line of thought carefully.

"If the times were too far apart, the rough time of death given by an autopsy might not extend to after 11.50, when the false Nishinohata was seen leaving the Orchid, which would have raised our suspicions of him as a decoy. Or else, the killer might have worried that people simply wouldn't take any notice of the decoy, reasoning that the man seen eating noodles at the Orchid just happened to bear a passing resemblance to the director but was clearly somebody else. In which case, there'd have been no point using a double at all."

"I see…"

"That's why I think Chita must have planned the murder for then. The real murderer committed the crime at 11.40, and Chita planned his for around 11.30. The two men, both of whom had their sights set on the director, were aiming for more or less the same time. It must have been a coincidence. If we refute this, then we'd also have to rethink the theory that it was Chita using Obata as the decoy, wouldn't we?"

Impressed, Seki took another look at the senior man. He may have seemed like an old codger from the backstreets, and he may not have looked the sharpest, but his long career as a detective had given him tremendous insight. Seki couldn't help but feel a little nervous, wondering whether he would be able to make such deductions by the time he reached the rank of inspector.

"Still, how on earth did you find the body in such an out-of-the-way spot?"

Sudo's words gave the policeman from the station in Nagaoka a jolt. The local officer turned to him as though in a panic. His face, bathed in the reflection of all the green leaves, looked strangely dark.

"Sorry, sir, I was listening to the cicadas. It's unusual to hear them so early." His excuse was a tad awkward, but it was understandable that he should tune out while Sudo and Seki exchanged their tiresome theories. "A farmer happened to be passing and found the body. He rang immediately to let us know. The officer stationed at the nearest police box came out to investigate and saw that it was a murder. That's when we rushed over here."

"Can we be confident that the estimated time of death was between 14.15 and 14.30?"

"Yes, we arrived shortly before three, and the blood was still wet."

The officer's cigarette had burnt down almost to the filter. He dropped it, extinguished it under the heel of his shoe, reached down to pluck a blade of grass and placed it in his mouth.

"I don't know if it's relevant, but today is the day of Nishinohata's funeral."

"What? Today?"

The two detectives turned to him, not even trying to hide their astonishment. Seki's mouth hung open, revealing a set of slightly yellowed teeth.

"You mean, there are people from the company here?"

"Oh, yes, a lot of them have made the journey down from Tokyo. And all the management from their factory in Zaomachi is there too. It looks like a big affair. Even the notorious chairman of the union and his deputy have come down for it."

The detectives from Tokyo looked at each other. At last, they thought, they'd hit upon the reason why the killer had summoned

Chita all the way to Nagaoka. At any rate, the killer was among the group now assembled in Nagaoka. Of that, they were sure.

"We can discount Koigakubo and Narumi," Sudo said after a moment.

"Yes, they both have the perfect alibi."

Seki's tone was confident. He was certain because he had gone in person to corroborate it.

"Correct. And besides, they'd have had no need to make Genkichi Obata play the role of the double."

This was something Seki hadn't considered before. When he thought about it, though, he realized that Sudo was right. The two union men had been on the Hokuriku mainline, and their alibi didn't depend on whether the director had been killed before or after 11.50 p.m. It was beginning to look as though their three suspects—Koigakubo, Narumi and Chita—were in fact innocent.

A long pause ensued. Both of them seemed acutely aware that there had to be a radical shift in their investigation.

Overhead, the cicadas suddenly began to chirp again. They sounded just the same as the ones in Tokyo.

4.

"He came down on me like a ton of bricks. When I said I was going to see a film, he told me off, saying it was the day of the director's funeral, so I should show some respect. I said I'd go for a walk instead, and then he suggested that I take Mother with me. But we should be fine. I don't think anybody's going to find us here."

Atsuko shrugged mischievously and laughed. It was the kind of laugh one would hear from a schoolgirl in her sailor uniform. The sense of security that she wouldn't be seen at the restaurant, as well as her intense joy at this reunion, had made her giddy. Since renting a room at a hotel was out of the question, Narumi had suggested they meet at a steakhouse he'd heard about on Suzuran Street, just in front of the railway station—one with private booths. And so that evening, skipping dinner, he'd gone to meet her there.

"I'm starving!" she said. "I only had a little bit of dinner, because I didn't want it to look suspicious."

As they ate, they tried to avoid any topics of conversation that might spoil their appetite. In other words, they deliberately ignored the funeral that day and the discovery of Chita's body in Kurojo, and talked instead about what sights they'd seen in town and the scenery they'd glimpsed from the train window.

"Who's treat is it tonight?" Narumi asked.

"Mine. I'm the one who invited you, after all."

"Is that right? Then I really must compliment you on your cooking. These potatoes are delicious!"

"Hah! Well, the joke's on you, because, as it just so happens, I can cook this sort of thing at home. Once we're married, I'll make you eat them every night."

"Ugh, who said I was going to marry *you*?!" he said, teasing.

They carried on laughing and joking throughout the meal, and, when the ice cream arrived at the end, Narumi asked the waiter to give them a moment undisturbed.

"So, what's all this about?" he said, leaning in.

"It's something I noticed last night. I think he might have done it…"

"Who might have done what?"

"You know… done the director in."

"What?!" Narumi raised his eyebrows in astonishment. His face suddenly turned serious. "You know who did it?"

"Yes. And I think I know why…"

"You do? You'd better tell me everything from the start!"

Despite everything, Narumi didn't despise Nishinohata's murderer. The sole reason that the now temporarily halted strike had any chance of success was because that tyrant had been killed—and he had only the murderer to thank for that. Deep down, the membership of the union in its entirety was probably grateful to whoever had done it.

While Atsuko had broached the subject herself, however, she was now hesitant to speak. How could she tell him that Haibara had tried to steal a kiss from her? If she said the wrong thing or gave him the wrong impression, there could be a lingering unpleasantness between them for some time to come.

"What's the matter?" Narumi asked impatiently, as Atsuko ate her ice cream in silence.

"I'm thinking! I need to get it all in the right order."

"Is it really that convoluted?"

"Mmm-hmm… Now don't get angry. In the end, nothing happened."

"What are you on about? Nothing happened to who? Him?"

He had a suspicion that she was trying to dodge something.

"No," she said. "Now, I want you to listen carefully and not jump to conclusions. It only happened last night. I went down to the hotel lounge by myself and read for a little. I'd found a book on the history of Nagaoka—it was actually quite interesting, so I lost myself in it completely. By the time I came to my senses, he was standing right beside me."

"Who was?"

"Mr Haibara!"

"The director's private secretary?"

As Atsuko had anticipated, Narumi's expression hardened. He put the wafer he was eating down on the plate in front of him.

155

"Yes. You remember, he's the one who, er, proposed to me through Mr Hishinuma's wife. Well, since I hadn't given him any answer, he must've been aching to know my decision. Evidently, he couldn't wait any longer and had opted to ask me himself."

"He doesn't know when to give up, that guy. I'd have clobbered him if I were you," he suggested spiritedly. But then his tone changed to one of sympathy. "Then again, I suppose it's understandable. If I were in his shoes, I probably wouldn't be able to sleep without an answer."

"Oh? Aren't you the magnanimous one!" Atsuko laughed. But even if it was just a silly joke, it was nice to hear such a thing from the man she loved. "He was insistent, I'll give him that. But when he was getting carried away with himself, trying to persuade me, that's when he let slip his big secret."

"His big secret? Meaning that he'd killed the director?"

"Hardly. He'd been caught by the director with a geisha."

"No!"

"He's convinced that the reason I rejected him was because the director had ratted on him to me. He got all worked up and spouted off this story about having forgotten something at a tea house after a banquet, saying that he'd only gone back to pick it up and that I shouldn't read anything into it. He claimed it was all innocent enough."

"So had you in fact heard this story from Nishinohata?"

"No, that's the thing. Yesterday was the first time I'd heard about it before. Of course, if I had heard about it, I'd have been even less inclined to accept him…"

"I see."

No sooner had Narumi said this than he looked away and pondered for a few moments. When he turned his head to the side, the line of his nose was well-defined, as though it had been embossed. Atsuko liked it very much.

Buses passed back and forth under the open window, and the voices of the women bus conductors carried on the breeze. There were no trams in this city.

"So, you're suggesting that he might have killed Nishinohata to get his own back because he thought the boss might have scuppered his chances with you?"

"Oh, for goodness' sake, keep up! I turned down Haibara's marriage proposal only the night before the director's funeral."

"Dear, oh, dear!" Narumi said facetiously, looking sheepish. "I must be losing my touch. If I made a blunder like that at the negotiating table, I'd be in big trouble. They'd laugh me out of the room!"

"Is everybody there really so hostile?"

Atsuko wasn't saddened by their antagonism so much as she was perplexed by it. Was the idea of cooperation between capital and labour really just an empty armchair theory?

"It was inevitable when dealing with the late director and Haibara. That's why we're praying that the new director, whoever he may be, will sympathize with our position. Even so, to paraphrase an old but observant Western scholar, the Japanese are an excitable lot, and they get riled up very easily. They deem anyone who isn't on their side to be an enemy, and enemies to be objects of hatred. It's a sorry state of affairs." He took out a cigarette, tapped it on the table and suddenly looked up. "So, why do you think Haibara killed the director?"

"Well, you see, he was so worried that the director *might* let slip his misconduct and that I'd get to hear about it. You should've seen his face. He looked as though he'd have gone to any lengths to prevent it."

"Please, that guy isn't man enough to risk doing something like that. Not with enemies as clever as his."

Narumi's difference of opinion frustrated Atsuko, so, as she tried to convince him, she got more and more carried away.

"But he's crazy, that man! Just last night…" she began to say, but suddenly stopped.

Narumi couldn't help noticing her alarm.

"Last night what?"

"No, it's nothing."

"Well, it must be something. I've never seen you so anxious before."

Narumi looked genuinely concerned, and although his eyes were smiling, he seemed determined to press this point. Atsuko knew that if she tried to hide it, she risked introducing a crack into their relationship. She wanted to avoid this and knew that, in order to do so, she'd have to confess at least part of the story.

"Oh, all right. I'll tell you. Just promise me you won't get angry. It wasn't a big deal."

"Am I the type to get angry? Go on."

"Haibara clasped my hand…"

"That bastard! And did he do anything else?"

"He sat down on the sofa and tried to take me in his arms."

"That son of a bitch… Next time I see him, he's going to pay for this. Anything else?"

This was the first time that Atsuko had witnessed Narumi's jealous side. His slender face was flushed, and his beautiful body seemed to glow as though it were on fire. Meanwhile, Atsuko, who had been upset, grew more relaxed when she realized that Narumi's jealousy was an expression of his love for her.

"No, that was all. Mrs Hishinuma came in and he darted out through the French doors."

"That bastard," Narumi said again. Evidently, his command of profanities was rather limited.

"At any rate, the police seem to think that whoever did it pulled a gun on the director and forced him to drive to Ueno Park. But the director had nerves of steel. He'd never have let a criminal intimidate him like that. He'd more likely have pulled over at a police box and had them arrest the guy. But suppose for a moment that it was Haibara. He could've lured the director to the scene of the crime without raising any suspicion. And if the director hadn't told anybody about Haibara's indiscretion, it would never have occurred to him that Haibara held this grudge against him. His guard would have been completely down."

"You've certainly got a point. In any case, it makes more sense than the police's theory. He seems to have been mad about you, so it stands to reason that his animosity towards the director would be equally intense. There's a Buddhist phrase for that, isn't there? *Gedo no sakaurami*—'the resentment of the other'."

"Well, I feel sorry for the other..."

"You do?" Narumi didn't appear to be listening. "So, did you turn him down because you'd already found your soulmate in me? Or did you just not like the guy?"

"Both, of course! But even if we'd never met, I still wouldn't have married Haibara. Not in a million years!"

"Oh? Why not?"

"Because I don't like him. He's fawns too much over his superiors, and yet he's so scathing to anyone beneath him. I also heard a story from somebody who went on last year's company trip to Izu: when they were fishing, Haibara caught a goby and gutted it, only to throw it back into the water. Apparently, the fish swam around unsteadily for a while, as though it were drunk, and Haibara just laughed. What an awful thing to do."

"Ugh… I'd heard that the junior employees have a low opinion of him. And that does seem rather cruel. Still, maybe it was an experiment of sorts," Narumi said, almost seeming to defend him. After all, those who are conscious of their superiority often subconsciously want to protect the weak.

Atsuko, however, would have none of it.

"Oh, come off it," she said indignantly. "He's an employee of a textiles company. Not a marine biologist. There was no need to 'experiment' at all."

"Yes, you're right."

"Anyway, do you suppose we ought to tell the police about this?"

"Hmm… We have to be careful. They might think it isn't a strong enough motive and decide not to look into it."

"I don't like ratting on people either. But then, we can't just sit back and do nothing, can we?"

Atsuko seemed oddly insistent. Unsure of what she was getting at, Narumi said nothing and just stared into her dazzling, pale-brown eyes.

"Well? Don't you think we should do a spot of investigating ourselves? If we're careful, he'll never know. It would cause less fuss than reporting him to the police."

"Playing at detectives?! And how exactly do you propose we do that?"

Narumi was joking, but, to his surprise, the look on Atsuko's face was serious.

"Well, we can't just go and question him ourselves, now, can we? That's why we have to check out his alibi. Tomorrow, I'll try to find out where he was and what he was doing when Hanpei Chita was killed. After you return to Tokyo, I want you to check his alibi for the night when the director was killed."

Having taken Atsuko's words with a pinch of salt, Narumi now saw how in earnest she was and adopted a more serious expression.

"But, darling, wanting to put a bell around a cat's neck is one thing; it's quite another to find somebody actually to do it."

"What do you mean?"

"I mean, how on earth are you going to find out what Haibara was doing? And I can't very well go up to him and ask, 'What were you doing on the night when the director was killed?'"

"No, I suppose not. So, how could we get it out of him?"

Atsuko's eyes suddenly darkened. It was an obvious question, but she hadn't appreciated the underlying difficulty.

Narumi sat there in silence, scooping up the melting ice cream with his spoon. It seemed so simple on the face of it, but it was proving difficult for Atsuko to come up with any good ideas.

But after thinking about it for few moments, Atsuko's face finally lit up.

"Well, if I can't just ask him myself, I've no choice but to get somebody else to do it for me. I'm sure *they* could find a pretext for it."

"Did you have anyone in mind?"

"Yes, somebody who's friendly with Haibara."

"Who?"

"Why, the very person who delivered his proposal! Mrs Hishinuma, of course."

All the executives from the head office and their wives would be leaving Nagaoka for Tokyo the following morning. Since they would probably all be travelling on the same train, Atsuko would have Fumie try to get it out of him on the journey back. Her tact could always be relied on. Surely, Atsuko thought, she'd find a way to extract the information.

NINE

What Did the Voice Actor Know?

1.

On the evening of the 17th, the day after they arrived back in Tokyo, Narumi took the bus from the factory in Adachi and got off at Tokyo Station. When he looked at the clock, he saw that he had ten minutes to spare, so he stood by the ticket office and waited for Atsuko to arrive.

It was 5.50 p.m. and the evening rush hour was almost over, but there were still a lot of office workers milling around. Office girls in light blouses and salarymen in white shirts, all having finished their work for the day, emerged in droves from the underpass directly in front of him, only to be sucked straight through the ticket barriers. Each of them seemed to have that same desire to get home as quickly as possible and not to miss out on a minute of the time that was finally theirs. The flow of people continued at a steady pace, on and on, like an infinitely repeating stream of numbers after a decimal point. As Narumi watched them idly, they all seemed like unfinished products on a conveyor belt.

"Shusaku!" came a voice from behind him. "What are you gawping at?"

Flustered, Narumi turned around. It was Atsuko, but she was wearing a pair of dark-green sunglasses. She looked like a different person altogether. She had on a neat pale-cream dress and a pair of shell earrings that were fitted snugly to her ears.

"Can that really be you?" Narumi said dubiously.

The two big dark-green lenses were like looking into a bottomless pit. Her red lips parted in a smile, revealing a beautiful row of white teeth. Narumi broke into a bashful smile.

"Now you'll never be able to get up to no good... I've actually been standing here for a while."

"That's not fair! I'd never recognize you in those sunglasses."

"Calm down," said Atsuko reassuringly. "I wanted to test myself. We can't let anybody see us walking together. But if *you* didn't even recognize me, then we should be OK."

She flashed another dazzlingly white smile. The fact that her eyes were shielded only made her red button lips seem more prominent than ever. As Narumi stole a glance at them, he couldn't help thinking back to the kiss they'd shared as they parted outside the restaurant in Nagaoka.

"Let's go. We won't feel so conspicuous once we're among the crowds."

Atsuko bought two tickets at the window and nudged Narumi towards the barriers.

"So, what about Haibara's alibi for the time of Chita's murder?" Narumi whispered.

An announcement for the departing train on the Chuo line platform came over the tannoy, so Atsuko waited for it to finish before answering.

"It's not entirely clear. He was running all over the place, seeing to the preparations for the director's funeral, wasn't he? So, it's not impossible that he could have gone there. It's two and a half miles from the factory to the scene of the crime. That's only a short drive. And besides, he'd been to Nagaoka several times before, so he had a *feel* for the area. That's why the real question is what he was doing on the night when the director was killed."

"And? What were his movements?"

"He claims he got blind drunk in some bar. So, we need to go there and find out whether what he says is true or not."

"And where exactly is this bar?"

"It's in the Ginza. A place called the Black Swan."

"It would be convenient if it turns out he's a regular there. That way they'd remember him."

"Well, according to Mrs Hishinuma, he's been going there an awful lot lately." Atsuko smiled. "She says he only started drinking recently—it's to try and take his mind off of me, apparently."

"I almost feel sorry for him. He's such a pathetic creature."

They made their way up the stairs, jostled by the crowd as they went.

"I'd like you to go to the Black Swan," she said. "It would be a little awkward if Haibara turned up while you were asking questions, though. So I'll stand guard at the café in front of his office, watching in case he comes out. I called earlier and they told me he'd be in meetings until around seven, so he should still be at work."

"Now there's some planning!"

Atsuko laughed, feeling pleased with herself. "I hope he'll go straight home, but it's not beyond the realms of possibility that he'll stop by the Black Swan on his way."

"To drown his sorrows?"

"Very likely. That's why I'll keep an eye on him. If he looks as though he's heading to the bar, I'll ring you there right away." There was a look in her eyes that said she was enjoying the thrill of it all. "I've got it all worked out: I'll say something that only you and I will understand."

"Such as?"

They'd reached the top of the stairs and were standing on the platform. It, too, was crowded with commuters, all rushing to get home. To avoid the crush, they walked over to the far end.

"We have to assume that the owner and the waitresses at the Black Swan will be on Haibara's side. If he comes to the bar later and finds out that you've been poking your nose in, there'll be a scandal. And if Haibara is the culprit, he might sense that he's in danger and make a break for it. And if that were to happen, the police would come down on us like a ton of bricks. So, I can't give your name when I call the bar."

"You want me to use a false name?"

"Yes. What was your mother's maiden name?"

"Sakanashi."

"Right, then I'll ask for a message to be given to Mr Sakanashi. The message will say that I've managed to get tickets for the express train. Got it? So, if the bartender tells you that there's a ticket for you for the express train, you're to get out of there at once."

"Got it. It's like we're in some kind of thriller, isn't it?"

"Yes. It's so exciting, don't you think? It's so exciting."

She was like a giddy schoolgirl. There was a childish naïveté to her plan, but nothing better had presented itself. In fact, Atsuko's plan made perfect sense.

"Where will you be waiting for me?"

"Hmm… Let's pick out a rendezvous along the way. I'm sure we can find somewhere nice."

Atsuko seemed to be genuinely looking forward to the adventure.

2.

Narumi and Atsuko parted ways at the crossroads at Sukiya Bridge, and, as soon as he was alone, he began to feel nervous. He was going to have to act like a private investigator now and wasn't at all confident that he could pull it off. He made his way towards the Ginza, picking his way through the stream of people bathed in neon light.

After crossing the intersection at Owaricho, he turned right down the first alley and clocked, about ten yards ahead on the wall, a sign with a large, long-necked black waterfowl. You couldn't miss it. All around him loitered businessmen carrying briefcases.

Perhaps it was a louche crowd, or it may have had something to do with the location, but even though it had just gone 6.30 p.m., almost half of the chairs inside the Black Swan were occupied by customers. Narumi had never been one for bars. He could never understand what was so interesting about having inane conversations with the waitresses or what was so entertaining about pawing at the hostesses over a drink. He would rather throw his money down the drain than spend it in a bar. And so, to Narumi, the men sitting there on stools or in booths with their arms around the hostesses just looked sleazy and seedy.

"Well, well, well, if it isn't Mr Tae! It's certainly been a while. I haven't seen you for almost three months."

One of the hostesses who was at a loose end sashayed over and plumped herself down beside him.

"Oh, I *am* sorry," she said. "I was so sure that you were Mr Tae. Is this your first time here?"

She wore blue eyeshadow to cover her puffy eyelids, but rather than hide them, it merely made them look swollen and bruised.

That she had supposedly mistaken him for this "Mr Tae" seemed like nothing more than an excuse to sidle up to him.

"Can I get you something to drink?"

"Yes, why not…"

Narumi surveyed the bar with a sense of foreboding. If this had been his usual diner, there would have been a menu stuck to the wall with the names of all the dishes they served. But this pretentious bar clearly didn't permit anything so uncouth.

"Yes, why not…"

He repeated the words, stalling for time. He tried his best to recall the name of a cocktail, but it was just as useless as trying to remember a piece of English vocabulary during an exam.

"… why not, indeed. I'll have what Mr Haibara drinks."

At last, he'd managed to say something.

"Ah! You're a friend of Mr Haibara's?" she said, casting off her show of reserve.

Although she wore the kimono of a young woman, she appeared to be considerably older, and, if you looked closely enough, you could see that her red-painted lips and the skin of her face were cracked.

"Why, yes! The name's Sakanashi. We go way back. As the old saying goes, we've long eaten rice out of the same pot."

"I'm partial to rice myself. You wouldn't happen to know any good restaurants in Nihonbashi, would you?" Seeming to get the wrong end of the stick, she pulled out a small business card from the *obi* sash of her kimono. It read: *Rirako*. "You must bring him next time."

"Ah, yes, the old boy's a regular here, isn't he?"

"I wouldn't exactly say that. He's been here three times, maybe."

"Is there anybody here he has his sights on?"

"Why me, of course!" she said, laughing aloud at her own joke.

The laughter made the wrinkles at the corners of her eyes more noticeable. If she was trying to hide her age, she would have done better, Narumi thought, to be a little more restrained.

"I'm only joking," she continued. "He just has a drink or two by himself. Maybe he likes the atmosphere."

It made Narumi all the angrier now to think that Haibara, with his shameless love of tea houses and bars, had asked the pure and innocent Atsuko to marry him. However, he couldn't afford to reveal his distaste.

"Will you join me for a drink?"

"With pleasure! What shall I order?"

"Have whatever you like! I'll have Haibara's usual."

Rirako stood up and went over to give the order to the barman.

"A Scotch on the rocks and a Mont Blanc."

"A Scotch on the rocks and a Mont Blanc," the barman echoed. "Coming right up!"

From his vantage in the booth, Narumi could see neither his face nor his silhouette, but, judging by his voice, he imagined him to be a handsome, sombre man in his thirties.

Narumi rested his chin on his hands, wondering what to do. He could no longer pretend to be a private investigator. If he was claiming to be an old friend of Haibara's, he'd need to ask in a way that was appropriate for one. He prayed inwardly for the answer. He recalled having read about a similar scene in a book once.

"What's the matter?" Rirako said, sitting down beside him. "You look miles away all of a sudden."

"It's just something that's been on my mind. I made a bet with Haibara the other day, you see."

"Oh? What kind of a bet?"

"Well, it's like this. The other evening, I saw Haibara on a train with the most beautiful woman. The next day, half out of jealousy,

I rang him up, but the bastard denied the whole thing! Said he had no recollection of any woman on the train."

"Goodness!"

Being a woman, she seemed very interested in the notion that Haibara had been spotted with a beauty. As she leant in, Narumi could smell her overpowering perfume.

"In the end, we decided to have a bet to see who was telling the truth."

"Oh?"

"We agreed that the loser would treat the other to a slap-up meal in the Ginza."

The drinks they had ordered arrived. It was the first time that Narumi had seen either of them.

"He's got a very short temper, does Mr Haibara, you know," he went on.

"Really? He's never like that here."

"That's because there are ladies present."

"Maybe, yes. But aren't all men like that? Before they marry, all they do is flatter women. Then, the moment the deed's done, they turn into tyrants."

"Oh? You've experience yourself, have you?"

Narumi peered at Rirako. The thick layer of powder and rouge that she'd applied to cover her rough skin seemed to suggest something sad about her past.

"Oh, you! No, I've never been married yet."

She tried to pull a face as though butter wouldn't melt, but her fine lines and crow's feet betrayed her efforts.

"Never been married yet, eh?"

Narumi was amused by her inadvertent turn of phrase and couldn't help repeating it back to her.

"Drink up!"

As Rirako reached out to the whisky on the rocks, Narumi realized that the Mont Blanc was for him. Smiling at him, she placed her lips to the glass and drank half of it. Even the way she looked at him as she drank concealed a technique that would arouse a man's heart. Though it may have been her job, she was undeniably good at it.

"Ah, that hits the spot," she said. "So, tell me: how did it all end with Mr Haibara?"

"Well, he came up with a very cunning excuse. The bastard said he spent the whole evening drinking here, so there was no way he could have been on that train."

"Which evening was this?"

"Hmm… Let me see now."

Narumi looked heavenward for effect. On the white stucco ceiling, which was indirectly lit, several black swans had been carved. He gazed at them, pretending to think. Rirako had taken the bait, but he would have to take even greater care not to tangle the line as he reeled her in.

"That's right, it was the night before I left on my trip to Tohoku, so it must have been on the first of the month. It would have been around 11.40."

"On the evening of the first? In that case, I'm afraid you must be mistaken. Mr Haibara was here."

"Really?" Surprised, Narumi looked at her with a mixture of disappointment and mistrust. "He was here?"

"I'm afraid so," she said resolutely with a nod.

"At 11.40?"

"That's right."

"And you're sure about the date?"

"Why, yes. Do you see that calendar over there behind the barman? He'd forgotten to turn it, and it still showed May. I realized it on the first and asked him to flip the leaf over. And just as he was doing it, Mr Haibara showed up. That's why it left such an impression on me."

"How terribly strange," Narumi said, as though speaking a line from a play. At the same time, however, it reflected his true feelings. He wondered whether Haibara might have bribed the people at the bar to tell this tale. "Oh, come on. I made a bet with Haibara. If I lose, I have to take him out for the best meal that money can buy. I don't mind that, of course. But it's a question of winning and losing. And I'm a man who hates to lose. So, how about it? If you tell me the truth, I could treat you instead. I'd be much happier treating a beautiful woman like you than Haibara. And if, hypothetically speaking, Haibara offered you, say, 2,000 yen not to tell me, then how about I make it worth your while and raise it to 3,000? What do you say? Tell me honestly."

It was a lame way of putting it, ignoring the woman's sense of *amour propre*, but Rirako didn't seem offended in the least, probably because Narumi's enthusiasm shone through so clearly.

"It wasn't me who kept Mr Haibara company that night. It was Mitsuko. Let me fetch her."

She twisted around to look back at a stool on the other side of the room and called out to a woman wearing a high-collared two-piece.

"Mitsuko, could you come over here for a moment?"

"What is it?"

"Just come and you'll find out."

The woman whispered something to the customer beside her and came down immediately from her perch. She was young, but both her clothes and face alike were sombre. She sat down facing Narumi and Rirako.

"Yes, he really was here," she said, gently touching her beautifully set hair, after hearing the story from Rirako. Her cherry-painted nails glimmered brilliantly. "It was his first time here that night. He said he'd been in meetings at work all day, and it was pretty late."

"What time did he arrive here?"

"Hmm, it would have been just after a quarter past. I heard the chime," she said, nodding towards the clock tower at the cross-roads in 4-chome.

Even Narumi, who was not very familiar with the Ginza, knew that the clock tower copied the one in Westminster and struck every quarter-hour.

"He had quite a few drinks. And the whole time he just kept sighing miserably."

"He looked like he was drowning his sorrows," Rirako jumped in, looking earnest. "He had five or six Mont Blancs, and in the end he just lay down on the sofa and fell asleep. When closing time came, since we had no other choice, the owner and I bundled him into a cab and sent him home. We're absolutely certain."

"Oh, I see. Then it must have been my mistake..."

"I'm afraid so. He'd have been sighing away at 11.40. In fact, he was doing it so much that it was beginning to get on my nerves. Is there something the matter with him?"

As she asked Narumi, there was an inquisitive gleam in Mitsuko's eyes.

3.

After Mitsuko left, having been called over by a customer, Narumi ordered another Mont Blanc and lit his fourth cigarette. He wondered whether he could really believe what the two waitresses had told him.

"You know," he said, "I really can't stand losing to Haibara. Are there any customers who saw him here at 11.40? Maybe one of your regulars?"

"Now let me think…"

As Rirako frowned and cocked her head, trying to think, a man appeared beside their booth. He had on a pale-brown beret and a red chequered short-sleeved shirt, and he was tall and imposing, like a bronze statue.

"Sorry to disturb, but there's something I'd like to ask," the man said in a nasal voice.

Narumi thought he'd heard that deep bass somewhere before, but he couldn't immediately place it. He looked at the man with a wary smile and indicated the seat that Mitsuko had just vacated.

"Rirako, you couldn't go and buy me some cigarettes, could you?"

She stood up, and, as she left, the man's face drew in closer to Narumi and he lowered his voice. His bulbous forehead was practically touching Narumi's.

"My ears pricked up when you started asking questions about 11.40 on the night of the first. You wouldn't happen to be investigating that case, would you?"

"'That case'?"

It was obvious that the man was referring to Nishinohata's murder, but Narumi played dumb, thinking it better to be cautious.

"Why, the case in which that man was killed, thrown over a bridge and carried off to some preposterous location."

"You mean, the murder of Gosuke Nishinohata?"

"Yes."

The statuesque man nodded and lowered his voice even further.

"You're investigating it, aren't you? You can't fool me. It's obvious." Drunk, he mopped his gleaming face with a handkerchief. "Hey, Rirako! Would you get me some water? And put a splash of

173

bitters in it, will you? There's a good girl. We're conducting some very important business, this gentleman and I, so don't disturb us."

His face seemed to be part of the furniture in this establishment, and nobody—neither Rirako nor the other staff—looked in the least put out by his forthrightness.

"Err, something like that," Narumi stammered, still on his guard. He had the distinct sense that he'd met this man somewhere before.

"Now, as for me," the man said, wagging his finger in front of Narumi's face. (He looked as though he was about to tell him something important.) "As for me, I know something that nobody else knows about it. When I rang the police this evening, some low-level officer answered and had the nerve to take some high-and-mighty tone with me, so I just slammed the phone down."

The man appeared to be drunk. He spoke with what sounded like a painfully blocked nose, and his speech was slurred.

"Where have all the good detectives gone?" Narumi lamented, pandering to him. He desperately wanted to find out what it was that the man knew.

"Ah, now you're talking!" he cried, slapping Narumi on the shoulder.

Despite the man's manifest inebriation, Narumi was mindful to keep Rirako away while he talked.

"Now, you see, I'd told this to the police before, but they clearly thought I was just some idiot off the street and wouldn't believe me. I won't rest, though. I'm determined to prove my theory. But just today I realized that an important clue had been staring me in the face all this time. I was at the studio, leafing through an old newspaper that isn't one of the ones I take at home, and—"

"By 'studio', you mean?"

"I work for a national broadcaster."

He reached into his trouser pocket, and, after putting his handkerchief, a lighter, a notebook, a wallet and a few other items on the table, he finally pulled out a business-card case.

When Narumi saw the name Toshio Murase, he finally realized why his voice sounded familiar. The man was a voice actor, so that feeling of familiarity must have come from hearing him on the radio. He hadn't expected him to be so large in person, but perhaps this fact accounted for the deep voice. As he surreptitiously compared his own slight frame to Murase's, Narumi frowned.

"What was it that you spotted?"

"It was that guy! The one who was poisoned on the ov—, *hic*, on the overnight train."

Apparently hearing the word "poisoned", Mitsuko looked over at the voice actor with a startled expression.

"You mean Genkichi Obata?"

"Yes, that's the chap! Obata. It said that this Genkichi Obata was a re—, *hic*, a real Tokyoite."

Murase's hiccoughing could have been because he was drunk or because he was so worked up. A drop of sweat beaded at the corner of his round nose. Narumi also recalled having read in the paper that Genkichi Obata was a native of Tokyo.

"It said he was proud of the fact that he'd never left Tokyo."

"But hadn't he supposedly been in Saitama for a period?"

"Well, yes, but that's neither here n—, *hic*, nor there. We can ignore that."

Murase waved his enormous hand, which made Narumi think of a glove. As Tokyo has been expanding in recent years, Saitama has become a part of Tokyo, so it wouldn't be wrong to say that Genkichi had never set foot outside of Tokyo, except for that fateful trip when he was poisoned.

Nevertheless, Narumi still couldn't fathom what the voice actor was getting at. What was the connection between Nishinohata's murder and the fact that Genkichi had never left Tokyo?

"So, does it matter then? The fact that Obata was a true Tokyoite, I mean."

"Oh, it matters all right! It fundamentally changes the Nishinohata case. The view taken by the investigative team has been wrong from the get-go. And now this gu—, *hic*, this guy called Hanpei Chita has been killed in Nagaoka… This evening's papers say that the case is close to being solved and that the police won't be outwitted. But if things carry on the way they are, the murderer's never going to be caught! Ever!"

"Would you care for a drink, Mr Murase? Then you can tell me your story," Narumi said with great interest. There was clearly some basis to what the man was saying, and Narumi could tell that this wasn't just some drunken joke.

"Oh, I'll tell you all right. I have to tell somebody. But I'm d—, *hic*, done with the police. I don't want to see another copper again."

The experience with the telephone seemed to have thoroughly riled him.

"You see, I noticed only because I'm a voice actor. Anybody else would have m—, *hic*, missed it."

These words piqued Narumi's curiosity. He wanted to get the actor drunk, but not too drunk—just enough so that he'd reveal his discovery.

"How about a Mont Blanc?" Narumi said, not knowing the names of any other cocktails to suggest. "Or maybe a Scotch on the rocks?"

"If it's your treat, make it a double," the voice actor said.

Just as Narumi turned to pass the order on, the telephone behind the bar began to ring. The barman said only a few words in reply before hanging up and looking around the room.

"Is there a Mr Sakanashi here?"

"I'm Sakanashi," Narumi said, standing up.

The barman was good-looking and a little older, just as Narumi had imagined. He had on a smart white jacket and a stylish bow tie that any man would have admired.

"There's a message for you, sir," he said when Narumi got to the bar, in a discreet whisper. "Apparently, they've managed to get you a ticket on the express train, so you're asked to come as quickly as possible."

A polite smile floated on his pallid cheeks.

"As quickly as possible?"

"Yes, it seemed to be a matter of some urgency."

"Thank you."

The barman flashed another forced smile and bowed slightly.

Perhaps Atsuko had been delayed making the call. In telling him to hurry, she must have meant that Haibara could appear at any moment. Narumi had to make a snap decision. He returned to his seat and, still standing, looked at the voice actor.

"Why don't we go for a bite to eat?" he suggested. "I know a nice place not far from here."

"I'm not hungry. Can't we just talk here?"

As he serenely extracted his cigarette case, Murase looked solidly ensconced.

"It's just, there's a girl I'd very much like you to meet."

"What's this?"

Desperate, Narumi mentioned Atsuko, whereupon the man in the beret, who until now had been slumped in the booth, suddenly perked up and grinned.

"A girl, you say?"

"Yes, she's a real beauty. I've agreed to meet her at a café just down the street. I'd like her to hear your story as well."

"Let's get going then. I, *hic*, I do love beautiful women."

He stood up, his belly pressing against the table, and tapped Rirako lightly on the shoulder.

"See you next time, dear!"

"What, you're leaving already?"

Rirako and the voice actor said goodbye to each other and exchanged a suggestive kiss in a manner that made Narumi want to raise an eyebrow.

"I do hope you'll visit us again."

Rirako flashed a smile at Narumi, who was blushing. Holding the door open with one hand, the actor turned to the woman and blew her another kiss.

The alley outside the Black Swan was bathed in the brightly coloured neon lights of the bars and restaurants that lined the street. After leaving the establishment, Murase began to stagger off in the wrong direction.

"This way's quicker!" Narumi called out.

"No, my—*hic!*—car's this way!"

When Narumi tried to lend a hand, the actor shook his head firmly and carried on, staggering as he went and narrowly avoiding a collision with two buskers who were playing a guitar and an accordion.

"Aren't you a bit merry, Mr Murase?" one called out.

"What are you talking about?!" he retorted angrily. "I've hardly touched a drop!"

The buskers laughed and hurried off.

There was a car parked at the end of the street. Narumi, who had no interest in cars, had no idea what make it was or how much it might have cost. He just thought it very glamorous that this voice actor drove around in his own car and went drinking in the watering holes of the Ginza.

"Come on, get in. Where is this place?"

"It's just by Yurakucho Station."

"That's only a minute away!"

"Will you be all right behind the wheel?" Narumi asked hesitantly, recalling the many accidents caused by drunk drivers.

"Don't worry! It's only down the road, isn't it? And I'm not even drunk."

Narumi had no choice. He was desperate to hear what Murase had to say. And besides, he was starting to get nervous that Haibara might see them.

"I'm in your hands… Just take it easy."

"Right you are!"

As Murase climbed into the driver's seat, the body of the car tilted to one side.

They set off immediately, and, before they knew it, they were approaching the crossroads at Owaricho. In the blink of an eye, the green lights turned to red, and, all at once, the pedestrians who had been waiting on the pavement began crossing the road.

Murase should have hit the brake and stopped the car, but instead the opposite happened. As drunkards often do, he hit the accelerator by accident, causing the people crossing the road to scream and scatter. The actor's face flushed, and he gripped the steering wheel in a daze.

The car came out of the crossroads with such force that it jerked violently, and the wheels screeched as it mounted the pavement. A woman shrieked. A red pillar box came flying towards them, and, with a tremendous bang, the car smashed right into it, coming to a halt.

The voice actor was thrown forwards, crying out in agony as his head went through the windscreen. Red blood began to trickle out of the car, dripping down onto the paving stones and forming a small pool as a crowd of bystanders looked on. Narumi, meanwhile, had been thrown from the car and, having hit his head on the ground, lay lifeless on the pavement.

TEN

The Cactus Club

1.

As the official investigation hit a dead end, the idea of having somebody review the case was raised by the top brass. That the job was entrusted to Onitsura was not so much because he was regarded as a safe pair of hands, but simply because those hands happened to be free. It was not uncommon for the metropolitan police to take this approach when the chief inspector wasn't up to the task. That way, the investigation could remain an internal matter, and, even if Onitsura were to succeed in saving the chief inspector's face, he wouldn't be the one to receive any of the glory. Still, that didn't mean that Onitsura didn't enjoy his work. He was just the kind of man to take satisfaction in a job well done. Perhaps that, too, was a part of the reason he'd been picked for the assignment.

Inspector Onitsura began his investigation on 25 June, almost a month after the first incident. He kept his trusty assistant, Tanna, on hand and sent away the rest of the detectives to support other incident rooms. Then he sat down leisurely at his desk and began to review the investigation so far. He read through the considerable volume of reports systematically, double-checking all the important points and making a note of those that hadn't been investigated in enough detail, as well as of the questionable behaviour on the part of the suspects. For example, it struck him that even if Mrs Nishinohata couldn't have killed her husband because of her bad legs, it was still possible that she could have entrusted the deed to a third party. The investigation thus far, he felt, had been inadequate on points such as this. He immediately dispatched Tanna to Kuroiso in Tochigi Prefecture to make a detailed report on Hisako Wakatake and her mother. It was an unfortunate rainy day, but Tanna traipsed up and down the country lanes, got covered in mud and found out that the deceased Tazuko Wakatake had been a naïve, unsophisticated girl who knew nothing but her home town and Tamagawa in Tokyo. He also brought back with him an official copy of the family register, which proved that Hisako Wakatake had not been acknowledged as Gosuke's child. Given this confirmation that the child had not been registered to the Nishinohata family, the widow's possible motive could be eliminated.

The alibis of each of the suspects in the murders of both the director and Chita, of course, were also rechecked with the relevant witnesses. For example, to confirm the alibis of Koigakubo and Narumi, Tanna was sent to the dormitory at the Miyahara Yard in Osaka to visit the conductor of the *Sea of Japan*, who was relaxing on his day off. And while Constable Seki may not have been best pleased about this, it was unavoidable if there was to be a thorough investigation.

Onitsura proceeded with the utmost caution and diligence. Neither Koigakubo nor Narumi had any obvious motive to kill Chita, but, despite this, he pursued the alibis of both men on the 14th and was finally satisfied after confirming that they'd both been on a train on the Joetsu line at the time of the murder.

After eight days of review and further investigation, Onitsura was left with the following two questions:

1. What was it that Toshio Murase had realized? He had said it was a major discovery that would fundamentally change the Nishinohata case.
2. What was the purpose of Gosuke Nishinohata's two visits to the safety deposit box?

"What are your thoughts on these questions, Tanna?" Onitsura said, laying down his pencil and turning to his diminutive, energetic colleague. "It seems to me that the solution to the case boils down to these two points."

Tanna, who had a naturally dark complexion, seemed to have caught the sun during his exertions over the past eight days. He raised his tanned face from the newspaper spread out on his desk.

"What Murase said has been weighing on my mind lately, so I've been going through these old newspapers."

Following the accident in Ginza 4-chome, Murase had been taken by ambulance to the hospital in Tsukiji. The artery in his neck had been half-severed, and his injuries were so severe that several times they thought he had died. Hence, it had been impossible thus far to learn what it was that he'd discovered, and now Tanna was trying to find out for himself what it could have been.

"I called Murase's home and asked for the names of all the newspapers he takes. I've been going through them all one by one, but I just can't imagine what it was that he might have found in them."

"Well, then, let's hope he makes a speedy recovery and can talk to us before long."

"It's touch and go. I thought modern cars were supposed to be fitted with safety glass. Then again, I suppose there's only so much that it can do if the car's travelling too fast."

Tanna had a pessimistic look in his eyes.

"If Murase is out of action for the time being, we'll just have to examine other avenues. Anyway, what are your thoughts on the second point, about Nishinohata's visits to the bank? I think we need to examine this more thoroughly."

Onitsura waited for Tanna to nod before he continued.

"The investigating team seems to have assessed this in a rather naïve way. Just because the director visited the safe twice doesn't necessarily mean that he took something the first time and put it back the second. That's a bit of a hasty conclusion, wouldn't you say?"

Tanna's response was noncommittal. He knew well enough that Onitsura was the sort of man to give everything due consideration, but for the life of him he couldn't see what could be wrong with the investigating team's assumption.

"All we know," Onitsura continued, "is that he went down twice into the bank's vault. Nothing more."

"I see…"

"The investigating team envisaged only one possible explanation, but I can imagine at least four of them. The more I think about it, perhaps even more than that."

"For instance?"

"I'll try to write them down in a way that's easy to understand."

Taking a pen, he noted down the following:

1. On the first visit he collected something, and on the second he returned it.
2. On the first visit he took something out, and on the second visit he did likewise.
3. On the first visit he deposited something, and on the second he took it out again.
4. On the first visit he deposited something, and on the second he did likewise.

"I see! When you put it like that, there are lots of possibilities, aren't there?"

"And there's more!" Even though Tanna looked as though he was developing a headache, Onitsura pressed on. "Take the first point, for instance. Strictly speaking, we can divide this into two possibilities. The first is that, when he opened the safe, he took out object A, and then put it back again when he opened the safe for the second time; but it could also be that he returned with object B, a completely different item."

"Ah, yes, of course."

"We can say the same for point three. He could have started out depositing object A and then taken it out again the second time, or he could conceivably have taken away object B with him."

"Yes, I see…"

"And there's more still! Theoretically, he could have opened the safe twice without depositing or removing anything from it at all. It could be that he just needed to make it look as though he stopped by the safety deposit box for some reason."

Tanna, however, was no longer following what the inspector was saying. Considering different possibilities was all well and good, but this sounded like hair-splitting.

"So, there you have it," Onitsura said gravely, seeming to sympathize with Tanna. "I just wanted to point out that the observations and deductions made by the investigating team were a little too pat. In other words, I think there may well be oversights in the investigation of the safety deposit box. I can't say for sure that they've made a mistake, but, if after re-evaluating all the evidence, all we're left with is this box, then I think we ought to take another look at it."

Tanna agreed. The two of them decided to go out that afternoon. First, they requested the presence of the lawyer, Nukariya, and then they contacted the Showa Bank.

2.

Nukariya had visited the bank vault before, but for Onitsura and Tanna it was their first time going down with the manager and the clerk, Koine. Tanna looked around furtively as they descended the stairs and reached the conclusion that it was better to be moderately poor and have nothing to do with safety deposit boxes whatsoever. The air conditioning down there was so effective that it sent a shiver down his spine.

The five men opened the doors to the vault as had been done on 3 June and pulled out the steel box with a clatter.

"Please, gentlemen. It's yours to examine."

The white-haired lawyer spoke briskly. He stood about four inches taller than the more ordinary-sized Onitsura, had a chiselled face and a skin tone that would have allowed him to pass for an Indian (if only he wore a turban).

"Tell me," Onitsura asked the clerk, whose head was still caked in pomade, "when the director visited the vault, did he bring anything with him? A bag, for instance, or a briefcase?"

"No, sir. He came empty-handed both times."

"Thank you. Then it must have been something small enough to fit in his pocket. If it was a document, it could have been only four or five pages at most," he grumbled, extracting the papers from the box with Tanna's help and examining them thoroughly.

The lawyer watched the inspector's hands silently, half in anticipation of what he would discover, and half-expecting that, no matter how hard he looked, no new facts would come to light.

One by one, Onitsura examined each and every share certificate. After about three minutes, the other men present began to show signs of boredom at the meticulousness of the process, but the inspector paid little mind to this and proceeded to examine the two photographs of Hisako Wakatake and the one that had been torn in half. Unsatisfied with merely looking at them, he then took out a magnifying glass from his pocket.

"Well, sir? Any luck?" the lawyer asked impatiently when Onitsura had finished with it. There was an unmistakeable trace of contempt in his voice.

"Nothing leaps out at me just yet. I'd like to take my time looking at this one though," he said, indicating the torn photo. "Would you mind if I borrowed it? A day ought to do it."

The lawyer granted his permission, and Onitsura placed the photograph nonchalantly inside his briefcase. He bowed to the vault manager and closed the safety deposit box, after which the five men headed back upstairs.

Even after they returned to the metropolitan police headquarters, Tanna had no idea what it was that Onitsura had spotted in the photograph. The copy of Hisako's family register made it clear that the matter of an inheritance had nothing to do with the case, so what could it have been in the photograph of Hisako's mother that had piqued the inspector's interest?

Onitsura went over to his desk, opened his briefcase and extracted the photograph, handling it as though it were a precious object. Unable to restrain himself any longer, Tanna finally asked the question, and the inspector's lips creased into a smile.

"Think again. Just because the three photos were found together, you and the others have assumed that they are of Hisako and Tazuko, but there isn't a shred of evidence to support that conclusion."

"So, you mean to say that the woman in this photo may not in fact be Tazuko but a perfect stranger?"

"I think it could well be somebody else. Take a look at this," he said, pointing to one part of the photo with the tip of his pencil and handing the magnifying glass to Tanna.

The woman in a rather dishevelled-looking kimono and with sandals was standing, facing the camera almost square on, but the absence of the upper half of the photo meant that her age and appearance could not be determined. She appeared to be standing by the front door of a building with the sort of window bars seen on urban houses. It was clear that she was in a city, because a paved road was in the shot. In the background, there was a single car parked on the road. Onitsura was pointing to the number plate.

"Take a close look. The car isn't from Tokyo."

"A-ha," Tanna exclaimed, struck by the discovery. "It's a Kyoto plate. KYO-98983. Then, do you suppose the photo was taken in Kyoto?"

"Possibly. According to your report, the late Tazuko had never ventured anywhere outside of her home town, except for Tamagawa in Tokyo. So there's no way she could have been photographed in Kyoto. And even if that car had come to Tokyo all the way from Kyoto, I'm pretty familiar with the streets of the capital and I've never seen one even remotely resembling the one in this photo. Then again, that could just be because half is missing. Still, common sense would dictate that the photo was taken in Kyoto, and, if that's the case, then logically this cannot be Tazuko Wakatake."

"Yes, you're right."

"Of all the items in the safety deposit box, this photo is by far the most mysterious. The very fact that it's missing the top half is suggestive, don't you think? Have a copy of it made as fast as you can. I'll take it with me when I go to Kyoto and try to identify the woman. Whether or not it'll help us crack the case will only become clear afterwards."

Onitsura was clearly in a hurry. He had already opened his desk drawer and pulled out a railway timetable.

3.

The express train *Izumo* left Tokyo at 10.30 p.m. and arrived in Kyoto at 8.40 the following morning. Although it was a little too early, there was no other express train that left Tokyo Station later and stopped at Kyoto. Travelling in the same berth as Onitsura was a newly-wed couple on their way to visit the great shrine at Izumo, and, although he was not exactly thrilled to see this picture of intimacy, he did at least manage to get some sleep that night.

The *Izumo* express glided into Kyoto Station's platform No. 5. It was an eleven-minute stop, so Inspector Onitsura was in no rush. He took his time getting to his feet and, after casting a friendly glance at the happy-looking couple, alighted from the train. Likely because of the hour, the platform was crowded with passengers wanting to buy bento boxes. Carrying his briefcase under his arm, he weaved through the crowd of people before making his way up over the footbridge and out through the ticket barrier.

The inspector had got off at Kyoto Station once during the war, and his abiding memory was of being accosted by a dirty-looking vagrant lying on a bench in the waiting room, begging him for food. He'd passed through the station any number of times since then, but even now he couldn't help recalling that pitiful sight. Even as he stood on the central concourse, with all the stylish beauties of the old capital passing around him, he could still see the dark shadow of war beneath the crowded scene, as though he were looking at an X-ray. He paused for a moment to look around, found a public telephone beside the information desk and placed a call to the prefectural police, informing them of his arrival and his desire to visit them once he'd eaten.

Kyoto has a reputation for sultry heat and humidity in summer. That morning, however—perhaps owing to the early hour—it was still relatively cool and altogether quite comfortable. As the inspector stood in front of the station still in his jacket, he deliberated where to have breakfast. After all, Kyoto was a place renowned for its food. Whenever he visited the old capital, he would always return with an upset stomach after guzzling down too many of the local delicacies, such as the exquisite tea-house dishes and freshwater fish cuisine. As a Tokyoite, he would never have said it out loud, but the truth was that he looked forward to his work trips to Kyoto very much. This time, all being well, he secretly hoped to sample some softshell turtle before he left.

Right now, however, the inspector had a strange craving for altogether simpler fare. He wanted *kitsune udon*—noodles in a light broth, served with pieces of sweet, deep-fried tofu on top—but the little noodle shop was not yet open. He had no choice but to go to a nearby canteen, where he had a run-of-the-mill sandwich and a cup of insipid, watery black tea. It was odd that even in Kyoto, a city that prided itself on its refined palate and sophisticated cuisine, one could find such little effort put into so scant a meal.

After finishing his breakfast, Inspector Onitsura hopped on a tram outside the station heading towards Takano and alighted on the west side of the Imperial Palace, at the point where Karasuma Street crosses Demizu Street. From there, it was a five-minute walk to the solid yet elegant building that was the prefectural police headquarters. It had just gone nine o'clock, but the sunlight on the white stone steps outside was already dazzling. The inspector wanted to take off his jacket.

The chief traffic inspector was a short man of around fifty by the name of Isono. For a brief moment, Onitsura was put in mind of a certain disgraced politician who had a similarly large, round face. The two men also shared the same narrow, piercing eyes. As he looked at him, Onitsura realized that the similarities had even given him the curious notion that this inspector was harbouring some dark secret.

"We checked it out as soon as your call came in…" Isono began after the initial introductions were over with.

The previous night, Inspector Onitsura had telephoned to request that their records be checked in order to identify the registered owner of KYO-98983.

"It belongs to a car club."

"Oh," Onitsura said, his heart sinking. "And what's the name of this club?"

Had the car been privately owned, the solution to his problem would have been simple enough. But if the car belonged to a hire club, there was no telling how many people might have used it. To go around, asking each and every one of them whether they'd parked it at the location shown in the photograph would cost the force dearly in terms of time, effort and money. Yet the inspector had come all the way from Tokyo, so he couldn't sidestep the issue just because it was difficult. Besides, his methods were based on patience and perseverance. And yet, no matter how much patience he was blessed with, the very thought of traipsing around in this sweltering heat was too exhausting for words.

"Would you like the address? It's on Chie no Koin Street in Tojimachi, Kamigyo Ward. Shall we get in touch with them directly?"

"You'll never get anywhere with them over the telephone."

"In that case, sir, maybe you'd care to take a look at a street map?"

Just as Isono was about to point to one on the wall, Inspector Onitsura took out a map of Kyoto that he had bought at the station and spread it out in front of him.

"Here it is. If you aim for the Toji pagoda, you should be able to find your way easily enough. If you get lost, just ask anybody on the street. Most people in Kyoto can speak standard Japanese reasonably well these days, so you shouldn't have any trouble communicating."

Inspector Isono followed this with a few suggestions on how to get there. That he neglected to mention taxis and spoke only of public transportation was indicative not only of the budgetary woes common to police forces, but also of the resignation of their officers who were all too accustomed to this.

Inspector Onitsura suppressed the wry smile that was about to form on his lips and bowed politely.

4.

The Cactus Club was located in the Toji temple precinct. The area was home to many small factories and workshops, and there was a yard enclosed by a fence, where twenty or so cars of various makes and models were parked. Standing on the far side of it, beneath an enormous willow, was a whitewashed bungalow, obviously an office of some kind. As Inspector Onitsura approached the main gate, a Nash returned and, as though trading places with it, a Datsun departed. In the driver's seat, gripping the wheel, sat an almost naked young lady in a solid colour sundress; she seemed to be pouring all her overflowing energy into driving the car, which turned onto the road and sped off, leaving behind only the faint echo of its engine. The inspector was a little unnerved to see her lax steering.

Carefully, lest he risk being run over, the inspector crossed the yard and made his way over to the office. Pushing open the screen door, he found a reception desk immediately to his right and a young woman sitting behind it.

"New membership?" she asked in a Kyoto accent.

The inspector introduced himself and informed her that he wished to speak to the manager. She hauled herself up and disappeared into the back room. Judging by her cheap blouse and flaking sandals, she must have been from a poor family, a world away from the bright young things who came here to enjoy themselves driving, albeit in a hired vehicle.

Presently, Onitsura was shown into the back office. Behind a round, varnished table sat a wiry middle-aged man in short sleeves, who, when he saw the inspector, got up to greet him. An old-fashioned black electric fan was whirling away, making an appalling racket. Stirring up the warm air was apparently the least they could do for their customers.

"Certainly is hot, isn't it?" he said. Perhaps it was the intonation of the dialect, but it almost sounded as though he were sneering at the inefficacy of the fan spinning beside him. "I'm the manager. What can I do for you?" he said, placing on the desk a business card naming him as Tsugio Tamai.

Inspector Onitsura opened his briefcase, took out the copy of the photograph that he'd had made and placed it in front of the manager. After glancing at the half-photograph with a bewildered expression on his face, Tamai gazed back silently at the inspector, lighting a cigarette and awaiting some kind of explanation.

"You see this car? It's a little hard to make out, but it's a Mercury…"

"That it is. The model is seven years old."

Onitsura took out a magnifying glass and had the manager read the number plate.

"Well? Does the number ring any bells?"

"Yes, it does. It's one of ours."

His sunken eyes open wide, the wiry man stared back at the inspector, wondering where he was going with this.

"I'm investigating a case, you see, and I'd very much like to know where this car was parked. You wouldn't happen to recognize the location, would you?"

"Now, let me see…"

Cigarette dangling from his mouth, the manager looked at the photograph again. There was a curious expression on his face, as he appeared to mull over the reasons that it might have been ripped in half. A brief silence ensued.

"I don't know," he said at last, still staring at the photograph. "I haven't even the foggiest."

He seemed to be more interested in the identity of the woman standing in the photograph than in the inspector's question.

"Am I right in thinking that only members can hire these cars?"

"Yes, you have to be a member in order to hire them."

"And do you keep records of which members borrow which cars?"

"We do. There's a book for each vehicle. The staff write down the date and time of the loan, the time it was returned, the name of the member who borrowed it and so forth."

"How convenient. Would you mind showing it to me? I'll have to go through everyone who's borrowed this car, asking them whether they know where it's parked."

"I wouldn't relish that in this heat!"

The manager frowned exaggeratedly, as though he were being asked to do it himself, before getting up and stepping out of the office. Onitsura extracted a notebook and a fountain pen from his jacket pocket and prepared to make notes.

The door opened, and in came the manager carrying a ledger bound in black leather. On the cover, inscribed in white enamel beside the words "Record of Loan", was the vehicle's number.

Onitsura bowed as he took the book from the manager and opened it to the first page.

Since the first entry was dated 10 January of the previous year, it was clear that only a year and a half had passed since the vehicle was purchased. Just as the manager had promised, the names were there, alongside the dates and times of the loans, all written in a woman's hand between red ruled columns. The remarks row at the bottom was always left blank, but after a couple of pages, Onitsura came across an entry recording that the car had been involved in an accident and that the bumper had been dented, requiring repairs. The cost of these repairs, as well as the name of the garage that had carried them out, was also recorded.

There were five people recorded on each of the sixteen pages, and the car had been hired out a total of seventy-seven times. Discounting those that had occurred after the murder on 1 June brought the total down to seventy-one possibilities. The very prospect of it made the inspector feel exhausted.

"This means that, on average, the car has been hired four times a month."

"That sounds about right."

"How does that compare with other cars? More frequently? Less frequently?"

"Once a week isn't very often. With our regular cars, it's common for them to be loaned out daily. We bought one of the new Hudsons back in the spring, and all our members have been after it. There's often a waiting list. We have just over forty members, you see."

There was a look of pride on the manager's face as he stated the number of members.

"Why isn't the Mercury so popular, then?"

"Well, it's because it's an old model, you see. Our members have very peculiar ways of thinking. Even when flagging down a taxi, they'll always try to find a newer one. So, when it comes to a car they're actually driving, they tend to steer clear of anything that's old-fashioned. And then there are those who grow used to a car and find that it has a special quality they like. You might say these favour the underdog."

The inspector took another look at the ledger and saw that, sure enough, just as the manager was explaining, the same names did indeed crop up again and again. He opened up his notebook and began to take down the names. Having sorted them, he discovered that there were seven regulars. One of these seven must have parked the Mercury at the spot in the photograph. Although his investigation had only just begun, the inspector was buoyed by the thought that it was progressing and that the truth would emerge sooner or later. In fact, he had already begun to forget how hot it was in Kyoto. He asked for the addresses and workplaces of the seven members, entered them into his notebook and left the car club. As he walked away, he casually glanced at the Mercury, which was sitting forlorn in a corner of the yard. Maybe it was the inspector's imagination, but there was something sad about its dull and lonely appearance.

5.

It was nearly an hour after the fierce sun set in the western mountains that Onitsura returned to his inn in Sanjo, dragging his weary feet. Although there had been only seven club members to see, it was exhausting to spend the day running around an unfamiliar city; going about by taxi would have been one thing, but the inspector had relied on buses and trams. To make matters worse, each of the club members, as though by tacit agreement, had kept him waiting; some being out of the office, others being detained with work, and so in some cases he'd had to come back a second time. It would have been worth it if all his efforts had been rewarded, but when the five men and two women saw the photograph, they shook their heads and denied not just having parked the car in that location, but knowing where the location was altogether. When the seventh and last club member, a bank employee, replied that she knew nothing about it, even the ordinarily patient Onitsura looked crestfallen and could distinctly feel a sense of fatigue slowly spreading through all the capillaries in his body at once.

The downside of staying in one of Kyoto's *ryokan* inns was that, despite being in a basin that suffered extremes of heat and cold, they had no heating in winter, nor any air conditioning in the summer. Watching the snow through a glass door in winter while having a drink by the *kotatsu* brazier might well have been more elegant, but not being able to shower after trudging home under the blazing sun was a decided inconvenience. It was pleasant to have a wind chime hanging under the eaves of the building, but the air was so still that its bells didn't ring even once. All the inspector could do was to fan himself when the need took him.

Given that each of the seven drivers of the Mercury claimed ignorance as to the location in the photograph, it seemed possible that one of them had loaned the car to somebody else, but they all insisted that they had never let anyone else drive it. With no alternative, Onitsura had come up with another theory: namely, that when the car had been in the garage for repair, one of the mechanics had taken it for a test drive and stopped at the location in the photograph. He had called the manager of the Cactus Club, Mr Tamai, from a telephone booth on a street corner and asked for the name and address of the garage, which he had then visited. He showed the photograph to all the mechanics and asked all the necessary questions, but still to no avail. When the inspector left the garage, his shoes felt very heavy indeed.

"I've run a bath, sir," the round-faced maid said, bowing.

The inspector replied that he would be along shortly. As he stood up, placing his hand to the belt of his trousers, the wind chime rang a little. The noise seemed to jolt him out of his stupor, and he realized something that he had overlooked until now. The Cactus Club had acquired the Mercury only in the January of the previous year, but, as the manager had pointed out, it hadn't been a new model then. Could the Cactus Club have bought it second-hand? And if so, could it have been the previous owner who had parked it at the location in the photograph?

Reticent by nature, Onitsura was a man who was rarely flustered. Having played sports as a young man, his reflexes were still quick and even now he was generally more poised than most. He rarely raised his voice or got excited or showed his emotions in public. This, however, was different. With his belt still unfastened, he picked up the receiver and excitedly asked the receptionist to put him through to the traffic department at the prefectural police headquarters. It was already past their official hours, but, with the telephone pressed firmly to his ear, he hoped that Inspector Isono would still be at his desk.

Onitsura was relieved when he finally heard the latter's voice at the other end of the line.

"Well, have you found something?" Isono asked.

Onitsura summarized his day and asked whether the inspector could tell him the name of the Mercury's original owner.

"Now, if the broker bought the vehicle from another prefecture, then it will be a little tricky, but if the previous owner lived in Kyoto, then it should be easy enough to find out. Shall I ring you back when I have an answer for you?"

Onitsura thanked him, gave him the number of the inn and replaced the receiver. It was only when the buckle knocked against the table that he realized his belt was still undone. Having fastened it, he sat down in a rattan chair by the veranda, feeling on edge. He kept looking at his wristwatch.

About three minutes later, the telephone rang.

"We've got it!" There was excitement in Isono's voice. "Do you have a pen? The address is Imadegawa Street, Kamigyo Ward. Just where it crosses Sembon Street. The name is Mikio Niikura. He's a dealer in textiles. He seemingly bought the car from an American four years ago. Who owned it before that, though, I can't say."

"Thank you," Onitsura said with genuine gratitude.

Before changing into a new shirt and getting ready to head out, he told the receptionist that he would forgo the bath. Whether because he had rested or because of this new excitement, who could say—but his former weariness had now vanished without trace.

6.

With singular extravagance, Onitsura ordered a taxi to collect him at the inn. As the car drove alongside the Kamo River, groups of people were already sitting on little piers overhanging the riverbank, drinking beer under the Gion lanterns and surrounded by geisha. Though unable to drink, Onitsura wasn't in the least envious of the beer, but he did think how refreshing it must be to sit there with the cooling breeze blowing from the river. Still, he felt a little sorry for the *maiko* with their heavy make-up and large *obi* tied at their backs.

The riverbank broadened as they crossed the Sanjo Bridge. By day, there could be glimpsed a beautiful scene of dyers washing traditional *yuzen* silks and modern prints in the river and drying them on the riverbank, but now, instead, the lights on the opposite bank were reflected on the dark surface of the water. This nightscape was even more beautiful, and Onitsura regretted somewhat the speed of the taxi.

Eventually, the car crossed the Kamo River, turned west and for about ten minutes drove towards Kitano Shrine, where it suddenly slowed down.

"This is the place, sir."

"We're at the textile wholesaler Niikura's?"

"Yes, it's the one on the corner."

The taxi came to a halt at the crossroads. In front of them was a large shop lit up by bright, daylight-coloured fluorescent lights, with a frontage wide enough to give the impression that it was a long-established business. Having paid the driver, Onitsura strode right in. There was a teenage beauty sitting on one side of the shop, picking her way through several rolls of fabric laid out beside her. As her pale, slender fingers clutched a red *yuzen*, they reminded the detective of icefish swimming in the Kamo River.

When Onitsura discreetly informed the shop manager of the purpose of his visit, handing him a business card, the manager took him aside and immediately ushered him through the shop to the reception room at the back. There was a television set fixed to the wall of the room, and the owner and his wife were engrossed in a soap opera that was being projected through the cathode-ray tube. Onitsura apologized for calling so late.

"These soap operas are all the same, anyway. If you've seen one, you've seen them all. A good thriller would be much more entertaining," said the woman, switching it off and greeting the inspector.

She appeared to be in her early forties and, as one might expect of the wife of a textile wholesaler, was dressed in a fine *yukata*. She had a slender frame and a pale complexion, and she wore a large opal on her finger. In contrast, her husband, Mikio Niikura, was a stout, red-faced man in his mid-fifties who, seemingly discontented with the electric fan in the room, sat there fanning the breast of his own *yukata* incessantly.

Having confirmed that the man had indeed been the owner of the Mercury, Onitsura took out the half-photograph and repeated the questions that he had asked so very many times that day already.

"Let's have a look then," Mr Niikura said, taking out a pair of large tortoiseshell reading glasses. He placed them on his nose and peered at the photograph calmly, looking every bit the wealthy merchant. Onitsura glanced at the fish tank on the stand beside the television. At the bottom of the large aquarium were pebbles and moss-covered stones, and among the green aquatic plants were guppies, angelfish and other beautiful tropical fish whose names he did not know. Tiny red shellfish clung to the water thermometer. An extravagant hobby, Onitsura thought.

"Well, I feel bad that you've had to trouble yourself coming all this way, but I'm afraid I've never parked the car in a place like this. I'm sorry that I can't be of more help to you. It must've been somebody else."

"That's what I've spent the day trying to find out…"

"You must be exhausted!" the woman said sympathetically.

With a pensive look about him, her husband stared silently at the pale-yellow screen of the television.

Onitsura felt dejected. His last hope had been dashed so very quickly. The polite thing to do would have been to leave as soon as possible. That Mrs Niikura had said the soap opera was dull might simply have been a show of feminine tact in front of her guest.

As the inspector put away the photo and got to his feet, he realized that there was yet another possibility. Generally, when a used car changes hands, the owner seldom looks for a buyer. Most of the time, they leave it to dealers. The Mercury had therefore very likely passed through a dealer before being sold to the Cactus Club—in which case, might it not have been the middleman who had taken the car and left it where it was photographed?

"No, I'm afraid not," Mr Niikura said. "The Cactus Club's Mr Tamai and I are old fishing buddies, so I sold it to him directly. There's nothing more foolish than letting a broker charge a handling fee. Mr Tamai seemed to be very pleased with it."

"I see. I might as well ask, since I'm here: have you ever lent your car to anyone or had it taken without your permission?"

Onitsura shifted his gaze to Mrs Niikura and back again to her husband. When the two of them shook their heads in unison, the inspector knew that his luck had deserted him completely. His sense of defeat was all the more onerous since everything had started out so promisingly. Now he was faced with a choice: either to return to Tokyo empty-handed or to start over again from the beginning. And yet, looking back on the day's work, Onitsura couldn't see where he'd gone wrong. He'd made every effort to ensure that he let nothing slip by unnoticed. Suddenly, the fatigue that he'd forgotten caught up with him. Apologizing again for the intrusion, he left the cloth shop, looking forward to a bath at the inn.

ELEVEN

The Search for a Head

1.

When he woke up the following morning, Inspector Onitsura found that a fine drizzle was falling soundlessly. He was not the kind of man to let the weather affect his mood, but, after the failure of his investigation the day before, the sight of gently falling rain only made him feel more depressed. He got up and removed the rain shutters himself, before washing his face and returning to his room, where the manager had arrived with his morning newspaper. The bed had already been folded away.

"Good morning!" the manager greeted him brightly.

As he replied, Onitsura mused that while the Kyoto dialect sounded elegant and charming when spoken by a woman, it seemed a little effete and disagreeable on the lips of a man. Then again, his impression was also partly because the manager didn't at all look the part: with his pale, slender face and spectacles, he looked more like a young man of letters.

"I'll be leaving after I've eaten," the inspector said. "Please have my bill made up."

"Of course, sir. It's such a pity about the rain."

"It's a relief after yesterday's unbearable heat."

"Ah, yes, it does get very hot here. My apologies," the manager said, bowing as though it were his fault. "By the way, sir, there was a telephone call from a Mr Niikura this morning."

"I beg your pardon?" said Onitsura, putting down his newspaper on the table and staring at the manager.

"I explained that you were still asleep, sir. He said he'd stop by at around half past eight this morning, and would I ask you to wait for him until then."

"Thank you. Please bring the bill after I've seen him."

"Very good, sir. In that case, I'll bring up your breakfast immediately."

The manager bowed and left.

What business did Mikio Niikura have with him? Onitsura wondered, recalling the man he had met only last night, with his *yukata*, folding fan and boar's neck.

The textile wholesaler arrived just as Onitsura was being served breakfast by the maid.

"I'm sorry to call on you so early," he said.

Likely due to the growing heat, the inspector had little appetite. Setting down a plate of fish, he moved over to the rattan chair by the veranda.

"I'm sorry to have wasted your time last night, but there's something I neglected to mention."

With his briefcase resting on his lap, Niikura looked as if he were about to make the rounds of his clients, dressed as he was in a short-sleeved cream-coloured shirt. His face was rosy, as though he'd already had a drink that morning, and his corpulent body looked rather hairy and unkempt. Onitsura had observed before that this type of man tended to have a fixation with money.

"I'm afraid, Inspector, my wife is a little too devoted, and, when we have guests, she doesn't ever stray from my side, so there are times, like last night, when I can't always say what I want to."

He pulled out a heavy silver cigarette case, and, after offering one to Onitsura, placed a cigarette in his mouth and lit it.

"You don't smoke? That's unusual."

"I never could get a taste for it."

"Well, I believe that a man should try everything at least once. That's my philosophy. I'd tried everything from smoking to drinking even before I entered the army. Even now, if I hear about something delicious to eat, I'll go straight there, and if I hear about a beautiful girl, then…" He cut himself short, realizing that he was digressing, and placed his cigarette in the ashtray. "The thing is, Inspector, I recognized the location of that photograph you showed me only too well."

"I see…"

The inspector suppressed his excitement as he waited for Niikura to get to the point. What was he going to tell him that he couldn't have said on the previous night?

"As I was saying, Inspector, I'll go to the ends of the earth for a beautiful woman. It must have been around four years ago. I'd heard about a real beauty. Smooth skin, the works. She was a former *yatona*… Well, a team of wild horses couldn't have held me back."

Onitsura nodded as he listened, but he didn't quite understand this Kyoto word—*yatona*. He imagined the man essentially meant something along the lines of a geisha, but he decided to hear out the textile wholesaler and clarify this later.

"I told my wife that I had to go and see a client, so took the car and spent the night there. The photograph must have been taken while it was parked there."

"Where was this?"

"It's in Tobita. The old pleasure quarter in Osaka."

Wearing a look of embarrassment, he mopped his face with a handkerchief. The fat of his double chin reminded Onitsura of a large sea turtle.

"Where exactly is it in this 'pleasure quarter'?"

"It's a place called the Old Pine. And it isn't just me, either. There are lots of well-known people who, unbeknownst to their wives, frequent this place."

His frequent excuses could, in all likelihood, be put down to a guilty conscience. Onitsura, however, was no Buddhist confessor, so such things did not concern him. All he wanted to know was what building was shown in the background of the photo.

"I don't really know the area well, you see, but, if my bearings are right, I think that place must be a little to the south of the Old Pine."

"To the south, you say? That's all I need to know. How big is Tobita?"

"It's not quite as big as Gion here in Kyoto, but it's certainly bigger than any other red-light district in western Japan. I haven't yet been to Yoshiwara in Tokyo, but no matter how impressive it might be, I doubt it could rival Tobita," he said proudly, replacing the cigarette in his mouth.

Onitsura had experienced the competitive spirit Kansai people fostered towards Tokyo in various ways, but this was the first and only time he had ever heard them boast of their brothels.

The inspector had Niikura draw him a rough map of Tobita and the Old Pine and saw him to the door of the inn.

Mikio Niikura bade farewell to the manager of the inn with all the pomp of a wealthy merchant, but, the moment he stepped outside, he lowered his voice once again and said to the inspector: "I truly am sorry about last night, but however much I might indulge, I'd never breathe a word of this in front of my wife."

The trip to Kyoto hadn't been a waste of time after all. As Inspector Onitsura watched Niikura's car vanish into the distance, he felt that worn-out fighting spirit begin to swell within him once more.

2.

From Kasumicho, if you pass under the bridge carrying the tram-line and the Kansai mainline, cross the main boulevard and carry on walking for about ten minutes, you'll find yourself in the Tobita red-light district. Much like San'ya in Tokyo, Kasumicho was lined with cheap eateries and hostels, but even Inspector Onitsura was surprised at the prices. Five yen for a slice of watermelon, four for a *kushikatsu* skewer and twenty for a whole plate of *nigirizushi*—these prices would be hard to beat even in the backstreets of San'ya. Standing at every shopfront was a young girl who, with a piercing cry, would try to lure customers in. What distinguished the scene from San'ya, however, was that here gentlemen in fine clothing would, without the least show of embarrassment, practically lick their plates clean. Though he had little appetite for a four-yen *kushikatsu*, Onitsura envied the locals who had no affectations or pretensions where food was concerned.

Once you crossed the main boulevard and entered the red-light district, however, the atmosphere changed entirely. No sooner had you set foot inside it than its cleanly swept, spotless streets and alleys, its aversion to bright colours and its buildings done in deliberately sombre tones announced that this was the renowned Tobita pleasure quarter. There was a sense that it wanted you not to miss it, that it was trying, with its incongruous austerity, to make a show of high status, that it was, in a word, overestimating itself.

It was before noon, and the place was practically deserted. The only vehicles the inspector passed were a pedicab carrying a woman with a traditional Japanese hairstyle, and a municipal rubbish truck. Thanks to the accurate map that Mikio Niikura had sketched, Onitsura found the Old Pine without any trouble, and it didn't take long before he was able to locate the exact spot he was looking for—a little to the south, just as Niikura had said.

As he looked across the street, Onitsura saw a rather large two-storey building. Situated on a crossroads, it had a corner portico that bore a slight resemblance to that of the Kabuki-za theatre in Tokyo. Heading off at ninety degrees from one another from the central entrance were two corridors done in frosted glass, while the streets outside were lined with a row of wooden posts that looked like sharp-pointed bollards. Onitsura surmised that they had probably been put there as a precaution to stop the patrons, or perhaps even the women, from jumping out of the windows. As with the ground floor, there were two long corridors stretching along the upper floor, both with wooden railings. Outside every other room on the upper floor was a round lamp hanging from the eaves and emitting a milky-white glow, but no matter which angle you looked at them from, they gave the impression of being, if anything, tacky and inappropriate on an establishment of this kind.

The inspector took the photograph from his jacket pocket and compared it with the scene in front of him. It was clear that the woman was standing in front of the entrance, a little to its left. In the background of the photo, he could see part of the latticework on the front door as well as the glass door of the ground-floor corridor and some of the spiked bollards—and then, in the distance, parked by the side of the road, the Mercury. He still hadn't the slightest idea why Gosuke Nishinohata had kept this photograph, but there could be no doubt that the spot captured in it was where the inspector now stood. Finally, he understood why the woman had been wearing such a garish and dishevelled kimono: she was no ordinary woman, but rather one of the girls who worked the red-light district.

As he approached the entrance to the building, he looked up and saw a carved wooden board on which was inscribed a name: Palace of Dreams. Though it bore the name of a brothel, the signboard was so large and imposing that it wouldn't have looked out of place hanging on any of the six great national shrines. Indeed, it was so solemn-looking that it might well have moved an impressionable person to tears.

As a rule, brothels and hotels that rent out rooms by the hour have the tact to install a side entrance that patrons can use to avoid being recognized. The main entrance is, in effect, nothing but window dressing. In all his attempts to find the side entrance, however, Inspector Onitsura was unsuccessful and had no choice but to enter through the front door. From the street, he could see through the latticework of the heavy, solid door into the interior of the brothel, so anyone inside must have been able to see this stranger looking around outside for some while. He opened the door and, before he could call out, saw a middle-aged woman standing there. She had applied peppermint oil to both her temples—a rare sight these days—and was looking down at him with suspicious eyes.

"If it's life insurance you're selling, I already have it!"

She appeared to be the owner of this establishment—that is, if her faded looks and haughty manner were anything to go by. The inspector produced his business card and stood there in silence as she read it. The place was as quiet as a temple; the women were probably taking a siesta to avoid the worst of the heat.

"Oh, I'm awfully sorry," she said, breaking into a smile as though to avert some punishment that might await her.

The forced smile combined with the headache oil on her temples to lend her a rather hysterical appearance.

"I'd just like to ask a few questions if I may. The building seen in this photograph is this establishment, is it not?"

Having taken the photograph from the inspector, she placed her hands to the bottom of her *yukata* and knelt by the entrance as a mark of respect. Immediately she nodded.

"Yes, sir, that's us all right."

"And do you have any idea who the woman in the photo might be?"

"Why, yes. It's Yayoi. She used to live here. Has she done something, Inspector?"

There was a brief pause while Onitsura considered his response.

"We can't really talk here," she continued before he could answer. "Would you care to follow me?"

"Well, if it's no inconvenience," the inspector said unhesitatingly.

She waited for the inspector to take off his shoes before offering him a pair of slippers and leading him down the corridor. A plush crimson carpet ran up the broad staircase directly in front of the entrance and down the corridors to the left and right. With every step he took, Onitsura's feet sank into the carpet as though he were treading on sponge. The downstairs corridor twisted and turned, zigzagging like a lightning bolt, until at the far end they came to a stone lantern upon a bed of gravel and a small vermilion-painted bridge with charming black *giboshi* finials on the handrails. The stone and paper lanterns were probably illuminated with electricity at night, giving the hallway a dreamlike atmosphere. Unlike the sombre exterior, the interior was done in the Japanese style, all opulent and gaudy.

When they at last reached the back staircase, the inspector spotted, off to one side, a room with a *noren* curtain hanging over the door frame. The owner looked back at him and ducked inside. It appeared to be her sitting room. It was a subdued Japanese-style *tatami* room, with a black-persimmon tea chest and a *maneki-neko* sitting on top of it, as though it were a mark of her refined taste. On a stand in a corner stood a shallow planter with Rodgers' bronze-leaf growing in it, and a shamisen in a bag. A world away from the gaudiness of the corridor, this room was elegant and sombre. She offered the inspector a folding fan and a summer floor cushion, switched on the electric fan, opened the lid of the Tsugaru-lacquer tea chest and began to prepare some tea.

"Here you are," she said, handing him a cup.

Onitsura bowed his head slightly. This was only natural, since it was high-quality tea, but both the water and the cup were lukewarm. It would have been one thing if they were scalding, but to drink something so tepid felt as though you were being infected with some strange illness, and so it proved to be a rather unwelcome favour.

"What a lovely cup," he said helplessly.

"I wouldn't say that, Inspector, but it is old Kutani ware," she said quietly, bringing over a cup for herself. "My late husband liked to collect such pieces, but he was forever giving them away or breaking them, so this is all I have left."

As she stared at the cup in front of her, she appeared to pine for her late husband. The initial harshness of her face seemed to soften as she drank the tea and chatted. Onitsura began to sympathize with her. He thought how difficult it must be for her to manage a large business alone, so it was perhaps inevitable that from time to time she should suffer from headaches or encounter situations that were wont to provoke hysteria.

Perfect silence reigned in the brothel still.

"To return to our earlier topic of conversation," Onitsura said. "Would I be correct in assuming that the girl called Yayoi no longer works here?"

"Yes, she was here for about four years after the war ended. She's gone now."

"And I assume Yayoi was her professional name? Do you happen to know her real name?"

"Correct, Inspector. We've always had girls known as Yayoi ever since the Edo period. The current Yayoi is the second reincarnation after the one you're interested in." Her voice seemed to lift as she boasted of carrying on the old traditions.

"So, what was the real name of the girl in the photo?"

"Hmm, I wonder. There were so many comings and goings until around 1950, so it's hard to remember now. What did the girl say her name was? Sakuko? Or maybe Sakiko? I think the surname was Saito, in any case. Whether or not that was her real name, though, I couldn't say."

"Do you have any photographs of her, or her letters perhaps?"

"You see, Inspector…" In the face of his dogged persistence, the proprietress rubbed the oil at her temples with her fingers, as though her headache was returning. "As you may be aware, in this business we generally try to forget those who have washed their hands of it and gone into something more respectable. If we should happen to run into one of our former girls in the street, it's one thing if she strikes up a conversation with us, but if she doesn't, we'll just pretend not to know her and look the other way. Really, it's a kind of courtesy that we afford them. That's why, whenever a girl leaves the profession, she puts everything in order and burns all her photographs and letters. We help her, too, and take pains to ensure that nothing is missed. And so I'm afraid I haven't any of her photographs or letters."

Hearing this explanation, Onitsura was impressed that this world, too, had its own customs and ways. And yet, without knowing so much as the real name of this girl, it would be impossible not only to establish her identity, but also to uncover what her connection to Gosuke Nishinohata was. To get to the bottom of the case, he would somehow have to meet this "Yayoi". Put simply, it was possible that she held the key to solving the Nishinohata case.

"Girls often want to take photographs with their friends. Might one of them not have a snapshot with her in it?"

The owner shook her head.

"For some reason, that girl had a terrible aversion to being photographed. The mere sight of a camera was enough to make her tremble. I doubt there's a single photo of her left anywhere." She looked at the photograph that the inspector was holding and seemed to recall something. "As for this one, the customer snapped it when she wasn't looking. She caused such a fuss over it... After she found out that he'd snuck a camera in, she got hold of the film and burnt it."

The inspector flashed a wry smile and nodded. The girl—this Sakuko or Sakiko Saito—seemed to have wanted to conceal her identity at all costs. The possibility that this could have been due to some shady criminal activity only intrigued him more.

"There'll be a record of her change of address at the ward office, though, won't there?"

If he could find that, it would give him an idea of where she might have gone afterwards. There was a note of excitement in the inspector's voice.

"I'm afraid she was never registered here in the first place. The girls arrive with only their bodies, so to speak."

"But then how do they get rations?"

"There's a place over in Kasumicho that sells rice and plenty of other things. So, it's easy enough to get by without a ration card."

It had all been easy enough for Yayoi. Or perhaps she had chosen the red-light district in Tobita for that very reason— because of its proximity to Kasumicho.

"Were there any problems when she left? With her advance, for example?"

The owner couldn't help but laugh at Onitsura's ignorance. She explained that, unlike the pre-war days, there were no advances paid to the girls, and, since they could come to work as they pleased, they could also leave whenever they wanted. As he listened, the inspector recalled having read an article to this effect in a newspaper.

"But she told you she was leaving the profession?"

"Yes."

"And why was that? Did she intend to marry?"

"She never said as much herself, but that's what I inferred, yes."

"I've heard tales of working girls falling in love with their clients and ending up marrying them. Was there any potential candidate in this Saito girl's affections?"

She placed her fingers to her temples again and appeared to think for a moment.

"It's nothing to boast of, Inspector, but our patrons are exclusively men of high standing—prefectural governors, cabinet ministers, the scions of wealthy families, that sort of thing... Naturally, these men are sensitive about their public image, so there's never yet been an instance of one of our girls becoming romantically involved with a client."

In that case, if there really were no love affairs to speak of, it was possible that she'd returned to her home town and a steady life, eventually marrying and becoming a housewife. When the inspector thought about her secretive behaviour, though, he found it hard to believe that she would simply have settled down into that sort of life.

Onitsura asked a variety of questions about the girl's age, appearance and character, and noted down the woman's answers.

If the age she had owned to was correct, this Sakuko or Sakiko would have turned thirty this year. If anything, she was on the thin side and had a good figure, and she had what looked like a little red mole on her left earlobe. For all the secrecy surrounding her identity, she'd seemingly had quite a cheerful nature, with none of the dark shadows that followed some of the other girls around.

"The girls once started a rumour that she'd previously been a streetwalker because they overheard her speaking fluent English with an American GI who'd lost his way. She was a very bright and spirited girl."

As evidence of this, one had only to consider the fact that she'd taken the film from a client's camera and burnt it. Yet all these details were of no use to him without knowing her exact name and whereabouts. He had to find out where she had gone.

Where she had gone... A thought suddenly popped into Onitsura's mind. It was a long shot, but he had run out of options. It had to do with the girl's belongings and how she had them sent on after she left the Palace of Dreams. For women in this profession, making their outfits was one of their few pleasures. A girl who'd worked there for a couple of years might have made half a dozen or so garments. So, what had become of them after she left? It was inconceivable that a woman, for whom clothes were so important, would have disposed of them by selling them off to a second-hand clothes shop. She must therefore have packed them into a suitcase and taken it herself, or, if there were a lot of them, perhaps she'd had them boxed and sent by courier. If the latter, she would have required an address, and, in that case, the shipping company or the baggage clerk at the station would have a record of its destination. If the records were kept, that is.

"Did Miss Yayoi take any luggage with her when she left?"

"Any luggage? Hmm… Yes, actually. Now that I think about it, she had the bath-house attendant go out and buy her a large wicker basket and packed a mountain of kimonos into it."

"I can't imagine she'd have carried something like that herself?" the inspector asked flatly.

At last, things seemed to be going his way.

"No, I seem to recall that she had him lug it away to be sent on."

She sounded a little vague, but then it was several years ago. She must have seen similar scenes play out many times over since then, so it was little wonder that this accumulation of memories would gradually get blurred.

"Who was the attendant?"

She hesitated.

"I'm sorry to say my memory isn't what it used to be. You see, I suffer from cerebral syphilis…" she said, trailing off pitifully.

For a moment, the inspector felt crestfallen, but then he thought better of it and realized that it probably wouldn't be too hard to guess where the luggage had been taken. If she were going to some far-away station, she'd have taken a taxi at the very outset. The fact that she'd had the old man carry it himself meant that the station or courier company must have been relatively nearby. The closest station to the red-light district was Tennoji, just over in Kasumicho. It was the station Onitsura had spotted on his way there.

"Are there any courier companies in the neighbourhood?" the inspector asked.

"Courier companies?" Though she understood Onitsura's words, this non-sequitur seemed to confuse her. "Well, there's Kinai Transport, which has a branch office about a five-minute drive from here. There must be dozens of others, but none, I think, in the local area."

Sure enough, Tennoji Station seemed to be the best bet, and it seemed safe to assume that both the girl and the attendant carrying her luggage had gone there. The inspector sipped politely from his already cold cup of tea, apologized to the hostess for staying so long and got up to leave.

3.

As soon as he stepped out into the street, Inspector Onitsura was blinded by the dazzling sunlight. His vision grew dim, as though it were being eclipsed, and even though his eyes were wide open, he couldn't see anything around him clearly. The heat being reflected up at him from the asphalt road engulfed his body. He had never experienced a Turkish bath, nor had he any desire to do so, but he imagined that the sensation would be akin to this.

Onitsura made his way through the deserted noonday red-light district, up a long slope, and finally arrived at Tennoji Station. By the entrance to the old and dingy building, a group of tourists with children, who were setting out on an insect-collecting trip to Nara, were chatting excitedly amongst themselves, carrying their insect nets and water bottles. The inspector wondered whether it was the weekend already. With no wife or children, however, it took him a good few minutes to realize that the children were on their summer holidays. He tried to avoid bumping into them as best he could while he looked around for the luggage desk.

It was to be expected that on a hot day like this, nobody would be carrying heavy baggage that needed to be checked. As Onitsura approached the counter, he saw an old man with a weary look about him, sitting idly in a chair.

"Sorry to bother you…" the inspector began.

The station attendant heaved himself out of the chair and placed his hands on the counter. His sluggish, oppressed movements reminded the inspector of a polar bear he'd once seen at Ueno Zoo during the height of summer.

"I know it's a long shot, but I wonder whether you could tell me the destination of some luggage that was sent from here a while ago."

"When exactly was this?" the station attendant replied in standard Japanese, almost without any accent.

When the inspector mentioned the date given him by the proprietress of the Palace of Dreams, a look of suspicion came over the man's acne-ridden face.

"I wonder whether we'll have records going back that far... What do you need it for?"

After Onitsura reluctantly told him that he required the information for an investigation he was conducting, the man said that he would check in the records cabinet and disappeared into a back room. He returned surprisingly quickly with a black-covered ledger.

"Here you are," he said in a weary tone, slamming the book down on the counter. "Take a look for yourself."

And with that, he went and sat back down in his chair.

Out on the platform, a train bound for Osaka was about to depart, and the tannoy kept repeating the names of the stations where it would stop. As he listened to the announcer's voice behind him, Onitsura flipped through the pages of the ledger, to find the date he was looking for. His first job was to ascertain whether the old records had in fact been kept: only then could he try to establish whether or not the luggage had been sent from this station. Based on the story that the old man had carried it on his back and gone out on foot, the inspector guessed that the luggage had been brought to Tennoji Station, which was only a short distance away from the brothel, but he didn't have any evidence. Naturally, he felt a degree of excitement, and his fingers began to tremble slightly as he neared the date in question.

There turned out to have been a total of sixteen items dispatched from the station that day. These were itemized as one trunk, five bundles containing futon covers, seven wooden boxes, one metal can, and two wicker baskets. The final two items drew Onitsura's attention. He looked at the "sender" column. By now, he had forgotten all about the heat. He could no longer even hear the voice of the station announcer over the tannoy. Every fibre of his being was focused on this old record of checked luggage.

The person who had sent the wicker basket proved to have been a man. This was not necessarily a problem, however. The inspector looked at the next column and found the name he had been looking for. Right there, written in the station attendant's scrawl, was the name Sakiko Saito. The sender's address was listed as the brothel where the inspector had just received that cup of expensive lukewarm tea. It didn't matter whether Sakiko Saito was her real name or not: the fact remained that, just as Onitsura had imagined, she had sent her luggage that day from Tennoji Station.

The inspector opened his notebook and, character by character, taking great care not to miss anything, copied down the delivery address. Having done so, he looked over the words once more before reading it aloud to himself.

Saitozaki Station (Kashii line)
Saitozaki 43, Kasuya, Fukuoka Prefecture
Sato Takizawa

The basket had been marked for home delivery. The address was on the island of Kyushu in the south of Japan. The line mentioned was a small branch line that ran from Saitozaki on the coast to the inland mining town of Umi and crossed Kagoshima mainline at Kashii. Whether this Sato Takizawa was Sakiko's family home or just the address she had moved to was not clear. What was certain, however, was that the inspector would have to pay a visit to Saitozaki.

Onitsura sat down on a bench and extracted the timetable from his briefcase. It showed half a dozen express trains bound for Kyushu, but they all departed from Osaka Station after seven o'clock in the evening. The very thought of having to kill time until then in this sweltering city was enough to make the inspector shudder. It surprised him to learn that the timetable was so exceedingly inconvenient for passengers wishing to travel from Osaka to Kyushu.

For the inspector, who had no interest in the cinema or the theatre, and who could not very well spend the day drinking, the question of what to do with the six or so hours that he had before boarding his train was a rather difficult one. Sensing that his joy at this discovery risked being crushed prematurely, he set about trying to come up with something good.

Eventually, an idea presented itself and, to put his plan into action, he got to his feet. All he had to do was find a hotel with air conditioning and take a nap there. If he wanted to spare his head, he would have to sacrifice his wallet.

4.

There was no express train that stopped at Kashii, so the inspector had to alight from the *Amakusa* service at Orio and spend twenty minutes sitting on a bench on the platform, waiting for the next train towards Kagoshima. Because he had napped at the hotel, he'd been unable to sleep on the night train, and because of this his mind was dulled.

Like Tokyo's Akihabara, the station at Orio consisted of a two-tier platform, which was unusual in Japan. The lower part was reserved for the Chikuho mainline and crossed the level above, forming a letter X. The shrill cry of a steam whistle prompted Onitsura to stand up, and he saw that a series of goods wagons were passing through on the Chikuho line, bound for Wakamatsu. The next station the freight train would pass through was Futajima, to the north. He couldn't help remembering an old case that had begun with luggage left at Futajima Station. He also remembered a woman he had loved as a student once upon a time, who had lived quietly in the little village, in an old house on the canal. His reminiscing continued until a diesel train bound for Hakata pulled in.

Kashii was a small station with a dead and dusty atmosphere. After waiting there for over an hour, the inspector transferred to a diesel train on the Kashii line. There were few passengers on this local service, and the locomotive ran slowly and unhurriedly with its thunderous drone. As soon as it departed Kashii Station, the train passed through a series of red-clay fields, but when it left the Kagoshima mainline and began heading north, the surrounding landscape changed to one of sandy soil. From the right-hand window, he could glimpse the sea through the gaps between the pine trees, while from the one on the left he could see only forest, but beyond this, he knew, lay the blue waters of Hakata Bay. The train was running along a narrow headland towards the tip of the cape.

After passing Wajiro and Gannosu, the train pulled into a rural station called Uminonakamichi. The branch line seemed to be running on and on, steadily into the sea itself. A writer of children's stories with a fantastical mindset might have imagined that the train were a tortoise and that he were riding on its back towards the Palace of the Dragon King. Yet the inspector himself was too much of a realist to have such fairy tales in his mind, and he was simply frustrated by the slow running of the train. That frustration seemed to increase exponentially, the closer he got to his destination.

With a single blast of its whistle, the train at last pulled into Saitozaki, its final stop. The passengers, who had been sitting spread out, got to their feet. Carrying under his arm the briefcase he'd had with him since the start of the trip, the inspector was the last to step down onto the platform. The terminal was a meagre affair, enclosed by a fence made of railway sleepers, but it had a certain rustic charm to it, bathed as it was in the bright southern sun and with yellow sunflowers growing right in the middle of the platform. After a couple of steps, the inspector saw a board bearing the name of the station; it was written in two different scripts—Chinese characters and Japanese phonetic—and only then did he realize that he had been misreading the Chinese characters this whole time.

When he handed over his ticket at the barrier, he asked the ticket inspector for directions and left the station, heading west. The whole place was covered in a desert-like sand, which was already hot enough to scorch the soles of his shoes, even though it was just after eleven o'clock in the morning. He kept having to mop the sweat beading on his brow with a handkerchief.

The area was replete with pine forests, between which were scattered shabby little huts that had been cobbled together from sheets of rusting corrugated iron. From one of them issued the voice of a woman shouting. She had all the intonations of Japanese but did not appear to be speaking the language. A man's voice followed, in a tone of profuse apology.

After walking 500 yards, as directed, he stepped into the shade of the pines, mopped his brow and caught his breath. The house belonging to Sato Takizawa had to be nearby. He looked around and spotted three middle-class houses. Two were two-storey Japanese-style houses, but the other was a bungalow with a cor-rugated slate roof and its outer walls painted in creosote.

"Excuse me," Onitsura said, doffing his hat to a young man walking past him.

The youth stopped. His open-necked shirt was drenched with sweat.

"Is there a Sato Takizawa living in this area?"

"Sato Takizawa? I don't know. Can't say I've ever heard the name, though."

"Is there anybody who's lived here for a while and knows the place well?"

"Try the old house over there," he said, pointing to the bungalow.

Having thanked the young man, Onitsura once again went out into sun and headed towards the odd-looking house. As he climbed the gentle slope, his field of vision suddenly widened, and there, before his very eyes, he could see the glittering blue waves of Hakata Bay. He knew that it had to be there from having seen it on a map, but its appearance now was so sudden that he almost thought it couldn't be real. Directly in front of him was a 3,000-tonne cargo vessel with a red belly, resting idly in the water. Another four or five ships were anchored in the distance. Some years ago, he too had crossed the bay on a passenger ferry to Tsushima. He walked on, recalling the blood-red camellias he'd seen blooming in the mountains of Izuhara.

When at last he found himself standing in front of the bun-galow, he saw the name "San Park" written on the nameplate. Surprised at this, he knocked and called out. The woman who

223

answered the door was, as he suspected, Korean—a beautiful middle-aged lady with a long face and smooth skin. Though it was the height of summer, she was dressed very presentably in a traditional *hanbok* and had not a hair out of place.

Standing there with a look of suspicion in her eyes, this Mrs Park heard the inspector out before turning her pale face and replying in precise Japanese:

"Mrs Takizawa passed away about four years ago. Her house used to be on the other side of that telegraph pole, but it's been demolished since."

The inspector turned to look at the telegraph pole. It stood halfway between the bungalow and the spot in the pine forest where he'd just paused to catch his breath.

"Did Mrs Takizawa live there alone?"

"No. Before the war, there were three of them: Mrs Takizawa, her husband and their daughter. The husband died in an air raid on Hakata. After the war, it was just the two of them."

"And what became of the daughter?"

Onitsura imagined that Mrs Takizawa's daughter must have been the girl who'd given her name as Sakiko Saito at the Palace of Dreams.

"Miss Kayoko headed straight for the city just after she left the girls' school in Hakata. How she must have hated living in the country-side. She rarely came back, even when her mother was still alive."

If Mrs Takizawa's only daughter had so loathed the monotony of rural life, yearning for the big city, Onitsura reflected, it was possible that she'd met with the fate typical of so many inexperienced girls there. He could imagine only too well how she'd been led down the path to corruption and come a cropper, selling her body in Osaka's red-light district. Was it too much to imagine that Sakiko Saito might in fact be Kayoko Takizawa?

"Do you happen to know where I might find Miss Kayoko?"

"I'm afraid not. I haven't seen her since her mother died. She was wearing that beautiful kimono of hers, crying something awful. But I've no idea where she is now. She said hello to me after the funeral, but I haven't heard anything since. There are times when I remember what she was like in primary school, and I miss her. We were together in the same class, you see."

Then, out of the blue, she offered the inspector a floor cushion and asked him if he would care for some tea. Onitsura declined the refreshment but sat down on the ledge of the entrance. His legs were tired, doubtless from all that walking on sand.

Her yearning for the big city, her subsequent flight, her very infrequent visits home—it all fitted perfectly with his theory that she had been employed in Tobita. If she'd been working as a prostitute, surely she wouldn't have been able to return home at the drop of a hat. Onitsura wanted to go one step further and find out whether his theory that Kayoko Takizawa and Sakiko Saito were the same person was correct. He regretted that the photograph had been torn in half. With her reputation for hysteria, it had probably been Mrs Nishinohata who'd done it. If only the top half showing the head had remained, the matter might have been cleared up already.

Suddenly he remembered what the owner of the Palace of Dreams had told him.

"This may sound like an odd question, but did Miss Kayoko have any identifying features?"

"*Identifying features*? Hmm…"

"A mole, for instance? Or a scar?"

She fumbled with the folds of her *hanbok*, as she searched among her memories.

"Perhaps on her nose? Or her ear?"

225

She placed her hands in her lap and stared at a spot on the wall. Truly, with her regular features and striking silhouette, Mrs Park looked beautiful.

"Ah, yes!" she said. "Now I remember. She had a little red mole on her left ear. I used to see it whenever we whispered to one another as children."

"Where exactly on her left ear?"

"Right here," she said, pointing a slender finger to her earlobe.

Just as he'd thought: the girl who worked as a prostitute at the Palace of Dreams must have been Kayoko Takizawa.

Perhaps Gosuke Nishinohata had spent the night at the Palace of Dreams on one of his trips to Osaka. Given his love of womanizing, it wasn't inconceivable that he might have fallen for Kayoko there. As for her, she could have lived the life of Riley if it was being paid for by a big industrialist like Nishinohata. And if she was the kind of girl who'd hated her life in the country and had run away, she'd have had few qualms about becoming a mistress. Even if he did wear the old-fashioned moustache of an army general, she'd have just had to put up with it.

If all this were true, it was easy to imagine both why a photograph of Kayoko was in Nishinohata's possession and the quarrel that might have ensued if his lawful wife had happened to catch sight of it. Mere conjecture was not enough to satisfy the inspector, though. If a single photograph of Kayoko Takizawa had something to do with the director's mysterious solo outing—and, by extension, had some significant bearing on his death—it was impossible to believe that Kayoko was not somehow mixed up in the case. In fact, the investigation was sure to make excellent progress by shining the spotlight on Kayoko, who until now had been in the shadows. If her whereabouts, moreover, were unknown, what he needed was a photograph of her.

"I'm sure I have one, but it'll be from primary school."

Mrs Park got up and cheerfully went to fetch her school-leaver's photo. It was a commemorative photograph of nearly two hundred schoolchildren, boys and girls, all lined up in rows, gazing intently into the lens. Even if they were to enlarge the pea-sized face, however, it would have been impossible to imagine the present Kayako from the cherubic face and bobbed hair of the child staring back at the camera.

"You don't have any from when she was older?"

"Not even one, I'm afraid."

"Do you happen to know if she had any friends from her high-school days?"

Her face in a photograph from that period in her life wouldn't look so different from the one she had now. If there was such a picture, Onitsura wanted to get his hands on it. And, if he could spare himself the trip to Hakata, then so much the better.

"She had two friends, but since we went to different schools, I never spoke to them."

"Do you at least remember their names?"

"I never knew their names, but I remember where they lived. One of them is the daughter of a *ryokan*-owner in Kashii. The other comes from a family of farmers."

Though she called them "daughters", they must have been grown women by now. When the inspector enquired about this, Mrs Park replied that the daughter of the *ryokan*-owner was married now and had opened a shop in the neighbourhood, while she'd heard a rumour that the farm daughter had let marriage slip her by and become a spinster.

She stood up once again, disappeared into the back room and returned, carrying a pencil and a notepad, on which she proceeded to make a quick sketch of Kashii for the inspector.

"Thank you," he said. "So, the farm is further away?"

"That's right, yes. The farm is a little out of town, whereas the *ryokan* is right by the station."

"I'll try my luck at the *ryokan* first in that case. You've been a great help."

Having left the bungalow, Onitsura retraced his steps towards the station. When he arrived there, however, he discovered that he would have to wait, sitting on a hard bench, until the next train came at 3.30 p.m.

5.

After he got off at Kashii Station, Inspector Onitsura made his way to the street that Mrs Park had told him about and soon found the *ryokan* he was looking for. He had imagined a traditional old inn in the Japanese style, but, much to his surprise, what he saw was a bleak building made of concrete, as square as a sugar cube. With its double windows and stone staircase at the entrance, it looked very much like the style of houses favoured by the Japanese who'd gone to Manchuria and northern China before the war. He wondered whether the owner hadn't perhaps returned from the continent and, in thrall to some feeling of nostalgia, had this dismal house built.

As soon as he'd got his hands on a photo, he'd no longer have any need of this place. The inspector intended to rest there until the evening, when he would return to Tokyo aboard the *Kirishima* or the *Western Sea*. In the meantime, he thought the best course of action was to call this former friend of Kayoko's to his room, have her show him a photograph and hear what she had to say about her.

After he was led upstairs to a north-facing room, Onitsura took a bath, picked up some things from the shop and had a late lunch before receiving the innkeeper's daughter. The girl worked at the local grocer's, so she stopped by her parents' house practically every day. When the inspector sent for her, she came right away.

"So, you're the gentleman who's looking for a photo of Kayoko, are you?" said the short, stout thirty-something-year-old woman, carrying an album.

"That's right, miss. It's about an inheritance, so I really must confirm her identity."

The inspector smiled as he told this white lie. His prominent jaw might have lent him a severe, unfriendly look, but when he smiled, a gentler expression would appear on his face, revealing his true, amicable nature. The woman seemed to relax completely when she saw this.

"Kayoko and I were the best of friends," she said. "We sat beside each other in class and always studied together. But that was only until we left school. I got married and became an ordinary housewife, whereas she—"

A train thundered by just below the window. The whole building shook, and the flower vase in the *toko-no-ma* alcove rattled in time to the vibrations. The innkeeper's daughter carried on talking unconcernedly, but Onitsura couldn't catch what she was saying. Eventually, the noise diminished, and a melancholy whistle could be heard far in the distance. Even the whistle sounded somewhat provincial.

By the time the train had passed, she had finished telling her story, opened the album on the table and was directing Onitsura's attention to something in it.

"This is the class photo taken when we started high school," she explained.

He saw the same rows of little faces that he'd seen in the photo Mrs Park had shown him, only this time there was not a single male pupil in sight.

One by one, she turned the pages of the album. They must have been very good friends indeed, for there were photographs of Kayoko on almost every page. There were snapshots of her on her own, some full portrait, others only half-portrait, and some with three of them laughing together—perhaps the two of them and the farmer's daughter. As the years went by, their childish bobs were replaced by more mature plaits, their breasts grew fuller, and they began to make a show of their femininity, craning their necks, putting on airs and flirting with the camera. The album could have been used scientifically as a teaching aid, illustrating the metamorphosis of a young woman from a chrysalis into a butterfly.

The woman turned the page again.

"There she is after school, wearing make-up for the first time. During the war, they were so strict about it—if they caught you even putting on face cream at school, you'd get a ticking-off. I used to take so much pleasure in putting it on after we graduated. Kayoko looked so pretty with it, too…"

Onitsura stared at Kayoko's face, his eyes wide. With her lined eyebrows and rouged cheeks, Kayoko indeed looked very different from the young girl in the school photos: almost like a different person. In the turn of a page, a young schoolgirl had matured into a beautiful woman. This was not what had caught the inspector's attention, however. Rather, it was the fact that he had seen the face in the photo somewhere before. He hadn't just seen her on the tram or in the street, either: this was a memory of seeing it at close quarters. But for all that, he hadn't the slightest recollection of where or when.

If Kayoko was Gosuke Nishinohata's mistress, he must have seen her somewhere since the murder. The idea that the director had had a mistress had presented itself to Onitsura while he was talking to Mrs Park; back in Tokyo, it hadn't even occurred to him as a possibility. Hence, if he had seen Kayoko before, it would not have been as Nishinohata's mistress, but as somebody else entirely.

"Are there any others?"

"Of Kayoko? I'm afraid not," she replied, with a shake of the head. "You see, she went to Tokyo after finishing school, and we gradually lost touch. I don't even know where she's living nowadays."

"She went to Tokyo? Not Osaka?" the inspector asked, looking surprised.

"No, it was a ladies' college in Tokyo."

"A ladies' college?"

"Yes, she enrolled in the English department. I was good at maths, and Kayoko was always good at English. She loved studying. You see, she always said she was determined to leave this place. She didn't have the easiest time at home…"

Onitsura just stared at the photo without replying. That Kayoko had once entered a ladies' college only to suffer the fate of a prostitute, and that afterwards this fallen angel had seen yet another reversal of fortune, living in the lap of luxury because of her attachment to a man of great power and wealth, seemed to exemplify the wretched lot of so many young women who had been thrown into the chaos of post-war Japan and made to fend for themselves.

The owner of the Palace of Dreams had told Onitsura that Yayoi had been good at English. In hindsight, this was no surprise, given she had studied it at college.

The photo of Kayoko seemed to smile back at him. Her lips seemed to part and dimples form on her cheeks. The image sparked

231

a memory. Why, yes, it must have been when he was research-ing back in the office, leafing through the heavy directory of company employees. It didn't just include the management, but also photos of their wives and daughters. Kayoko must have been among them...

The inspector kept staring at the photograph in front of him, trying to remember. She was one of the wives. Yes, he was sure of it...

Suddenly, the fog clouding his mind lifted. He could see the name of the executive's wife clearly before his eyes. Kayoko wasn't the director's mistress: she was Fumie Hishinuma.

TWELVE
Two Alibis

1.

Because he had got off at Osaka en route, Inspector Onitsura didn't arrive back in Tokyo until the following evening. His whistle-stop trip came to an end the very moment the soles of his summer shoes touched the platform at Tokyo Station.

When he reached police headquarters, he found the chief inspector already gone and Tanna sitting alone in his office with a weekly magazine.

"Ah, welcome back!" said Tanna, putting down the publication and getting to his feet. "I've been expecting you. How was it in Kansai? Hot, I imagine."

For some reason, the detective's face looked a little gaunt.

"It looks as though the chief's already gone home for the day. I'll make my report tomorrow. How about it? Do you fancy grabbing something to eat? I'm famished."

"Sorry," Tanna said, looking genuinely disappointed. "I've got a stomach bug. I haven't been able to keep anything down. I'd much rather hear about what you found to take my mind off it."

"Oh, I see... Well, Tanna, you'd better brace yourself. I've got something to show you."

They sat down facing each other at a desk by the window. During the day, the temperature had risen above 33°C, but as the sun had set, it had cooled, and every now and then a feeble breeze would blow in.

"I ended up going all the way to Kyushu! Almost as far as Hakata…"

Watching the surprise on Tanna's face, Onitsura proceeded to tell him about his trip, from the beginning all the way up to Saitozaki.

"Here's a photo of Kayoko Takizawa."

Tanna scrutinized it for several moments. He then got to his feet, fetched the company directory and opened it to the page on Hishinuma, comparing the photo with that of Hishinuma's wife, Fumie.

"It's her, all right!"

"If she'd had a sister of a similar age, I mightn't have been so quick to jump to that conclusion. But given that she had no siblings, I don't think it's too much of a stretch to assume that Mrs Hishinuma is in fact Kayoko Takizawa."

The inspector was wary of jumping to rash conclusions, not because this involved the wife of a socially prominent businessman, but because it was his nature to exercise caution and discretion at all times. He continued:

"Well, there's one quick way to find out whether Mrs Hishinuma is Kayoko. We need to establish whether or not she has a red mole on her left earlobe. That's the first thing that needs to be checked out. There's no way you can go traipsing around in your state, though, so let's have somebody else do it. They should be able to ascertain that information easily enough if they check with her family doctor or regular beauty salon."

"No, I'd like to do it myself," Tanna said, handing the photograph back to the inspector.

"On my way back, I stopped off at Osaka and paid another visit to the Palace of Dreams," Onitsura said, pointing to the photo.

"Just to be sure, I showed the owner this photo and asked whether it was the woman who'd called herself Sakiko Saito. She said there was no doubt about it. In other words, we can be certain that the woman in the photo that was discovered in the safety deposit box at the bank is none other than Kayoko Takizawa."

"But sir, how did the director come by a photo of this Takizawa woman from her days working as a prostitute?"

"How, indeed? That's precisely why I went back to Osaka."

Onitsura reached into his briefcase, and, just as Tanna was expecting him to produce some important documents, he set down two bars of chocolate on the desk.

"How about it? I'm sure it'll do you a world of good."

Though he didn't smoke, the inspector had a sweet tooth, and since it was not yet dinner time, he wanted to quell his hunger pangs temporarily with some chocolate.

Tanna pushed them back.

"I don't think I could stomach it right now. I'd kill for a cup of *senburi* tea though."

"That's a pity," the inspector said, putting the chocolate back in his briefcase. It would have been cruel of him to eat the confectionery in front of Tanna while he was in that condition. "After I pressed the owner of the Palace of Dreams, she finally admitted that the photograph had originally been in her possession. I should point out, however, that she hadn't realized this as the photo had got lost her bureau drawer. Recently, though, Gosuke Nishinohata happened to stop by the Palace of Dreams and—"

"Hang on, isn't it a bit odd that a big businessman like him would just *happen* to show up at a brothel?"

"Not at all! To put it plainly, there are all sorts of brothels out there, catering to every taste. The Palace of Dreams is one of Osaka's most exclusive establishments. It's been in business since the days of the shogun, and many famous people from history have visited it. As payment they even used to take swords and armour, which have become family heirlooms. So it's a very prestigious place. Even if it does seem rather funny to attach prestige to a brothel… At any rate, it's still only wealthy libertines and playboys who can afford to frequent it. The director himself once spent the night there several years ago when he went down to inspect the factory in Osaka."

"The pompous, moustache-wearing old creep…" said Tanna, giving full vent to his outrage.

"Back then, the owner would greet people at the door, so she remembered him. She was apparently quite flustered when he turned up unannounced not so long ago. He told her that he hadn't come to avail himself of her services again, but that he hadn't been able to forget the girl he'd spent the night with the last time he was there. He offered her all manner of rewards if she—the owner, that is—could find a photograph of her for him. Well, after asking around, it came to light that the girl in question was Sakiko Saito, but all the photos of her had been thrown away after she'd left, so the owner had to hunt high and low for one. It was probably the reward that induced her to go to all that trouble, but she also seemed to feel sorry for the old boy as he pined away for her."

"And in the end, she found this photo stashed away in her bureau?"

"Exactly. Clearly, 'Sakiko' hadn't gone so far as to check there. At any rate, Nishinohata apparently took the photo and left in high spirits, having told the owner never to breathe a word of this to anyone. Naturally, out of consideration for the man, she swore not to tell anyone about it. That's why she pretended even to me that she knew nothing."

Tanna fumbled around in his pockets, retrieved a crumpled pack of cigarettes, placed the last remaining one in his mouth and lit it. He inhaled the fragrant smoke into his lungs and was overcome by a sense of giddiness. The inspector's voice seemed to be coming from somewhere far away.

"What I can't understand is why the director needed a photo of Kayoko, but let's leave that to one side for now and consider the woman in question. During the war, she left high school with top marks and enrolled in a ladies' college in Tokyo, originally intending to take her studies seriously and telling her classmates that she would do whatever it took to succeed. Then came the defeat. Every institution collapsed, the government, whose power we had believed to be absolute, fell, and starvation and chaos flooded the country. If she had to resort to prostitution in circumstances like that, I wouldn't reproach or blame her. There were any number of examples of college girls who had no choice but to do it back then. What's difficult to imagine, though, is how she came to wash her hands of it so suddenly and became the wife of the senior executive director. Then again, it was an era of extremes, so perhaps it isn't so odd after all."

"Maybe he visited the Palace of Dreams, too, and fell in love with her. They do say that a soldier's discipline depends on his general's, so perhaps Mr Hishinuma is a playboy, too, just like the director."

"Yes, it's certainly a possibility." Onitsura paused for a moment and turned his angular profile to the window, savouring the chill of the night breeze. "At any rate, when she married Hishinuma, she'd have to conceal her shameful past. The fact that she goes by the name Fumie rather than Kayoko these days is probably intended to avoid people finding out about it."

"Agreed."

"Which brings us back to the question: why did the director want a photo of Kayoko? Was it, as the owner of the Palace of Dreams believes, because he was still pining for a girl he'd spent a night with? Because she was an old flame, as it were? I doubt it. Now that Kayoko was married to one of his employees, he didn't have to go all the way to Osaka to beg for it. If a picture was all he wanted, he could have looked at one whenever he wanted right here. So, he must have wanted Kayoko's photograph for some reason other than the one he gave to the brothel madam."

"Agreed on that point, too."

As he tapped away the ash from his cigarette, Tanna nodded. A blue ring of smoke drifted out of the dark window, carried on the breeze. For several silent moments, the two men were transfixed by the movement of the smoke.

Tanna could well imagine why the womanizer Gosuke Nishinohata had wanted the photograph of Kayoko. He could picture Kayoko's astonishment as the director confronted her with a photograph from those days and pressed her to do what he wanted, telling her that if she didn't, he would reveal the truth about her past.

"Once we've got confirmation that she has a red mole on her ear, our job's as good as done. It's time to go home, Tanna," the inspector said, sounding relieved. There was a distinct note of weariness in his voice.

The issuing of arrest warrants was a task for the criminal investigations department, not for Onitsura or Tanna. Both men believed that the case was almost closed.

2.

The criminal investigations department requested the presence of Mrs Hishinuma the following evening. They had already learnt from the Red Peony, a beauty salon she visited regularly in the Ginza, that she did indeed have a red mark on her left ear. However, even though they were now certain that she was the murderer, since she was the wife of a well-known figure, they couldn't just pick her up like a young delinquent. If by some chance they'd got it wrong, there'd be hell to pay. The reason they had asked Fumie Hishinuma to present herself at the chief inspector's office in the headquarters of the metropolitan police, and not at the station in Ueno, was ostensibly to protect her from the cameras, but in reality it was also because this ruse would work to their advantage.

She arrived in a silver-grey twin set, the lawyer, Nukariya, by her side. From beginning to end, the short-tempered old boy did his best to protect her, objecting vehemently if they asked even the slightest off-topic question. In reality, though, Fumie didn't need the old lawyer's help one bit, for she had a watertight alibi proving that she wasn't the murderer.

Calm and composed, she took a seat and fixed the chief inspector and Lead Investigator Kaya square in the eye without a hint of guilt or fear in those deep black pupils of hers.

"Is this a joke? You're really asking whether I killed the director?"

When she was informed that she was being treated as a suspect in Nishinohata's murder, she grew indignant. Both her facial expression and tone of voice remained the same, but her anger was apparent from the bluntness of her words.

As a matter of course, Inspector Kaya did have to raise the question of her alibi.

"And when exactly did the director meet his end, gentlemen? I don't recall. The date and time, if you please?"

"It was on the first of June. The place was Ryodaishi Bridge in Ueno, and the time was eleven-forty in the evening."

"Eleven-forty…" Fumie repeated in a well-rehearsed whisper, opening her crocodile handbag. "I'd probably switched off the television and gone to bed. The maid will know."

She extracted from her bag a little traditionally bound notebook and small gold mechanical pencil. She read over the words in the notebook as though she were trying to memorize them carefully, but then let out a soft cry.

"Ah! I was wrong. I gave the maid some time off at the end of May and let her go home to see her family for a week. So, I'm afraid I'd have been alone at the time."

"Then there's nobody who can corroborate your alibi?"

The suspect's eyes looked pityingly at Kaya, who had just offered this hasty conclusion.

"Oh, but there is, Inspector."

"And who might that be?"

"I was suffering from stomach cramps, so I went to the local pharmacy."

"Would you care to elaborate on that?" the chief inspector cut in.

He was rumoured to have one of the best minds in the force, and his piercing eyes gazed over the top of his glasses, looking for the slightest discrepancy in Fumie's story.

"Of course," said Fumie, returning her attention to the notebook. "I went to bed a little after ten o'clock on the night of the first. With the maid gone and my husband away on his business trip, I had nothing but sleep to while away the hours. Just after I drifted off, though, there was a sharp pain in the pit of my stomach, which woke me up. I switched on my bedside lamp and looked at the clock. It was eleven exactly. I tried to ignore it for a while, but in the end I couldn't bear it any longer, so I got up and went to the local pharmacy. As I already said, the maid had gone home, so I had no choice but to go there myself, clutching my aching stomach. The pharmacy is usually open until eleven, but when I got there, the door was locked and the lights were off. I felt bad, but I decided to knock on the door anyway and wake the owner up. I don't know whether he'll remember, but this was at half past eleven. So, as you see, there's no way I could have killed the director."

The small bound notebook appeared to be a pocket diary, and as she looked at it, she reeled off her explanation. To the chief inspector, at least, she appeared to be lying.

The Hishinumas lived in Omiya, in Saitama Prefecture, and, when he wasn't travelling abroad, the senior executive director commuted to the Tokyo head office every morning in a car driven by his wife. If Fumie had been buying medicine at a pharmacy in Omiya at half past eleven, there was no way that she could have killed the director in Ueno, some fifteen miles away, only ten minutes later.

"What is the name of this pharmacy?"

"The Hoashi Pharmacy. It's in Daimoncho, the next town over. It's a four- or five-minute walk from the house."

"And who answered the door?"

"It was the pharmacist himself."

Kaya took down each of her unfaltering answers.

"And the name of the medicine?"

"I don't know. It was a preparation they made up themselves."

Kaya put several other questions to her. These were all indirect, pertaining to the weather that night and what sort of clothes she had been wearing, but, aside from having no clear recollection of the weather that night, she answered each of them without hesitation.

After the preliminary questions were over, Kaya moved on to the next stage. Fumie kept dabbing her broad forehead with a handkerchief—not because she had come out in a cold sweat, but rather because the room was so hot. Though Nukariya specialized in commercial law, it must have been reassuring for her to have such an esteemed lawyer beside her, chivalrously taking notes. Indeed, she appeared altogether calm and composed.

"I'd also like to ask you about the fourteenth of June," Kaya said, "that is, the day when Chita Hanpei was killed."

The lead investigator's face was so devoid of identifying marks that it almost constituted an identifying mark in itself.

"And why would Mrs Hishinuma have anything to do with that?" the old lawyer asked.

His silver hair was dyed red in the crimson light of the setting sun.

Kaya explained briefly that they believed Chita had witnessed the murder of the director and had used it as leverage to blackmail the murderer.

"Mrs Hishinuma, Chita was killed sometime between a quarter past and half past two in the afternoon. Where were you during this time?"

"I was on a train," Fumie shot back immediately, turning her notebook to another page.

"I'm afraid I haven't a timetable to hand, so I can't tell you exactly where I was, but I boarded the train from Omiya at around six-thirty in the morning and arrived in Nagaoka at around half past five in the afternoon. So, I would have been on the train the whole time."

"One moment... Kaya, would you mind fetching a railway timetable?"

242

There was a slight feeling of anxiety welling in the chief inspector's chest. What if there had been some terrible mistake?

Fumie extracted a *cloisonné* cigarette case, which she graciously offered to the chief inspector, and, as she puffed on a cigarette, she told him all about the adorable squirrels that lived in the garden of their country villa in Karuizawa.

After Kaya brought over the railway timetable, the chief inspector returned his gaze to Fumie.

"I'm sorry, which train did you say you boarded?"

"May I see that a moment? Ah, yes, it was this one. The one that goes to Niigata."

"Now, let me see…"

As the chief inspector took back the timetable, Kaya peered over his shoulder. The train that Fumie had indicated was the No. 311 on the Shin'etsu mainline, which departed Ueno at 5.50 a.m. and arrived at Niigata Station, its final destination, at 19.48 that same evening.

"Then between two-fifteen and two-thirty you would have been…"

"… somewhere between Sekiyama and Wakinoda," Kaya said, his rough fingers pointing to the names of the two stations. Around his ragged nails, the tips of his fingers had yellowed with nicotine.

"That's Nagano Prefecture, isn't it?"

"Yes, sir. Shall I find it on the map?"

Kaya flicked back to the start of the book and opened it at the map. Contrary to expectations, they found that both Sekiyama and Wakinoda were just beyond the border, lying in Niigata Prefecture. The chief inspector looked up at Fumie.

"Were you with anybody on the train?"

"Yes, my maid had returned from the countryside, so I took her with me."

TAKASAKI – NAGANO – NAGAOKA (SHIN'ETSU MAINLINE) (DOWN TRAINS)

	Naoetsu	Naoetsu	Niigata	Naoetsu	Niigata	Nagano	Niigata	Niigata	Nagaoka	Niigata	Kanazawa	Naoetsu	Nagano	Kashiwazaki
	349	349	523	917	335	321	119	311	337	313	603	919	2305	315
Ueno dep.	0 15	…	…	…	…	…	…	5 50	…	6 55	9 10	…	9 40	10 10
Takasaki dep.	4 10	…	…	…	…	7 10	…	8 26	*2nd & 3rd cl.*	9 45	10 50	↱	11 26	12 32
Kita-Takasaki "	4 16	…	…	…	…	7 15	…	8 32		9 53	*2nd & 3rd cl. Semi-Express*	*Runs until 11.11*	*2nd & 3rd cl. Semi-Express*	12 37
Gunma-Yawata "	4 23	…	…	…	…	7 21	…	8 39		10 00				12 43
Annaka "	4 30	…	…	…	…	7 28	…	8 47		10 10				12 49
Isobe "	4 51	…	…	…	…	7 43	…	9 00		10 23				13 01
Matsuida "	5 05	…	…	…	…	7 57	…	9 19		10 38				13 15
Yokokawa "	5 25	…	…	…	…	8 15	…	9 38		11 03	11 29		12 11	13 33
Kumanotaira "	5 52	…	…	…	…	8 42	…	10 05		11 30	11 55		12 38	14 00
Karuizawa arr.	6 13		…	…	…	9 03	…	10 26		11 51	12 16		12 59	14 21
dep.		*Ueno–Karuizawa: Extended running every weekend until 4.11*	6 50	…	…	9 10	…	10 32		12 01	12 21	↱	13 05	14 40
Naka-Karuizawa "			6 57	…	…	9 17	…	10 39		12 08	12 28		13 11	14 47
Shinano-Oiwake "			7 03	…	…	9 23	…	10 45		12 14	↓	*Stopping at Naka-Karuizawa only until 10.11*	13 20	14 53
Miyota "			7 12	…	…	9 33	…	10 53		12 46	↓		↓	15 01
Hirahara "			7 22	…	…	9 44	…	11 02		13 01	↓		↓	15 16
Komoro arr.			7 27	…	…	9 49	…	11 07		13 06	12 49		13 37	15 22
dep.			7 35	…	9 10	9 55	…	11 10		13 23	12 49		13 38	15 42
Shigeno "			7 43	…	9 21	10 03	…	11 18		13 31	↓		↓	15 50
Tanaka "			7 50	…	9 25	10 09	…	11 24		13 37	↓		↓	15 56
Uya "			7 57	…	9 32	10 15	…	11 30		13 43	↓		13 53	16 06
Ueda arr.			8 03	…	9 38	10 22	…	11 36		13 50	13 09		14 00	16 12
dep.			8 08	…	9 41	10 28	…	11 40		14 08	13 10		14 00	16 20
Nishi-Ueda "			8 14	…	9 47	10 34	…	11 46		14 14	↓		↓	16 29
Sakaki "			8 22	…	9 55	10 41	…	11 53		14 25	↓		↓	16 37
Togura "			8 30	…	10 05	10 48	…	12 01		14 33	13 28		14 18	16 46
Yashiro "			8 37	…	10 12	10 55	…	12 07		14 40	↓		14 25	16 53
Shinonoi arr.			8 43	…	10 18	11 02	…	12 14		14 46	↓		14 31	16 59
dep.			8 44	…	10 20	11 04	…	12 15		14 48	↓		14 32	17 01
Kawanakajima "			8 51	…	10 27	11 11	…	12 22		14 55	↓		↓	17 08
Nagano arr.			8 58	…	10 34	11 18	…	12 29		15 02	13 49		14 43	17 15
dep.			9 06	…	10 44		…	12 35		15 33	13 56			17 30
Yoshida "			9 13		10 50			12 41		15 39	↓			17 36
Toyono "			9 22		10 59			12 50		15 49	↓			17 47
Mure "			9 39		11 17			13 08		16 06	↓			18 05
Furuma "			9 55		11 33			13 24		16 21	↓			18 22
Kashiwabara "			10 05		11 48			13 36		16 30	14 38	*Naoetsu*		18 33
Taguchi "	*Aomori*		10 17		12 01			13 48		16 43	14 50			18 44
Sekiyama "			10 27		12 15			14 04	*Diesel locomotive*	16 53	↓	*Diesel locomotive*		18 55
Nihongi "			10 36		12 26			14 16		17 07	↓	921		19 09
Arai "	501		10 45	12 02	12 41		12 56	14 25		17 16	15 12	15 44	18 29	19 18
Kita-Arai "			↓	12 07	↓		13 01	↓		↓	↓	15 49	18 34	↓
Wakinoda "	*Osaka, dep. 22.30*		10 53	12 16			13 06	14 33		17 24	↓	15 55	18 42	19 26
Takada "		*Osaka, dep. 2.17*	10 59	12 24	12 58		13 15	14 39	16 05	17 31	15 23	16 30	18 50	19 32
Kasugayama "			11 05	12 30	13 04		13 25	14 45	16 13	17 37	↓	16 37	18 56	19 38
Naoetsu arr.	10 20		11 03	12 35	13 09		13 30	14 50	16 18	17 42	15 32	16 42	19 02	19 43
dep.	10 32	*Sea of Japan Special Express*	11 16			13 19	13 34	15 00	16 30	17 48	15 38			19 54
Kuroi "	↓		11 21			↓	13 38	15 06	16 35	17 54	*Kanazawa arr. 19 07*			19 59
Saigata "	↓		11 28			↓	13 44	15 14	16 42	18 01				20 07
Katamachi "	↓		11 34			↓	13 50	15 21	16 49	18 08				20 14
Jogehama "	↓		11 39			↓	13 55	15 26	16 54	18 13				20 19
Kakizaki "	↓		11 45		13 39		13 59	15 34	17 01	18 19				20 25
Hassaki "	↓		11 53		↓		14 07	15 42	17 12	18 28				20 34
Kasashima "	↓		11 59		↓		14 12	15 48	17 18	18 34				20 40
Omigawa "	↓		12 04		↓		14 17	15 54	17 23	18 39				20 50
Kujiranami "	↓		12 10		↓		14 22	16 04	17 28	18 46				20 56
Kashiwazaki arr.	11 12		12 16		14 01		14 27	16 11	17 34	18 53				21 03
dep.	11 14		12 19		14 04		14 34	16 20	17 36	18 54				
Yasuda "	↓		12 27		14 12		*To Niigata (via Echigo Line) arr. 17 00*	16 30	17 44	19 03				
Kitajo "	↓		12 32		14 17			16 40	17 49	19 08				
Echigo-Hirota "	↓		12 38		14 23			16 46	17 54	19 14			*Nagaoka*	
Nagatori "	↓		12 44		14 29			16 53	18 02	19 20				
Tsukayama "	↓		12 53		14 37			17 03	18 11	19 29				*Nishi-Ojiya 18 43*
Echigo-Iwatsuka "	↓		12 59		14 44			17 10	18 18	19 36			30	
Raikoji "	↓		13 05		14 49			17 19	18 24	19 42			20 08	↵
Miyauchi "	↓		13 14		14 57			17 28	18 31	19 51			20 23	
Nagaoka arr.	11 56		13 19		15 02			17 33	18 39	19 57			20 31	
Higashi-Sanjo arr.	12 24	*Aomori arr. 22.28*	14 13		15 34			18 26		20 52				
Niitsu "	12 54		14 56		16 18			19 12		21 37				
Niigata "	↓		15 38		16 38			19 48		22 18				

"Your maid, eh?" There was a note of frustration in the chief inspector's voice. A maid's testimony couldn't be trusted. There was no telling what lies she might spin after being bribed by her mistress. "Anybody else?"

"I'm afraid there's nobody but the maid who can vouch for me for the time between Sekiyama and Wakinoda. But it's a fact that I was on the train the entire time. I'm sure if you ask my maid she'll be able to confirm this."

"Of that I've no doubt. All the same, we'd very much like to hear evidence from somebody *other* than your maid. It would help us a great deal if there were another person who could confirm that you were on this train."

Fumie looked down and thought—or rather, perhaps it would have been more accurate to say that she looked as though she was thinking. Either way, the chief inspector and Kaya could only take this gesture at face value.

"I don't know if this will satisfy you," she said, "but there's a trustworthy girl, a student I hired to look after the house while I was away. She saw us both to the station. I'm sure she could vouch for us. And the conductor is another possibility: just after the train left Kashiwazaki, I went to his compartment to report some lost property."

"And what was it, this 'lost property'?" the chief inspector pressed immediately.

"A stamp book. You see, I have a hobby of collecting station stamps. I'd chosen to go on the Shin'etsu line this time because I wanted to get the stamps from Karuizawa onwards. I've been to Karuizawa countless times before, so I've got all those ones. And I've already got all the stations along the Joetsu line, because of all my husband's business trips to the factory in Nagaoka. I don't have any stamps from Nagano Prefecture, though."

245

The chief inspector nodded, making a show of understanding. He had been wondering why Fumie had taken the time-consuming option of the stopping train on the Shin'etsu line.

"And what exactly went missing?"

"Why, the book itself. After I'd got the stamp at Kashiwazaki, I went to buy some rice crackers for my maid and I must have dropped it. I wouldn't have minded so much, had it just been stamps from that line, but the book had all the stamps from my trip to Tohoku last year. So, I couldn't just let it go and went to report it to the conductor. It was a waste of time in the end…"

Fumie looked crestfallen, while Kaya kept scribbling away with his pencil.

"This student you employed… What's her name?"

"She's a second-year student in the English faculty at the ladies' college. Her name's Seiko Mano."

"And is your maid at home right now?"

"She is, yes. She's from somewhere up in the mountains in Chiba. Tai Okuwa is her name. A real country girl!"

"Thank you, Mrs Hishinuma. Will you excuse me for a moment?"

With a slight bow, he got up and left the room. Naturally, this was so that he could contact headquarters and dispatch some detectives there. There was still light in the western sky.

"There's one thing I neglected to ask you, Mrs Hishinuma," he said when he returned. "This No. 311 train left Omiya Station at 6.26, didn't it?"

"That's correct, yes."

"I just wonder: why did you take such an early train? For instance, you could have taken the No. 313, which left an hour later. If you'd done that, you wouldn't have had to get up so early."

"I wouldn't have been in time for the big dinner at the hotel, otherwise. Everybody had to be there for six-thirty, and I had to show my face there. The No. 313 got in too late."

The chief inspector checked the timetable once again. Just as she said, while the train left Ueno only an hour or so later, it took its time along the way and pulled into Nagaoka almost two and half hours after the earlier one. A train arriving at 7.57 p.m. would indeed have meant missing an event that started at 6.30.

A silence ensued.

"Well, if you've quite finished with your questions," the lawyer ventured at last, "there's something I'd like to ask."

"By all means, Mr Nukariya."

"You seem to think that it was my client who killed both the director and Hanpei Chita. Are you suggesting, therefore, that she was also responsible for the death of Genkichi Obata?"

There was a note of belligerence in his voice.

"I cannot deny it," the chief inspector replied.

He agreed with Inspector Sudo's theory that the person pulling the strings behind the scenes—the same person who had sent Genkichi Obata to the Orchid as a decoy that night—had to be Nishinohata's killer. It hadn't been Hanpei Chita. Nor had it been the chairman or the vice-chairman of the labour union. That much could be proven logically. In the end, given that the body had happened to fall on top of a moving train, thus revealing the time of the murder, the decoy himself had become irrelevant. Only, the murderer hadn't trusted him to keep quiet about it—and the only way to ensure his silence had been to kill him.

As he answered the lawyer, the chief inspector found himself going over the logic, one step at a time.

"Very well. Then permit me to ask a few questions of my own. After my client returned home from the chemists, she went straight to bed. In other words, there is nobody to confirm her actions after—say—eleven-thirty. Right?" The two little eyes on his berry-brown face looked at the chief inspector almost triumphantly. "Why, then, would my client have sent the decoy to the Chinese restaurant to make it look as though the director was still alive at ten to midnight, when she herself had no alibi for that time? Making it look as though the director had been killed *after* eleven-fifty would only be to her disadvantage."

The chief inspector, too, had a quick mind, and he didn't have to hear out the old lawyer's explanation before he grasped his point. To be told all this in such a smug, tedious manner was infuriating. With a bitter look on his face, the chief inspector looked out of the window.

"My client, you see, had no need to create a decoy—much less, to kill Genkichi Obata."

"Yes, I see," the chief inspector replied, without looking at him.

What the lawyer said certainly made sense. Until now, there had been no doubt that whoever murdered Nishinohata had also been the person responsible for the decoy. Yet the hypothesis that Fumie Hishinuma was the murderer could invalidate this theory. The chief inspector had been careless not to realize this. It was bad enough that he had unwittingly let a suspect off the hook, but even worse that it had taken the lawyer to point this out.

3.

After the call came through from headquarters, Sudo and Seki were dispatched to Omiya.

"I'm learning an awful lot on this case!" Seki said cheerfully, as they waited for a Keihin–Tohoku-line train on the platform at Ueno Station.

Until now, he had carried out only background checks and low-level investigative work, but these were rather humble, unsung jobs. It was only after he'd teamed up with the veteran detective that he was at last able to get stuck in. Sudo replied with a toothy grin, the meaning of which Seki couldn't quite fathom. He wanted to ask about it, but, with so many people crowding the platform, there was a terrific din, and so he decided to maintain a discreet, sensible silence.

The journey from Ueno to Omiya took forty minutes. The packed carriage began to empty out after they passed Urawa, and at Yono they were finally able to get a seat. The toe of Seki's shoe collided with a lady's folding fan, which had accidentally been left on the floor. It was a small, pretty object, made of carved bone, and, as he watched it roll away, he instinctively checked that his own fan was secure in his belt, fearing the scalding from his wife that would inevitably follow if he lost it.

When they passed through the ticket barrier, the scene that met them in front of the station was much the same as you'd see anywhere. Cafés alternated with booking offices for taxis, and over in a corner a university student in an academic cap was shouting hoarsely, making a speech attacking the government. It seemed a pity that, during the bustle of rush hour, not a single person stopped to listen to him.

Across the street from them was a large beer hall. When he spotted it, Inspector Sudo licked his lips.

"Say, here's an idea. Since what Hishinuma's wife said will probably turn out to be a load of codswallop, this shouldn't take long. Why don't we stop off there for a drink and a bite to eat on the way back? My treat."

As they went past the beer hall, the inspector was unable to keep his eyes off it.

The Hoashi Pharmacy was in the Daimoncho neighbourhood, about a fifteen-minute walk from the station. They'd memorized the street names from a map, so found their way without getting lost. Among the many old shops in the area, the Hoashi Pharmacy alone was new, and gave an impression of cleanliness and good hygiene.

At the back of the shop there was a glass-walled room lined with display cases, on the door of which was written in gold lettering: DISPENSING ROOM. Through the glass, lined up on the shelves, medicine bottles, scales and mortars could be glimpsed.

As the two men entered, the white-coated owner stood up, ready to take their order. He was a fair-skinned man of around forty, with light-brown hair and eyes.

They had been ordered to tread very carefully. In other words, they were not to give any indication that Mrs Hishinuma was being treated as a suspect in a case.

"You wouldn't happen to know a Mrs Hishinuma, would you?" the inspector began in a familiar tone. With his unassuming, ordinary appearance, Sudo had an uncanny ability to get the other person to open up to him right away—a wonder that Seki had observed many times already.

"I certainly know her face, yes."

"Is she a regular customer of yours?"

"No, she doesn't come here all that often."

"You mean she usually sends her maid instead?"

"No, I just mean that she doesn't come in very often. She's a beautiful woman—that's why I remember her face."

"Yes, I see. Well, we're here because a cat burglar broke into Mrs Hishinuma's house recently."

"Oh? I wasn't aware of that."

The pharmacist's face suddenly turned serious.

"The fact that we don't yet know when exactly it happened is hampering the investigation somewhat. Mrs Hishinuma told us that she once went out in the middle of the night without locking the door and believes it must have been then. Apparently, she came here to get some medicine."

"Oh, yes, I see," the pharmacist said, appearing now to realize why they had come.

"It would be a tremendous help to us if you could tell us the date and time. You wouldn't happen to remember, would you?"

"Let me see, now. I wonder whether it could be the night when I prescribed her some painkillers?"

"Yes, I believe she said she had a headache."

"Oh, it wasn't a headache. She had stomach cramps. I gave her a preparation of scopolamine, camphor and phenacetin. She told me how well it had worked for her."

"And when was this?"

The pharmacist shouted to somebody in the back room and left the two men, returning soon afterwards with a prescription card.

"It was on the night of the first of June. At eleven-thirty. I remember it well, because I'd actually just closed the shop."

"That's very useful to know. And you're sure about the time?" Sudo asked, staring at the owner's pale face. After taking the long route, he had finally arrived at the question.

"Absolutely. As I say, it was just after I closed the shop for the night, so I remember it well. And I have it written down on the prescription right here. A good pharmacist always keeps a record of these things—we're responsible for what we prescribe, after all."

The man handed them the prescription, and, sure enough, written there in ink was the name Fumie Hishinuma, alongside the date and the name of the medicine dispensed. Seeing that the time had been recorded at the bottom of the page in the same pen and handwriting, both Sudo and Seki were satisfied with the man's testimony.

4.

Leaving the pharmacy and carrying on eastward along the road, you reached the historic Nakasendo Road. Cutting across it and turning left would then take you onto the approach towards the Hikawa shrine, where there was a rather ramshackle-looking shopping precinct that had been thrown up just after war. Follow the street up, and, just before you enter the grounds of this Shinto shrine, turn right, and you'll find yourself in Takahanacho. As this newly developed residential area was intended for salarymen, it had already lost the rustic charm of the old post-station town that it had once been.

There, within the fenced gardens, husbands, who had just come home from work, had already changed into shorts and were out watering their lawns with a hose, or, having changed into their *yukata* after a quick bath, now stood admiring the pale-white blossom of their calabashes. Each house exuded a sense of peace and tranquillity. For a busy police detective, it was an unfamiliar sight.

The Hishinumas' house lay just beyond this middle-class neighbourhood. The first thing anybody approaching the house would see was a steeply sloping red roof set behind mature cypress trees. It was a rather old mock-Tudor building with what looked to be quite a few rooms inside, and through the dusk the white plaster walls and criss-crossing black timbers displayed a beautiful harmony. There was a lawn at the front and a small shed that looked like a garage at the rear. One of the house windows was lit up, and a small plump woman, who appeared to be in the middle of preparing dinner, kept going in and out through the wide-open kitchen door.

"That must be the maid, Tai Okuwa," Sudo said as they stood by the gate.

"I don't see lights on in any of the other rooms."

"The husband probably isn't back yet. Let's go round the side and ask."

The detectives entered the property, walked through the garden and round to the back door. There was a smell of cooking oil in the air, and they could hear the sizzling of something frying. Seki looked at the inspector. His eyes seemed to be saying: this'll be easy.

"Hello?" Seki called.

The roar of frying oil was fierce, and the maid seemed not to be able to hear him. Finally, though, after the third attempt, he got a response. The woman squealed like a wild pig when she saw the two strange men standing in the twilit garden. By the time they got her to understand the reason for their visit, the food in the pot had burnt, and she began to wail again.

"Have you ever been to Nagaoka?" Inspector Sudo asked, sitting down in the nearest chair after they were permitted to enter. The kitchen, as one would expect of an upper-middle-class house, was furnished with a stainless-steel sink, a large electric refrigerator, a gas range and a small radio hanging on the wall. The maid would always hum along to popular songs while she cooked.

"Yes," she replied.

She had removed the pan from the heat, turned off the gas and now sat down opposite the inspector. Because of a bad nose, she had to breathe through her mouth, so her lips were constantly parted, revealing a set of horse-like teeth. There was no light in her eyes, and she looked rather dim-witted.

"And when was this?"

The maid held out her fingers and began to count, folding her fingers one by one.

Though she may have been simple, she was also honest to a fault.

"On the fourteenth of June."

"And who did you go with?"

"The mistress."

"The mistress? Which one? Next door's?"

"Oh, no! *My* mistress."

Lest he frighten her, Sudo asked his questions slowly and with a kindly expression on his face. She in turn responded slowly, as it appeared was her wont.

"And when did you take the train?"

"You'd have to ask the mistress."

"All right, we'll do that when she gets home. And were you with her the whole time?"

A brief silence followed. The maid seemed not to understand the question and just played with her hair without saying anything.

"When you left Omiya and went all the way to Nagaoka, were you sitting with your mistress all the time?"

"Yes," she replied at last. "Only, she'd go down onto the platform from time to time. She had to get her book stamped."

"And does she still have her stamp book?"

The maid shook her round, reddish face.

"What happened to it?"

"She dropped it."

"Oh? Then what happened?"

"She reported it to the conductor. He told her that somebody would pick it up and hand it in."

"And where was this?"

"I don't remember the name of the station. But it was just a little before we arrived in Nagaoka."

The detectives looked at each other instinctively. The more they asked, the more it looked as though Fumie Hishinuma's story checked out.

Suddenly, the sound of the front door being opened reached them.

"Tai!… Tai!…" a woman's voice called out.

"Welcome home, mistress!" the maid shouted, flustered.

If the mistress found out that she'd allowed not one but two strange men into the kitchen, she knew she'd be reprimanded.

"It's the mistress," she said. "She's home."

In contrast to her panic, Sudo was cool and composed. He still had questions to ask.

"What on earth's the matter with you?!… Are you there?!"

Receiving no response, Fumie seemed angry, her voice now rising imperiously. Looking bewildered, the maid was about to get up to greet her, when suddenly the door flew open and in came Fumie.

"We're from the criminal investigations department, madam. We've come to verify your story."

"Well, well! Tell me, gentlemen, what have you found?"

The inspector didn't know what material it was made of, but in the light hanging from the ceiling, her silver dress was the most beautiful colour. Her chest seemed to undulate with every deep breath she took.

"Well? Out with it!"

Fumie's penetrating gaze moved from the inspector to Seki and then back.

"It's just as you say, madam."

"Well, of course it is! I was telling the truth."

"Since you're here, though, there are one or two other things I'd like to ask," Sudo persisted.

He wanted her to answer the questions he hadn't yet had time to ask the maid.

"And those are?"

"When you travelled to Nagaoka, which class did you travel in?"

"Third class," she replied. "Tai, the bus will be coming soon, so get ready."

When the maid had left, Fumie stood in front of the electric refrigerator and leant lightly against its pale-cream-coloured rectangular body.

"I'd never say it in front of her, but I'd feel rather sorry for her if she rode in second class with me. She knows well enough that she's unsightly and isn't the right sort of person to be in second class. Despite how she looks, she's actually quite intelligent and isn't entirely oblivious to such things. Then again, if I were to travel in second class by myself, it would be like rubbing her face in it. That's why I prefer to sit in third with her."

"And what about hotels?"

"That's different. I always put her up at a nice little inn in town. I'd hate to put her among pretentious people and make a laughing stock of her, but I have to do as the others do. And not just where the hotel's concerned. On the way back, I travelled with the rest of them in second class and sent her on ahead with a third-class ticket on the overnight train."

Though her tone was matter of fact, she exhibited considerable tact where this bumpkin of a maid was concerned. Or at least that was the impression she gave.

5.

By now, the sun had completely set. When they reached the station, there were a lot of people milling around, many of whom were carrying fans and had on *yukata*. From the right-hand side of the station came the sound of *taiko* drummers, beating time for the evening dances that began the summer night's festivities. All the young men and women in traditional dress were flowing towards the music.

"What do you say then?"

"About what?"

"The beer hall! We didn't really find out anything interesting. But maybe Takeda's having a better time of it. Let's have a drink and toast to his success."

Inspector Takeda and his partner had gone to take a statement from the conductor on train No. 311. Sudo appeared to want a drink under any pretext.

"Why not!"

Seki was all for the idea. The prospect of cracking open a cold beer made his empty stomach gurgle in delight.

"I'll go and find out how they're getting on."

There was a red public telephone just outside the tobacconist's, next door to the station. Sudo placed an out-of-town call, while Seki stood by the side of the road and lit a cigarette. As he looked across the road, the neon lights of the beer hall were gaily flashing red, blue and magenta, trying to provoke a feeling of longing in his stomach. In the window beside the entrance, there were rows of waxwork fried prawns, eel *kabayaki*, *nigirizushi* and other delicacies that would make you drool even on a full stomach; each one the idealized representation of its real-life counterpart. When Seki thought about it, it had been a long time since he had last seen any of these dishes.

After the call, Sudo returned. His forehead was drenched in perspiration. He took a damp handkerchief from his pocket and mopped his brow and dabbed his little moustache.

"Well, sir?"

"Damn it! It looks like we'll have to postpone those celebratory beers."

"But why?"

"The results of Takeda's investigation weren't great either. Apparently, the Mano girl who was employed to watch the house also confirmed Mrs Hishinuma's story. She said she was certain that the lady boarded the No. 311 at Omiya Station early on the morning of the fourteenth. The conductor on duty also confirmed that she reported her stamp book missing. It would appear she's been telling the truth this whole time!"

"So, Mrs Hishinuma could be innocent?"

"It's starting to look that way, yes. And if she is, then somebody else must be responsible for the deaths of Chita, Obata and the director…"

The two men stood there in silence, looking deflated. And not just because a cold beer was off the menu. There had been a faint flicker of light, hinting that the case had been solved, but it had lasted for only a moment. Now, yet again, the investigation had been plunged into darkness. Truly, their disappointment was justified.

THIRTEEN

Bamboo-Leaf Toffee

1.

"If only the voice actor had said something…" Tanna kept repeating to himself as he turned to Inspector Onitsura.

The chief inspector had ordered the two men to re-examine Fumie's alibi. According to the hospital, both Murase and Narumi were still in a critical condition, and were still unconscious.

The hostess from the Black Swan said that Murase had been scornful of the authorities' approach to the investigation, and that he believed they'd made a grave and fundamental error of which they weren't even aware. No matter what he did, the criminal investigation headquarters hadn't paid him the slightest bit of notice. Only, with things the way they were, they could no longer afford to ignore his claims.

"It must be awfully hard to sleep when you're wrapped up in bandages in this heat," Tanna observed flatly.

"Apparently, as they're both unconscious I doubt they can feel heat or pain. They'd be better off staying in a coma until their wounds heal."

"What? So, it's only us poor sods who have to deal with it?!"

As he wiped his sweaty forehead with a starched handkerchief, Tanna squinted out of the window, which was reflecting the intense sunlight. Onitsura stood up, lowered the blind and returned to his desk to face his partner.

"There was something that struck me while I was listening to the chief inspector's report on her alibis. I wonder whether you spotted it, too?"

Tanna rifled through the witness statements, but he couldn't immediately think what it was that the inspector was hinting at.

"Hmm… I'm not sure I did, sir. What was it that you noticed?"

"It was in the statement given by Matsuoka, the conductor on the No. 311."

As he weighed the inspector's words, a look of perplexity appeared on Tanna's tanned face and stayed there without fading. Fumie Hishinuma had claimed that she had dropped her stamp book on the platform of Kashiwazaki Station while on her way to Nagaoka, while the conductor, Matsuoka, had testified that she had come to his compartment directly after that to report the loss. There was no discrepancy between the two statements in terms of date or time, and the story had also been corroborated by the maid, Tai Okuwa. No matter how he scrutinized it, Tanna could find nothing suspicious in the conductor's statement.

"Do you see?"

"I'm afraid not, sir…"

Onitsura smiled. His chin seemed to jut out even more whenever there was that look of confidence on his face.

"If I hadn't been paying attention, I might not have noticed it myself. She boarded the train in question on the fourteenth of last month, right? Whereas the conductor provided his statement on the eighth of this month. Almost four weeks have passed between those two dates."

"That's correct, sir."

"Have you ever glimpsed a woman on the train and still remembered her face clearly after so much time?"

"I don't think so, sir... Not unless there was something particularly memorable about it."

Tanna finally grasped what the inspector was getting at. And, having understood it, he also knew what Onitsura would try to do next. Tanna could tell that he was pinning a lot of hope on this.

"Would you like me to go?"

"No," the inspector said, snapping his fan shut. "This time, I'll go myself."

2.

The train conductor's house was in Ogumachi, in Tokyo's Arakawa Ward. Although located on a lowland near the Arakawa River, the land was always dry, dusty and grey due to the poor quality of the soil. Because of this, everything there grew slowly, and there were no tree-lined avenues. The sooty factories and workshops that were nestled among the houses lent the area an even bleaker impression. The area was home to numerous cottage industries, so it was only natural there should be many factory workers living there, but second to these in number were the railway workers, who were employed either at Oku Station on the Tohoku line or at the local depot. This was a distinctive feature of the town.

Mr Matsuoka lived at the end of a narrow alley just beyond the ring road. In his garden, he had a trellis growing sponge gourds, and, when Inspector Onitsura called on him, he was watering them dressed only in his underwear. For all his efforts, the gourds were rather measly, no bigger than regular cucumbers.

"What can I do for you, Inspector?" he asked, looking up from the business card Onitsura had given him. Set against his protruding cheekbones, his eyes had a look of sincerity about them.

Before he explained the reason for his visit, Onitsura took in the appearance of the house. They couldn't very well discuss his business standing outside, but at the same time he hated to intrude on the conductor's family in their cramped quarters.

"Is there a quiet café where we could go and talk?" Onitsura asked.

Matsuoka ducked into the house and soon reappeared, wearing a short-sleeved shirt and white trousers.

The two walked down the now slightly softened paved road towards the large avenue that led back to Showa-machi and entered a smart café that seemed out of place in this dusty part of the city. The narrow shopfront opened to reveal an equally small interior. Placed with great care on a counter in the middle was a display of early chrysanthemums and carnations encased in ice. The heat had melted the block halfway, and the tips of the red petals were already peeking out.

They were lucky that the place was empty. The inspector sat down in a corner and ordered something cold. On the wall beside him hung a picture of a mermaid done in the style of Seiji Togo; her soft, hazy features somehow reminded him of Fumie.

"I'm sorry to make demands on your time outside of working hours," the inspector apologized, returning his gaze from the picture to Matsuoka.

"It must be a real nuisance to be visited and questioned over and again by the police."

"Not at all, Inspector," the conductor answered succinctly.

There was a glimmer of a smile in his little eyes that could easily have been missed.

"Would you mind confirming for me once more that Mrs Hishinuma was on the train?"

Instead of answering directly, Matsuoka launched into the following story.

"It was on the fourteenth of last month. I was on duty on the No. 311, the down train to Niigata, and the lady came to my compartment to tell me that she'd lost her stamp book on the platform at Kashiwazaki Station. She said she wasn't sure whether she'd dropped it or it had been stolen, but said that, since nobody was very likely to steal a stamp book, she'd probably just dropped it somewhere, and would I please return it to her if it turned up? I asked for her name and address there and then and passed them on to the station staff at Kashiwazaki."

"And when was this?"

The conductor paused for a moment and said: "Let's see now, it was just after we left Echigo–Hirota, so it must have been around ten to five."

When Onitsura took out his timetable, he saw that the train was due to depart Echigo–Hirota at 16.46. It was therefore plausible that Fumie had indeed gone to see the conductor around 16.50. At any rate, it couldn't have been much earlier than this.

Two ice creams arrived. They picked up their spoons at the same time and set about tackling the white mass. The coldness numbed their tongues and stung their teeth. Meanwhile, outside on the ring road, a trolleybus tottered past, as though its great bulk were too big for the street.

"Allow me to change the subject, Mr Matsuoka."

Without realizing it, the inspector had adopted a more formal tone. As Matsuoka placed his spoon down on his plate, the expression on his face slightly hardened as he looked at the inspector.

"As you just said, Mrs Hishinuma reported the loss to you on the fourteenth of last month. How is it that you can remember her face so distinctly after all this time?"

Perhaps because of Onitsura's deadpan expression, the conductor didn't seem to understand what he was being asked and just sat there, blinking repeatedly. The inspector had to repeat his question.

"It's really quite simple, Inspector," he said eventually. "Twice after that, she returned to my compartment to check whether or not the stamp book had been found. All in all, I got a good look at her face. The book never did get handed in, but the lady must have given up, since she never came back after that."

With that, the conductor picked up his spoon again. Because of the terrific heat, both ice creams had already half-melted.

Though the inspector didn't let it show, deep down he felt rather disappointed. It wasn't in the least surprising that a person who'd lost a cherished stamp book would return to the conductor's compartment several times to see whether it had been found. The fact that Matsuoka had remembered Fumie's face had seemed odd at first, but, after hearing this story, it seemed perfectly natural. There had been only one avenue left to exploit in the sole suspect's alibi, and now, in a flash, that had been blocked off. Fumie's alibi was watertight: unassailable from every angle.

Though despairing at first, Onitsura soon felt further motivation to crack this alibi. It was the very perfection of it that lit a fire under him.

So: how and where should he start? There was only one thing for it. He had to go and visit the two remaining witnesses, listen to their witness statements and take a magnifying glass to them. He needed to find any mistakes, oversights or inconsistencies that might have been missed.

3.

First, Onitsura had to pay a visit to the student, Seiko Mano; then he would make his way to Omiya. Enrolled at the same ladies' college where Fumie and Atsuko Suma had once studied, Seiko was the girl who had been employed by Fumie to watch over the house while she was away in Nagaoka. When Onitsura rang her apartment, he was informed that she had gone to study at the college library.

Having said goodbye to the conductor, the inspector walked back to Oku Station, where he caught a train down to Ueno, changed to the Yamanote line and then travelled on to Meguro, where Seiko's college was.

It was a mere mile and a half from Meguro Station to the ladies' college, but nevertheless there was a regular bus service, which Onitsura took. The journey reminded him of a time several years ago when he happened to ride this jam-packed bus along with a gaggle of college girls. Confirmed bachelor that he was, he was unfamiliar with the fairer sex and had never shared a space with them so intimately. The cramped bus had soon filled with the piquant smell of their bodies, a kind of sweet and sour aroma that was not at all the sort of odour that would charm a man, but rather one that provoked in him a sense of psychological discomfort, one he wished never to experience again. Arriving at his destination, he had stepped out into the fresh air and, with a sense of acute sympathy for the driver, breathed deeply.

This day, however, the bus was empty. During the summer holiday, hardly anybody used the service. Eventually, it reached its final destination, where Onitsura got off. He crossed the wide street and found himself in front of a big iron gate. The college was young, having been founded only in the late 1920s, but it had a reputation for its liberal education. Naturally, when the second Sino-Japanese War broke out in the late thirties, the college had become a target for numerous crackdowns by the military authorities, and several of its teachers had even been forced out.

The gate was firmly closed, but beside it there was a small service entrance. From there, he could see a grass-covered court with a gently curving gravel path leading to a white schoolhouse with a clock tower in the middle. It was deserted but for a large Chinese peacock butterfly that was fluttering about over the dark-green lawn. Guessing that the oblong russet building opposite the schoolhouse must be the library, Onitsura proceeded in that direction.

Plane trees, laurels, metasequoias and other rare trees, which must have been planted to commemorate certain events, surrounded the library, creating a lovely shade. Perhaps because of this, the air in the library felt surprisingly cool. Onitsura asked a student who was perusing the noticeboard about Seiko Mano, whereupon she disappeared into the stacks, only to return with Seiko moments later.

This was the first time that the inspector had set eyes on the girl. Her large, robust frame was covered by a white dress, and, with no trace of powder or lipstick on her face, she wasn't at all pretty, but instead she had a healthy brightness about her. She led Onitsura over to the shade of a eucalyptus tree and sat down on a bench, facing him.

"If it's about Mrs Hishinuma, I spoke to the police just the other day…"

She looked up at the inspector who was standing in front of her. There was a note of protest in her voice, probably occasioned by annoyance at being questioned by the police yet again or else at having her studies interrupted. As if to pacify her, Onitsura sat down and, in his innately calm tone, began to enquire how it was that she came to be asked to look after Fumie's house.

"I saw an advertisement for it at the school club. She was looking for somebody who wasn't going away for the summer break, and since I don't like travelling all that much, I was a perfect fit, so I answered it. Why are you so interested in this lady anyway?"

It was an obvious question for the girl to ask. It was also one that Onitsura had anticipated.

"We're making a range of enquiries, not only concerning Mrs Hishinuma. It all has to do with a case we're investigating, so we're questioning everybody without exception—that is to say, eleven individuals in total."

The explanation was plausible enough, and the girl seemed to accept it without question.

"It must be hard having to work in this heat," she said sympathetically.

"It's all part of the job, I'm afraid… Incidentally, would you mind telling me at what time Mrs Hishinuma left you in charge of the house?"

Onitsura reached out and brushed off a caterpillar that was clinging to her clothes. No woman likes caterpillars, after all. Although it wasn't his intention, his action seemed to make a good impression on her, and, brightening up, she lost a little of her reserve.

"I visited the house the day before she went away and was given the grand tour. Then, the morning after that, I got up early and saw her off at Omiya Station. Her suitcases seemed awfully small, but then again, I suppose there were five of them, stuffed full of her mourning clothes and various other things. She and the maid couldn't carry them all by themselves."

"When you say 'the morning after that', which day do you mean exactly?"

"The fourteenth of last month."

"And which train did Mrs Hishinuma take?"

"It was the one going to Niigata."

"What time did it depart?"

"The other inspector asked me the same question just the other day, so I remember it clearly. It left Omiya at 6.26," she said briskly, without any hesitation.

Naturally, Onitsura also recalled the time at which the No. 311 left Omiya Station.

"And you're sure she didn't take the train that left for Niigata an hour later?"

Seiko nodded vigorously.

"That detective asked me the same question. She took the 6.26 train. The train you're asking about left Omiya at 7.34, so there can't be any mistaking it. At half past seven, everybody's already awake, but when we went to the station, the whole town was still asleep."

"One more question, if I may. Did anybody accompany Mrs Hishinuma on the trip?"

"Yes, her maid. She's fat—if you don't mind my saying so—and a bit slow. The two of them sat side by side in a third-class carriage. I remember her saying how glad she was that they'd managed to get a seat."

"What did you make of Mrs Hishinuma?"

"She's clever. And she has a mind of her own. No other wife of an executive would ever have ridden in third class with her maid. I hate to speak ill of my sisters, but it isn't easy for a woman to have that kind of empathy."

Once again, Onitsura's questioning had been in vain. If anything, Seiko's answers had only lent further credence to Fumie's

268

alibi and reinforced the inspector's impression of her as a particularly determined woman. This was supported by what the proprietress of the brothel in Tobita had told him. It was, moreover, clear to him that a woman possessed of such strength of character wouldn't hesitate to kill a man once she had made up her mind to do so.

4.

Inspector Onitsura got off at Omiya Station and, although he had memorized the route beforehand, mistakenly took the east exit. His mind must have been hazy because of the heat. The town of Omiya spread out to the west of the station, while to the east lay almost entirely undeveloped land. As soon as he stepped out of the ticket gate, he noticed the vast gulf between the bustling west exit and the gloomy eastern one. He tutted at the blunder and, taking the overpass, crossed the tracks back to the western side.

As he walked westward through Daimoncho, he came upon the Hoashi Pharmacy just as he was about to reach the Nakasendo Road. He could see what looked to be the owner in a white coat deep in conversation with a man who had a bandage wrapped around his head. Half a dozen medicine bottles of varying sizes were lined up in front of the customer. The pharmacist appeared to be describing the efficacy of each one with a mix of words and gestures.

Onitsura crossed the Nakasendo Road and turned left, heading up the shop-lined street towards the Hikawa shrine. In the chaos after the war, these ramshackle shopping precincts were wont to spring up in the unlikeliest of places. Though the shops on this approach had a well-worn look about them, they all had a certain vitality, more typical of a new, up-and-coming area. There was a florist's, a confectioner's, a tofu-monger's and a butcher's. As he walked along, Onitsura's eye was suddenly caught by a pharmacy with a signboard that read: Temple of Remedy. The number of medicines on display was as great as that in Hoashi Pharmacy in Daimoncho. Perhaps because of the rivalry between these two pharmacies, this shop, too, was large and clean and had a magnificent room with the words "DISPENSING ROOM" written in gold lettering. Yet it was not these baubles that attracted the inspector's attention, so much as the unnatural fact that Fumie, who'd been suffering from stomach cramps, went all the way to the far-flung Hoashi Pharmacy, when she could have gone to the Temple of Remedy so much more easily. Onitsura had himself suffered stomach cramps before and knew that they caused no ordinary pain. He also knew that it was human nature to want to stop the pain as soon as possible. So why then had Fumie made the trip to Daimoncho?

As Onitsura saw it, there were two possible explanations for Fumie's visit to the Hoashi Pharmacy. The first was that the Temple of Remedy didn't have the medicine she was looking for. This would be understandable enough. But, given that the Hoashi Pharmacy was so crucial to her alibi, the other possible reason was that by going to the Temple of Remedy there would have been something lacking in her alibi; something that only the Hoashi Pharmacy would supply.

Onitsura stopped in his tracks to avoid an oncoming bicycle. What did the Hoashi Pharmacy have that the Temple of Remedy didn't?

He took a few slow steps forward. It seemed as though it ought to be a relatively easy problem to solve. Fumie's alibi was predicated on the evidence of the owner of the Hoashi Pharmacy, which was corroborated by the dispensing record card. It was the card itself that lent credence to the pharmacist's testimony. It could be inferred, then, that the card was the only thing that established the alibi, and that, unlike the Hoashi Pharmacy, the Temple of Remedy kept no records of the medicines they dispensed. Whether this was true could easily be determined by testing it, and so the inspector turned around and purposefully walked back to the Temple of Remedy.

The owner of the pharmacy was a healthy-looking woman in her fifties. She had a mole by the corner of her right eye, traditionally said to be the result of too much weeping, which jarred with her cheerful demeanour.

"What can I do for you?"

"I'd like some medicine for stomach cramps," Onitsura replied vaguely.

The owner turned around to look at the shelves behind her and fetched down a couple of boxes, each one containing the sorts of painkillers one often sees advertised in the newspapers.

"It must be my wife's constitution," the inspector said, "but I'm afraid the over-the-counter ones don't work for her. Could you make up something stronger?"

The pharmacist nodded, entered the dispensing room, took two bottles, one blue, one brown, from the medicine cabinet and mixed their contents in a mortar. Onitsura kept a close eye on her throughout the process, but, as expected, she didn't bother to fill out a dispensing card. Perhaps Fumie, who knew from years of experience which chemists would and would not fill out a card, had come up with the idea of using it as a means to establish a false alibi.

"That'll be 300 yen, please. There's enough here for three doses. Please tell your wife to take one whenever she has an attack."

Having paid and pocketed the paper sachets, the inspector turned to leave, but stopped and asked:

"Could you point me in the direction of Mrs Hishinuma's house? She's the young, good-looking woman who lives nearby…"

"Turn right in front of the *torii* gate, then go straight ahead. You'll see it on your left. It's a big house, so you can't miss it."

Onitsura could see from her expression the fondness she had for her customers. It was clear that the Hishinumas were regulars here.

So, even though the Temple of Remedy could have dispensed prescription medicine, Fumie had avoided it and opted to go to the Hoashi Pharmacy instead.

Onitsura had just glimpsed the artifice of her alibi.

5.

As the inspector neared the Hishinumas' house, the back door opened, and out came a young girl carrying a shopping basket. The coverall apron that she wore only made her portly figure seem larger. Even from a distance, it was clear to see that this was the maid, Tai Okuwa.

Onitsura called her over and soon learnt that he had been correct in his assumption. At first, the maid was mute and seemed shy, but soon enough the inspector's friendly smile put her at her ease, and she told him that she was heading out to buy lard for frying, hence the tin can in her basket. Walking in step with her, they started back the way he had come. They made an odd couple, and several housewives passed them by, giving them strange looks.

The inspector's questioning would surely reach Fumie's ears sooner or later. It wasn't something that could be hidden from her, so he introduced himself properly and took the maid into the Hikawa temple grounds. She was hesitant about going with him, saying that she'd be told off if she was late, but she appeared to be unused to asserting herself, and, in the end gave up and followed him obediently.

After climbing the stone steps and passing the guardian lion, they happened upon a bench in the middle of a grove of old cedars. Wiping away the dust with his handkerchief, he bid the maid take a seat before sitting down beside her. The chirring of the cicadas was relentless. Apart from four or five children wandering around with insect nets, there was nobody else in sight.

"Do you remember the time you went to Nagaoka with your mistress?" he said with a look of encouragement.

Her mouth hung open and her expression was vacant, so much so that he wasn't entirely sure that she had understood the question.

"… Yes."

"And who did you go with?"

"… The mistress."

"And did the mistress go off at any point, leaving you alone on the train?"

"No, we were together the whole time."

The maid replied slowly, as though she didn't understand why she was being asked the question. Onitsura sat there patiently, trying each point from various angles, making sure of it before moving on to the next. It took so long that he began to feel sorry for the maid and the scolding she'd get from Fumie, but he couldn't stop now.

In the end, however, despite his efforts, he was unable to get anything out of her that she hadn't already told Seki and Sudo. She and Fumie had gone to Omiya Station early in the morning and boarded a train bound for Nagaoka. She insisted that the student, Seiko Mano, had come to see them off at Omiya, helping with the luggage, and that she and Fumie had been together all the way to Nagaoka. That it was all told in that same dull, emotionless tone of voice only made it seem all the more credible. It was more than just credible, though: by all accounts, it had to be true. As he looked at the blank, guileless face of Tai Okuwa, not only did he believe that she wasn't lying: he believed that she was incapable of it. Even if Fumie had told her to lie, it was unimaginable that this slow-witted girl would have been able to pull the wool over the eyes of the experienced Inspector Sudo. Not only that, but she also corroborated what Seiko Mano had said only a few hours previously: that the train they had boarded at Omiya Station on the 14th was the 6.26 a.m. Nagaoka-bound service. Taken together, these two statements appeared to confirm that, just as she had claimed, Fumie had been on a train between Sekiyama and Wakinoda at the time when Hanpei Chita was killed in Kurojo.

Onitsura lapsed deep into thought. Anxious about the time, the maid began to fidget. Beside the temple, some children began to fight over a cicada, and a little girl burst into tears. There, in the cedar grove, the evening colours were growing darker.

"Umm… may I go now?"

"Yes," Onitsura replied listlessly.

He sounded resigned. No matter how he questioned her, he was unlikely to find out anything new. He had neither the cause nor the pretext to detain her any longer. If anything else came up later, he would have to telephone her.

"I'm sorry to have kept you," he said, after thanking her. "If the mistress scolds you, tell her it was my fault."

He had no way of knowing whether Fumie would be assuaged by this excuse for the delay with her dinner, or whether she would forgive the maid. Thinking this, he felt sorry for this good-natured girl and regretted having detained her so long.

"If I want to ask you anything else, I'll call. What's your telephone number?" the inspector asked, standing up and dusting off his trousers.

Tai Okuwa stood there, holding her shopping basket with great care. She placed her hand into the pocket of her apron and began to rummage around for something.

"… I have it written on a piece of paper. Otherwise I'd forget it," she said, her hand still moving.

"Let me help you with that," the inspector said, indicating the basket.

"Thank you."

She handed the basket to him and carried on rifling through her pocket, until at last she pulled out a scrap of green paper. She unfolded it clumsily with her fat fingers and proceeded to read out the telephone number that had been scribbled down on the back of it.

"Thanks," the inspector said, closing his notebook and casually glancing at the piece of paper she was still holding.

Onitsura recognized the plain wrapper. Lithographed onto the green background was some red calligraphy, which read: *Bamboo-Leaf Toffee. An Echigo–Yuzawa Speciality*. The inspector may not have been much of a drinker, but he did have a sweet tooth. When he'd travelled to Niigata about five years after the war, he'd seen and bought one of these on the platform at Yuzawa Station. However, it had turned out to be a rather boring and tasteless confection, made by simply pouring boiled white sugar onto a bamboo leaf and folding it in half. Even Onitsura had been disappointed by it. He found himself wondering whether they'd improved the flavour of it enough now to satisfy his taste buds.

"Bamboo-leaf toffee! When did you buy this?"

"On the trip we just went on. The people sitting in front of me bought some and offered me a piece."

"It doesn't have much flavour, does it?"

The girl looked at him in surprise, evidently thinking that it wasn't too bad. Perhaps a girl like her, who had been raised in the privations of the countryside, would find almost any food delicious.

"… I tried to buy some on the way back," she said with a hint of resentment and regret. "But it was a night train, and I didn't know the name of the station, so I couldn't get any in the end."

Onitsura had only been half-listening, but now, like a thorn, her words seemed to pierce his ears.

"So, you were given it on the outbound train?"

"Yes."

"The one where you were together with the mistress all the way to Nagaoka."

"That's right."

This was rather odd, Onitsura thought. What caught his attention was that Echigo–Yuzawa Station was on the Joetsu line. This implied that she had travelled to Nagaoka on that line, whereas she and Fumie would have had him believe that they'd gone together on the Shin'etsu line, a claim that had been corroborated not only by Seiko Mano, the college student, but also by the conductor, Matsuoka.

Given the number of witnesses and the credibility of their statements, he had believed that they'd travelled on the Shin'etsu line without a second thought. Yet the episode with the toffee interested him because, although both lines passed through Nagaoka, the Joetsu line was a good sixty miles shorter. What if Fumie's claim to have travelled on the Shin'etsu line was a lie, and she had in fact gone to Nagaoka via the shorter Joetsu route? In terms of distance alone, it would certainly have saved time. But would it have been enough to commit the murder?...

When he returned to his senses, Onitsura realized that the maid was still fidgeting with her basket, her habitually rosy face now even redder in the light of the evening sun that was filtering through the leaves.

6.

When he returned to the office, Onitsura found Tanna alone and, as usual, leafing through a newspaper idly. He had already read most of the articles and appeared to be ogling a photograph of a model in one of the advertisements.

"Ah, you're back! We've just had a call from—"

"The call can wait," Onitsura shot back. "You've got to listen to this."

He wanted to go over his findings as soon as possible and see where they would lead him. Seizing a towel, he mopped his face, sat down and began fanning himself furiously.

"As you know, I thought that Mrs Hishinuma's alibi *had* to be a fabrication, so I set out to break it. Only, Matsuoka and Seiko— that is, the conductor and the college girl—both testified that it was true. Despite my efforts, I didn't learn anything that Sudo hadn't already got out of them. The sun was beating down on me, and I felt totally defeated."

After working with Onitsura for so many years, Tanna could read him like a book. Judging by the expression on his face and the tone of his voice, Tanna knew that he must have struck gold, and he wanted to hear about it right away.

Still fanning himself with one hand, Onitsura extracted the railway timetable from his briefcase with the other and plumped it down on the desk.

"But I refused to give up. I'd resolved to go out and question every one of them. And do you know what? I learnt something very interesting from that maid."

With this preamble, Onitsura proceeded to recount in detail the conversation that he and Tai Okuwa had had at the Hikawa shrine. As the conversation went on, Tanna's fan grew more and more listless, until it suddenly stopped moving altogether. A look of excitement was written across his dark face. Once Onitsura had finished, Tanna just sat there in silence, trying to gather his thoughts.

"We need to follow up this discrepancy immediately," Tanna said.

"Agreed."

"One thought does immediately suggest itself, though…"

"Yes? Come on, out with it!" Onitsura said, mopping the sweat from his brow. His voice sounded a little nasal because he'd just blown his nose.

Tanna licked his lips.

"Couldn't the maid have taken another trip to Nagaoka, before or after the fourteenth? She could have taken the Shin'etsu line one time and the Joetsu line another time. If she was given the toffee while she was travelling on the Joetsu line, then the story still fits."

"I checked that point as well. She says she's never taken such a long trip before or since—be it to Nagaoka or anywhere else."

"It's an odd one, isn't it? Bamboo-leaf toffee *is* also sold at Naoetsu Station on the Shin'etsu line, though. Did the one she was given definitely come from Yuzawa?"

"The wrapper had Echigo–Yuzawa written on it."

"Right, but for argument's sake," Tanna continued unflinchingly, tapping his folded fan on the desk as though to punctuate his words, "let's say that the passenger who gave it to her had travelled on the Joetsu line the day before, then just happened to be on the Shin'etsu line on the day in question. That way, she could easily have bought the toffee at Yuzawa Station on the Joetsu line and offered it to the maid after she met her while travelling on the Shin'etsu line a day later. In which case, it wouldn't be so odd, now, would it?"

"That possibility already occurred to me. But the maid told me that she saw the couple sitting in front of her buy it from a vendor at one of the stops en route. She was absolutely clear on that, so there's no way they could have bought it the day before. It's unthinkable that a speciality of the Joetsu line would be sold at a station on the Shin'etsu line, so this couple must have bought it at a station on the Joetsu line—Echigo–Yuzawa Station, to be precise—and so, you see, the train on which the maid was travelling must also have been on the Joetsu line."

Onitsura spoke slowly, as though trying to persuade his colleague.

"What's more, if Fumie Hishinuma had actually been sitting beside her maid, I guarantee you that she would have confiscated the wrapper and destroyed it. But she didn't, and that's why we are where we are. Now, think about it the other way around: the fact that Fumie didn't destroy it means that she can't have known about it. And the fact that she didn't know about it means that she can't have been with her maid at the time. They can't have been on the Shin'etsu line!"

Tanna tried to find every chink in Onitsura's theory. This was his usual tactic in such cases. But now, the more he tried, the more the gaps closed, and the more watertight the theory became.

"The couple offered her the toffee when the train stopped at the next station, Ishiuchi. That must have been when Mrs Hishinuma went down to the platform with her stamp book. Of course, this was a mere formality and just for show. Meanwhile, Tai Okuwa, being the oblivious sort that she is, must have pocketed the bamboo-leaf toffee without showing it to her mistress or just scoffed it while she was gone."

"The greedy so-and-so," Tanna said.

Though abusing the poor girl like this, he looked cheerful, seeming to have accepted Onitsura's theory at last. He too knew that the journey time to Nagaoka was much reduced by taking the Joetsu line.

"So, it's quite a quandary, Tanna. The witness statements made by the conductor *and* the college girl hold that Mrs Hishinuma and her maid took the Shin'etsu line. But what I heard from the maid gives us little choice but to conclude that they took the Joetsu line. First things first, we have to decide which of these is true."

"Joetsu, surely. It's a much shorter journey, so she'd have arrived in time to commit the murder. Otherwise, it wouldn't be worth considering."

"I'd like to think so as well. But the college girl gave a statement saying that she saw them board the No. 311, which left Omiya at 6.26 a.m. And the conductor, Matsuoka, remembers Mrs Hishinuma coming to see him in his compartment. How do we account for that?"

"They must be lying."

"Then the question follows: how did Mrs Hishinuma get them both to provide false witness statements? Did she bribe them?"

"Hmm…"

Although he'd said it, Tanna was unsure. He knew well from past cases how dangerous it was to bribe somebody, and how difficult to keep it all under wraps.

"I would've thought it impossible to bribe the conductor and the student," Onitsura said. "But then we'd have to accept that they travelled on the Shin'etsu line. I'd therefore like not only to believe their witness statements, but also to propose that Mrs Hishinuma and her maid travelled on the Joetsu line to Nagaoka."

Thinking that he was joking, Tanna looked at the inspector. But his face, with its protruding jaw, was the very picture of seriousness. He didn't appear to consider what he'd just said a contradiction in terms.

"But is that even possible?"

"Well, listen to this. I was wondering this myself, so I decided to ask the maid two questions. The first was as follows. Given her abilities, I surmised that she'd at least remember the names of the stations they passed through."

"And? What did she say?"

"She didn't remember any of them! Or rather, she hadn't paid much attention to them, so she couldn't say. Knowing this, it would have been easy for Mrs Hishinuma to take the Joetsu line and pass it off as the other one. Besides, the maid is a good and trusting sort: it would never occur to her to doubt the words of others."

"I see."

"The second question was to see whether she knew when they arrived at Echigo–Yuzawa Station, since that would settle the question of whether they were on the Joetsu line. It would also tell us what time the train arrived in Nagaoka, which in turn would make it clear whether or not she was in time to commit the murder."

As he said this, there was a distinct note of confidence in Onitsura's voice.

7.

Tanna, however, could not imagine that Tai Okuwa had a watch, let alone that she could ever have remembered the times at which her train had departed the stations along the route.

"I was lucky," Onitsura said. "Oh, how lucky I was! She couldn't remember the exact time, of course, but she did remember eating her bento at noon. She certainly has her priorities, that one. At any rate, she said that the couple bought the toffees around an hour before that, so that would put the stop at Yuzawa at around eleven o'clock. Shall we take a look at the timetable?"

With a practised hand, Onitsura opened the book at the page showing times for downbound Joetsu line services and looked down to the row for Echigo–Yuzawa Station. Unlike the Tokaido mainline, this was a quiet branch line, with only fourteen down trains stopping at this station each day, averaging out to around one every two hours. Consequently, it was easy to find what he was looking for. The No. 725, which left at 11.16, was a stopping service bound for Nagaoka. The previous train left at 8.48, while the one after left at 13.49, so there could be no confusion over a train that left at around eleven o'clock. Leaving his seat and joining Onitsura on the other side of the desk, Tanna sat down beside the inspector and together they looked at the timetable.

"Here, look! It must have been the No. 725."

"You're right. The timings don't work for any of the other trains."

Onitsura traced his finger down the column for the No. 725 train and stopped at the arrival time in Nagaoka: it read 13.14 p.m.

"Hanpei Chita was killed sometime between two-fifteen and two-thirty," the inspector said. "So, if Mrs Hishinuma arrived in

282

Dist. from Tokyo	Station	Nagaoka 723	Numata 731	Niigata 521	Aomori 501	Nagaoka 725	Niigata 523	Niigata 943	Minakami 335	Niigata 733	Niigata 713	Nagaoka 311	Niigata 727	Niigata 701	Niigata 313
2.1	Ueno dep.	...	...	...	...	5 50	...	...	...	6 55	8 20	...	11 00	12 30	...
102.1	Takasaki arr.	...	...	...	...	8 10	...	...	...	9 19	10 41	...	13 20	14 03	...
102.1	Takasaki dep.	6 08	7 06	...	...	8 17	...	...	9 35	10 58	11 19	→	13 26	14 06	→
109.4	Shin-Maebashi	6 19	7 18	...	...	8 30	...	...	9 50	11 09	...		13 45	↓	
114.2	Gunma-Soja	6 27	7 25	...	...	8 38	...	...	9 58	11 17	...	(2nd & 3rd cl. Special Express)	13 52	↓	(2nd & 3rd cl. Special Express)
119.8	Yagihara	6 35	7 34	...	...	8 46	...	...	10 09	11 26	...		14 00	↓	
123.2	Shibukawa	6 47	7 40	...	...	8 53	...	...	10 23	11 35	...		14 07	14 28	
129.6	Shikishima	6 57	7 50	...	...	9 03	...	...	10 38	11 45	...		14 17	↓	
132.6	Tsukuda	7 03	7 57	...	...	9 11	...	...	10 45	11 51	...		14 25	↓	
138.4	Iwamoto	7 13	8 07	...	...	9 22	...	...	10 55	12 01	...		14 33	↓	
143.5	Numata	7 22	8 15	...	...	9 32	...	...	11 04	12 11	...		14 41	14 50	
148.7	Gokan	7 31	...	...	...	9 40	...	...	11 12	12 19	...		15 04	↓	
155.8	Kamimoku	7 44	...	...	...	9 55	...	...	11 24	12 32	...		15 17	↓	
161.2	**Minakami** arr.	7 52	...	...	...	10 04	...	...	11 35	12 42	...		15 25	15 09	
161.2	**Minakami** dep.	7 57	...	...	...	10 15	...	...	...	12 50	...		15 32	15 20	
168.0	Yubiso	8 08	...	...	...	10 27	...	...	...	13 03	...		15 44	↓	
171.4	Doai	8 15	...	...	...	10 35	...	...	...	13 10	...		15 51	↓	
182.2	Tsuchitaru	8 30	...	...	...	10 54	...	...	...	13 31	...		16 06	↓	
189.5	Echigo-Nakazato	8 39	...	...	...	11 05	...	...	...	13 40	...		16 17	↓	
196.3	Echigo-Yuzawa	8 48	...	...	...	11 16	...	...	...	13 49	...		16 26	15 58	
202.7	**Ishiuchi** arr.	8 56	...	...	...	11 25	...	...	...	13 57	...		16 34	↓	
202.7	**Ishiuchi** dep.	9 00	...	...	...	11 30	...	...	...	14 03	...		16 44	↓	
206.7	Osawa	9 06	...	...	...	11 36	...	...	...	14 09	...		16 50	↓	
210.0	Shiozawa	9 11	...	...	...	11 42	...	...	...	14 15	...		16 56	↓	
213.9	Muikamachi	9 17	...	...	...	11 49	...	...	...	14 25	...		17 02	↓	
220.5	Itsukamachi	9 25	...	...	...	11 58	...	...	...	14 33	...		17 11	↓	
226.0	Urasa	9 32	...	...	...	12 10	...	...	...	14 40	...		17 20	↓	
234.3	Koide	9 43	...	...	...	12 20	...	...	...	14 51	...		17 31	16 36	
236.8	Echigo-Horino-Uchi	9 47	...	(2nd & 3rd cl.)	(Osaka dep. 20 12)	12 25	(2nd & 3rd cl.)	...	...	14 56	(2nd & 3rd cl.)	...	17 37	(2nd & 3rd cl.)
240.2	Kita-Horino-Uchi	9 53	...			12 31		...	...	15 01		...	17 42		
244.9	Echigo-Kawaguchi	10 01	...		(Osaka dep. 22 30)	12 43	(Osaka dep. 22 17)	(Komoro dep. 9 10)	...	15 09	(Ueno dep. 5 50 via Shinetsu Mainline)	...	17 52	(Ueno dep. 6 55 via Shinetsu Mainline)
251.5	Ojiya	10 10	...			12 52			...	15 18		...	18 02	16 56	
258.7	Echigo-Takiya	10 20	...			13 02			...	15 28		...	18 12	↓	
264.7	Miyauchi	10 28	...	11 10			13 09	13 14	14 57	15 36	17 28	18 22	...	...	19 51
267.7	**Nagaoka** arr.	10 34	...	11 16	11 56	13 14	13 19	...	15 02	15 42	17 33	18 28	...	17 13	19 57
267.7	**Nagaoka** dep.	...	...	11 24	12 00	...	13 33	13 38	15 06	15 58	17 40	...	...	17 18	20 05
270.2	Kita-Nagaoka	...	...	11 29	...	(Sea of Japan Special Express)	13 38	(2nd & 3rd cl.)	↓	16 05	17 47	...	(2nd & 3rd cl.)	↓	20 10
274.5	Oshikiri	...	...	11 35	...		13 44		↓	16 13	17 54	...		↓	20 22
279.1	Mitsuke	...	...	11 42	...		13 51		15 19	16 22	18 02	...		17 30	20 29
283.2	Obiori	...	...	11 48	...		13 58		↓	16 30	18 09	...		↓	20 36
285.8	Tokoji	...	...	11 53	...		14 03		↓	16 38	18 14	...		↓	20 41
289.3	Sanji	...	...	12 00	12 24		14 09		15 31	16 42	18 21	...		↓	20 48
290.9	**Higashi-Sanjo** arr.	...	...	12 03	12 24		14 13		15 34	16 50	18 25	...		17 43	20 52
290.9	**Higashi-Sanjo** dep.	(Niigata)	(Niigata)	12 06	12 25	(Niigata)	14 15	(Niigata)	15 37	16 58	18 29	(Niigata)		17 43	20 54
294.7	Honai			12 12	↓		14 21		15 43	17 04	18 35			↓	21 00
298.5	Kamo			12 19	↓		14 27		15 49	17 11	18 42			17 52	21 07
302.6	Hanyuda	**912**	**217**	12 25	↓	**922**	14 34	(Koriyama dep. 7 15)	15 56	17 18	18 49	**221**		**225**	21 14
305.8	Tagami	(Shibata dep. 11 02)	(Koriyama dep. 7 15)	12 31	↓	(Akita dep. 5 44)	14 39		16 01	17 23	18 55	(Koriyama dep. 12 00)		(Koriyama dep. 13 20)	21 20
309.5	Yashiroda			12 36	↓		14 45		16 07	17 30	19 01				21 26
213.6	Furutsu			12 42	↓		14 50		16 12	17 35	19 07				21 32
315.8	**Niitsu** arr.	11 42	12 22	12 48	12 54	13 30	14 56	...	16 18	17 10	17 41	19 12	18 18	18 09	21 37
315.8	**Niitsu** dep.	11 50	12 28	13 04	13 00	13 43	15 11	16 25	16 20	17 17	17 46	19 18	18 25	18 12	21 42
319.6	Ogikawa	11 56	12 34	13 11	(Aomori arr. 22 28)	13 51	15 17	16 30	↓	17 23	17 52	19 25	18 33	↓	21 49
324.5	Kameda	12 02	12 42	13 18		13 59	15 25	16 37	↓	17 31	18 00	19 33	18 43	↓	21 57
330.9	Nuttari	12 15	12 52	13 31		14 08	15 34	16 46	↓	17 45	18 13	19 44	18 52	↓	22 14
332.8	**Niigata** arr.	12 19	12 56	13 35	...	14 12	15 38	16 50	16 38	17 49	18 17	19 48	18 56	18 30	22 18

Nagaoka at 13.14 p.m., she'd have had ample time to commit the murder."

"You're right," said Tanna, nodding.

Chita had left the Okesa inn at half past noon, so the two of them must have arranged in advance to meet somewhere: for Chita to think he was collecting his money, and for Fumie to take his life…

"Then what do you suppose the maid did? Surely she didn't go with her mistress?"

"She was taken to the *ryokan* in the city and left on her own to relax. According to the maid, Fumie said that since she must be tired, she should have a leisurely bath and take a breather. The Shin'etsu route would have got them into Nagaoka in the evening, but, as we've just seen, the Joetsu train arrived in the early afternoon. No matter how awful her memory, the maid must surely have remembered whether she arrived in the afternoon or in the evening. If only we'd asked what time she arrived, I think we'd have got to the bottom of this much sooner."

Onitsura sounded a little choked. He must have been laughing at his own foolishness. However, when his finger reached the top of the same column and found the departure time from Ueno, his voice regained its composure.

"Take a look at this, Tanna! The departure time is 5.50."

"Yes, sir."

"Don't 'yes, sir' me!" he said breathlessly. "The departure time is the same as the No. 311, the Shin'etsu line train they claimed to have taken!"

He quickly turned to the page listing downbound Shin'etsu line services and pointed to the No. 311's departure time at Ueno Station. It was just as he'd said: the Joetsu and Shin'etsu trains were scheduled to leave at precisely the same time. In other words, there had been two trains—the Nos. 311 and 725—that departed Ueno at the same time and were headed in the same direction.

Still, Tanna still couldn't quite fathom what Onitsura was getting at.

"Don't you see? This is a major discovery!" the inspector said, a little frustrated by Tanna's lack of quick thinking. "Two trains can't leave Ueno at exactly the same time, because there's only one track. That means that the 311 and the 725 leave together. Or, to be more precise, both trains are pulled by the same locomotive until they reach Takasaki, where the train divides. So, between Ueno and Takasaki, there's no way to tell from the outside which is No. 311 and which is No. 725."

"But then…"

"Exactly! Mrs Hishinuma pretended that she was going to Nagaoka on the No. 311 Shin'etsu line service, whereas in fact she boarded a carriage belonging to the No. 725. The college girl who saw them off would have had been none the wiser and accepted that it was the No. 311 without question. Unless she'd taken the trouble to check the timetable for the Joetsu line, she'd never have spotted the deception."

Tanna wrinkled his nose and looked embarrassed. Although they had both been looking at the timetable in front of them, he hadn't realized this possibility until it was pointed out to him.

"I forgot to mention this earlier, but when Mrs Hishinuma hired Seiko Mano to look after the house while she was gone, she placed an advertisement for a girl who didn't like to travel and was going to stay in Tokyo for the summer. But this, in fact, must also have been so that her plan wouldn't be discovered." Onitsura quenched his thirst with a sip of lukewarm tea before continuing slowly. "We're making way with this. We've discovered that Mrs Hishinuma could have taken the Joetsu line without contradicting the witness statement of the college girl, Seiko Mano. What we have to do now is look at the one given by the conductor, Matsuoka. We've got to consider the problem of Mrs Hishinuma being on the No. 311 train on the fourteenth of June, when he was on duty."

Onitsura closed the little book and turned to Tanna. Even though it was evening, the heat had not let up and both of them were drenched in sweat. Only their eyes seemed to shine on their grimy faces.

"For the reasons I've already outlined, I don't believe that the conductor would have twisted the truth and given a false witness statement. Therefore, having already been in Nagaoka, she must have somehow caught the No. 311 while it was still on its way to the city and gone to see the conductor then."

"So, saying that she'd lost her stamp book at Kashiwazaki Station was nothing more than a pretext?"

"Precisely. Now let's think. I believe she had two aims in using the stamp book as a prop: firstly, to mask her peculiar choice to take the Shin'etsu line, which is a very long journey; and secondly, to create a very natural alibi by appearing in the conductor's compartment, claiming that she'd lost it."

Tanna was annoyed at himself for having been so bewildered by this likely-fictitious stamp book and for having failed to glimpse the truth through Fumie's elaborate intrigue.

"I can't imagine she'd have taken a taxi or hired a car from Nagaoka to catch the No. 311. Somebody would have been liable to remember her face."

"Yes, and especially a good-looking woman like her. So, she must have taken a train. Or, to be more precise, she must have caught a train at Nagaoka—or another one nearby, like Nagaoka North Station—and taken an upbound on the Shin'etsu line."

"I'll take a look," Tanna said, seizing the timetable.

His frustration at having been duped by Fumie made him want to solve this last problem by himself.

"There's no rush," Onitsura said. "There's bound to be a convenient up train. In the meantime, how about some dinner? My treat, to celebrate. Surely your stomach's better by now?"

The inspector's face, which only moments ago had looked so serious, was smiling now. It struck Tanna that the smile lent his eyes a certain softness.

"That's awfully good of you."

"What are you in the mood for?"

A pang of hunger assailed Tanna. He'd been intending to go home and eat his wife's cooking, but now that Onitsura had offered to treat him, he felt ravenous, as though a gaping hole at the bottom of his stomach had opened up all of a sudden.

"Well, *hayashi* rice might be nice…"

"Come on, I don't mean the canteen! I'm talking about proper restaurant food. How does some eel *donburi* sound?"

"Oh-ho, now you're talking!" said Tanna, licking his lips.

Once Onitsura had finished placing their order over the telephone, he slipped his hand into his pocket, as though suddenly remembering something, produced the sachets of medicine he had bought earlier and laid them down on the desk in front of a perplexed-looking Tanna.

"What's this? It looks like some kind of painkiller," he said, placing a white sachet in the palm of his hand and looking at Onitsura.

"It's proof that her alibi for the time of Nishinohata's murder is also a fabrication."

The inspector proceeded to tell Tanna about the experiment he'd conducted at the Temple of Remedy. Forgetting all about his hunger, Tanna hung on his every word.

"There's definitely something fishy about it, as the saying goes."

Tanna's eyes grew pensive. Fumie had done at the Hoashi Pharmacy what she'd done with the conductor on the No. 311 train. Her intention to give the impression of her presence, and to use it in case of need at a later date, was as transparent as looking through a pane of glass.

Knowing that it was a false alibi, however, simply wasn't enough. The real question was how to break it. And in that respect, Onitsura wasn't having much luck.

"We have to find out what it was that the voice actor discovered, what it was that he spotted. What I'd give to know his basis for concluding that our investigation is fundamentally flawed."

"But, sir…"

"He must have discovered something about the decoy. You remember, that poor chap Obata. I really hope he recovers soon. We need answers from him!"

"But, sir…" Tanna said again, sounding agitated. "That's just what I've been wanting to tell you."

"Tell me what?"

"We received a call from the hospital an hour ago."

"From the hospital?"

"Yes, sir. It seems that Mr Murase's dead."

"Murase? Dead?… Damn it!"

Onitsura fell silent.

They seemed to have broken Fumie's alibi for the murder of Chita. But the key to solving Nishinohata's murder had just slipped out of reach for good.

FOURTEEN

A Surprising Fact

1.

There were now fewer than half the number of officers working on the investigation that there had been at the start of it. This was because the suspects had been identified, and, more than a month after the incident, most of the detectives had moved on to new cases. Inspector Sudo and Constable Seki, however, had not been reassigned and continued to operate out of their base on the first floor of Ueno police station.

Just as Fumie Hishinuma's alibi at the Hoashi Pharmacy had been established, and as Onitsura and Tanna were facing difficulties with their investigation, Sudo and Seki were summoned to the lead investigator's office.

"Please, have a seat."

With a blank expression, he indicated a chair and waited for the two men to sit down before continuing.

"Ogawa's team are currently examining the clothes that Genkichi Obata was given to wear. I'd like you two to look into any connections between Obata and Fumie Hishinuma."

"Of course, sir."

"No matter how desperate he was for money or how much he liked to drink, it's inconceivable that he'd simply have gone along with all this if she were a total stranger to him."

"Agreed, sir."

"For a day labourer, wearing a Western suit alone would be something out of the ordinary. And then to be made to go to a Chinese restaurant, wearing false whiskers… Any reasonable man would have had his doubts."

Inspector Kaya was right, of course. Striking up a conversation with a perfect stranger just because he happened to bear a passing resemblance to Gosuke Nishinohata would have been suspicious, no matter what.

"Therefore, I suspect that Fumie and Obata must have been acquainted for some time."

"It would certainly stand to reason, sir," Sudo agreed, allowing for some leeway.

After all Sudo's years of service, the job had rubbed off on him so much that he could no longer just accept things without at least a degree of doubt. There were times when it depressed and tormented him to realize this.

"Obata was a real Tokyoite. According to the owner of the Tachibana-ya, he was proud of having never set foot out of the capital, but for the fact that he'd once gone to Saitama. Yet this visit to Saitama could be interpreted as having been a day trip, or it could have lasted several days if he'd gone there for work. Hell, it could even mean that he'd been there for several weeks, months, maybe even a year! Now, you two were the ones who took that statement from her. What do you suppose she meant by it?"

"Well…" Sudo said, turning his moustache towards Seki.

Seki hesitated, looking bashful. "Umm…"

The question was one to which they hadn't paid much attention until now, and their memories of it had grown rather hazy, so neither of them could offer a definitive answer.

"I see…" said the lead inspector, intuiting all this from the looks on their faces. "'Saitama' is a pretty vague term, and I wonder whether it mightn't in fact mean Omiya."

"Omiya?" replied Sudo.

"Could he have lived in Omiya for a couple of years, do you think?"

"It's possible, sir."

"Didn't the woman say that Obata used to work as a gardener? Do you suppose he could have worked as a gardener for the Hishinumas before falling on hard times?"

"That's a very good point, sir. I hadn't thought of that." Until now, Sudo had been listening with a look of scepticism on his face, but now he piped up, intrigued. He folded the fan he'd been using with a snap and leant across the desk. "We can check that out right away."

"Do that. As it so happens, there's a gardener who visits the house these days called Tatsugoro. Apparently, his face is pretty well known in Omiya. Who knows what you may find out if you talk to him."

"Where does he live, this Tatsugoro?"

The lead investigator looked down at the notebook lying open in front of him.

"Miyacho."

"I wonder which part," Sudo said, turning to Seki. Before Seki could say anything, however, the detective inspector muttered something about figuring it out once they got there.

The two set out for Omiya under a leaden sky. The fact that it was hot and overcast only added to the sultriness. No matter how much they fanned themselves, the perspiration continued to seep out of them unchecked.

Just outside Omiya Station there was a police box, where Seki asked the way to Miyacho. As directed, the two then headed east.

The neighbourhood where the gardener lived was a bit of a walk from the station, but it was a lively place, although not as bustling as Daimoncho. They reached a corner where a pickler's shop stood and turned into a side street. There, on both sides of the alley, they found display racks with row upon row of Japanese sacred lilies, and above them a signboard bearing the name of the shop. Seki felt that the arrogance of this Tatsugoro could be seen in the fact that he'd built these racks with total disregard for the inconvenience it would cause his neighbours. It didn't dispose him well towards the owner.

At the end of the alley was a gate made of cedar. When they stepped inside, they found the entire garden covered with trees and shrubs and potted plants. To the right, there was an area with a dense planting of hedgerow trees such as photinia, sasanqua, yew plum-pine and Japanese spindle, while across the path on the left were cherry trees, maples and a large, magnificent tree that looked like a magnolia, although it was hard to tell because of the lack of flowers. Past these were peaches, plums, persimmons with small green berries and other fruit trees with their roots tied to ropes so that they could be unearthed at any time.

As they delved further and further back, the noise of the street died away and was replaced by silence that was broken only by a periodic ringing that came from up ahead.

"I love that sound!" Sudo exclaimed, stopping all of a sudden to listen.

To the inspector, who had been chasing after a case all day without a moment's rest, there was certainly a refreshing quality to that metallic sound, one that seemed to cleanse the ears.

The two men carried on. Turning a corner, they came to a plot reserved for shrubs and found a man in a faded brown-straw hat crouching down, cutting the branches of a nandina with a pair of shears, while a small cabbage white perched on the back of his livery coat. His broad back seemed to give the butterfly a sense of stability, like a large rock.

"Excuse us!" Sudo called out to him in a friendly voice.

Wearing a look of annoyance, a berry-brown face turned towards them. It was not only his straw hat that had been scorched by the sun.

"Yes?"

Resting in one corner of his mouth was a fat pipe, from the end of which rose puffs of blue smoke. He stared up at Sudo and Seki with a glance more brazen than it was it blasé. No sooner had he looked the men over, however, than his scowl was replaced with a smile. He got to his feet, proving himself to be even taller than Seki.

"D'you have a moment?" Sudo asked brusquely. "We've got a couple of questions for you."

His overly familiar tone didn't arouse the gardener's antipathy because of his unpretentious appearance and the smile on his face.

"I was just about to take a break, as it so happens."

The gardener extracted himself from the shrubbery and sat down on the edge of the path.

"Those are some nice lilies you've got. We saw them on the way in."

"They're all right, I s'pose. I've only got the giant *rasha* ones at the moment. Come autumn, I'll have to split them."

"Really? The ones outside looked pretty good to me."

"I wouldn't put good ones out there. Somebody'd pinch 'em!"

The gardener laughed, his lips parting to reveal a set of gold teeth, which Seki thought lent him a greedy and vulgar appearance.

"Do you like sacred lilies, sir?" Seki asked his partner.

"I do, although I don't have a garden. I've just got five pots. I would like another one, though. A nice *gashi* dragon lily."

Inspector Sudo and the old gardener then became engrossed in their discussion of sacred lilies, talking about which *negishi* were best, how the *kinshiden* was cultivated, and how *chojuraku* gave off a finer scent than *sekko-kan*. They reeled off so many exotic names, all of which, to the young Seki, sounded more like brands of sake. He couldn't understand a word of it. As he stood there, puffing away on his cigarette, he thought it was the ultimate tragedy to be old and interested in things like lilies and cactuses.

"Anyway," the inspector said when his own cigarette was nearly finished. At last, it was time to get down to business. "I don't suppose you've ever heard of a man called Genkichi Obata?"

"I surely have. He's a good worker." He suddenly fixed the inspector in his gaze with a questioning look. "You know, it's a funny thing. Somebody else was 'ere, asking me about Genkichi not so long ago."

"Who?"

"Nobody you'd know."

"It wasn't Mr Hishinuma's wife, by any chance, was it?"

Inspector Sudo asked the question in a friendly enough tone. Not only his voice, but also the look in his eyes appeared to express admiration for Mrs Hishinuma. As usual, the little moustache under his nose added to the overall effect.

"You know the Hishinumas?" asked Tatsugoro.

"I wouldn't say I 'know' them exactly. But I *have* visited their house a few times. I heard the rocks in the garden were put there by Genkichi."

Sudo laughed as he tried to trick the old man into revealing his hand. Seki had also spotted the large rocks set in the lawn when they went to question the maid the other day.

"Oh, no, that wasn't him. The rocks were put in by another gardener when the mansion was built. Genkichi only came to Omiya

294

after the war. His home in Tokyo burnt down, and his children died in the fire. He was all alone in the world when he rolled up at my door. Well, I felt sorry for him, didn't I, so I'd take him along to help out here and there. He couldn't handle his drink, though, and in the end, it just couldn't go on."

"He just couldn't keep up with you, you mean?"

"No, I don't touch a drop myself. He never used to be much of a drinker, neither, mind you, but what with the firebombing and the death of his wife and kids, I guess he just couldn't help it."

Despite these apparently offhand words, his tone hinted at a genuine feeling of friendship for Genkichi. Seki could feel his initial impression of the man gradually changing. However, since Tatsugoro didn't appear to be in mourning for him, it seemed likely that he hadn't yet learnt of the man's death.

"What could Mrs Hishinuma have wanted with Genkichi, I wonder?" Sudo pretended to ask himself as he stroked his chin. "Maybe she had a job for him..."

"That's right. He may have gone off the rails a bit, but he's a decent chap. And then, he *is* very good at what he does. I s'pose she must've had something she wanted taking care of. Last I heard, he was working as a day labourer down in San'ya, and when I told the lady... oh, she was heartbroken, she was."

Tatsugoro tapped the ashes out of his pipe and extracted some pale-brown shredded tobacco from the pouch hanging at his waist. He then patiently rolled the tobacco into a ball before placing it into the bowl.

Sudo proceeded to touch on other topics, casually enquiring about Fumie, but the gardener seemed to know nothing else of interest. It was clear from what he'd just said, however, that Mrs Hishinuma had been interested in Genkichi Obata's whereabouts and that, in order to find out, she had sounded out her gardener.

With that, Sudo brought the conversation to a swift close, and he and his colleague took their leave.

"It's astonishing, the knowledge that comes in handy when you're a detective," Sudo whispered as they left the gate, glancing at the pots on both sides of the alley. "I hardly know anything about sacred lilies, but the little bit I do know certainly came in handy in getting him to let his guard down. If it weren't for that, I doubt the old boy would have told us half the things he did."

"So, now we know that Fumie Hishinuma was looking for Genkichi. But how did she find him?"

As they exited onto the main street, Sudo turned to look at Seki.

"She must have done it herself. Leaving it to somebody else would risk causing problems for her later. In which case, where would she have gone to look for him?"

"What about the job centre in Minowa? After all, they're the ones who found him the work as a day labourer."

"Yes, you're right. That's where she must have gone. And if she couldn't get a definite answer at the job centre, she'd have probably tried a 'private' one next."

By "private", Sudo meant the gangs of men who would hang around the street corners in Minowa, hunting for out-of-work labourers whom they'd load onto trucks, bypassing the official channels.

The two headed straight for the station at Omiya. Because of this latest case, they'd already become quite familiar with the streets of the town. Right by the station was that same canteen, with the same delicious-looking waxwork simulacra of their fare displayed in the window—just as they'd seen the other day.

2.

The detectives got off at Ueno and, without stopping at the office, headed straight for Minowa on a tram. The building that housed the job centre was much like any other, and, just like any other, it looked grimy, faded and drab.

It was almost the end of the working day, and the job centre was practically deserted. The recruitment office had several benches and tables where the centre's staff and the job-seekers would talk, each of which sat empty. They were all dull and gloomy, as though having soaked in the hardships of those who had lost their jobs.

Three young members of staff sat arranging cards, their eyes trained on the desks. Sudo spoke to the nearest of them, then sat down in a chair beside Seki. It looked as though they'd come to find employment themselves.

"Genkichi Obata?… Oh, the old guy? Used to work as a gardener?" The man had a misty look in his eye as he recalled the elderly labourer. "I heard he took ill on a train and died, poor guy."

"Had anybody been looking for him?"

"Looking for him? Hmm… A man or a woman?"

"A woman. Thirty-ish. I've got a photo here. She's a real looker."

From the pages of his notebook, Sudo extracted a copy of the photo from the company directory and handed it to the employee. With hair hanging over a face caked in sweat, the young man took in the photograph, his worldly interest piqued by the beauty before him.

"Well?"

"I don't remember her. Do either of you remember her?"

The man turned to his two colleagues and held out the picture. They had both been listening to the conversation already, so he didn't have to explain things again.

The first shook his head, but the other, who had a flat head, nodded.

"I think I remember her," he said, walking over to their table and picking up the photograph. "She was wearing sunglasses, though, so I can't say for sure that it was her. But I do remember the outline of her face."

"When was this?"

"I can't be sure of that, either. A month ago, maybe? Perhaps longer."

He was large and fair-skinned, and he seemed like a nice man.

"Could you tell us from the very beginning?"

"Of course…"

He turned away as though trying to think. Right above his head hung a leaflet with the terms and conditions for a job. Because he was so tall, the leaflet brushed against his hair.

"As I said, it was a month, maybe a month and a half ago. It must have been around the same time of day. The office was quiet, at any rate. A beautiful woman wearing sunglasses came in and asked me whether I knew a man called Genkichi Obata, who she'd heard was staying at a modest *ryokan* in the San'ya neighbourhood."

"Did she say why she was looking for him?"

"No, nothing like that… Anyway, since we know Mr Obata well here, I told her that he was staying at a *ryokan* called the Tachibana-ya, and that he came here every morning with his labour book."

The man could never have known that Fumie was sharpening her blade. Moreover, Sudo could easily imagine why the appearance of a beauty like her in this drab office would have inclined the staff to give their answers more freely.

The connection between Fumie Hishinuma and Genkichi Obata had been clarified somewhat. As the two detectives mopped their perspiring brows with their handkerchiefs and continually fanned themselves, they thanked the staff and took their leave.

"I'm starting to feel as though I've lost my job," Sudo said.

"They're not exactly cheery places, job centres, are they?"

Seki felt as though he could well understand the anxious, hopeless state of mind of those who turned up there every morning, job-seeker's card in hand, worrying about tomorrow's bread.

3.

It had been five days since Murase died. In the meantime, Onitsura and Tanna had made little progress. No matter how they tried, they just couldn't break Fumie's alibi of having been buying painkillers at a pharmacy in Omiya, a long way from the spot where Gosuke Nishinohata was killed on Ryodaishi Bridge. When Tanna went to requestion the witness for this alibi, the pharmacist lost his temper, his pale face flushed crimson right to the roots of his reddish hair, and he shouted that he'd already answered the police's questions and didn't have to answer them again. Tanna was so taken aback by this that he'd run out of the shop with his tail between his legs.

It's common for fishermen to have the persistent delusion of a having just missed a big fish. And so, Tanna couldn't help feeling sorry when he learnt of Murase's death. If only they'd known what it was that he'd realized, the Nishinohata mystery would be as good as solved. Yet this was nothing but a fool's lament.

Murase said that he'd been having dinner with a friend that night at the Orchid. Now, it was likely that this friend had seen the same thing as the voice actor, so, if they could find this friend, there was a chance he could give them a clue to what Murase had discovered. With this in mind, Tanna had been making enquiries everywhere, trying to identify this friend, but so far without any result. They couldn't wait for ever, though, and, even supposing they did find him, there was no guarantee that he had in fact spotted the same thing that Murase did.

Both Onitsura and Tanna knew they had to do something proactive to break the deadlock in the investigation, but as for what those next steps were, they were at a loss. What's more, they were trying their best to avoid the chief inspector. Word had reached the top brass that a connection between Fumie and Genkichi had been uncovered by another pair of detectives, and this was only adding to the impatience upstairs.

It was hot again that morning. There was a vigorous-looking arrangement of large pink dahlias in a vase, but their green leaves had already lost the strength to draw water and were starting to wilt. Tanna felt exceptionally thirsty.

Onitsura was sitting at his desk, reading through the case notes. He had gone through them several times already, so he wasn't expecting to make any new discoveries. However, having exhausted all other options, he had no choice but to go over everything again. If nothing else, it looked better than sitting there with his head in his hands.

Tanna turned over a clean teacup and poured himself a cup of lukewarm tea. As he sipped it, the faint smell of bleaching powder tickled his nose. The tea was dreadful. When he was a child, there'd been a well with drinking water at the back of his house, and that water had tasted so cool and indescribably fresh. Every time he was forced to drink this lukewarm tea made from tap water, Tanna would think wistfully back to his boyhood.

He suddenly heard a rotary dial being operated. Looking up, he saw Onitsura holding the receiver, an unaccountable glint in his eye, and wondered what was going on. The inspector's expression was inscrutable. His emotions rarely showed themselves on his face; even in moments of comedy, he would never give a hearty belly laugh, but only smile faintly. Now, too, he was trying to contain his emotions, but the look in his eye betrayed him. Holding a pencil in his other hand, he tapped the desk impatiently.

"Hello? Is that the Oku depot?"

Tanna was surprised to hear these words. The diminutive constable could scarcely imagine what Onitsura had in mind, ringing them up like this out of the blue.

"… there was a collision on the approach to Shimojujo Station on the night of the first of June, wasn't there? Yes, yes…"

Onitsura's piercing gaze was fixed on the pink dahlias on the desk.

Hearing the name of the station sparked Tanna's memory. At 11.10 that night, a goods train heading out of Tokyo had collided with a truck, causing casualties and bringing traffic on the Tohoku mainline and the Keihin–Tohoku line to a standstill for several hours. But why was the inspector enquiring about this only now?

"What I'm really interested in is the Aomori-bound stopping train that left Ueno Station right after the accident took place. It's the No. 117, which was scheduled to depart at eleven-forty."

Tanna's auditory nerves suddenly twitched. By the No. 117, he was referring to the train had carried Gosuke Nishinohata's body off on its roof.

"I believe the Tohoku mainline was closed at the time due to the accident in Shimojujo, so which line did this No. 117 train take?"

It was only when Tanna heard this that he realized what the inspector was really asking. The incident had occurred thirty minutes before train No. 117 was due to leave Ueno, and both tracks had supposedly been out of use until a little after 2 a.m. Yet later that same morning, the train had pulled into Shiroishi Station in Miyagi Prefecture only twenty minutes behind schedule. This had been confirmed by the painters and the station staff. In which case, the No. 117 train couldn't have stood idle until the accident at Shimojujo was cleared up at around 2 a.m. It must have been put on a different track.

"… via Ikebukuro? So, on the Akabane line, then?"

Onitsura thanked the voice on the other end and put down the receiver. Tanna noticed that, even though there was no change in his facial expression, there was a hint of satisfaction in the way the inspector moved.

"Have you found something?" Tanna asked, still holding his cup of insipid tea.

"Maybe."

Onitsura jumped to his feet.

"Are you heading out?"

"Yes. I've finally seen the light. Now I need to go and put my theory to the test."

"What do you mean?"

"Come and find out," Onitsura said in an uncharacteristically brusque manner before rushing out of the room.

Tanna grabbed his hat and followed him. It was obvious that the inspector's lack of explanation meant something big.

4.

When they boarded the second bus, Tanna noticed that it was bound for Koiwa, so he had a rough idea of where they were heading. The inspector, however, had sat in quiet contemplation the whole way, so, not wanting to distract him, Tanna likewise remained silent.

Just as he expected, Onitsura nudged him to stand up as the bus approached Namidabashi. It seemed likely that they were going to pay a visit to the Tachibana-ya, the down-at-heel lodgings where Genkichi Obata had been living. Yet Tanna still had no idea what they were there to investigate. In the end, he had no choice but to follow the inspector blindly.

Just as Inspector Sudo had done before him, Onitsura stood in front of the street map and checked the location of the Tachibana-ya.

"So, we have to turn the corner when we reach a cobbler's," he muttered to himself, before setting off again.

When they got to the *ryokan*, they found two women standing on the road outside it, both sucking on ice lollies and gossiping loudly about someone. They were clapping their hands and doubled over, laughing no doubt at something amusing. Behind them was a bicycle with a trailer attached to it, and a man who was ringing his bell, trying to get past.

"Hey, are you deaf or what, you stupid woman?!"

"What did you just call me?!" one of the women retorted, suddenly looking deadly serious.

All trace of levity had vanished, and they were now staring daggers at the man. With a look of determination on her face, the offended party threw her ice lolly down on the road and grabbed the handlebars.

"I dare you to say that again!"

"I didn't mean to offend you. I'm sorry, all right?"

The young man on the bicycle was frightened by the two women and tried to offer them a grovelling smile. Seeing this pathetic spectacle, the two women suddenly recovered their good spirits.

"Talking like that... You ought to conduct yourself more like a gentleman!"

"I just said I was sorry, didn't I?!"

His face looked more and more pitiful. Tanna decided he could not stand idly by, and so, wearing a wry smile, he staged an intervention.

The woman with her hands on the handlebars turned out to be the proprietress of the Tachibana-ya.

"Well, I can't stand here chatting all day, looking like this," she said, suddenly acting bashful and touching up her hair. "I'll see you later," she said to the other inn owner, while showing Onitsura and Tanna into the narrow entrance hall, where she took off her sandals and plumped herself down on the ledge.

"Well, what's he done now? I really don't know what to do with that husband of mine," she said flirtatiously.

"We aren't here about your husband, madam. We've come to ask a few questions regarding Genkichi Obata, who we believe lodged here for a while."

"Oh, my heart breaks for that man, it does. Will they ever catch who done him in? When I think about what happened, it just makes me so, so angry."

She spoke in a very rapid patter.

"Yes, about Mr Obata…" Onitsura began in a calm voice.

"What do you want to know?"

"I'd like you to think back. Do you remember what he was doing on the night of the first of June?"

Her eyes widened, and she looked at him in astonishment. Why ask this now, after all this time? her face seemed to say.

"Obviously, the day before was the last day in May, in case that's any help."

The woman cast a glance at the two swallows perched on the telegraph wires outside the inn. She had a good eye, Tanna thought.

"I remember the last of the month, all right. When I went to ask for the money he owed, he was pretending to be asleep in his room."

"So, it's the night after that that we're interested in," Onitsura gently pressed her.

In cases like this, he would never rush the witness.

The woman rested her hands on the knees of her neat, starched dress and looked up at the electric wires in the eaves again. Tanna was enchanted by her eyes.

"The night of the first…" she muttered to herself.

The night of 1 June was when Gosuke Nishinohata had been killed and also when, at the same time, Genkichi Obata had turned up as a decoy at the Orchid restaurant. Yet Tanna still couldn't fathom why the inspector was so interested in this point.

"Ah, yes, I remember now!" the woman exclaimed. Her nose was twitching. "As I say, I went to ask him for the money he owed on the evening of the thirty-first. Pretended to be asleep, so he did, at the time, but he must've felt bad about it, because the very next day he came back with a bottle of *shochu* and started drinking with my husband. He even brought me some red-bean-paste sweets as a gift. He could be such a thoughtful person. Mind you, I'd rather he just paid the money than went bringing us sake and sweets…"

"You don't happen to recall at what time they finished drinking, do you?"

"Hmm… It must have gone on until around midnight. I remember telling them to break it up, otherwise they'd disturb the other guests."

Tanna looked at the woman in surprise. There was nothing on her pale face to suggest she was lying, but then, if she was telling the truth, what did that mean for the story about Obata having turned up at the Orchid and eaten a plate of noodles?

Tanna glanced furtively at Onitsura, but the inspector seemed perfectly composed, as though he'd been expecting this all along.

"And you're absolutely sure that your husband and Mr Obata stayed up drinking until around midnight?"

"Why do you ask?" The woman gave the inspector a cold look, as if she didn't understand why she was being asked twice. "I asked for the money on the thirty-first, and then he came back with the bottle of sake on the first. I'm certain of it."

"Thank you, madam," Onitsura said all of a sudden, apparently satisfied. "You've been a great help."

She raised her eyebrows. The abruptness of the inspector's volte-face seemed to have startled her.

As the two men were about to leave, she leant against the lattice door at the entrance and quietly recalled: "He liked whale meat topped with vinegar miso."

She seemed a totally different person from the one they'd encountered earlier.

5.

"Well, now I'm *totally* confused," Tanna said once they were outside.

A man in black sunglasses was walking towards them. As he passed, he turned his head and eyed the two detectives suspiciously.

"What makes you say that? Surely, everything's falling into place…"

"But if we're to credit what we just heard, doesn't that mean that Genkichi wasn't in fact the person who played the decoy at the Orchid that night?"

"Precisely. That's why we came here: to hear it from her lips."

"But how did you know that it wasn't him?"

"Because of what it said in the report. It showed from the very outset that it couldn't have been Genkichi Obata who dined at the Orchid. I just never spotted it until this morning."

"Spotted what?"

"Read it for yourself. If you pay careful attention, you'll see what I mean."

The inspector wasn't trying to be cruel. Though his eyes were fixed firmly ahead, there was a smile on his face, teasing Tanna.

The two turned the corner at the cobbler's and made their way along to the street with the tramline.

"Very good, sir. I'll take a look when we get back," Tanna said, determined to rise to the challenge. "But if Genkichi had nothing to do with the case, why was he killed? I'd always assumed that he'd acted as the decoy and then been silenced to make sure he'd never reveal the secret."

"No, that wasn't the reason. But the killer did have to get rid of him. It was absolutely vital."

"Hmm," Tanna said, half-sounding as though he agreed. He was annoyed, because if he were to ask the real reason, he'd have been told, as with his previous question, to work it out for himself.

"Shall we find somewhere to have a cold drink?" Onitsura asked. "We can talk about it there."

When they reached the street with the tramline, the inspector looked around. Only, there were no decent cafés in the San'ya area, so in the end they made their way back to Asakusa, where the found an *okonomiyaki* restaurant that didn't seem to be very popular and headed upstairs.

"This is the perfect place to have a chat," the inspector said. "It's like the *Mary Celeste* in here."

"I've never had *okonomiyaki* before. I thought it was something only women ate."

Tanna knelt down on a summer floor cushion, mindful of the knees of his trousers, and looked about the restaurant curiously. Dotted around the walls were framed portraits of actresses playing female samurai, done in brush and black ink, and drawings done on coloured paper.

Taking the damp towels offered them, the two detectives cleaned their hands and wiped the perspiration from their foreheads.

"It certainly is quiet today. Is it always like this?" Tanna asked the waitress.

"These days, yes. We don't get many customers in summer," she replied, taking the used towels.

Above her head, the large blades of an electric fan rotated like an upside-down helicopter.

"I'll be back in a moment," Onitsura said, seeming to have remembered something all of a sudden. "I need to make a telephone call."

He got up and stepped out into the corridor. Five minutes later, he came back and sat down again.

"So," he said, resting both elbows on the table. "Regarding your question… The investigation has now revealed that, on the night in question, Genkichi Obata was at the Tachibana-ya, drinking with the owner's husband. In other words, he wasn't the man who had dinner at the Orchid restaurant that night, as we'd previously believed."

"Right, so this means that it must have been somebody else who acted as the decoy?"

As Tanna spoke, Onitsura stared at him sceptically.

"Does it? Even you can see that having somebody play the role of a decoy was a dangerous thing to do—so dangerous, in fact, that it might have cost Genkichi Obata his life. Would the murderer really have compounded the risk by having to kill a second person?"

"But the killer *did* have somebody besides Genkichi play the part... Or do you mean that it's the owner of the Tachibana-ya who's lying?"

"You're only considering the story from one angle. You've got it into your head that the person who showed up at the Orchid was a decoy."

Tanna stared hard into the inspector's eyes and for a moment held his breath. He could tell that what Onitsura was suggesting was terribly important, but it took him some time to appreciate what he meant.

"... so you're saying the man who went to the Orchid *wasn't* a decoy?"

"Precisely."

"But then, are you saying it was Gosuke Nishinohata?"

"I am. It was the man himself." In contrast to Tanna's uncertainty, Onitsura's voice was brimming with confidence. "Remember what the report said, Tanna. That evening, he hadn't had dinner: he'd just had a light snack, a sandwich. He would have been famished by eleven o'clock. It's little wonder then that when he was walking through Ikebukuro, he spotted the Orchid's neon sign and felt like having a bite to eat."

"But, sir..." The words that came out were startlingly loud, but Tanna immediately took control of his voice again. "I remember the sandwich, too, so I don't doubt that he was hungry on the way home. But Nishinohata was lying on the roof of that train at eleven-forty. How could he have been seen eating Chinese food at the same time?"

Tanna's protests, however, did not perturb the inspector in the slightest. Instead, he opened his fan, and, as he cooled his face, he slowly, convincingly set out his theory.

"Because our assumption that he was thrown from Ryodaishi Bridge has been wrong all along. I think that is what the voice actor must have meant when he said that our thinking was fundamentally flawed. But how he came to realize this is still a mystery to me."

Though the inspector said he didn't know how Murase had discovered this, Tanna, for his part, was baffled by how Onitsura himself had reached this conclusion. He wanted to get back to the office to review the reports as soon as possible.

"Then, the bloodstains on Ryodaishi Bridge were…"

"… planted there, to make it look as though it was the scene of the crime. Abandoning the victim's car in front of the National Museum was also, I think, part of the murderer's plan to make it look as though the crime took place in Ueno."

"By 'murderer', you still mean Fumie Hishinuma?" Tanna asked, just to make sure. Now that his working hypothesis had collapsed, he'd lost confidence in all his previous assumptions.

"Yes," Onitsura replied.

"Then, where do you suppose the real crime scene was? Given the body was thrown on top of a train, surely we need to find somewhere with an overpass?"

"Correct… It's getting late, isn't it? I'm hungry," said Onitsura, looking towards the corridor and then back at Tanna. "There are constraints on both time and distance. You'd also have to know the area around the overpass well. Taking all these factors into account, I think Omiya would be our best guess."

"Is there an overpass there?"

When he'd gone there the other day, Tanna hadn't spotted anything like that.

"If you're heading out of Tokyo, it's just after the station. When I went there recently, I mistakenly took the east exit and had no choice but to double-back across an overpass to reach the west one. At the time, I never imagined that it could have been the scene of the crime."

From the way he spoke, it was clear that Onitsura was almost certain that this was where the murder had been committed.

There were several overpasses between Ueno and Omiya on the line passing via Ikebukuro, but throwing a body over the railing would naturally have left traces of the victim's blood, so a forensics team could easily reach a conclusion on that score. This was one point on which they could be optimistic.

Tanna was surprised to see that, in the blink of an eye, the barrier in front of him had been silently lifted.

"So, then… Fumie's alibi that she was buying medicine at the pharmacy is worthless, isn't it, sir?"

"Exactly. I just rang Omiya Station to check, and that night, train No. 117 pulled out of the station at midnight forty-nine—that is, almost a full half-hour after the scheduled time. It was late because of the extra time required on the route through Ikebukuro."

"I see," Tanna said, nodding.

After leaving Omiya, the No. 117 must have increased its speed, reducing the late running to only twenty minutes by the time it pulled into Shiroishi Station.

"So, if she pushed the body over the railing at midnight forty-nine, her alibi of having bought painkillers at half past eleven is absolutely irrelevant, irrespective of whether it's true or not."

Hearing this explanation, Tanna finally understood the reason for Onitsura's quiet excitement that morning. He knew that he himself would never have been able to hide his emotions as well as the inspector.

"Then we're done here?" Tanna asked after a brief pause.

"Yes, we can leave the rest to the criminal investigation department."

"Do you think they serve beer at *okonomiyaki* restaurants?" said Tanna, licking his lips. "I think this deserves a celebratory drink."

FIFTEEN

A Conversation on a Rooftop

1.

Shusaku Narumi had breathed his last a week before the voice actor Murase did. After the accident, Atsuko saw him only once, and even then only after much effort. Since the union had drafted in female employees to take turns tending his sickbed, Atsuko wasn't officially permitted to visit him at the hospital. Therefore, she'd claimed to be a cousin from Narumi's home town, who'd come to find out how he was, but she found Narumi still unconscious, his entire head wrapped up in white bandages, covering every trace of his formerly elegant, handsome features. As she placed the straw of his feeding cup to his lips and tried to give him some cold juice, tears dampened her cheeks for the first time since she'd met him. Never before had their bright and happy romance called for tears.

She was informed of Narumi's death by her father exactly two days after that. Naturally, there was no solemnity to the announcement: as they sat there after dinner, chatting away happily, he mentioned it in passing, as though just happening to recall the fact. In that moment, everything turned dark, as though Atsuko had lost her eyesight, and only narrowly did she manage to hold back a fit of vomiting.

It was perhaps to be expected that news of Narumi's death wouldn't immediately reach Atsuko, given that she had no formal relation to him, but the time lag had only been exacerbated by the physical distance between them, which had kept the two of them apart to the very end. She couldn't attend the funeral. She couldn't even let grief show on her face. She had no choice but to fix a mourning band secretly about her heart, so that nobody else should know about it.

On the day of Narumi's funeral, Atsuko hid herself away in her room, citing a headache as the reason. There, she savoured the memories of her first encounter with Narumi the previous summer. Having wearied of the seaside by her family villa in Zushi, she'd gone to swim alone at Morito Beach, just past Hayama. She'd very nearly drowned there, after she developed a cramp when swimming a hundred yards out in the open sea. It was Narumi who'd saved her. As she'd lain there on the sand, she'd gazed up at him and his slender frame, wondering where he had got all that strength from. She also remembered that, as they reached the shore, her eyes had been drawn to a jellyfish sting on his back, which was so red that it looked as though he had been whipped.

As vice-chairman of the union, Narumi had fought the company's unfair practices tooth and nail, and he'd never lost the conviction of his principles. The reason he'd always rejected support from other unions and done everything under his own steam was that he didn't want to entangle himself in obligations to others. He despised the leaders who would organize demonstrations and parade down main streets, blocking the traffic. When one of his fellow committee members tried to get him to don a white headband, it was Narumi who'd scoffed at him, saying, "What do you think we are?! A kamikaze squadron?" No, Narumi was no leftist

313

poseur. And while Atsuko loved him, she also respected him deeply for this. What's more, she knew only too well how rare a man worthy of respect was these days.

Yet this happy love of hers had been but a fleeting dream that lasted less than a single year.

The day after the funeral, Atsuko was invited out by Fumie to go for an evening stroll in the Ginza. Atsuko wasn't especially keen on the idea, but, finding no reason to refuse, she agreed and they arranged a time and a place to meet. She hadn't seen Fumie in a while and thought that a trip out might help her to forget her sorrows. Though Atsuko wanted to cherish Narumi's memory for ever, she also wanted to get rid of this heart-breaking sadness as quickly as possible.

That day, in contrast to Atsuko's heart, the sky was so bright that she felt as though she were about to faint. As she stood under the awning of the National Theatre, where they'd agreed to meet, Atsuko could see, even though she tried not to look at them, the figures of young men and women in loud Hawaiian shirts and sundresses, all looking bright and cheerful, as though their happiness could never end. Not one of them seemed to realize that all this was only an illusion, and that they were standing on fragile foundations, which could crumble at any moment.

Until just the other day, when she and Narumi had strolled side by side, or rather until after Narumi had his accident and was taken away by ambulance, Atsuko too had believed, as she sat in a booth in a café, awaiting his arrival, that happiness would last for ever. Now, having gone out to try to forget her sorrows, she was, on the contrary, conscious of becoming more and more despondent.

And so, Atsuko was relieved when Fumie showed up at five o'clock on the dot, as promised. She was wearing an unusual white

Chinese dress and carrying on her slender arm a matching white bag. With each step in her white pumps, her graceful legs could be glimpsed through the plunging split in her dress.

When she was standing in front of Atsuko, Fumie asked:

"Have you been waiting long?"

"No, I've just got here myself."

"That's a relief! Right, let's go to the Ginza and find something to cool us down," she suggested, lightly applying a lawn handkerchief to her forehead.

Even though it was a weekday, there was a constant flow of people on the street running between Yurakucho and the Ginza. Carried by the wave of people, the two women crossed the intersection at Sukiya Bridge. As the traffic light turned from green to amber and Atsuko picked up her pace, she recalled crossing that road with Narumi by her side on the night when he'd gone to the Black Swan to check out Haibara's alibi. Holding his hand before they parted on the pavement was the last time she'd seen him as she remembered him.

The closer they got to Owaricho, the more vividly the memory came back to her. Right in front of her, she could see Murase's car careening through the red light and hear the screams of passers-by.

"Let's go that way," she said, suddenly grabbing Fumie's arm and turning right.

In that moment, she was thinking only of herself, and, after a few moments, she finally realized that they were on tree-lined Namiki Street.

"What is it?" Fumie asked, looking puzzled.

"Nothing," Atsuko snapped back.

Perhaps sensing from her tone that Atsuko didn't wish to be pressed further, Fumie dropped the matter.

"We walked down this street the last time we were here, didn't we?" said Fumie, as she peered into the window of a jeweller's.

Atsuko had just remembered the same thing. The appearance of all the shops and boutiques, as well as the layout of their display windows, had hardly changed since they strolled around them a month and a half ago. The only thing that had changed was Atsuko herself. The gold pendant she had wanted still glinted preciously on the uppermost glass shelf. But today it held no allure for her. Without her beloved Narumi, she had no cause to adorn herself.

Suddenly, she recalled that she'd come out that day to forget her grief. Besides, if she started sobbing, Fumie was bound to suspect something. So far, she'd been so preoccupied with peering into each and every shop window that she seemed entirely oblivious to Atsuko's sombre mood.

"Oh, no! They've sold that sabre-shaped tiepin you had your eye on," she called out cheerfully, turning to Fumie. "Or did you buy it in the end?"

"It wasn't me, no. What a pity… Oh, yes, of course." A look of recollection seemed to come over Fumie. "It's a little early, but what do you say we have dinner at Posillipo again?"

"That would be nice. But it's my treat this evening."

"I won't hear of it! I just invited you, didn't I?"

Leaving the shop window behind, they slowly picked their way towards the Italian restaurant. Since it was summer, it was still light, despite the late hour, but all the shopfronts were already lit with neon lighting. The hazy glow revealed the dazed expression on Atsuko's sleep-deprived face.

Arriving at Posillipo, the two women went upstairs and took a seat by a large flowerpot. Unlike on their last visit, the tables were now mostly occupied, and the Chinese windmill had been replaced by a date palm. The only things that hadn't changed were the tiled fountains and the dark-skinned waiter who came to take their order. He appeared to remember them and smiled as he bowed.

"What will you have, Atsuko?"

"I think I'll go for the macaroni Caruso. It was so delicious last time."

"An excellent choice, miss," the waiter said amiably. "Everybody seems to love that one."

Atsuko tried to lighten the atmosphere by forcing herself to be more animated than usual. Although it wasn't the most appropriate topic of conversation, they discussed the company: the death of the director had proved to be a turning point in the negotiations, and, now that a resolution had been reached, both the workers and the management had heaved a sigh of relief. Both women in fact found the conversation rather enjoyable.

If Narumi were alive, he'd be terribly pleased with the outcome, the thought struck Atsuko. She shook her head and tried to sweep the thought aside.

"I understand how you must feel," Fumie said all of a sudden, as she lit a cigarette while they were enjoying an after-dinner cup of coffee.

Cup in hand, Atsuko had been in a world of her own, daydreaming about Narumi again. In that instant, she couldn't understand what Fumie meant.

"I'm sorry?"

"I understand why you feel so low."

When she saw those big eyes, with their unfathomable depths, gazing intently into her own, Atsuko panicked.

"… so low?"

"You were in love with Mr Narumi, weren't you? I thought as much."

"… with Mr Narumi?"

317

"There's no use hiding it, you know. When I told you about Mr Haibara and the Black Swan, he just up and went to the bar, asking all sorts of questions about Mr Haibara. When I heard that, I knew straight away that you two had to be together."

"…"

"Even just now, you turned away from that street because you didn't want to see the spot where he had his accident."

"…"

"It's fine—you needn't worry. I wouldn't dream of telling anybody," she said warmly, placing her coffee cup to her lips.

It wasn't just her voice: there was a note of kindness and sympathy in her big eyes, too. As she returned Fumie's gaze, Atsuko could feel a sense of calm returning to her. The suddenness of the remark had taken her off guard, but Fumie couldn't have any ulterior motive; very likely, she just wanted to confirm what she had already guessed.

Atsuko placed her cup back on its saucer.

"Please, you mustn't breathe a word of it…"

"Don't worry, I won't."

"I've gone to a lot of trouble to keep it a secret."

"I can well imagine."

"That man who was killed in Nagaoka—you know, that Hanpei Chita—he tried to blackmail me about it."

"What?!" Fumie seemed startled and set her cup down with a clatter. "When?"

"Do you remember the last time we came here? It was just after that, as I was on my way home. He came up to me in Shibuya Station. I can't say I'm sorry he met his end like that."

"So, he was a blackmailer through and through…"

Fumie weighed her words. But Atsuko neither understood nor was interested in the sentiment behind them.

318

"Anyway, you have to promise me you won't tell a soul."

"Pinkie promise," Fumie said, reaching her hand across the table and linking her little finger with Atsuko's. "There is one thing I'd like to ask in return though. In fact, it's why I asked you here today."

"I'm all ears. What is it?"

"There's no rush," Fumie said, flashing a smile. "We can discuss it later."

She almost seemed to be evading the question.

2.

They entered the department store around half an hour before closing time. Fumie strode casually through the door, with Atsuko following her, thinking they were going to do some shopping. The lift stopped at every floor, but Fumie went up and up, all the way to the very top.

"They have the cutest little bear cub up here!"

Fumie turned around as she stepped out onto the open-air rooftop. Until now, she'd shown hardly any interest in children or small animals. In fact, she'd never once regretted not having children with her husband. Consequently, Atsuko found her sudden desire to see a bear cub rather peculiar, even if only for a moment. Be that as it may, Atsuko, who had a love of cats and dogs, had never seen a bear cub, so she gave the oddness of the situation no further thought.

Fumie took out some change and bought some food, which she tossed into the cub's cage, making the furry animal happy. She then crossed the rooftop and leant against the bulky concrete railing.

It was nearing closing time, but there were still plenty of customers and their children around. The concession stand was busy with parents trying to get their children to drink cold milk or juice, and, around the flower garden, there were several fathers anxiously adjusting the aperture of their lenses in order to take pictures of their beloved little ones with all the flowers in the background. There were also many parents who simply let their children run riot, while they themselves sat idly on benches.

"What was it you wanted to ask me?" Atsuko said, returning Fumie's gaze.

The latter placed her hand on the railing and stared out at the sea of neon lights that were becoming more and more vivid.

"Promise me you won't be shocked," Fumie said, turning around again.

"Why would I be shocked?"

"Don't ask why. Just promise me."

Her tone was assertive, as though she was trying to extract the promise forcibly from her. Atsuko looked at her with a mix of trepidation and curiosity and nodded silently; she seemed wary, as though having realized that there was no way out now.

Fumie looked around.

"Well, then, let's talk," she said, suddenly lowering her voice. "It was me who killed the director."

"What did you just say?"

"It was me who killed Hanpei Chita, too. And I killed the day labourer who died in the waiting room at Hamamatsu Station."

Atsuko was not the least bit surprised. Or, it wasn't that she *wasn't* surprised per se, but rather that she *couldn't* be surprised. There was no space in her mind to comprehend it. It was as if she'd been shot repeatedly by a machine gun.

Fumie kept her mouth shut and, with her characteristically beautiful eyes, looked at Atsuko, as though waiting for a reaction.

"I imagine this must come as something of a surprise."

"I am surprised… And yet, I'm not surprised at all. If it's true, you must have had good reason to kill them."

"Thank you for being so understanding."

"Who knows, I might kill somebody myself if I had reason enough. All I'd lack is the courage to do it."

"Thank you again. You're the only one who understands me. That's why I wanted you to hear my confession. I don't need your judgement. I'm a stubborn person, and I don't like to be judged. I just want you to listen to me."

"I understand."

Atsuko herself cared little for unsolicited criticism—unless, of course, it was called for.

For a moment, Fumie was silent, as though plotting her next move. Bathed in the slanting light of the setting sun, her eyes and nose stood out clearly, and only her lips were in the shadows.

"My father died when I was in college," she said. "He was shot by a Grumman plane during a raid on Hakata. It was in the spring of the closing year of the war."

Fumie began her tale in such a matter-of-fact manner that, when it came to it, she didn't seem at all embarrassed about revealing that she'd sold herself to a brothel in Osaka to pay for her schooling. Because of her fastidious nature, Atsuko had always despised and scorned prostitutes, but when she heard that Fumie had become one simply to pursue her studies, she wasn't in the least inclined to view her differently; she even admired her determination.

"I left as soon as I'd made enough to cover four years of schooling. I went home and waited for the new school year to begin.

That's when I went back to my old school. I hadn't seen any friends in Osaka, so nobody knew that I'd been there. Everybody believed me when I told them I'd been recovering from pleurisy."

After describing the joys of campus life, she told Atsuko how she'd met Shintaro Hishinuma, then head of a department, at a Christmas bazaar at the university, and how they'd fallen in love and embarked on married life together after she gradu-ated. Perhaps it was the glow of the golden hour, but her cheeks appeared to flush as she described that first encounter.

Atsuko had heard from her own mother that Shintaro Hishinuma's first marriage had been a failure. His wife had been a luxurious, vain, theatrical woman, and he'd been tormented constantly by her behaviour. In this second marriage, Shintaro had sought in his new wife the love he hadn't found in his previ-ous one, while Fumie, on the other hand, had cared tenderly for her husband's emotional wounds. Six months after their wedding, Shintaro had been promoted, and so Atsuko could well imagine that their marriage had been a happy one, blessed in both love and wealth.

It was at her wedding reception that Fumie first met the direc-tor. Even as they chatted, she'd no idea that here was a man who'd once been a client of hers in her days at the Palace of Dreams. The director had now grown his characteristic moustache, so this was perhaps unsurprising. In fact, it wasn't until around two years later that Fumie realized who he was. For his part, the director didn't seem to know that his employee's new wife was the woman with whom he'd spent the night all those years ago, or, if he did, possibly he just hadn't yet seen fit to do anything about it; in any case, nothing happened during those first two years.

"I suspect the reason he sent my husband to Lancashire was so that he'd be able to get me on my own. Maybe that's just my imagination, though. At any rate, it was that same evening when the director called."

"What did he want?"

"Put simply, he wanted to see me. At first, he used my husband as a pretext and said he had some company matters to discuss. We met a couple of times at restaurants in Tsukiji and Yanagibashi, but his tone soon turned nasty. It was when I got up to leave that he mentioned the Palace of Dreams. He started saying things like, 'What do you suppose will happen when Hishinuma finds out about this?' I've heard blackmail described as being like having the life choked out of you, but in this case I really did think I was going to pass out. It was as though an enormous crack had suddenly appeared in the happy marriage I'd taken such pains to build for us, and now it threatened to collapse at any moment..."

She stopped and sighed heavily. During her time at the Palace of Dreams, she'd been so careful not to have her picture taken, lest her former identity ever come to light. Even after changing her name and getting married, Fumie always took every precaution: she rarely went out in public and, whenever she did, she always wore sunglasses. After all, the Palace of Dreams catered to high society: as the wife of a businessman, she never knew whom she might run into. In the end, though, these precautions had all been for naught.

Atsuko looked around. There were fewer guests remaining on the rooftop now.

"I never knew the director was that kind of man. I'd heard rumours that he had a weakness for women, but I'd no idea he was so despicable."

Fumie simply nodded. She seemed to be trying to suppress the rising tide of her emotions.

"… On the afternoon of the first of June, he left his private secretary behind and drove out to meet me at the Museum of Modern Art. I don't know where he got it, but he showed me a picture from my days at the Palace of Dreams and threatened me, saying that, unless I did as he said, he'd make it public. I leapt at him and tried to snatch the picture away. In the struggle, the picture was torn in half, and I was left with the upper part. In my rage, I ripped it up into tiny pieces and threw them at him. Only…" Here, she lowered her voice. "It was one thing to tear up the photo, but I couldn't let anyone who knew my secret go on living. Don't you think that every human being has the right to protect her own happiness? That's why I did it, to protect my happiness."

"… I understand, yes—"

"I couldn't sleep because of the director's threats. Then, it suddenly dawned on me that if I were to kill him, there'd be nothing left to worry about. I'd lie there, tossing and turning, thinking up all kinds of ways to keep myself safe if I went through with it. That day at the museum, I'd already hatched a plan, and I told him to meet me later on at my house. He didn't suspect a thing: he thought I was finally relenting, so he was in a good mood. He'd no idea that he'd been sentenced to death…"

It was half past six already, but it was still light all around. Atsuko could clearly see Fumie's eyes glinting.

"I told him to meet me at the east exit of Omiya Station at midnight, on the pretext of not wanting the maid or the neighbours to spot us. You see, the first step in my plan was to throw his body onto a train that left the station a little after midnight."

Atsuko, who'd thought that the body had been dropped from Ryodaishi Bridge in Ueno, looked at her in surprise, but decided to hear her story without asking any questions.

"As I was waiting by the station for the director's car to arrive, I heard an announcement saying that the train would be thirty minutes late because of an accident at Shimojujo. It was poor timing for an accident, I thought, but then, it didn't really affect me, since I'd only to extend the schedule by that much. If I hadn't heard the announcement, though, I'd have been really confused, because the train I was counting on wouldn't have come for a long time."

"So, it wasn't in Ueno that he died?"

"No, it was in Omiya. As the train pulled into the station, I led the director out onto the overpass and fired the pistol just as the locomotive blew its whistle, about to depart. All that remained was to push the body over the railing. The train wasn't going fast, so I couldn't miss. It was easy."

"You were lucky that nobody saw you," Atsuko said, as though congratulating her.

"It was the middle of the night, so there were no passers-by. Even if there had been any, they'd have used the level crossing below. Nobody would have bothered taking the stairs, going all the way up and down again. For three nights in a row, I had stood there, testing it out."

Atsuko was silently impressed with Fumie's meticulous planning. But still, she couldn't quite fathom why Fumie had placed the bloodstains on Ryodaishi Bridge to make it look like the scene of the crime.

3.

As the customers on the roof thinned out, quiet gradually descended. Once again, Fumie began to speak in her soft whisper.

"My plan wasn't even half over. Next, I had to get in his car, which he'd left under the overpass, and drive to Ueno Park. I needed to make it look as though the crime had been committed in Ueno so as to give myself an alibi... Why don't we sit down over there on that bench?" Fumie suggested, walking over and taking a seat. "That's better. Now, where was I? Ah, yes, my alibi... You see, the train onto which I pushed the director's body was scheduled to pass under Ryodaishi Bridge in Ueno at 11.40, so by making it look as though he'd been killed there, the police would assume that was when the murder had taken place. But at that time, I'd go to a pharmacy in Omiya on the pretext of getting some medicine for stomach cramps. That was my plan."

"I see," Atsuko said. "But how could you possibly find such a convenient train?"

"You need only look at a timetable and any number of ideas will present themselves. I've always been interested in the railway, and I like travelling," Fumie said nonchalantly.

She told Atsuko that she'd abandoned the director's car outside the National Museum, leaving his hat inside the car and the door open, in order to make it look as though he'd fled the vehicle. She smiled proudly when she said that that was how the police had interpreted it, too. Atsuko nodded, recognizing that the bullish company director would indeed never have allowed himself to be led into Ueno Park like that.

"After that, I smeared the director's blood, which I'd soaked up with a sponge, on the railings of Ryodaishi Bridge and threw one of his shoes away at Uguisudani. The Yamanote, Keihin–Tohoku, Joban and various other lines all run together there, so it was imperative that I got the right one. I'd worked all this out in advance and had remembered which track was the downbound Tohoku line."

Having done all that, she'd then taken six taxis and returned home to Omiya at around four o'clock in the morning. Each time she changed vehicles, she would make herself out to be a different woman, now a wealthy lady, now a maid, and would have the drivers make detours and double-back, just in case anybody should have been following her.

"You must've been quite relieved by the time you got home."

"Only I wasn't," Fumie said. "I hadn't finished. You see, there was still one more tedious thing I had to do."

"What was that?"

"The director happened to let slip that he'd stopped off for some Chinese food on his way to Omiya."

"But why did tha—"

"The problem was the time he'd eaten. Surprised by this, I delved deeper and learnt that he'd left the restaurant in Ikebukuro a little before midnight. Do you follow me? He ought to have died at Ryodaishi Bridge by then."

"Why, yes…"

"He's got such distinctive features, I was sure somebody would remember seeing him. And if the police got wind of this, my carefully constructed alibi would come crumbling down."

No sooner had she returned home and breathed a sigh of relief than she'd had to come up with another plan.

Drawn in by Fumie's story, Atsuko had even forgotten her sorrow at losing Narumi.

By now, there was hardly anybody else left on the rooftop. Although it was just after midsummer and the days were long, the corners of the building were gradually growing darker and darker.

"It took all my wits, but eventually, two hours later, just as day was breaking, I had an idea. I realized that I could make them think that the man who'd shown up at the Orchid in Ikebukuro wasn't in fact the director, but a decoy who was the spitting image of him. In other words, I could turn the facts to my advantage. I could make it look as though the murderer had killed him at Ryodaishi Bridge at 11.40 and was trying to create a false alibi by having it appear that he was still alive ten minutes later."

"But could you really find someone who looked like him so easily? He was very distinctive with that moustache, after all…"

"The moustache in fact only made it easier. Put a false one on someone of roughly the same age and with more or less the same build, and you'll be so fixated on it that you won't really pay much attention to the facial features. The human eye is a fickle thing. I thought that, if I was bold enough, I'd be sure to succeed."

"Yes, you may well be right about that…"

Atsuko recalled reading in a psychology book that human sight could be unreliable. Yet Gosuke Nishinohata was a well-known figure, whose face had appeared in weekly magazines and newspapers, and no matter how similar the body might have been, if the face itself were too different, it would surely have raised suspicions.

As Atsuko pondered these misgivings, Fumie spoke of Genkichi Obata.

"The idea came to me because I remembered that a gardener who used to come to our house, a man named Genkichi, looked a lot like the director—not only in build but also in his features."

Genkichi's whereabouts, however, were a mystery. Fumie had heard a rumour that he'd lost several jobs because of his drinking and was now eking out a wretched existence somewhere in Tokyo, working as a day labourer. So, Fumie had asked her gardener, Tatsugoro, to find out where he was as quickly as possible.

Genkichi was a good man at heart. Never would he have suspected her of harbouring any murderous intent towards him, not least since she was a former client of his.

"If I could have done it any other way without killing him, I would have done. But in order to save myself, I had to close my ears to the mercy of my heart. Unsuspecting of any foul play, Genkichi believed my story that a very wealthy man in Kansai wanted to take him on as a gardener, and so he set off for a fictitious interview in high spirits. I secretly slipped a photograph of the director into his pocket along with a false moustache. That way, the people who discovered him would assume he'd used the photo as a reference to disguise himself."

Atsuko couldn't quite bring herself to agree that, in order to save her own skin, Fumie, for all her ingenuity, had no other choice than to sacrifice Genkichi. She thought that Fumie had probably had this part in mind when she admonished her at the very outset not to judge her.

In any case, she'd bought the man clothes and even some whisky as going-away presents, before sending him off on his merry way to Osaka. But en route he died from poisoning, just as she had planned.

By now, Atsuko and Fumie were the only ones left on the rooftop. Perhaps hoping to finish her tale before the security guard came to announce closing time, Fumie now began to speak more rapidly, leaving Atsuko no time to ask questions.

"But once again, I found that I couldn't rest easy," she continued. "I decided not to mention this earlier, lest the story get too confusing, but two days after the death of the director, Hanpei Chita turned up out of the blue."

Fumie had no truck with the Shaman's hard man. When she tried to turn him away at the door, his white eyes flashed and he began to make threats, informing her that he'd witnessed the murder of the director.

"'I was after the director, too,' he said, grinning. 'I was even planning to beat the bastard to a pulp, and that's why I was following him. So, imagine my surprise when you did the job for me. I saw everything, from the bridge in Omiya to Ryodaishi Bridge in Ueno.'"

To think that, of all men, this scorpion should have witnessed the crime. It was as great a shock to her as when the director had thrust in her face that photograph from her days working as a prostitute. She just stood there, breath held.

"'When it comes to the director,' he continued, 'we're comrades in arms, you and I. Depending on the circumstances, I could be a very good ally to you. Depending on the circumstances, mind.'

"'So, you mean to blackmail me?' I said.

"'Blackmail is such an ugly word, don't you think? Better let's call it a deal. Only, we can't talk here. We'll have a little chat in the parlour, shall we?' he said, becoming more and more brazen."

As she recovered from the shock, Fumie had already decided that she was going to avert this fast-approaching disaster. She didn't know how she was going to do it exactly, but she knew that she had no choice but to kill him, too.

"'I think 5,000,000 should just about do it,' he said as though it were nothing, when we were sitting on the sofa. 'How does that sound?'"

As Atsuko listened to the story, she recalled her own bleak encounter with the man in Shibuya and reflected that his demeanour had been the same when he tried to blackmail her.

"'That's a lot of money,' I said. 'I can't get it for you right away.'"

It wasn't a good idea to reject him out of hand. But since Fumie had no intention of paying him, she had to reassure him by pretending to compromise.

"'I never said anything about getting it all at once. We wouldn't want your husband finding out about it now, would we?'

"'Come back again. I'll have a better idea of how exactly to do it by then.'

"'Now, now, don't try to stall for time… The police are after me because they think *I* did it. We need to get this sorted out as soon as possible.'

"'But that's impossible! Even if I were to pay in instalments, 5,000,000 yen is a lot of money. It's not the sort of thing I can get my hands on just like that. And besides, my head is spinning right now. I can't give you a proper answer. You'll have to come back in five days' time. I'll have an answer for you then…'"

Of course, those five days were not to prepare the money, but to work out a strategy. If she was going to take on the formidable Chita, she needed time to think it through carefully.

Chita had then left, placated with surprising ease by Fumie's pleas. The skills she'd mastered during her time as a prostitute had come in handy once again.

4.

It was decided very early on that the director's ashes would be buried in Nagaoka. By the time Chita came back five days later, Fumie had already perfected her plan to kill him, using the funeral as a ploy. She'd already summoned her maid, Tai Okuwa, back from her family home in Chiba, where she'd sent her, lest she obstruct her plans to kill the director. She'd also posted the advertisement at her alma mater, looking for a student to watch the house while she was gone. Now all that remained was to set her plan in motion.

Fumie knew from the newspapers and radio bulletins that the police were hunting for Chita. On the appointed day, he turned up at her house from god only knew where, calm and composed, bearing no signs of exhaustion from being on the run. In fact, he seemed rather to enjoy the thrill of the chase.

"Before we get down to business," Fumie said, ushering him into the parlour, "just what are you going to do with the money afterwards? The police think that you're the murderer and they'll catch you sooner or later. You'll be in a lot of trouble if you give them my name under questioning."

"I'm going to catch a boat to Taiwan and join the National Army. I'll go on the rampage again. My friends over there keep telling me to join them."

"Really?"

"Why would I lie about it? Even if the statute of limitations expires, I doubt I'll ever come back. It may be a cliché, but I'm getting fed up living on this cramped island."

The blackmailer puffed out his chest, emulating a proud nationalist. Fumie heaved a sigh of relief.

"Anyway, how's my money coming along?"

"I've got a plan," Fumie said, moving closer and getting down to business. "The funeral's taking place in Nagaoka on the fifteenth. I have to attend. I can give you 3,000,000 there. The remainder will have to be in four monthly instalments of 500,000. How does that sound?"

"What can I say? It looks as though I don't have much choice in the matter. I suppose I'll have to wait."

"Good. You go ahead. I'll give you 100,000 now for your train ticket and accommodation."

"Fine."

"You aren't safe here in Tokyo. And as I said, if you're arrested and my name comes up—"

"Oh, calm down, will you? I used to work for the intelligence services. If I decide not to talk about something, then the words won't pass my lips. Not even under torture. Not that the Japanese police know much about that…"

The ordinarily expressionless face smiled for the first time.

Having specified a *ryokan*, Fumie told him where and how to contact her, gave him 100,000 yen and sent him on his way. The plan was on track.

"People may well look down on the techniques employed by prostitutes, but they do come in handy when you're dealing with men. It was because of them that I was able to manipulate Chita right to the end. It's probably down to them that my marriage has been so happy and harmonious, as well. Joking aside, I really do think that girls ought to learn these skills before they get married. They could set up a 'charm school' where they teach them how to attract and seduce men. Wasn't it Weininger who said that the prostitute's techniques were essential in a marriage?"

Atsuko had never heard of Weininger, but she could see Fumie's point. She even took it as a piece of well-meaning, almost sisterly advice.

Fumie suddenly looked at the clock. Atsuko in turn looked at her watch. It was already ten minutes after closing time. The guard would be making his rounds shortly.

"Quick, I have to explain—there isn't any time to lose!" she said, speaking even more rapidly now. "The plan was to make it look as though I went to Nagaoka on the Shin'etsu line, when in fact I took a Joetsu-line service."

She began by explaining that the Nos. 311 and 725 both departed from Ueno Station as a single train, albeit with different numbers, and that the service running via Joetsu arrived in Nagaoka four hours and nineteen minutes earlier.

"To be specific, the 725 arrived in Nagaoka at 13.14. I immediately sent the maid to relax at the *ryokan* and went to meet Chita,

333

just as we'd arranged, at a spot near Nagaoka North Station. I lured him to an out-of-the-way spot and stabbed him. I'd given him tea laced with sleeping pills, so he was already half out of it. It was like leading a lamb to the slaughter."

Atsuko had no objection to Chita's murder. If only she'd had the courage herself, she too would have gladly rid society of that vermin by plunging the knife in.

"At that time, I was still supposed to be on the 311 train, so I had to rush back so that somebody would actually see me on board."

Fumie was speaking faster and faster. The lights of the Ginza were reflected up in the clouds overhead, making it look as though an aurora had appeared in the sky. The department store was about to close its back door. If she didn't hurry, Atsuko feared they'd both be locked in.

"In practical terms, it was a simple enough matter, and there was no immediate rush. I had plenty of time to catch the 15.38 bound for Osaka at Nagaoka Station. The sixth stop was Echigo–Hirota, and it was due to arrive there at 16.24, stopping only for a minute. The 311 Shin'etsu service was scheduled to pull in twenty-two minutes later, at 16.46, so I could just get off and change trains there."

Fumie's gaze drifted to another part of the rooftop as she tried to avoid looking at Atsuko. It was getting dark, but her eyes were still glittering.

She hurriedly told Atsuko how she had gone to the conductor's compartment on the pretext of having dropped her stamp book and had him take down her name and address. Atsuko watched on as her dark lips moved, revealing glimpses of her white teeth. Then at last her tale was done.

A hush suddenly fell between them. From far below came the sound of a car's exhaust, but Fumie just carried on staring off into the distance.

"There's just one thing I don't understand," Atsuko whispered, as though overwhelmed by the silence.

"And what's that?"

"Why you're telling me all this."

"Because I no longer have to keep it a secret," Fumie replied, taking out a handkerchief and mopping her brow.

Atsuko did likewise. She had been so engrossed in the story that she hadn't even noticed how much she was perspiring.

"People are always apt to say all sorts of things about each other. But I want there to be at least one person who knows the truth."

"But then, why don't you need to keep it a secret any more?"

"Because the police have already worked out most of it. Some detectives have been looking into why I asked Tatsugoro about Genkichi's whereabouts. He came and told me about it the other day."

"Oh..."

"And one of their inspectors has managed to find out from the maid that we took the Joetsu line rather than the Shin'etsu."

"I see..."

"I also got wind that a forensics team was spotted checking for blood on the overpass at Omiya Station. So, they must have already pieced together about nine-tenths of the picture. The only thing I can't understand is how they worked out that the murder didn't take place in Ueno..." She began to trail off, a faint tremor of emotion in her voice. "A detective's been tailing me ever since I left home. Haven't you noticed?"

"I can't say that I have, no."

"He's hiding around the corner in that grey building over there behind the bear cage. He's been watching us for a while now."

Fumie's gaze reached over to a concrete pen, where elephants had once been kept.

"Watch and see. His face will pop out any minute. He's a miserable-looking guy in a hunting cap."

Atsuko did as she was told and waited for the man to appear.

The silhouette of the building formed a black triangle on the dark-brown tiled floor. At any moment, the figure in the hunting cap could peer out from the shadow of the animal pen. And yet, for all that she tried, Atsuko couldn't see a thing.

Time went by. Suddenly, there was a noise behind her. It sounded like a shoe scraping against a hard surface. Instinctively, Atsuko turned around, not even daring to breathe.

Fumie's bag and handkerchief were lying on the broad ledge, but she was nowhere to be seen. Bathed in the salmon-pink light of the setting sun, the handkerchief looked like a solitary rose.

A gust of wind blew in from Tokyo Bay, bringing with it the refreshing cool air of a summer's evening. But in that moment, a look of horror written across her face, Atsuko felt as though a cold autumnal wind were blowing straight through her hollow chest.

Epilogue

1.

At the Viktoria restaurant in Hibiya, Onitsura and Tanna were drinking kvass as they waited for their guest. Although he didn't drink alcohol, the inspector was rather fond of this Russian drink, which tasted like a mixture of beer and cider.

"Is this alcoholic?" Tanna asked, looking mystified by the brown, foamy liquid.

"It's not really alcohol. But then, I suppose it is a bit like beer. It's made from barley flour and malt, so it's only natural."

"I'm a bit disappointed by the lack of alcohol, but it's actually quite drinkable."

Despite his criticisms, Tanna finished the drink in a single draught.

"If you like that, there's another kind of kvass called *boza*, which is made with apples or pears and is white and smooth and sweet, with slight sourness to it."

"I'll have to give it a try—for research purposes," Tanna said, licking his lips.

Onitsura was relaxing after tying up various loose ends, and this evening he was intending to celebrate the Nishinohata case being cracked with an intimate dinner at this Russian establishment. Perhaps because Russian cuisine was not well known in Japan, there were few customers in the spacious restaurant. The only others were a handful of left-wing students, sitting in the far corner, drinking vodka and nibbling on little fried sausages as they argued amongst themselves. For Onitsura, the lack of customers was a boon.

While Tanna took out a cigarette and began to puff away on it, the inspector attracted the waiter's attention and ordered a glass of *boza*.

"Who's joining us tonight?"

"Somebody you don't know. In fact, I've never met him before either."

"He must be running late," Tanna said, looking at the clock.

"Yes, he's a busy man. He said he could spare only ten or fifteen minutes. There won't even be enough time to treat him to dinner."

"Is he a reporter?" Tanna took a stab in the dark.

"No, he's an actor. I wonder where he's got to…"

"An actor?"

"Yes, on stage, mainly, but he also does some television and radio work. His name's Sensuke Hirota."

"Sensuke Hirota? Now, where have I heard that name before?… But why have you invited an actor along?"

Tanna exhaled a cloud of smoke, a look of puzzlement on his dark face.

"Do you remember that the late Mr Murase was having dinner with a friend at the Orchid when he saw the victim? Well, Mr Hirota was that friend."

"Oh, I see."

"We searched high and low for him but without any result. But it turns out that his theatre troupe was off playing in Hokkaido. It was only after he returned to Tokyo that he found out about everything. He said he'll tell us this evening, albeit somewhat belatedly, what it was that the voice actor noticed."

Hirota, who specialized in Western-style theatre, finally arrived when the glass of *boza* was almost empty.

"I have to be back in time for the third act," he said, "so I'm afraid I can spare you only ten minutes."

He was a slender man in his thirties. The hair at the front of his head was beginning to thin, and his eyes were bulging. However, he seemed to have a vocation for acting, as was clear from his spirited demeanour.

Onitsura ordered some tea and pirozhki. These fried meat buns were like little sandwiches and went down a treat.

"Let's set aside the question of what old Murase realized for now and have ourselves a think about Japanese pronunciation," Hirota said out of the blue, as he bit into one of the pirozhki.

Taken aback by this bizarre non-sequitur, Tanna stared at the actor in perplexity.

"In recent years, the arrival of people from the provinces in the capital has had a considerable impact on the native population of Tokyo. Take, for instance, the word *negi*. Before the war, if you asked for a *negi*, people would think you meant a Japanese spring onion, but nowadays you have to call it a 'long *negi*', so that people don't confuse it with a 'round' one—that is to say, an onion. And to top it off, you even see these words used in the newspapers and hear them spoken on TV and radio now. Another immediate example is the Tokyo way of preparing saury: they cut it down the middle and place both halves on a wire grill. Tokyoites have always had an appreciation for elegance, so, even when grilling a cheap fish like saury, they always knew that it was more beautiful to cut it in two, given its length. But now, even on TV, they just leave the fish whole. It's proof that we're being squeezed out by these incomers!"

"I see," the inspector said.

"And the way they mangle the language, trying to make themselves sound more eloquent… I think it's a great pity that Tokyo is being poisoned by these people from the provinces."

Thinking they were going to hear a lecture on Japanese pronunciation, the detectives instead had to listen to this rant about onions and fish. Onitsura was paying careful attention to his words, but Tanna, hailing from those very provinces, felt a little uncomfortable whenever he heard them being talked about in this way, so he just sat there, pouting as he ate his pirozhki.

"It's the same with pronunciation," the actor went on. "For those of use who've been trained in the language and are very sensitive to it, it's lamentable that young people these days can no longer pronounce the nasalized '-ng' sound correctly."

"What do you mean by that?" asked Tanna, who had little interest in linguistics.

"In Japanese the phonemes *ga, gi, gu, ge* and *go* are usually pronounced with a hard 'g', but in some cases it ought to be nasalized: *nga, ngi, ngu, nge, ngo.* Hear the difference?"

"I never knew that…"

"It usually occurs only in the middle of a word."

"But there are exceptions? It seems very tricky. I suppose I'll never tread the boards now if I have to study all this!"

"No, your pronunciation is fine. In fact, people from the eastern provinces—Hokkaido, Tohoku, Kanto, and even parts of Kansai—are naturally able to make these sounds. It's people from Kyushu who can't, and, strangely enough, the natives of Gunma Prefecture. Try listening to radio programmes from Takasaki and Ota. You'll think they've been produced in Kyushu."

"It's true enough. It isn't very easy on the ear listening to Japanese spoken without those sounds," Onitsura agreed.

"Just so, Inspector, just so. But as I say, perhaps because of the influence of all those people coming from west of Yamaguchi, there are quite a few youths in Tokyo nowadays who can't pronounce them correctly. Just turn on the radio and you'll see what I mean. And yet…"

The actor gulped down another pirozhki before continuing.

"… maybe it's down to the influence of jazz singers. I don't know why, but when jazz singers sing in Japanese, they don't use these nasal sounds either. One theory holds that the first jazz singers in the country were from Gunma Prefecture, so they couldn't do it, and those who came after them just followed suit without thinking. Whatever the truth of the matter, we ought to be conscious of these things and look after the language. Especially when it comes to the language used by politicians…"

Tanna was not in the least interested in all this. Yet Hirota was clearly enjoying himself. He seemed to think that if he was having a gay old time of it, the others would be too.

"Of course, Tokyoites do tend to overdo it. Why, I once heard on the radio—"

"Fascinating, Mr Hirota. You really are an expert on this subject," Tanna cut in, playing it straight.

"Oh, I don't know about that!" the actor replied, looking back at him earnestly.

Flustered, Tanna averted his eyes.

"Another problem with standard Japanese is that people from the provinces can't easily master the voiceless 'k' or 'ts'…"

Wearing a look of utter boredom, Tanna looked up. The expression on his face seemed to say: Will you just get to the point?!

"Say, for example, you see snow—*yuki*—falling in winter and decide to call your little girl Yukiko. The 'ki' in the word for snow is voiced, whereas in the child's name it isn't. If you pronounce them

341

both in the same way, then your Japanese begins to sound a little hazy, almost as though you have a Korean accent. It's the same with the sound 'tsu'. When you say the word for desk—*tsukue*—the 'tsu' is unvoiced and you drop the 'u'. If you romanize it, it should really be written *tskue*. I realize this is all something of a digression, but the reason I disagree with those advocating for the romanization of Japanese is that the language will become increasingly distorted if you write it that way. That being said, I suspect it will come in handy for you detectives to appreciate some of these finer points."

"No doubt," Tanna said, looking decidedly unimpressed.

"All of which brings me back to old Murase, who, I understand, placed great importance on the fact that the gentleman who died in the waiting room at Hamamatsu had never set foot out of Tokyo in his life."

"Yes," Onitsura said, nodding. "We believe he must have read the newspaper article at the broadcaster's and reached his own conclusion."

Tanna had suddenly perked up now that the conversation had turned to Murase.

"Well, I believe I can come to the same conclusion on that basis, gentlemen. If that what's-his-name Obata was a true-born Tokyoite and took pride in having never set foot out of the capital, then he must have spoken with a Tokyo accent. Strictly speaking, he'll have spoken the dialect used in the Shitamachi, so it's not exactly standard Japanese, but still, it will have been close enough."

"Yes, I see."

"Well, the man who dined at the Orchid that night may have spoken standard Japanese, but he couldn't make those nasal sounds I've just described. What's more, he often used voiced sounds where he ought to have used unvoiced ones. Just as a painter is sensitive to colour, and a musician is to pitch and

342

harmony, this is the sort of thing that the likes of us actors never miss. The account of Mr Nishinohata's biography said that he was raised in Kyushu as a child, so it's not surprising that he pronounced things in this way. Hence, there was no way that it could have been the old man, Obata, who went to the restaurant in disguise, as the investigating team seemed to think."

Before he'd even finished speaking, the actor looked at his watch. When he'd said all he had to say, he got to his feet, apologizing that he had to get back to the theatre, and thanked the inspector for the meal before rushing out. It suddenly became very quiet, as when an engine that's been revving suddenly stops.

After a few moments, the detectives looked at each other and grinned. It was the natural response to the sense of liberation they felt after seeing this long-standing mystery solved—and to their despondency at how obvious that solution had been.

"So that's how he worked it out!" Tanna said to himself ponderously.

He looked embarrassed at not having taken the actor's talk more seriously.

"Well, Tanna, you can't be full just yet," Onitsura said. "I know it's summer, but how about some borscht?"

2.

As they tucked into their big bowls of warm beetroot broth, sweat began to roll off them. As Onitsura had implied, this was a dish more fitting for winter.

"This must be a dish you serve up in snowy Siberia," Tanna said, stuffing his mouth with morsels of black rye bread. "It certainly warms you up."

Truly, it was a well-prepared soup: the beef in it was delicious, and the vegetables were full of flavour. As he was savouring it, mopping the beads of sweat on his brow, Tanna was quietly pondering the questions lingering in his mind. The voice actor had been able to tell that the man dining at the Chinese restaurant wasn't Genkichi Obata from the way he spoke. Yet Onitsura had realized the same thing because of something contained in the case notes. Tanna had gone over them any number of times in recent days, but, no matter how he tried, he just couldn't find anything. Feeling ashamed of himself, he had no choice but to ask the inspector.

Coffee was served after the meal. The drink didn't agree with Onitsura, so he sat there, silently taking in his surroundings. Here was Tanna's opportunity.

"I just can't work it out, sir. How did you deduce that Obata wasn't the man at the Orchid?"

"Oh, is that what's bothering you? I'd put it a little differently, my dear Tanna. It's tantamount to the same thing, but what I realized from the case notes was rather that it wasn't *necessarily* Obata who showed up at the restaurant, and that there was no reason it couldn't have been Nishinohata himself. That's why I asked at the Tachibana-ya. When I heard that the man in question hadn't gone out all night, I was able to conclude that the man who was spotted in the Orchid must have been the director."

"But what was it in the notes that made you realize that in the first place?" Tanna asked, setting down his coffee cup.

The inspector opened his briefcase, took out a large notebook, spread it out on the table and drew a large circle on it with a fountain pen. Next, he drew two tangents from a single point outside the circle.

"I'm afraid I'm no good with geometry," Tanna said. "In fact, I'm worried it might give me indigestion."

"Don't worry. This circle is the Yamanote line. These two lines are the Akabane line, which connects Ikebukuro and Akabane, and the Tohoku mainline, which runs from Ueno to Omiya via Akabane."

"Right, I see."

Tanna leant in, a look of concentration on his face. He couldn't wait to hear the explanation he was about to be given. Having read over the notes so many times, he couldn't help thinking: What did I miss?

One by one, Onitsura filled in the names of the stations of the Yamanote line on the circle, marking an X beside Shimojujo Station.

"Here's where the collision took place at ten past eleven on the evening of the first of June," he said. "As you know, the tracks in and out of Tokyo were closed. Hence, the No. 117 train bound for Aomori, which was due to depart thirty minutes later and was the last train out of Ueno, couldn't pass through Shimojujo. When I telephoned the station controller, I was informed that the train had been diverted via Ikebukuro on the Akabane line. This much you already know, right?"

"Yes, sir."

"And yet, I could have told you this even without making the call. The very fact that the train departed Shiroishi Station only twenty minutes late the following morning meant that it had to have taken the Akabane line. If one side of the triangle is blocked, the only other way is to go around it."

"I see."

"Let's pretend that this match box is the No. 117."

Onitsura picked up a box of matches advertising the Viktoria and placed it on the notebook at the spot marking Ueno Station.

"You see, Tanna, if this train joins the Akabane line at Ikebukuro..." he said, moving the match box along the track,

345

"... it can't just continue on its way. As you can see, it has to be taken down towards Shinjuku, where the locomotive has to be detached and a new one attached to the rear of the train. In other words, the rear becomes the front, and it ends up travelling in the opposite direction."

"Understood," Tanna replied. It was all clear to see right in front of him.

"Good. Now, let's return the No. 117 to its starting point. It leaves Ueno Station twenty minutes before midnight and a minute later passes under Ryodaishi Bridge. Let's imagine that the body is dumped on the train at this point. The blood flowing out of the corpse would be pushed back by wind pressure, forming what looked like exclamation marks, wouldn't it?"

Using his pen, he inscribed an exclamation mark onto the back of the match box and moved it towards Ikebukuro.

"Now, here we are at Ikebukuro. The locomotive has switched ends and is now at the rear of the train, and like this the train carries on up the Akabane line on its way to Sendai, passing through Omiya en route. Do you see the problem?"

Onitsura looked up at Tanna expectantly.

"As you may recall, the report from Sendai said that all the bloodstains on the roof of the train were blown backwards. In reality, however, the direction of the train was reversed at Ikebukuro, so the bloodstains should have been pointing in the opposite direction. As you can see from the box, the exclamation marks, by rights, should have been the other way around when the train pulled into Sendai."

"Of course!"

"As I just said, though, the report from Sendai said that their tails were facing away from the direction of travel. And there's only one possible explanation for this. That is, the body had to have

346

been pushed onto the train *after* the locomotive was changed. More specifically, it had to have been done after the train left Ikebukuro, so Ryodaishi Bridge in Ueno couldn't have been the scene of the crime."

The inspector spoke passionately but with deliberation, almost seeming to chew the words over in his mouth.

At long last, everything seemed to be falling into place for Tanna.

"And the fact that Ryodaishi Bridge wasn't the scene of the crime meant that the murder couldn't have taken place at eleven-forty. In which case, it was safe to assume that the man seen eating at the Orchid was none other than the victim himself. That was the starting point for my theory."

Suddenly, the inspector stopped talking, and his ears pricked up. He could hear the opening strains of the Russian folk song "Black Eyes" being played on the gramophone. Soon, accompanied by a strumming balalaika, a Russian soprano sang a tremulous, gypsy-style melody: *"Ochi chornye, ochi zhguchie…"* "Black eyes, smouldering eyes!"

"I hear Mrs Hishinuma had beautiful eyes…" Onitsura muttered to himself.

Tanna, who had no interest in Russian folk songs, couldn't help but wonder why the inspector had suddenly mentioned Fumie.

"Yes, so they said," he replied indistinctly, his voice trailing off.

AVAILABLE AND COMING SOON
FROM PUSHKIN VERTIGO

Yukito Ayatsuji

The Decagon House Murders
The Mill House Murders

Boileau-Narcejac

Vertigo
She Who Was No More

María Angélica Bosco

Death Going Down

Piero Chiara

*The Disappearance of
Signora Giulia*

Frédéric Dard

Bird in a Cage
The Wicked Go to Hell
Crush
The Executioner Weeps
The King of Fools
The Gravediggers' Bread

Friedrich Dürrenmatt

The Pledge
The Execution of Justice
Suspicion
The Judge and His Hangman

Margaret Millar

Vanish in an Instant
A Stranger in My Grave
The Listening Walls

Baroness Orczy

The Old Man in the Corner
The Case of Miss Elliott
Unravelled Knots

Edgar Allan Poe

The Paris Mysteries

Soji Shimada

The Tokyo Zodiac Murders
Murder in the Crooked House

Akimitsu Takagi

The Tattoo Murder

Josephine Tey

The Daughter of Time
The Man in the Queue

Masako Togawa

The Master Key
The Lady Killer

S. S. Van Dine

The Bishop Murder Case

Futaro Yamada

The Meiji Guillotine Murders

Seishi Yokomizo

Death on Gokumon Island
The Honjin Murders
The Inugami Curse
The Village of Eight Graves
The Devil's Flute Murders